CONTENTS

HORATIA'S SECRET

New edition

On the verge of nervous breakdown, a respectable Victorian grandmother turns to an old friend, but ongoing visions make her face her deepest fear.

FOREWORD

I'm telling this story because I believe it needs telling, and I've released this majorly overhauled, second edition because I believe it needs telling in the best way I can.

It's the story of a life ruined by misogynistic Victorian society in its bid to rewrite history to frame men as heroes, and women as sluts or saints.

It's the story of my direct ancestors, of whom Lord Nelson was all but canonised as the British Empire's paradigm of manly valour, whilst the love of his life, Lady Hamilton, was demonised in equal measure for having dared, as a poor-born woman, to rise above her station and achieve great things. And it's the story of their only child, Horatia, who lived her long life under the legacy of this misogyny.

Horatia's cold, public stance towards Lady Hamilton vexed me until my intuition suggested she'd carried a secret. I needed to communicate my hunch as a fiction.

I was experienced in writing fact-based pieces for naval history publications, but was all at sea when it came to putting a work of fiction together.

My first draft of Horatia's Secret, published in 2020, was rich in detail, character, mood, motivation and description, but lacked shape, like intricately woven cloth in need of a good tailor. This new, tailored version of Horatia's Secret is trimmed in many places and extended in others to create, I hope, a narrative that flows, engages and rings true.

LIST OF CHARACTERS

Residents of Woodridings, Pinner

No. 2 Beaufort Villas
Horatia Nelson Ward. Only child of Lord Nelson, and doting grandmother. B. circa 29th January 1801.

Servants appearing in the book
Honeysett, Walter. Butler. B. 1828 in Herstmonceux, Sussex.
Bryant, Beth. Housemaid. B. 1850 in Chipperfield, Hertfordshire.
Squires, Lettie. Cook. B. 1850 in Poplar, Middlesex.

No. 1 Cornwall Villas
Major William George Ward, Madras Staff Corps. Fifth child of Horatia. B. 1830 in Bircham Newton, Norfolk.
Tori (Catherine Parker Nelson Toriana Ward née Blanckley). B. 1835 in Plymouth, Devon.

Children
Nellie (Ellen Catherine) B. 1865 in the British cantonment, Jaulnah, Madras.
Ethel (Ethel Mary) B. 1866 "
Carrie (Caroline Gertrude) B. 1868 "
Evie (Evelyn Hervey) B. 1870 "
Ada / Oddy (Ada Blanche) B. 1871 "
Baby Alice (Alice Lilian) B. 1873 in Woodridings, Pinner.

Servants appearing in book
Kajri. Ayah. B. circa 1854 in Jaulnah, Madras.
Cummings, Mary. Maid of all work. B. 1853 in Pinner.
Mr. Ensten, James. Part-time gardener. B. circa 1818 in Stoke Poges, Buckinghamshire.

No. 2 Onslow Villas
Nelson Ward. Principal clerk to the Registrar of the Court of Chancery. B. 1828 in Bircham Newton, Norfolk.
Mrs. Jessie Ward. B. 1842 in Marylebone, Middlesex.

Children
Jack (Nelson). B. 1865 in Pinner.
Florence. B. 1867 "
Rose. B. "
Jessie. B. 1868 "
Mary (twin). B 1869 "
Kathleen (twin). B. "
Agnes. B 1871 "
Tom (Maurice Suckling). B. 1873 "

Servant appearing in book
Jones, Maud. Parlourmaid. B. 1859 in Hackney, London.

Tori's relatives living elsewhere

Paternal Blanckley family
Lizzie (Elizabeth Henrietta Blanckley Broughton). B. 1844 in Edinburgh, Scotland.

Henrietta Blanckley. B. circa 1804 in Minorca.
Bradford, Lucy. Housemaid. B. 1852 in Exmouth, Devon.

Horace (Captain Horatio Charles Nelson Blanckley, Royal Marines). B. 1831 in Versailles, France.
Joan. Horace's lover. B. circa 1853 in Plymouth, Devon.

Maternal Matcham family
Susan Moore. Tori's aunt and foster mother. Daughter of Lord Nelson's sister, Kitty. B. 1802 in Bath, Somerset.

The Cookes

Otho Cooke. Withycombe House near Budleigh Salterton. B. 1803 in Peterborough, Northamptonshire.
Mrs. Julia Mary Cooke. Sole heiress of General Garnault. B. circa 1831 in India.

Children
Francis Thomas Cooke. B. 1833 in Mylor, Cornwall
Amanda Verlander. Francis's half-sister. B. circa 1853 in Exmouth, Devon.

Residents of South Brent

The Royal Oak
William Petherbridge Arscott. Innkeeper. B. 1830 in Buckfastleigh, six-miles from South Brent
Mrs. Sarah Arscott. B. 1832 in Buckfastleigh.

Children
Ellen. B. 1854 in Buckfastleigh.
Jimmy. B. 1853 in South Brent.

Sopers
Harry Soper. South Brent's only coachman. B. 1822 in South Brent.
Mrs. Eliza Soper. B. circa 1824 in South Brent.

Harry's children
Billy. Apprentice shoemaker. B. 1854 in South Brent
Harry. Farm labourer. B. 1855 "
Sarah. Shoddy mill worker. B 1857 "
Lucy. Scholar. B. 1859 "
Mary. Scholar. B. 1862 "
George. Scholar. B. 1864 "
John. Scholar. B. 1867 "

Bill Soper. Harry's cousin. South Brent grocer. B. 1825 in South Brent.
Mrs. Eliza Soper. Co-manages their front-room shop. B. 1813 in South Brent.

Lutton House
Tom Matthews. Tenant. Retired wine merchant. B. 1832 in Penzance, Cornwall.
Mrs. Elizabeth Matthews. B. circa 1837 in Tavistock, Devon.

Hawton, Elizabeth. Housemaid. B. circa 1822 in Dartmouth, Devon.

Nelson Family Tree

Showing the relationships of characters in the book to Lord Nelson and to each other

Blanckley Family Tree

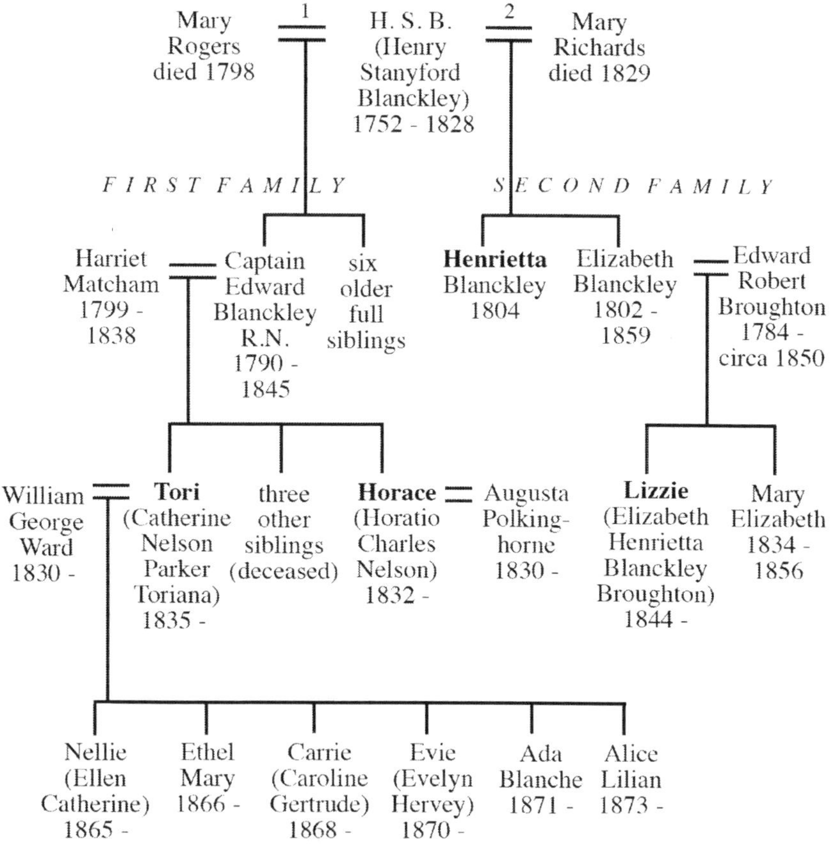

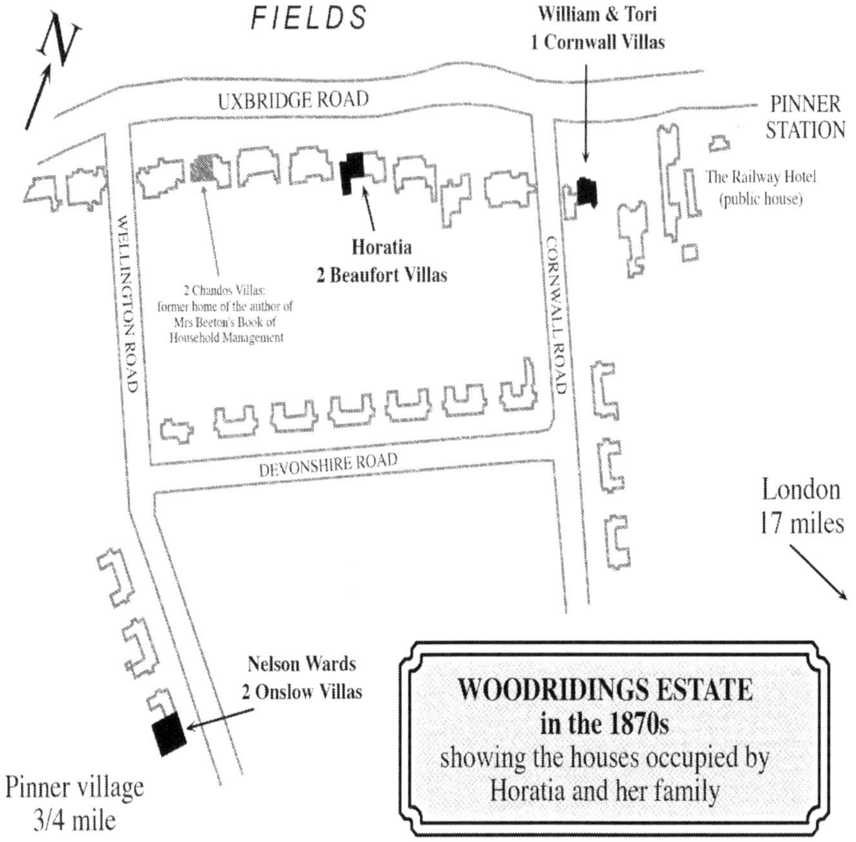
N
FIELDS
William & Tori
1 Cornwall Villas
UXBRIDGE ROAD
PINNER
STATION
The Railway Hotel
(public house)
Horatia
2 Beaufort Villas
2 Chandos Villas:
former home of the author of
Mrs Beeton's Book of
Household Management
WELLINGTON ROAD
CORNWALL ROAD
DEVONSHIRE ROAD
London
17 miles
Nelson Wards
2 Onslow Villas
Pinner village
3/4 mile
WOODRIDINGS ESTATE
in the 1870s
showing the houses occupied by
Horatia and her family

THEATRE ROYAL

Lessee and Manager, Mr. NEEBE.

SPECIAL TRAINS to and from Crediton, on Friday, 26th December.
Exmouth on Monday 29th December. Newton Abbot, on Thursday, 1st January.
Tiverton, on Friday, 2nd January.
For particulars see railway Bills.

MORNING PERFORMANCES of the PANTOMIME on FRIDAY, 2nd Jan., and FRIDAY, 9th Jan, at 2 p.m.
TUESDAY EVENING, December 30th, under the Patronage of Lady POLTIMORE

THIS EVENING WILL BE PRODUCED THE
GRAND COMIC CHRISTMAS PANTOMIME
ENTITLED, HARLEQUIN
SINDBAD THE SAILOR!
Or, the Captain, the King, and the Cabinet : and the Fairy Prosperity of the Valley of Dymonds.

(Written expressly for this Theatre by J. BANNISTER, Esq.)
New and Elaborate Scenery, and the Transformation Scene by Mr. H. Lancaster and numerous Assistants. The Music arranged by Mr. J. W. Fielder and Mr. Rendle. The dresses by Miss Thorne. The Lime Light effects by Mr. Carter. The Properties by Mr. Candy. Machinery by Mr. Lang. The whole produced under the immediate superintendence of Mr. G. W. HARRIS and Mr. NEEBE.

Scene I.——Abode of Hunkey.
Scene II.——Port of Balsorn.
Scene III.——The Valley of Dymonds.
GRAND BALLET!
Scene IV.——Island of the Old Man of the Sea.
Scene V.——Bungaboo.
Scene VI. Ante-room in the Palace.
Scene VII.——Gardens of the Palace.
Scene VIII.——Ante-Chamber.
Scene IX.——A Wild Spot.

Doors Open at 6.30, Commence at 7.——Dress Circle, 3s. ; Upper Circle, 2s. ; Pit, 1s. ; Gallery, 6d.
Box Office at Messrs. ROBERTS'S, 265, High-street, where the Box Plan may be seen and Tickets procured.

Exeter and Plymouth Gazette 26th December 1873

CHAPTER ONE

It was a sunny day and the breeze was warm, but her heart felt chilled as ice. The gardens of Merton Place were lush despite the late season, though weeds had run amok. Glimpses of the country house's new, brick frontage were strikingly red against the greenery. The wrought iron gate bar was cold in her small fist. Emma tugged her again. 'Let go, Horatia. The coach is waiting.'

'But I don't want to go!' Her words sounded shrill after her guardian's rich voice. Emma towered above her. People said she was statuesque and the epitome of fashion and grace, but Horatia had heard people whispering about Emma, Lady Hamilton being past her prime and gone to fat. Horatia thought Emma was splendid anyway, albeit currently heartless in her determination to drag her from the grounds of Merton Place, and her last link with her dead father, Lord Nelson. Emma pulled her harder, and her grip gave way. There were specks of black on the pink of her palm. She realised the iron gateway, once glossy black and tipped with gold, was lacklustre and flaking. The grand gateway, the house, the gardens, and everything here had been slowly dying since Lord Nelson's death three years before.

'Are you well?'

The male voice startled her. Merton's gates were no longer there. How could that be? She realised she was seated. Gnarled hands were clasping her waist. She recoiled, and the hands moved with her. Something was very wrong. She steeled her will to lift her right hand, and the gnarled hand on the right side of her waist lifted too. She felt the pain of its swollen joints.

'Mother, are you quite alright?'

It was that male voice again. She drew her eyes upward, scarce daring to learn the speaker's identity. The man was well-dressed and middle aged, with a square-jawed face dominated by a prominent nose and gingery brown sideburns. She knew him in an instant of cold dread. He was Nelson, her lawyer son. She was in the parlour of her house in Woodridings, seventeen miles north-west of London, and she was going mad. 'Ah, Nelson,' she willed her smile to appear relaxed and motherly. 'I apologise. I must have nodded off. You know how we old ladies are!'

Her son studied her with narrowed eyes. 'You turned quite white, Mother. I confess to having been concerned. We were talking normally, then you suddenly went blank. It was disconcerting, indeed!'

Her heart hammered as if beaten by a maniac drummer. *Please, sweet Jesus, don't let him see my insanity!* 'I can only apologise again for alarming you. I'm afraid I get very tired these days in my old age. I hope you'll forgive your old mama for startling you?'

'Of course I forgive you, Mother, and I'm sorry if my question tired you.'

'Oh dear, I'm afraid I have no memory of you asking me anything.'

Forty-five-year-old Nelson Ward leant closer. 'I'd been telling you of my great good fortune in meeting Mr. Archibald, Eton College's governor, at my club; and that he'd told me Jack has a good chance of being accepted with the January intake because he's turning eight in February.'

Horatia perked up. 'Jack would be accepted into Eton?'

'Yes, exactly that! The boost this will give his career is incalculable because of the connections he'll make with lads from the higher class. As they say, it's not what you know, but who you know.'

Horatia smiled back, giddily happy because the success of her sons and grandsons was the most important thing in the world.

Nelson continued. 'If you recall, I brought a rather, umm, sticky issue to your attention?' His grey eyes flicked briefly to hers. 'Mr. Archibald advised me, man to man, that Jack's acceptance into Eton will be guaranteed if his lineage is affirmed. You must write to attest the falsehood of those silly, annoying rumours that Lady Hamilton was your mother.'

'What a peculiar thing for them to ask of me.' Horatia felt suddenly dizzy.

Nelson's eyes hooked hers like magnets. 'Peculiar, perhaps, and decidedly indelicate, but, Mother, you must appreciate the necessity? Eton's reputation would be destroyed by the slightest whiff of bad blood. Jack can only go there if you confirm that Lady Hamilton is not his great-grandmother.' He flashed his polished, lawyer's smile. 'It would aid his case if you mention Lady Hamilton's statement that your true mother was too great to mention. Follow this with a brief account of Lady Hamilton's friendship with the Queen of Naples.'

Horatia's dizziness increased. She pressed herself against the back of her chair to support her spine so she could hold her head high and straight. 'Son, I've told you already that, as I have no certainty, I can make no public declaration about my maternity.'

'Mother, the statements I suggest are truths... Mother?' Horatia's pupils had rolled so her open eyes were as white as her hair.

****

When, three days later, Horatia was busily preparing for the visit of her old friend, Rietta Blanckley, she was fretful that she'd have another lapse of consciousness in front of Rietta and her other guests. She'd heard enough tales of elderly ladies being locked up in asylums because they could no longer tell fantasy from reality. It wasn't so much that she cared for her liberty, but about the effect the stigma her insanity would have on her sons and grandsons. Incarceration in a lunatic asylum would damage them far worse than rumours that Lady Hamilton was her mother.

'Will we do?' She asked her son, William. She was grateful that he'd come to help with the preparations for Rietta's visit, though his presence increased her anxiety in case she blacked out whilst he was there. Willing her mind to stay focused, she surveyed the room. All looked good.

'Yes, I think we will do, Mother.' William's bushy beard tickled her when he planted a kiss on her cheek.

****

Tori raised herself slowly, carefully holding sleeping Baby Alice against the slippery silk of her best day dress. 'They're here, they're here!' a high voice called again. It was most likely Ethel, the loudest of her older girls. Her guests' arrival was both exciting and worrying. She'd not seen Aunt Henrietta since her wedding nine years before, when she'd been her usual prickly self (although her aunt's sourness had been offset by Tori's own joy and the plethora of less prickly guests, including Lizzie). Cousin Lizzie had been one of Tori's four bridesmaids, and would be arriving now with their aunt. The thought of seeing her was infinitely more cheering. Glancing at the brass-framed mirror above the fireplace, her long oval face looked decidedly gaunt. She smoothed her dark, rolled hair with one hand, and made her way down to the front hall, Baby Alice still sleeping against her bosom. Her bottle-green, bustled skirt swooshed on the floor as she approached the front door, where, as suspected, six-year-old Ethel was hopping up and down to peer through the stained glass panes. Her firstborn, Nellie, was halfway down the stairs, also lured by Ethel's ruckus. Of the younger girls, Carrie, Evie and tiny Ada, there was no sight, but plenty of sound (her maternal brain was ever alert for signs of her six children's whereabouts). Her husband William was with his frail, elderly mother in Beaufort Villas, a hundred yards westwards along Uxbridge Road.

She suspected William was purposefully avoiding Aunt Henrietta. A British Army major seasoned in Madras he may be, but equal to Aunt Henrietta, perhaps not – and who could really blame him? Tori sighed, she'd really prefer not to see her herself... she was jolted back to composure by a sharp *rat a tat tat* on the door which caused Ethel to shriek excitedly and Baby Alice to launch into full-throated screams. Cummings, her maid of all work, scurried from the kitchen to see to the door.

Tori, shushing Alice, quick-stepped after the maid, and grabbed Nellie's hand en route to adeptly arrange her beside Ethel, before Cummings finished opening the door, 'Good aftern'n,' the maid bobbed to a red faced cabby.

'Af'noon,' the cabbie doffed his top hat. 'Miss Blanckley and Miss Broughton for Mrs. Ward.'

Tori constructed her most gracious, welcoming and confident smile, but realised her loudly crying baby was spoiling the effect. She passed the squalling infant to Cummings, and inclined her head politely. 'I am Mrs. Ward. I shall be pleased to receive the Misses Blanckley and Broughton.'

'Me too!' Ethel piped.

'I shall accompany you to the carriage,' Tori declared. 'Girls, you may come too, but *quietly*.'

'Yes, ma'am.' The cabby set forth back down the path. The top of a covered Clarence was visible over the hedge. While Nellie obediently matched step, Tori kept a steadying hand on Ethel's shoulder to prevent her bolting indecorously ahead.

'I can see them!' Ethel squealed. And sure enough, framed by gate and carriage window, Aunt Henrietta, looking older, plumper and very pale under a large, orange wig, could be seen studiously ignoring their existence. Cousin Lizzie leaned around their aunt's high hairpiece.

'Tori,' she beamed, 'it's so good to see you!'

The cabby's light knock on the Clarence door caused Aunt Henrietta to affect awareness of her arrival. Regarding Tori briefly with sharp, grey eyes framed in blue steel, she inclined her head and told the cabby, 'Very well, you may assist me to disembark, then take our cases to the house.' She finally acknowledged Tori. 'Good afternoon, Niece. I see two children and no husband. Is this all my greeting?'

Tori was about to speak when, to her deep mortification, her daughters' excitable spaniel, Patch, bounded out of the gate and jumped at the carriage, barking loudly. 'Nellie, take Patch to the rear garden, and see that the door is properly shut this time.'

'Yes, Mama.' The eight-year-old hauled the spaniel up, and carried him around the side of the house.

Once Henrietta had descended from the cab, she was revealed as a stout old lady, whose diminutive height was more than adequately compensated by an elaborate, orange wig and the fierceness of her steel-rimmed glare. Lizzie, for her part, was taller (though still a good three inches shorter than Tori) with a long face, fashionably wasp-thin waist, and a mane of red hair, which would have looked bright were it not for her aunt's brighter wig.

'Aunt Henrietta,' Tori bobbed, determined not to fluster. 'I am so glad to see you. Major Ward sends his fondest regards. He regrets to having been waylaid assisting his mother prepare for the meal in your honour.'

'Hmph, hiding more like it,' she muttered. 'I suspect he still sports a ridiculously long beard. Lizzie, you may recall my frequent observation that young men of today are as short on manners as they are long of beard.'

Lizzie took Tori's arm. 'Tis so very good to see you again! And these are your beautiful daughters?'

'Yes,' Tori smiled. 'The taller one is, or was, Nellie, I mean Ellen, our eldest. She will be back momentarily.'

Nellie reappeared with perfect timing and curtseyed. 'Good afternoon, Aunt Henrietta. Good afternoon, Aunt Elizabeth.'

Aunt Henrietta sniffed, while Lizzie gushed, 'And good afternoon to you, young Miss Nellie!'

'And this,' Tori tapped Ethel's shoulder, silently praying she'd somehow display well-bred manners, 'is our second eldest, Ethel–'

'Hello!' Ethel cut her off mid-sentence, and impertinently grasped her great aunt's podgy hand. 'You're Aunt Henrietta, and I'm Ethel Mary Ward!'

To Tori's astonishment, Henrietta met Ethel's enthusiasm with a yellow-toothed smile of her own. 'What a pretty introduction, Ethel Mary Ward. Well met.'

The female company made their way sedately (bar Ethel) up the garden path of No. 1 Cornwall Villas, heedless of the cabby huffing and puffing with various iron-bound trunks.

'Your house is smart enough,' Henrietta squinted at the white-painted building with a jutting front wing that soared upwards, like a church tower, culminating in three high-arched windows under a pointed, red-tiled roof. 'Although I see you are next to a public house.'

'Aftern'n ladies,' a moderately kempt, late-middle-aged man appeared from the trees flanking the eastern, pub side of the house.

'Ah,' said Tori, 'this is Mr Ensten who normally does the garden, but will assist with your bags.' The gardener hefted two large trunks with strong hands, and manoeuvred them, grunting, into the house.

'Perhaps you'd like to come into the parlour?' Tori enquired.

'Come into my parlour, said the spider to the fly.'

'Ethel!' Tori cut her off. 'I do apologise–'

'No need,' Aunt Henrietta overrode. 'I find my young great-niece quite enchanting. Ethel, do you like the works of Mary Howitt?'

Ethel stared at her blankly.

Tori reinstated her gracious, welcoming, and confident smile. 'Aunt, Cousin, please do come in and I shall call for tea, or if you prefer…'

'Tea will be perfect!' Lizzie interposed. 'Won't it, Aunt?'

****

The party set out from No. 1 Cornwall Villas resplendent in evening attire. The younger ladies, twenty-nine-year-old Lizzie, and thirty-eight-year-old Tori, had donned fashionable bustled gowns (purple and cornflower blue respectively) with low necklines and short, off-the-shoulder sleeves. Lizzie's auburn hair was teased into ringlets, while Tori had pulled her dark brown hair into a high knot surmounted with a small, pale blue bonnet. Aunt Henrietta wore a midnight blue three-quarter-length cape over a somewhat dated, mauve dress decorated with gold embroidery and a white lace collar. A green velvet hairnet clashed with the garish orange of her wig.

Nellie, Ethel and Carrie sped ahead along blustery Uxbridge Road. A lamplighter approached from the other direction, a string of warmly glowing lamps in his wake. He paused at every tall, iron post to hook its glass case open with his pole, light the lamp and re-close it before moving on to the next. A brief shower of rain had sprinkled the street with silver highlights, and the paired villas to their left stood rain-cleansed and sharp against the darkening sky. The leaves of beeches and elms in gardens, still visible in the twilight, were flecked with autumnal gold.

'Here we are,' Tori told the party when they arrived at the hedge-bordered gate of her mother-in-law's home. 'I hope the walk was not tiring?'

Aunt Henrietta sniffed. 'It was as you promised: brief, level and free from foul air. I surmise this to be one benefit of residing in a modern estate.'

'Good,' Tori breathed, composure maintained. 'This way, if you please.' Her three little girls were already half way up the path, coiffed curls and half-length skirts swirling amidst their clatter of hard shoes.

as this, but it was no comfort to realise she'd slipped into the past again. The episodes were increasing, like a drowning man might slip below the waves more frequently, and for longer periods, until he never rose again. She shuddered, then frowned. Something from her latest recollection niggled her. Horatia wondered how it could have been that her younger self, just four years of age, had possibly known. Perhaps, she mused, her memory was false: concocted from hearsay and later-learned facts? But she'd had such a strong sense of her child self's certainty and dread. Perhaps, she reflected, we sometimes just know, and they'd all *just known*. It is a misconstruction to assume knowledge enables explanation. Firstly, there is baffling knowledge of the type that defies explanation; secondly, there is the type of knowledge we are held by oath to withhold; and, thirdly, there is knowledge that could be explained, but can never be uttered even to one's own self. Horatia was familiar with all three forms of inexplicable knowledge.

Henrietta joined the dining room at No. 1 Cornwall Villas to partake of breakfast at a leisurely late hour. There was no sign of Tori, William or Susan, but the three eldest girls were still present, hovered over by the maid, and loudly chattering as they devoured poached eggs and kidneys on toast.

'Good morning, girls!' Henrietta plopped herself onto a high-backed chair. 'I see your mama doesn't hold with the custom of feeding children plain food.'

'Yuck!' Ethel screwed up her face. 'I would rather starve than eat boring nursery food!'

'Ethel!' Nellie hissed.

Henrietta chuckled. 'I quite agree, Ethel dear. My parents, God rest their souls, never forced plain food on us either. I suspect your mama gained the habit from her own papa, who was my half-brother.' She addressed the maid, 'Cummings, I too would like poached eggs and kidneys, if Cook can provide.'

'Certainly, and would you like anything to drink?'

'Tea, thank you.' She picked up The Morning Post, which had, as per usual, been placed thoughtfully to the right of her breakfast plate. The front page was the usual mass of small advertisements – Vienna Exhibition will Close on 31st October... Madame Florence Lancia as Eily, at the Crystal Palace Opera this day... she flicked through the pages idly, with more than half an ear on the girls' lively talk, until a passage of text hooked her eye: Today is the 68th anniversary of the Battle of Trafalgar. Subjoined is a list of the veteran surviving officers who contributed to that victory...

****

Henrietta found Horatia sitting statue-still on a bench among her roses. 'I do not wish to intrude, Ratia dear, but I only just realised the significance of today's date. I am here to convey friendship and support only. I shall go immediately, with no offence taken, if you so much as nod. It is you I am here for, not I.'

'Dear Rietta,' Horatia held her arms wide. 'Oh Rietta, I cannot tell you how wholesome it is to have you with me!'

'Dear friend, know that I am here.'

'Rietta, tell me please, how am I supposed to respond to this annual celebration of the worst day of my life?'

'Just as you are, my dearest. No one thinks of you when they earmark this day. They think of victory and national salvation, and clap their hands at what a great hero your father was: the perfect candidate for ceremonial toasts. But they do not think, not even for a moment, of how his sacrifice hit his family.'

Horatia considered this. ‘Why should they? We mere mortals play small parts in grand schemes. Nations would count few victories if individual losses were weighed in the balance. Our great nation celebrates the anniversary of…’ she winced, ‘the battle of Trafalgar, as is only right. That I endure it as a square peg failing to fit into a round hole is of no consequence to the greater scheme of things.’

‘But it doesn’t make it easier for you.’

‘You’re right, it doesn’t make it easier, but I’m used to it, so I don’t mind.’

‘Your son, Nelson, has invited me, along with the whole of Cornwall Villas, to dinner this evening. I hadn’t realised until now that it’s to commemorate Trafalgar. You’ll think me the worst type of immodest fool, but when Nelson told me, with a big smile, that the dinner is to celebrate the high importance of today, I’d assumed he meant it was because Lizzie and I are here!’

Horatia chuckled. ‘In truth, friend, your presence here is of far higher import to me. But my Nelson does love to celebrate the anniversary of Trafalgar with his family, and I am happy he honours his grandfather’s memory.’

‘But you cannot honour it thus?’

‘How can I, Rietta? It was no token loss for me. I admire Lord Nelson’s courage. I am humbled by his sacrifice, and truly appreciative of the freedom his victory bestowed upon us all as a people; but he was my father, and his death tore my whole life apart.’

‘So what shall you do?’

‘As always, I shall spend the anniversary in prayer and quiet contemplation. My children respect this.'

'And I respect this too, dearest friend,' Henrietta touched Horatia's soft, wrinkled cheek gently. 'Tis a time of highest personal import for you.'

Horatia met her friend's eyes. 'I say again that I do very much like that you are here with me on this occasion. That you were there... not in the same place as me, but in the same time: this is of high import also, perhaps even greater. Rietta, I have spent too many Trafalgar Days wrapped in grim memory, whilst my nearest and dearest have let me be... but not, I think, understood. Now here with you, and believing that you actually do understand, I feel unexpectedly liberated.'

****

No. 2 Onslow Villas was full to brimming with merry hustle and bustle. Nelson and his brother, William, were surveying proceedings from a quiet corner. The seven eldest of Nelson's eight children were running amok with William's older girls. Nine-month-old Tom and three-month-old Alice gurgled on a sheepskin rug under the watchful eye of the brightly-dressed ayah William had brought back from India. Nelson noticed that his sister-in-law, Tori, looked very pale and skinny. She was wearing her dark green day dress again. Nelson wouldn't dream of embarrassing his brother by querying his finances, but he suspected it was a tight stretch for his British Army salary to support a wife and six daughters, as well as their small body of servants. He stole a sideways glance at his brother. William had always been sickly, even as a child, but now he looked emaciated. William never complained, but Nelson suspected he'd never fully recovered from the severe liver illness he contracted ten years ago. It had been severe enough for the army doctor to grant him twenty-months sick leave which, in turn, had enabled him to marry Tori and take her back to India with him. The concerning thing was that their younger brother, Philip, had contracted a similar liver illness in India which had actually killed him.

Nelson knew he was fortunate that their father had paid for his lawyer training. As a leading member of the bar, his income was very comfortable. He had his eye on West House, a large property on the other side of Pinner village. In the meantime, although Onslow Villas was a squash for his large family, it was good to be in the Woodridings Estate close to their elderly mother and William and his family, now they'd returned from India. It pleased him to aid their finances by inviting their girls join his children's tutor sessions. His six girls got along famously with William's daughters. Thankfully, his eldest and youngest were boys (another thing not to mention to William, for the poor chap hadn't yet produced a male heir). His wife, Jessie, and Tori got along very well too. They currently looked happy together arranging red, white and blue silk flowers in a large vase, whilst their children giggled and squabbled good-naturedly trying to craft paper chains of the same colour scheme. Today was all about family, and the decorative chains they were producing, no matter how misshapen, were family-made. No amount of mangling detracted from their patriotic red, white and blueness. His parlourmaid, busy too, was perching on a stool to pin Union Jack bunting to the picture rail. Yes, the dining room was shaping up to look terrific. 'Jones!' he projected his voice to the maid, courtroom style, across the noisy room. 'Be sure to save some bunting for my Lord Nelson painting.'

The maid followed his eyes to a gilt framed oil portrait of Lord Nelson, with his trademark bicorn and glittering medals, hanging pride of place on the red, flock-papered wall. 'Certainly, Mr. Ward. There's another roll of bunting in the trunk.'

Nelson turned to his brother. 'I say, William, I do very much enjoy this annual celebration of our grandfather's triumph. One shouldn't be immodest, but I confess to a degree of personal pleasure that the whole nation is celebrating with us.'

William's bushy beard twitched. 'Quite so. Tis splendid to be in England for the anniversary of Trafalgar. It is, of course, celebrated in the British cantonments in India, but there's nothing like being here in England where our grandfather is praised on every street corner.'

Nelson gripped his brother's shoulder excitedly. 'Exactly this! Not that I've been abroad for Trafalgar Day myself, but it's the all pervading excitement that makes it so special.'

Jessie smacked his hand playfully. 'This year's Trafalgar dinner is even more special because dear William and his family are with us!'

One of the things he loved about his wife was her amicable, round-cheeked smile which always lifted his heart. 'My dear, your observation is prudent and timely! I say, Toriana, will you forgive my clumsy failure to mention my delight that you'll be joining us?'

Tori stilled partway into planting a red silk rose into the display she was constructing with Jessie.'There's nothing to forgive, Brother, for you and yours have made us feel more welcome than words could convey.'

William frowned. 'I must say, I think it a damnable shame that our mother won't join us. As Lord Nelson's only child, one would think she'd enjoy the celebration of his memory more than anyone.'

Nelson batted a speck of dust from his lapel. 'We invite her every year, of course, but her unswerving wish is to observe the anniversary in silent vigil.'

'Just as she did when we were children,' William nodded. 'Though it must surely comfort her to know her father's sacrifice is venerated by every British subject, regardless of creed and caste.'

The brothers turned in unison to regard the ayah quietly minding their babies. The young Indian woman looked up as if sensing their scrutiny. Her eyes were white and bright against the chocolate dark of her face. William addressed her, 'Kajri, are you aware of Lord Nelson's victory and sacrifice?'

The ayah studied the leather straps of her sandals protruding from the hem of her scarlet sari. 'Yes, Major Ward. Your grandfather's victory changed the fate of all my people.'

Nelson lent towards her. 'Lord Nelson's victory gave Britain the power to keep India safe from the French. If the French ruled you, they'd make you all Christians.'

Kajri continued to stare at her feet. 'We are grateful that Britain permits us to keep our own religions.'

Nelson smiled. 'And what about the opportunities our empire gives you? You'd not be here with us now, if it wasn't for the British army, and specifically my brother taking his lovely wife back to Jaulnah with him to start his family there, hey?'

William chuckled, but Kajri's answer was a mumble. 'Yes, Mr. Ward.'

Nelson warmed to the theme. 'So here you are now with a good job, living in a respectable English suburb, and earning money to send to your mother.'

'Yes, Mr. Ward. My mother is very grateful when the British help.'

****

Horatia's parlour was an island of calm refinement. She lent back contentedly in her fireside armchair, whilst Henrietta lolled on the settee and Susan sat in the window seat flicking through the West London Times. Susan held the paper aloft. 'What the journalist says here is a very pretty sentiment: "A good lady upholds her mother's virtue before her own". What say you, Henrietta? Oh dear, are you asleep?' She addressed Horatia instead, 'What do you think of the sentiment, Cousin?'

The mantel clock ticked like a relaxed heart, and the fire's glow was warm. Horatia blinked heavily. 'I agree that the sentiment is pretty, but I think it unrealistic.'

'Unrealistic?' Susan furrowed her brow. 'My mother's virtue, god rest her soul, is a continual source of inspiration to me – oh, Horatia, I'm so sorry. I didn't think.'

Horatia shrugged. 'Tis no matter. Your mother was an inspiration to us all. I was a happy girl when under her care.'

Henrietta coughed, spluttered, and snorted indelicately. 'Did I hear you say you were a happy girl, Ratia dear?'

'Ah, you're awake!' Susan plonked herself down on the sofa, bird-light, beside Henrietta's small, heavy bulk.

Horatia joined them, equally birdlike in weight. Henrietta, in a brick-red dress and orange wig, was a splash of colour between their black on black attire. Horatia said, 'I truly was a happy girl back then. Do you remember Paris when we were first there, all together, right after the war?'

Susan brightened. 'Wasn't it fun? Such adventure! Do you remember how excited my papa was tasting olives?'

'And my papa too!' Henrietta smiled at the memory. 'They were both over sixty, but like children unleashed!'

'They were quite mad for them,' Susan laughed. 'They tried to force us to eat them, but we squealed and refused!'

'We said "you can't make us like olives!"' All three old ladies laughed.

'Your papas were such fine-spirited men,' Horatia sighed, and slumped like a deflated hot air balloon. She appeared suddenly grey and shrunken. Nothing more than a husk.

Henrietta was instantly contrite. 'Ratia, I'm so sorry, we were clumsy. We forgot...'

'Really, please don't worry.' Horatia rallied herself to project calm confidence. 'Your fathers were as fathers to me. You were all my family. I felt embraced. Our days touring Europe were a much needed tonic, and of the very best kind.'

'Not like the olives, then?' Susan grinned impishly.

Henrietta chuckled. 'Susan, do you remember the fuss you made when Harriet pranked you by putting olives in your bed?'

'Oh yes, how funny! I jumped right out of my bed!'

'While shrieking loud enough to wake the whole street!'

'Oh we laughed so much, didn't we?' Horatia smiled. 'Those days were so sunny, and we had so much fun.'

'You know,' Henrietta declared, 'I am truly glad to meet up with you both again. In life, it is too easy for months to slip into years, and before we know it, all those years have passed us by with nothing of merit having been done in a single one of them.' The three ladies were thoughtful. 'Here's the thing,' Henrietta resumed, 'I firmly feel this trip to see you is one of my seldomly un-wasted ventures and, realising perhaps belatedly (although better late than never, without a doubt), that family and friends are the greatest treasures I have, I should like to spend more time with you both – and the children – before... well, we're none of us young, and I fear we have scant time ahead.'

'Oh, Henrietta,' Susan replied, 'these things, our family and friends, are treasures indeed and, yes, it is wonderful to reminisce together.'

Horatia gripped Henrietta's hand. 'Rietta, you are always in my heart, and it is true that being with you is better by far than our being apart. Your company today,' she turned to Susan, 'nd I mean both of you, is a tonic indeed for my soul.'

'Renewing our acquaintance is, indeed, a tonic for me too!' Henrietta's blue steel rimmed eyes sparkled.

Horatia grew tentative. 'Then might you, dear Rietta and Susan, consider keeping the company of this misfitting old lady for supper tonight?'

Henrietta's yellow, toothy smile broadened. 'Ratia, my most dear friend, I would be both honoured and delighted.'

'As would I,' said Susan.

Henrietta stood up dramatically, although the effect was somewhat limited because her full height, diminutive as she was, was barely higher than that of Horatia and Susan in their seats. She made a flourish with her hands. 'In place of Trafalgar Day, I suggest we have an "other days" celebration of our own. My most wonderful friends, I think we might all very much enjoy reminiscing on shared non-Trafalgar memories. What do you say?'

Susan frowned. 'I'm afraid I've accepted a dinner invitation from William's brother.'

Horatia patted her arm. 'I'm certain my son, Nelson, won't begrudge your attendance of an impromptu old ladies' nostalgia party. He, along with my other children, has oft voiced concern for my custom of solitary vigils on the anniversary of Trafalgar. With your leave, I shall send Honeysett to him with a note.'

Henrietta clapped her podgy hands. 'Splendid! Tonight we shall celebrate Other Days!'

CHAPTER THREE

Emma was hurrying towards her in a swirl of white muslin and bright patterned hems. Her short cropped hair was as lustrous as polished mahogany, 'Come quick, little angel! I do believe he's coming: good Lord Nelson!' a brilliant smile lit her face, 'Dear one, I'm quite certain! I can feel it right here,' she slapped a hand to her heart.

Horatia was excited. Although she remembered Lord Nelson only vaguely, the memories she had were all positive and, besides, he'd sent her loving letters which Emma read to her again and again. Emma's enthusiasm merely served to increase her own. The two of them, elegant woman and four-year-old girl, ran excitedly out of the house onto the gravel drive.

'Oh I just know he's coming,' Emma said, 'we'll be here to greet him, right on the drive, and we'll be smiling and waving so joyfully he'll think us his honour guard!'

And he really did come – how had Emma known? – the coach clattered round the corner and up the drive to find them jumping up and down, laughing with joy. The driver halted the horses with a light tug to the reins, and a slight, yet bright, and very solid man jumped out, resplendent in dark blue festooned with gold and jewels. His bicorn hat, topped with a plume of sparkling diamonds, was tucked under his one good arm. His craggy face was jubilant, 'My most dear ones! What great pleasure to find you awaiting a-ready. You are most clever indeed. And the most precious people in all the world!'

'Oh, my Nelson!' Emma flung herself at him.

'Horatia,' he beamed through the tangle of Emma's embrace, 'come to me, sweet one! My, but you have grown, and so very prettily!'

Horatia, feeling all the sunshine in the world lifting her heart high, ran to him and grinned up at his scarred, gentle face. All three, man, woman and child remained blissfully embraced on Merton

Place's drive for a long moment of the sweetest infinity.

'Mrs. Ward?' An immaculately dressed man with a thin face and balding head was watching her with patient expectance. She realised it was her butler, and that she'd slipped into the past again. She drew a steadying breath and nodded for him to speak. 'Your guests are arrived, shall I escort them to the dining room, or would you like to greet them here in the parlour first?'

****

Horatia's dining table was lit with a brass table candelabra holding a dozen beeswax candles. Three place settings, covered with silver cloches, had been laid at one end of the table. Susan and Henrietta sat either side of Horatia. Horatia led grace, then told her maid, 'Bryant, please reveal the first course.'

Horatia's plump, neatly dressed maid stepped forward from her discreet vigil beside the dresser to lift Susan's cloche. The revealed plate held a dozen green olives. Her guests shrieked with laughter.

'Would you care for a little wine with your olives?' Horatia asked her giggling guests. 'It's a *French* vintage.'

'Oh, Ratia,' Henrietta enthused, 'this is perfect! But would you be offended if I don't partake of the olive course?'

'They're actually quite tasty,' Susan speared a second olive with the cake fork provided.

'The olives were, of course, my jest,' Horatia smiled. 'Bryant, bring the next course.'

'Please don't take my plate yet,' Susan held a guarding hand over her olives. 'May I keep them to nibble on?'

'Who'd have guessed, Susan, that you'd grow up to be an olive-lover?'

Bryant cleared the other plates as Susan speared a third olive with relish. 'My child-self had no idea what she was missing!'

'Ah,' said Horatia, 'here comes the main course.'

Susan, seated nearest the door, was again served first. 'Roast chicken with potatoes and vegetables.'

'Not chicken,' Horatia winked, 'but eagle.'

Susan dropped her fork with a small shriek.

Henrietta chuckled. 'Is this a reference, Ratia, to the story of our Italian cook cooking our pet eagle during my childhood in Algiers?'

'It is, dear friend, I couldn't resist. After all, this is a celebration of Other Days.'

'I'm touched that you remembered the anecdote, but dare I ask where you procured an eagle?'

'I must confess Squires failed in her mission, and returned from the butcher with a guinea fowl instead. Will it suffice?'

'Thank goodness!' said Susan. 'Your prank gave me quite a fright.'

'This seems fair,' Henrietta laughed, 'as you survived Horatia's olive surprise completely unflustered.'

'Oh, I am thoroughly pleased we have concocted this gathering, dear friends,' Horatia declared. 'My spirits are quite lifted. I even feel merry, and this is a marvel after the succession of October twenty-firsts I've endured in dismal solitude.'

'My spirits too are lifted,' Susan concurred. 'Although, of course, this anniversary has been of lower import to me, for Lord Nelson was an uncle who, although much loved, I scarce knew. However, to sit here with good friends remembering happier times, and with Horatia artfully pranking us, this is a breath of much-needed air to my soul.'

Horatia lifted her glass. 'Ladies, may I propose a toast to Other Days?'

Her guests raised their crystal glasses smiling. 'To Other Days!'

'Shall we play a game of fond remembrance?' Susan asked. 'We could take turns relating tales of happy times from our pasts?'

'A marvellous idea, don't you think, Ratia?'

'Perfect,' Horatia agreed. 'Who shall begin?'

'Shall I?' Henrietta offered. 'I'm thinking of the happy time I had in spring of 1816, before we left for Europe, when my sister and I – freed from school – were at our parents' house in Bath with our half-brother Edward, who'd been newly promoted to lieutenant, and was wonderfully merry! He went out dancing every night, which quite vexed Mama, but Papa indulged him saying he'd earned his fun after ten years' fag as midshipman. It was one long party. So much fun!'

'Tori's father-to-be,' Susan smiled. 'Your story reminds me of… and I know such great grief later followed, but you've conjured a picture in my mind of my sister, Harriet's bright smile and the shine in her eyes whenever she beheld your merry half-brother!'

'Oh yes,' Henrietta breathed, 'and whenever Edward looked at Harriet his joy intensified. I was only twelve or thirteen, but it was apparent even to me. Yet he and Harriet thought their budding romance quite the secret!'

Susan laughed. 'We used to bait Harriet by talking about Edward just to see how she'd react, and she always tried to hide it, but her cheeks would flush bright red. We'd say things like, "Don't you think him handsome, Sister?" and she would grow even redder, and snap that it was none of our business to speculate about Papa's best friend's son!'

The three friends laughed, eyes soft with memories.

'She was the best of us, wasn't she?' Susan murmured. 'I don't mean to disparage anyone else, but Harriet was special...'

'She was golden,' Henrietta agreed.

'Oh,' Susan said, 'I feel grief coming back. Would someone please offer another happy memory?'

Henrietta touched Susan's hand across the table. 'Do you remember that time in Paris when we insisted on sharing a four-seater for the premiere of The Barber of Seville?'

Horatia exclaimed, 'Yes! We were so squashed! How many of us did we squeeze in?'

'I remember!' said Susan, 'It was the three of us, and Henrietta's sister, Lizzie, and my four sisters too!'

Henrietta clapped her hands. 'Eight of us it was. I was on my sister's lap, and she said I weighed as much a young heifer!'

Horatia laughed. 'She was vexed that you were creasing her new gown! It was green, as I recall.'

'No, I can picture her now, her dress was ivory silk, but she was wearing a green Spencer. Do you remember those silly, short jackets we were so enamoured of?'

'And those Paris-style dresses with waists up to our breasts!' Susan rolled her eyes at the memory.

'Didn't we think ourselves fine?' Henrietta laughed. 'And do you remember my mama rushing down the drive telling Pierre to stop? She was trying so hard to set a decorous example that she ran as slowly as she could, and shouted very quietly, *"Pierre, arrêtez maintenant!"*'

'I suppose, it was a good thing Pierre did stop,' Horatia mused, 'but we were by no means happy at the time.'

'Imagine though,' Henrietta said, 'if Pierre had driven us all the way into central Paris unchaperoned!?'

'I shudder to think,' Susan giggled.

After a comradely pause, Henrietta said, 'I must say, these carrots are quite delicious, very sweet.'

Horatia smiled modestly. 'They are from my garden. I keep a small kitchen garden to the rear of the house. My arthritic joints are no longer up to much labour, but I have a man, Mr. Ensten, who comes in a few times a week, and I must say he does wonders. The broccoli is his cultivation also.'

'Delicious,' Susan proclaimed. 'Cousin, would you perchance like to contribute a happy memory?'

Horatia frowned. 'A good challenge, and not, if I am honest, an easy one, but this is why I merit the challenge to be good. To remember good over ill is both Christian and redeeming. Allow me a short time to ponder… ah yes, I recall our shared delight in Lisbon on first sampling those delectable little custard tarts.'

'Pastéis de nata!' Henrietta cried, 'Weren't they divine?'

'Have we all finished the *eagle* course?' Horatia enquired. 'Good. Bryant, please clear our plates and bring in the sweet…'

'Voila!' Susan smiled when her dessert was placed before her a

few minutes later. 'You have surpassed yourself, dear Cousin-hostess: *pastéis de nata!*'

'Well,' Horatia shrugged, 'this is Squires' interpretation, but to my palette quite agreeable.'

'Your cook is superb,' Henrietta unceremoniously licked her fork. 'They take me straight back to Lisbon.'

'Oh, wasn't it marvellous?' Susan gushed. 'Do you remember Governor Beresford's grand ball? It was spectacular!'

'I do,' Horatia said. 'Poor Rietta and I were quite intimidated.'

'We were terrified,' Henrietta concurred. 'All that rigid etiquette, and we were only aware of half of it at best!'

'Oh yes, wasn't it complex? But so very gracious and beautiful too,' Susan smiled. 'Horatia, I had assumed you were quite at home, having previously met the royal princes?'

'Ah, but I had never attended a ball.'

'No,' Susan conceded, 'I should have realised that... but, oh, that music! Do you remember the dancers waltzing beneath those incredible chandeliers?'

'It really was extraordinarily grand. Quite a spectacle. Very gay.'

'And we did have fun despite our shyness, did we not, dear Ratia? Do you recall all our handsome suitors?'

Horatia smiled. 'I recall them queuing up to be introduced to you, Rietta.'

'But when I did dance, I was frightfully clumsy,' Henrietta laughed.

Susan looked wistful. 'When our mamas and papas took their

turn on the floor, they looked positively ancient! But weren't they aglow?'

'Messrs. and Mistresses Matcham and Blanckley were a joy to behold – and far more adept upon the dance floor than I!' Horatia reminisced with a laugh. 'I later heard your papas talking with Governor Beresford. Can you guess the subject of their debate?'

'Their unruly children?' Susan suggested.

'Why no,' Horatia smirked, 'it was about the viability of exporting local olives to England.'

Tears of laughter welled in Henrietta's eyes. 'Olives, oh how they did love them!'

'Were they really talking to the governor about olives during his grand ball?' Susan asked. 'Oh, how funny!'

'Mr. Matcham and my papa were certainly keen,' Henrietta owned, and added, eyes a twinkle, 'but thinking of keenness, do you remember Harriet dancing with Edward Blanckley?'

'Weren't they a picture?' Susan enthused. 'Harriet was in the most beautiful, sea blue gown with her golden hair in a knot, and Edward was so handsome in his lieutenant's uniform with his bicorn hat, shiny buttons, and starched white cuffs?'

'My mama thought him a popinjay,' Henrietta chuckled.

Horatia frowned. 'I suppose your mama did perhaps seem somewhat cold towards him.'

'Mayhap we should think on happier things?' Susan suggested.

Henrietta raised her hand to still Susan's concern, 'I should like to say my brief piece, if you'll permit? There's something I've much wished to broach, but haven't formerly known how. I swear that, whilst initially joyless, it proves joy to be attainable and, further more, this is the reason I journeyed here.'

Horatia leant forwards. 'I'm intrigued. Susan, shall we permit the brief respite from joy Rietta warns us of?'

'I say let's!'

Their eyes turned to Henrietta, whose aquiline nose and long face were rendered as orange as her wig in the flickering candlelight. 'I'm unsure what to say... well, I'll start at the beginning, whilst aiming to keep my account brief. My mother, as Ratia observed, was cold towards Edward. Never overtly so, but as her daughter, I sensed it. For example, when Edward surprised us by accompanying the officers of his ship to visit us at Algiers, my father and sister were as delighted as I to see him. We hadn't seen him for five years, and now here he was twenty-years-of-age and grown so tall! But my mother was cool. In those days, we children, of course, did not question our elders, and I assumed Edward had somehow offended my mama, though I had no idea what he might have done, as he was such an amicable chap... and it wasn't just towards Edward that Mama was cool. My eldest sister, Ann, was married to our father's clerk, Ned Dalzel. They lived in a little house adjacent to our villa. We were very fond of Ann and her Ned, who behaved to us as an affectionate elder brother, but Mama was cool towards them too. I again had no idea as to why this might be. She was similarly cold to my other half-siblings, Harry and Maria. I became cool towards them too without realising it. In retrospect, I believe my bond with my mother was so ingrained that it overrode my natural love for the children of our father's first wife. Like my mother, I was never explicit in my disregard. I maintained courteous relations, but only as far as etiquette demanded.'

A howl of wind caught in the chimney rallied a cascade of dancing sparks and sharp smelling smoke.

'Our mothers have strong holds on our hearts,' Susan murmured.

'For good, and sometimes ill, I fear, Susan. My antipathy towards my half-siblings' families was so entrenched that, to my deep regret, I bore it without thought. I would have continued this way had I not overheard my maid talking outside my parlour window to a friend. This friend of hers was lamenting that her husband preferred his first wife and the children she'd borne him. I was struck with a clear image of my mama holding herself aloof from my half-siblings and all their beautiful children. I knew, with sudden certainty, that her coldness was birthed in unfounded insecurity that Papa favoured his first family more!'

Susan sighed. 'Your poor mama.'

'My pity is for the families of my half-siblings! I have treated them with undeserved contempt.'

Horatia, who'd been silent for a time, asked, 'Toriana?'

'Yes, I'm deeply ashamed to say I have treated Tori with spite.'

'You wish to make amends?'

'I do, and I shall.' Henrietta brightened, 'This is the joyful ending I promised. My realisation of past injustice has empowered me to mend the rift.'

'Have you spoken of this to Toriana?'

'I've endeavoured to be warm towards her, and to her dear girls, but no, I've not broached the subject explicitly.'

'Henrietta, dearest,' Susan touched her friend's hand, 'tis brave to own our mistakes, and honourable to seek amendment. Toriana will feel your warmth, even if you don't explain the reason.'

****

Lizzie was regaling the company at Onslow Villas with tales of her family's genealogical prowess. 'We Blanckleys came to England with the Normans. Our surname originates from the French *blanc lis* meaning white lily or field.'

Ethel, impressed, asked, 'What is the Norman Con...Conk...?"

Lizzie was delighted by the opportunity to show off further. 'The Norman Conquest took place eight hundred years ago in 1066, when the Norman Duke William, later named *the Conqueror,* invaded Saxon England.'

'Oh,' said Ethel, looking confused.

'It was a big battle,' Jack clarified. The same age as Nellie, he was the eldest of Nelson and Jessie's eight children.

'You are correct, Son,' his lawyer father affirmed from an ornate armchair by the fire. 'Tis gratifying to hear evidence that you've absorbed your tutor's words. You're most certainly ripe to start college!'

Nelson's wife, Jessie, was sitting on an opulent settee with Tori and the loquacious Lizzie. William had a replica of his brother's armchair on the other side of the hearth, whilst their combined children, barring the two babies, were sprawled on a Turkey rug in a mass of fidgeting limbs. Their celebratory meal, which had started with giblet soup and progressed through eight further courses to a finale of sugar-stewed plums, had been delicious and satisfying. Nelson had provided fine wine to toast his grandfather's victory. Tongues had rapidly loosened, and the gathering's rendition of Rule Britannia had been loud and climaxed with back slaps.

Lizzie, the only person present not related to Lord Nelson by blood or marriage (or in Tori's case both) felt jealously excluded. It was this, along with her tipsiness, that was prompting her ramblings about the Blanckley family's prowess. 'So, Ethel dear, your Blanckley heritage is very ancient...'

Tori, who was also tipsy, interrupted, 'My papa told me the Blanckley surname derived from a place in the north of England. Lincolnshire, I believe: *Blankene* or something, which is actually recorded in the Domesday Book!'

Lizzie looked annoyed. 'I expect our bold Norman forebear gave his name to that town. How marvellous!'

'What's the Domesday–' Ethel began, but her aunt cut her short.

'Certainly the Blanckley family has been prominent in recent times. My great-grandfather was governor of Gibraltar–"

Tori interrupted again. 'Wasn't he Clerk of the Store?'

Lizzie ignored her. 'And our grandfather was British Consul to the Balearics and Algiers during the Napoleonic wars. Did you know,' she asked their host, 'that he was a good friend of Lord Nelson?'

'Umm,' Nelson spluttered, startled from a wine-induced semi-coma. 'Yes, I certainly am aware of this, and am now brought to mind of your dear mama's excellent book Six Years Residence in Algiers, which I found, umm, fascinating.'

****

'Lizzie's a lovely girl,' Horatia commented as they settled into her parlour after their "other days" dinner.

'She is lovely,' Henrietta eased her plump body into an armchair, 'although she is very much my sister's daughter.'

'How so?' Susan beckoned Horatia to join her on the settee, 'She has the Blanckley auburn hair and a long, oval face, but I sense you are referring to something else?'

Horatia sat beside Susan, who leant affectionately closer. 'I do see that Lizzie shares her mother's vibrancy...'

'Vibrancy in abundance!' Henrietta snorted. 'Oh, but I shouldn't laugh. I'm unaccustomed to wine and port!'

Susan eyed her eagerly. 'Please elaborate.'

'Well, not wishing to speak ill of the dead... especially with reference to my dear sister...' Henrietta took a sip of port, 'but she was a lickspittle.'

Susan gasped, and burst into laughter. Horatia, chuckling too, said, 'Oh Rietta, I'd never have said so without your owning it first, but I cannot disagree.'

All three old women shook with laughter. 'Oh dear,' Horatia gasped, 'laughing this much hurts my ribs!'

'It's the word you used,' Susan giggled, 'but I shan't say it again for fear of poor Horatia splitting her sides.'

'So, yes, Lizzie,' Henrietta's booming voice was distinctly slurred, 'I mean my sister, well, my niece too– it's so confusing with them both being Lizzies.'

'I remember your sister was very particular about her appearance,' Horatia observed.

'She was a vain, silly fool.' Henrietta clapped a hand over her mouth, 'I cannot believe I just said this of my own, dear sister! However, I regret to say I've detected the same inclination in her daughter.'

Susan raised her brows. 'But your niece, Lizzie's so charming and sweet!'

'Mark my words, if my niece wants something, she'll drop her charm before you can blink– I say, Ratia, are you well?'

Susan gasped. 'Oh my, Horatia's gone quite blank!' She shook her cousin's arm and patted her face but Horatia didn't respond.

Henrietta squinted at Horatia through her blue steel spectacles. 'Has she fallen asleep with her eyes open?' She cupped Horatia's face and shouted, 'Wake up!'

Horatia's eyes regained focus, but she looked confused. 'I, umm, I think I nodded off.'

Henrietta pursed her lips. 'Ratia, I am for a second time this evening a little lost for words. I sense that you're holding something back. I hope you take no offence at my saying this, but you have no need to hold any pretence with us. We're your friends.'

Horatia stiffened. 'What is it that you think I'm pretending?'

Susan intervened. 'I think what Henrietta's trying to say is that we've guessed, dear cousin.'

Horatia screwed her eyes shut. So much emotion was welling, but it mustn't burst. She must, as always, keep it tightly reined in. She'd devoted her life to not standing out. Although her sons were proud of being Lord Nelson's grandsons, she'd asked them not to mention it to their Pinner neighbours. She didn't want the attention. Her life goal, beyond the successes of her sons and grandsons, was to be considered virtuous, but not thought about. Unwanted tears brimmed beneath her eyelids.

'Sometimes,' she said slowly, 'I want to scream. Sometimes, I want to shout profanities, although, of course, I never do.' She smiled wryly. 'Sometimes I want to grab people's lapels, even my own sons', and tell them that Trafalgar Day is a memory of blood, destruction and immeasurable pain, and that to celebrate it is ugly. Oh, I know the selfishness of these urges, and have never voiced them, but in my heart of hearts I'm disgusted by these celebrations of my father's death.'

'This is completely understandable,' Henrietta's booming voice was gentle. Susan stroked Horatia's tense shoulder.

Horatia breathed in deeply. 'It haunts me. It sits on me. It squashes me.' She caught Henrietta's non-judging eyes, 'It feels like a huge, dirty, festering scab grown all over my head and weighing me down.'

'Maybe you should just let yourself shout?'

'How could I? People would hear.'

CHAPTER FOUR

'They're coming, darling!' Emma excitedly tugged seven-year-old Horatia's hand. 'I feared they'd change their minds and not come, but look, Horatia, here they are!' She pulled aside one of the anchor-patterned drapes framing Merton Place's bayed withdrawing-room windows so Horatia could see. Sure enough, a cavalcade of gilt coaches pulled by fine, matched horses, was clattering regally way up the freshly raked drive. Emma crouched to look her in the eyes and, after deftly readjusting an unruly lock of her short-cropped, strawberry blonde hair. 'Remember you must curtsey first to the Prince of Wales, then to his brother, Prince William, and then to my dear friend Prince Augustus. Now show me how you curtsey, quick, they are nearly here!' Horatia lowered her head and grasped the sides of her skirt as she bent her knees. 'Very good,' Emma beamed, 'they will be quite smitten with you, I know. Now remember, do not speak unless they ask you a direct question, and even then say only a few words. Do you understand?'

Horatia nodded.

'Good girl.' Satisfied, Emma faced the enormous mirror above the grand fireplace that was flanked with portraits of herself and Lord Nelson. She patted her chestnut curls, which were artfully pinned and beribboned into her signature chignon. Her flowing, high-waisted dress was pure white trimmed with glinting gold. Her short puffed sleeves revealed long, sinuous arms, that reminded Horatia of a bronze statue on the mantel shelf of a spread-armed lady wearing a similar dress and strange hat, was very old and something called Etruscan. Emma jumped and span back round. 'I hear their carriages, come quickly!' Emma whisked Horatia into the front hall in time to see Grandmama Cadogan pulling the doors wide open. Outside, all was sparkle and pomp. A wall of smart, gilt-emblazoned staff parted, smooth as theatre curtains, to reveal three imposingly stocky men in shiny boots, pale breeches,

and jackets with collars right up to their ample chins. Horatia felt Emma quiver before stepping forwards to greet their royal guests with an extravagant, full curtsey. The fattest of the trio, whose self-assurance made him seem larger still, bent awkwardly to kiss Emma's proffered hand, 'Your famed beauty is yet unfaded,' he proclaimed. Booming voice. Vowels clipped.

'Tis a high honour, your Majesty, that you visit our humble home.' Emma beckoned Horatia to stand beside her. 'Your Majesty, please allow me to introduce my ward, Miss Nelson, the true daughter of our beloved, lost hero.'

Horatia realised, in a shock, that this giant man would one day be the King of England. Knees trembling, she fumbled a clumsy curtsey. She panicked that she'd messed it up, but the portly giant smiled, 'charming!' He squatted closer. Eyes shiny as marbles, and breath that reeked of stale wine and cigars. 'I see good Lady Hamilton has trained you well.' Horatia, not sure what to do, looked at her feet, but the giant prince's belly was so close to her face that it kept luring her eyes to look up again. 'Lovely girl!' He ruffled her hair with such force that she was nearly knocked to the ground.

Henrietta, feeling remarkably well, was seated at the breakfast table with William, Tori and their chattering girls. 'Is there any sign of Susan?'

Tori flinched at the loudness of Henrietta's voice. 'I sent Cummings up with a tray of tea.'

Henrietta addressed the maid, 'How was Mrs. Moore when you took her tea?'

Cummings curtseyed. 'She said she were quite well, Ma'am.'

'And did she appear to be "quite well"?'

'Umm, no, Ma'am, she did not... but I asked her two times, and she said she was perfectly fine.'

'Did she take her tea?'

'No, Ma'am, she was laying in 'er bed with her eyes shut, and looking most pale, she were.'

'Hmm, this is a worry, do you not think, Niece?'

Tori flinched again. 'Perhaps she just needs a little time to compose herself?'

'Perhaps,' Henrietta interposed, 'your good aunt is unwell, and in need of assistance.'

'Oh,' said Tori, 'mayhap I have been remiss? Perhaps I should visit her room to see how she is?'

'It would be far better for me to visit her, Niece,' Henrietta declared haughtily. 'I have known Susan since childhood.'

Tori, looking upset, started to speak, but William spoke in her stead. 'I respect your counsel as you are my good wife's aunt, and so an aunt of my own, and furthermore, a guest in my house. However, my good wife,' he looked to Tori, 'was, as you are aware, adopted by Mrs. Moore after the death of her own mother when she was just three years old, and, in consequence, has come to know Aunt Susan, I should say Mrs. Moore, to a highly sensitive degree.'

'You are, of course, quite right,' Henrietta concurred, 'and I am bound to your will as the man of this household. However, please grant that it is I who know dear Susan as a peer, and, through obvious consequence, am the most appropriate party to attend her. Major Ward, I presume you will honour my prerogative of attending to your wife's aunt first. Would you deny me this, Major?' Without bothering to wait for William's assent, she turned to the maid, 'Cummings, do you have laudanum?'

'Yes, Ma'am, but–'

'Good, bring me the bottle and a glass.'

'Are you unwell, Ma'am?'

'I require it for Mrs. Moore.'

'Shall I take it to her, Ma'am?'

'Just bring it to me and I shall take it to her. Quick now!'

****

Henrietta rapped loudly on Susan's door and swept in without waiting for her answer. Susan was crouching on her unmade bed with her eyes closed and her hands pressed over her ears. 'Cummings, please, I need nothing further,' she muttered, without opening her eyes.

'Good morning, Susan dear!' Henrietta chirped.

Susan's eyes blinked open. 'Henrietta, I thought you were the maid. Ouch, my head!'

Henrietta peered at her intently. 'How are you?'

'I expect I look as bad as I feel.'

Henrietta flourished the bottle of laudanum. 'Then I have just the thing for you. A drop of this will work wonders.'

'Thank you,' Susan said faintly. 'I need a wonder worked upon me.'

Henrietta poured a good measure of the opium mixture into the glass Cummings had provided. Susan swallowed it in a single, unladylike gulp and grimaced at the bitter aftertaste.

'You'll feel fine within twenty minutes.' Susan winced at the church bell loudness of Henrietta's voice. 'Lie back on the bed for a bit, and I'll return to check on you in half an hour.'

'Don't go, please. I may feel wretched, but I do appreciate your company. And, besides, I can't sleep.'

'As you wish, dear friend.'

'I'm worried about Horatia,' Susan confessed. 'I feel she is carrying an unendurable burden, but cannot share it.'

'I agree with your appraisal. May I sit on the bed beside you?'

'Please do, but I'm afraid it isn't made.'

Henrietta grinned. 'I'm reminded of Paris when we were forced to endure boarding school after Ratia left us for Norfolk.'

'Do you remember sneaking into each other's bedrooms after lights out?'

'I've not forgotten. We had a wild old time trying to laugh silently so as not to alert Madame!'

'Do you think we were too wild for Ratia? Do you think that's why she chose to leave us and stay with her Bolton relatives in Norfolk?'

Susan mulled it over. 'My head's not very clear right now, but I recall having had the sense that she'd enjoyed touring Europe with us. Who could argue that she wasn't merry in Lisbon?'

'Quite true.'

'What was I saying?'

'You were speculating on Ratia's reasons for parting with us to settle in Norfolk.'

'Oh yes, I remember. Thank you. My thoughts were, I recall,

that Horatia, even against her own girlish wishes, felt driven to adopt a quiet and respectable life.'

'Yes, this rings true for me also, and, upon reflection, I sensed a similar thing myself, although I don't think I put it into words.'

Susan was thoughtful. 'Horatia's always carried so much unspoken weight, even as a child. My mama was very loyal to poor Lady Hamilton after Nelson's death. Mama's brother, Reverend William Nelson – he was a mean old sod! – anyway, he turned his back the moment he caught a sniff that the wind of public opinion had turned against Lady Hamilton. He always was a lickspittle. Keen to boast of his fraternity to Lord Nelson to advance himself, but with no compassion whatsoever for poor Lady Hamilton, even in the face of his brother's last codicil. We Matchams did our best to look after Lady Hamilton and Horatia. I was just a girl, but my eldest brother, George, was at college in London and helped Mama and Papa watch out for them. We sent them food, and invited them to stay at Ashfold... you know, we bought the house after the government granted Mama money for being Lord Nelson's sister? We felt it most unfair that they refused to grant even a penny to Lady Hamilton, especially as she was Horatia's guardian.'

'Do you remember Lady Hamilton? I only met her once. It was after we returned from Algiers. I remember being excited that she'd be there with you at Ashfold Lodge. I'd heard she was a famous beauty who set fashions. She felt to me like a character from the Arabian Nights, but I remember being disappointed because, when I saw her, she was an old woman. Not the glamorous goddess I'd expected. I remember Horatia as well. It was the first time I met her. She struck me as unnaturally serious and tense for a child not much older than me.'

'Poor Horatia. Those years were very hard for her.'

'Yes, it was a wretched affair. I remember you and your sisters at Ashfold. Do you remember us there?'

'Oh yes... well vaguely. I recall us playing on the lawn. It must have been summer. How old would we have been?'

'Oh, quite young. I would have been nine or ten. You were perhaps eleven. You had a lovely house. I remember it was a distinctly singular building with a criss-cross pattern along the front. Your Matchams were merry and lively. Did Lady Hamilton visit often?'

'Yes, she was a frequent visitor after Lord Nelson's death. Mama treated Lady Hamilton's visits as gala days. We children would be hopping up and down with excitement by the time she and Horatia arrived... although my papa, alas, never warmed to her.'

'Did she seem as old to you as my child-self perceived her?'

'I think she had perhaps faded, although she seemed a very fine woman to me. She was imposing. Statuesque, I think they call it. She had a very beautiful singing voice. She was a marvellous entertainer. You heard, of course, of her Attitudes?'

'Of course. They were famous. Classical tableaux of her own invention, which she performed to much acclaim.'

'Yes, even in her final years, despite her hardship and heartbreak, she performed for us at Ashfold Lodge. She was spellbinding. One minute she would be Aggripina conveying terrible grief; the next she was Circe standing bold and fierce. She'd switch from one character to the next in the blink of an eye. Each persona most lifelike!'

'Did she seem merry?'

'No, not merry. She carried a cloud of grief which was

unsettling, if I'm honest, but she was always good with us children. When I think upon it, it was a little odd. She was enthusiastic to spend time with us, but when she did, her mind seemed elsewhere. I suspect it was grief. She and Mama would often huddle together and cry, yet she never talked of her sorrow to us children... she was very much like Horatia in that respect.'

'How so?'

'She kept her problems hidden. For example, she never told us of her debt. We, I mean Mama, Papa and my brother George, guessed she was struggling, but they had no idea quite how badly. I think she was still proud despite having fallen so low.'

'You think Horatia similarly proud?'

Susan sucked her lips. 'No, not proud– or at least, not in the same way. She's protective, I think.'

'I wish she'd just talk to us openly. I'm sure she would feel better if she did.'

'I don't think she can. She's always so determined to seem virtuous, but invisible.'

'You may be right, but I feel her secrecy is tearing her apart inside.'

'I concur.'

'So our Christian duty is to coax her into sharing it,' Henrietta watched Susan, eager to see how she reacted.

'She looked as if she would cry when we pressed her to reveal her secret last night.'

'Why does she just not say?'

Susan shook her head. 'How can she?' Think how society

would judge her.'

'Well, I'd tell people and not give a hoot what they thought. My own mother was the orphaned daughter of the last born son of a last born son, or something like that. No money, anyway. At the time of her marriage to my father she was living on the charity of a more prosperous, prime-line second or third cousin whose grandfather had had the fortune of marrying into the Sulham Wilders, but,' Henrietta paused to collect her thoughts, 'Well, Mama didn't like to talk of her at all. She'd become visibly agitated if I pressed her for information, but my papa, ever open to my girlish wiles, eventually disclosed that Mama's mama was a farm labourer's daughter who dallied with my grandfather out of wedlock…' Henrietta stilled and frowned at the closed door, 'Is there someone there?' She pushed herself up off Susan's unmade bed and went to investigate, but the corridor was empty. 'No one there,' she told Susan, 'I was perhaps hearing things.'

'I didn't hear anything,' Susan admitted, 'but returning to your story, much as I feel for your mama's plight, I believe that, in society's eyes, being born to an unmarried farm labourer's daughter is entirely different from Horatia's delicate circumstance.'

Henrietta frowned. 'I am sad to say I agree. Poor Lady Hamilton has been rendered an anathema of evil– and yet, surely Ratia could talk to her family?'

'And how do you think her family would take it? Being the illegitimate descendants of Lord Nelson is bearable because his status as national hero amply compensates for her birth out of wedlock. However, proud her children may be to have Nelson's blood, any mention of Lady Hamilton being her childhood guardian sends them into apoplexy! Poor Lady Hamilton has been thoroughly demonised.'

'Do you believe Horatia came to hate her, as is widely assumed?'

'Well, we knew at the time that she didn't, or at least I knew. I sensed it. Did you not?'

'You're quite right. I fear the relentless barrage of propaganda against Lady Hamilton has muddied my thoughts.'

'If we heeded propaganda,' Susan said, 'we'd soon forget every fact we ever knew.'

****

The chair was far too small. Ethel had seen fit to inform Lizzie, repeatedly, that the room was normally hers. The furnishings were accordingly whimsical, but Lizzie paid them no heed, for her mind was racing wildly. What if people found out that her grandmother was both illegitimate and lowborn? They'd disown her. Society would shun her. Worse, that Susan woman now knew! What if she told Tori? Or Horatia and her sons? It was already bad enough that Tori's family were related to Lord Nelson, but now her own blood – blood Tori didn't share – was demeaned to that of a harlot pauper's. How they would look down upon her! It was unbearable!

And what of her marriage prospects? Lizzie's outward sweetness belied a steely ambition. She'd turned down many adequate suitors knowing that, if she held out until she inherited Aunt Henrietta's fortune, the windfall would attract gentlemen with titles. Lizzie wanted to gain a title with her marriage. Her aunt's unremitting good health was vexing, not least because Lizzie's eligibility decreased with each passing year. She was turning thirty in February. Men only looked for brides this old if they came with money, and this all-important money was dependent on Henrietta's good will.

Lizzie had rented an apartment in dreary, provincial Exmouth purely to spend more time with Aunt Henrietta, despite the embarrassment of her loud-mouth and clown-like red wig. When her smelly old aunt's health at last started to give way, she'd grit her teeth and invite her to move to live with her in Exmouth. Lizzie was prepared to endure all manner of hardships to make her dream wedding come true.

She'd planned it all out. Her eyes misted as she recounted her fantasy. She would sail to Paris to be fitted for a House of Worth gown with yards upon yards of silk and satin and sleeves so puffed as to be perfectly round. She'd have lavish lace trimmings, columns of satin bows, diamonds glinting in her hair and, of course, her most admirably wasp-thin waist! She would be entirely à la mode: as elegant as Princess Eugénie in her Charles Worth dress when she married Prince Louis Napoléon twenty years ago. She would glide down the aisle as a graceful swan with her back as straight as a church spire and her chin tilted high to denote her pride in her lineage and the cost of her dress. Six... no eight matched bridesmaids would carry her train. The church, no, it would be a cathedral – St Paul's would be perfect – would be filled with flowers and the crème de la crème of society. The best newspapers would print long descriptions of her wedding, entitled "A Most Fashionable Affair". Reporters would gushingly describe her arrival in a gilt carriage pulled by six perfectly white geldings with ostrich plumes on their heads, and streets crowded with cheering onlookers desperate to glimpse her House of Worth gown. Lizzie tensed. If word got out that... her mind quailed from naming the horror she'd overheard Aunt Henrietta blab to that damned Susan woman, but if Susan tittle tattled on her, then her dream marriage would never happen. Worse, she'd make no good marriage at all, not even with Henrietta's fortune.

Lizzie's tight-laced corset was, of a sudden, unbearably constricting. She felt breathless and sick. Her mouth was dry and, had she looked in the mirror, she'd have seen that her long Blanckley face had turned white. 'They must not know,' she muttered through tightly clenched teeth. 'They mustn't. They cannot. I don't care what it takes.'

CHAPTER FIVE

Emma clutched a mug of porter as tightly as a dying soldier grasping a shield.

'I'm fed up with you!' Horatia yelled. 'You're an embarrassment and always drunk. And I hate this apartment too. It has rats.'

Emma sighed. 'We have to take what we can afford.'

'You sold Merton Place!'

Emma gazed at her levelly. 'Do you think this doesn't tear my heart every day that I remain breathing?'

'It's all because of you spending too much on stupid parties.'

Emma remained calm. 'Darling, you know quite well that these "stupid" parties are necessary? I have to entertain my supporters. The Prince Regent has already vowed to stand as your guardian if anything befalls me. You did so well with him, my dear! More importantly for us now, he'll exert his influence for Nelson's codicil to be honoured so we're awarded those state pensions he requested. All the money I'm spending on parties will set us right before long.'

'Well, you don't have to spend so much on them, you stupid woman!'

'Good! Store up your anger against me, and hold it fast in your heart. It will be your insurance if I fail.'

Susan was fumbling in her travel chest for a clean dress. 'I'm fretting about Horatia. Imagine wanting to scream, but never being able to for fear of being heard? She's always so tense in public. Too worried about what people might think.'

'I have a solution,' Henrietta's smile revealed uneven yellow teeth. 'I didn't just come here on a whim, nice as it is to see you all – and I mean that! – I came here to invite all of you, including William, Tori and their girls, for Christmas with me in Budleigh Salterton!'

'I beg your pardon, did you just invite Horatia, Tori, William, their girls, and me to spend Christmas in your south Devon seaside resort?'

'Yes. It'd be fun! Think of it as much needed holiday spirit, if you will. Everyone here is far too serious. Not least Horatia, who certainly needs to stop worrying about what people think of her. In fact, all of you need to forget about the constant demands of etiquette, and focus on what we actually do need instead, which is being ourselves and not giving a hoot what we look like!'

'Golly,' said Susan. 'What a strange idea! Are you suggesting we cast away all social constraint? I can't say I think this advisable!'

'Oh, it does sound very reckless, doesn't it? But I'm not suggesting high jinks at our advanced age! I simply feel that you'd all benefit from letting your social guards down, and walking the streets without worrying about being judged for smiling too much, or showing sorrow.' She patted Susan's unmade mattress for dramatic emphasis, 'Joining me for Christmas will enable us to spend more time together, and, better still, give dear Ratia the opportunity to scream out her woes. The beach at Budleigh Salterton is deserted in the winter and, with the roaring tide to her aid, she'll be able to scream away to her heart's content without a single soul hearing!'

'I can't imagine Horatia, with her arthritis, fancying the idea of standing on a beach in the winter.'

Henrietta remained optimistic. 'We'd wrap her up warm. It would do her the power of good. As you said, she needs to scream without being heard. Budleigh Salterton beach is the perfect place for her to do this.'

'Why not wait until next summer? It would be easier for her when the weather's warm.'

Henrietta was uncharacteristically silent, before looking up with tear-rimmed eyes. 'I don't think I have that long left.'

'Oh, Henrietta! Surely not? You seem so hale.'

'Alas, my days are numbered.'

'I've only just re-found you. I couldn't bear to lose you again so soon!'

'I'm sorry, Susan dearest. I never intended to wound you. If I'm honest, I've never thought of myself as someone who's passing would be of consequence.'

'You are of the highest consequence to me! We've known each other since childhood. We share memories no one else has. We understand each other, do we not? Furthermore, we understand Horatia.'

'Well, yes, this is true. And, fear not, I feel perfectly fine today.'

'Then how can you be certain you have but a short time ahead?'

It was Henrietta's turn to frown. 'Promise to hear me out. Please don't laugh, but a fortune teller told me.'

'A *fortune teller?* But, Henrietta, I didn't think you'd pay heed to superstition!'

'For the most part I don't, but the circumstances of meeting this particular fortune teller were most singular.'

'Do tell,' Susan urged, excited at the prospect of a good tale.

'It was just a few months ago. I was walking along the high street of Budleigh Salterton and nearing my house, when a young woman, thin and pale she was and her dress was faded and worn. Well, she suddenly started. I hadn't observed her before. She must have been standing in the little lane beside my house, concealed in the shadows. As I say, she suddenly started, flinging her arms up and letting forth a little yelp. I was quite surprised, as you may imagine, and thought perhaps the woman had had a turn, but she looked me directly in the face, her eyes very wide and fearful, and told me urgently, "you have spurned the children of your half-brothers, and must make amends soon!" I was, of course, quite taken aback. I asked her what she meant. She seemed confused and shook her head as if clearing her thoughts. "I don't know, Ma'am," said she, "I think I had a funny turn. I apologise if I was importune or startled you." I asked her what she meant, and she explained that when she saw me approach she'd been gripped by an overwhelming clarity in which, as if in a dream, she was imparted with urgent knowledge concerning my person. She was quite contrite and apologised profusely for having blurted out the nonsense that had come, unbidden, into her mind. I'd have thought no more of it, as women of her age are prone to hysterical outbursts, but I was intrigued by her reference to spurning the children of my half-brothers, for I had indeed done this, as I confessed to you and Ratia last night.'

'So you did!' Susan gasped. 'What a fascinating tale!'

'I asked the woman to elaborate further on her strange vision, but she was reluctant to say more. She said she feared it would distress me needlessly, for her vision was the result of a funny turn, and had no sense to it. When I pressed her further, she began to cry and begged me to turn away for my own good.'

'Goodness! I'd have been terrified!'

'I confess to having been fearful, Susan dear, but I was determined. I took her by the shoulders and repeated that I wished to learn what had transpired in her vision. She at last relented and, sobbing, confessed that she had heard or felt – she couldn't properly describe the sensation – a powerful pronouncement that I must hastily make amends with my half-brothers' children because, and here she whimpered in sheer dread, I will be dead before the next year is out.' Henrietta attempted a brave smile, but tears glistened in her sharp, grey eyes. 'So you see, my determination to reconcile with Tori is the prime motivation for this visit. I've decided to leave her, and her brother, Horace, provision in my will.'

****

The Ward brothers had withdrawn to William's russet and cream-papered study. 'What I've been pondering,' Nelson divulged, 'is why our noble grandfather wrote his remarkable last codicil.'

'In which he asked the state to recompense Lady Hamilton for her so called "war contributions"?'

'That very one. It's perplexed me, perhaps because I'm a lawyer so duty-bound to question the motivations behind unusual codicils such as this. However, Lady Hamilton cannot be suspected of direct interference, because the document was witnessed on Victory, proving beyond doubt that she was not present at the time of its writing.'

'I believe the "war contributions" our grandpapa ascribed to her were her own exaggeration,' William opined.

'Invented, more likely. Lord Nelson, great man as he was, had his Achilles heel in that woman. That he believed she released provisions for the British fleet and couriered vital intelligence to the British was, with the utmost respect to our esteemed grandfather, utter poppycock. No doubt Lady Hamilton did have the ear of that foreign Queen – all women together – yet note that our own sovereign's wife, Queen Charlotte, refused to receive her. It's nonsense to think for one moment that a jumped up, low-born harlot served a genuine part in our war effort. Except, perhaps by making numerous sailors happier for one night at a time!'

'Our poor grandpapa was ensnared by her charms,' William sighed.

'Alas, all men are fallible, even the greatest of us. Our dear, open-hearted grandpapa was so bewitched by that scheming harlot that her claws continued to dig into him aboard Victory, hundreds of miles from her fluttering eyelashes and rouged lips. Yet, for all the money she inveigled from our hapless grandpapa, she spent every last farthing like water, thus soon finding herself in debtor's jail.'

William snorted. 'She had no financial acumen. Brought it all on herself.'

'Quite so.'

'It's our dear mama, then just a child, for whom I have sympathy. I can't imagine how greatly she suffered when Lady Hamilton's negligence dragged her into debtor's jail.' William exhaled a smoke ring, 'My wife, though, is of the opinion that Lady Hamilton was a fine lady who suffered unjustly following our grandfather's demise. This is what her aunt Susan told her, who apparently heard it from her mother, who was, as you know, our grandfather's sister, and Lady Hamilton's close friend.'

Nelson scoffed. 'Ladies are prone to believing fantasy. The hard facts, in the case of Lady Hamilton, are,' he counted each upon his fingers, 'she was base-born. She used easy charms to climb above her station. She was unable to maintain her ill-gotten rank due to a fundamental lack of financial sense, and her alcoholism.'

‘Quite so. Although one had best not voice such sentiments to my good wife.’

‘Let the women keep their harmless fantasies, for it’s we men who set policies.’

‘There is though our Queen,’ William pointed out, quietly.

‘And she, noble though she is, is fully guided by her ministers, of whom all are male.’

‘Quite so.’

Susan, now feeling much better, beckoned to Henrietta. ‘Please, would you help me dress? I am conscious of still wearing my clothes from yestereve. Fear not, I shan’t change my corset!’

‘You wear a corset?’

‘Laced very loosely,’ Susan winked.

‘The trend for tight lacing reeks to me of self-flagellation.’

‘But you do wear a corset, Henrietta?’

‘Very rarely.’

Susan giggled. ‘That’s quite scandalous!’

‘Susan dearest, I am a very old lady. It’s been many years since my purpose in dressing was to present my slim, girl-like figure to best advantage. In fact, even when young, with my long face and small stature, the best I could hope for was to resemble a well-groomed miniature pony ready for a show.’

‘Oh Henrietta, you do say the most outlandish things! You have never looked remotely thus.’

'My chief concern in these latter days of life,' she boomed on, 'is to clothe my ageing, much-expanded body,' she patted her rotund gut, 'in the greatest comfort I can accord it.'

'But... well, golly, please don't take this the wrong way, but, I mean that wig you wear...'

'What, this old thing?' Henrietta patted her hairpiece, 'Perhaps it's a vanity, but it's a comfortable one, and I do so detest being dull!'

****

Tori was enjoying her needlework when her elderly aunts let themselves into her parlour. 'Good morning,' she told them with a practiced smile.

'I hope we're not disturbing you?' Susan's own smile was frail.

'You don't disturb me at all. I've been working on this cushion cover without company since my brother-in-law called and William took him to his study. Aunt Susan, are you well? Aunt Henrietta was concerned about you.'

'I am quite well now, thanks to the laudanum.Henrietta rightly guessed that I was somewhat debilitated by fatigue after our uncustomary late evening.'

Tori politely refrained from mentioning the drunken state she'd found them in, and said instead, 'Please be seated.'

'Are you well yourself, Niece?' Henrietta enquired pleasantly.

'My thanks. I am very well.'

'You seem to have been somewhat unsettled by my question.'

'I didn't mean to. Umm, what I meant to say is that I did not mean to give that appearance.'

'I am certain you did not, Niece. However, the fact remains that you did.'

'I am sorry, Aunt.'

'Quite the contrary, Toriana, tis I that should apologise to you.'

'Whatever for?'

'For startling you, of course.'

Susan intervened. 'Henrietta, I fear you are merely startling Tori further.'

'Am I? Oh dear.' Henrietta returned her gaze to their bemused niece. 'Toriana, do please forgive me. I have made up my mind to be pleasant towards you, but I'm finding it harder than expected.'

'Tori, please don't mind Henrietta's clumsy and poisonous tongue. She means you no ill.' Henrietta raised her eyebrows but let Susan's comment pass.

'This I do not,' Henrietta agreed. Then asked Susan, 'Should I tell her?'

'I say yes.'

'But only in outline?'

'As you wish.'

'Toriana,' Henrietta looked Tori earnestly in the eyes, 'I own that I have, hitherto, been quite beastly towards you.'

'Aunt, I–' she began to protest.

'Hear me out,' Henrietta overrode. 'I know full well that I've been beastly, so there is no need for you to pretend otherwise. I have been similarly beastly towards your brother, Horace, and to every single one of your cousins, bar my own sister. So you see, I have been extremely beastly indeed.' She turned to Susan, 'I feel quite light-headed for having finally said this!'

'Perhaps tell this to Tori?'

'I suspect she heard me.'

'This is not the point.'

'Oh. Toriana, I apologise once again for having been rude towards you.'

Tori, by now rendered quite speechless, gaped at Henrietta in astonishment.

'I suspect you're wondering why I treated you all in such beastly fashion?'

When Tori gave no answer, Henrietta continued unabashed. 'It was an attitude I soaked up from my mama, who was averse to "the first family", in other words, the children of my papa's first wife; your grandmother. I did not think to question my mother's judgement, such a thing would have been disrespectful, so I assumed Mama's ill-judgement was correct.'

'Oh,' Tori managed to say.

'And now you wish to make amends, don't you?' Susan prompted.

'This is correct, yes. Toriana, on realising my injustice towards yourself, your brothers and cousins, I determined immediately to arrange this trip to you with the express purpose in mind of setting things right.'

'Thank you, Aunt,' Tori mumbled.

'With this in mind, there are two matters I wish to put to you.'

'Thank you, Aunt,' Tori parroted herself.

'Very good, although you really do not have to thank me. Firstly, I have decided to provide for you in my will. No, you don't have to thank me again. I also should like to sponsor Baby Alice. Now, I realise I am far too old to stand as her godmother, but I should like to make a bequest to support her in whichever way she wishes (though I favour education) once she turns twenty-one. Is this acceptable?'

'It is most unexpectedly generous.'

'Most unexpected, I am sure, considering what an old dragon I've been!' Henrietta chuckled, thoroughly enjoying her role as beneficiary aunt. 'My second proposal is for you all to spend Christmas at Budleigh Salterton. I shall rent rooms for you in the Rolle Hotel, which is a fine establishment with excellent sea views.'

Tori was again flabbergasted. 'Your offer is…'

'Don't worry Niece, I'm happy for you to find my offers unexpected.'

'Well then, your offer is most unexpected.'

'I knew it!' Henrietta chortled. 'Now affirm my offer.'

'I regret I cannot affirm without my husband's consent, and, besides, we are bound to care for his dear mama.'

'I've invited Ratia too,' Henrietta's grin revealed a daunting display of yellow, uneven teeth.

'We think it would be good for her to make the journey,' Susan chipped in, 'Your aunt's visit has raised your mother-in-law's spirits to the highest point I've observed since the loss of her husband, and I truly believe a visit to Budleigh Salterton would do her the power of good.'

'I really do have to consult my husband.'

'Of course, dear, most proper.' Henrietta rang the servant's bell. 'Ah, Cummings, fetch Mr. Ward immediately.'

'Ma'am?' The maid looked to Tori, unsure how to respond to their house-guest's imperious manner. Tori, flustered, looked, in turn, to Susan.

Henrietta ignored Tori and the maid's uncertainty, and barked, 'Quick now, Mr. Ward is needed here immediately.'

Cummings, overwhelmed, scurried off to fetch William.

'Henrietta,' Susan admonished, 'I do declare you a bossy-boots!'

She sniffed. 'Well I do declare you judgmental and rude.'

'You are naming *me* rude?'

'That I am. You have, in front of our niece, insulted my Christian endeavours to mend our family rift and save dear Ratia.'

'Poppycock! I have merely challenged your imperious way of going about it.'

'Oh look, Cummings has returned.'

The maid shot Henrietta an anxious glance, but addressed Tori. 'Your husband, Ma'am, he says he cannot come to the parlour because he's engaged with his brother.'

'This is no problem,' Henrietta pronounced grandly, and, without so much as a by-your-leave, strode out of the parlour.

****

William was irritated by a second knock on his study door within as many minutes. Expecting Cummings to have returned with another message from the womenfolk, he sighed and said, 'Come!' He was, however, thoroughly nonplussed when his wife's short, rotund Blanckley aunt burst in.

Henrietta briefly acknowledged William's brother with a booming, 'Good morning!' then stopped two feet from William and fixed him with a blue steel-rimmed glare, 'Nephew, I fear your maid may be failing in her duties, as she claimed you're too busy to heed your mother's needs!' Noticing that William looked discomforted, and remembering her resolution to behave kindly towards Tori's kin, she conceded, 'Your brother does not have to leave immediately. I think it permissible for him to wait here while you see to the business at hand. Agreed?'

William regarded her open-mouthed, very much as his wife had done ten minutes before. It was his brother, Nelson, lawyer-trained, who had the presence of mind to respond. 'Miss Blanckley, I'm charmed to see you again. It has been many years. I think we last met at William's wedding?'

Henrietta grabbed his proffered hand. 'Ah yes, Toriana's wedding in Clevedon. It was a lovely affair, was it not? Now, William, you are required immediately in the parlour to assure your wife of your intent to spend Christmas at Budleigh Salterton.'

'But–'

'Do not delay! This trip is for your mother's health. Nelson, do you deny that your mother needs cheering, and that my visit to Pinner has cheered her?'

'In point of fact, umm... yes, I do feel bound to declare that our mother has been cheered–'

'Exactly. Now come along William.' Henrietta ushered him briskly into his own parlour, and, with a self-satisfied smile, informed Tori, 'Your husband is keen to support his mama's best interests, and is in full agreement with my plan for you all to stay at Budleigh Salterton for Christmas.'

Tori, flabbergasted for the countless time that morning, studied her husband's sharp-nosed face. He appeared more surprised than keen, and, when their eyes met, his raised brows spoke volumes.

Henrietta continued. 'The next step is to persuade dear Ratia of the merit of my plan.'

'William, dear,' Susan interjected, 'I do hope Henrietta has not been forceful toward you.'

He bristled. 'I am man enough to have weighed the pros and cons of her plan and judged it, umm, meretricious.'

'Well, good,' Susan shot Henrietta an assessing glance nonetheless. Henrietta simpered back sweetly.

'I am unsure whether Mama will wish to embark upon such a long journey,' William pondered.

'No need to worry on that account,' Henrietta replied, 'I've already informed her that the train journey is comfortable and swift. When shall we tell her you've agreed to come too?'

He shuffled uneasily from foot to foot. 'It should also be borne in mind that, umm, well it is likely I will be called back to duty in Madras–'

Tori stiffened. 'Husband, do you know when?'

'Umm, well, Wife, as it so happens–'

She turned white. 'You do know?'

'Err, yes, umm, that is to say the papers arrived yesterday, but I didn't like to, umm, that is I did not wish to interfere with the celebration.' He knelt to clasp Tori's hands, and looked beseechingly into her eyes. 'Darling, as you know, my leave was for eighteen months, and that term has already expired.'

Tori sobbed helplessly. 'I cannot bear it. What of your health?'

'I shall be perfectly diligent in taking whichever tonics the doctor prescribes.'

She pulled herself together. 'When do you leave?'

'I am to board the S. S. Tanjore at Southampton in the first week of November.'

'We could come with you–'

'You know, darling, that the climate is not good for the girls, and that they need to be raised within the graces of civilised society... and think of taking Baby Alice on that horrendous journey.'

'She cries more than my older girls did as babes. I believe this is a result of the cooler climate–'

He laid a hand on her shoulder. 'We've talked all of this through at length.'

'It's just that you are leaving so soon, and I won't be with you this time to care for you.' Tori threw her arms tightly around William's thin shoulders. They were oblivious of the old ladies' discreet departure.

****

Ethel, who'd been eavesdropping behind a large urn in the downstairs hallway, burst into the nursery. 'We're going to Buddy Salty... where Aunt Henrietta lives for Christmas!'

'They have not spoken to me of this,' Kajri observed, bouncing fretful Alice on her knee. 'Will they have me come to this place too? Will it be more cold than Pinner?'

'Aunt Henrietta said it's warmer there, but I don't know if they'll ask you to come with us, Kajri, for the news is quite new,' the six-year-old, proud to possess important information, continued grandly, 'and Papa's going back to India!'

The older girls gasped. Nellie proclaimed, 'Mama will be heartbroken!'

'I'll be heartbroken too,' Ethel countered, 'and you'll miss Papa as well, won't you?' she asked Carrie, who burst into tears.

'What's bubbly-salty-bum, and will it hurt?' Little Evie asked anxiously.

CHAPTER SIX

'You're a stupid, old, drunk!' Horatia spat at Emma when she emerged in the morning with a shaky hand clamped to her brow.

Emma stopped in her tracks. 'What did you just say?'

'I said you are a stupid, old drunk.'

'Do not speak to me with those cruel words!'

'You told me to harness my anger, so here it is: what you *wanted.'*

'What has come over you, child?'

'You. You have come over me. It's your stupid, drunkenness…' Horatia was upset and annoyed when another fit of whooping coughs racked her body so she couldn't speak, or even think. She braced one hand against the mildewed wall to support herself, glaring at Emma the whole time.

'Horatia, I know times are hard, but–'

'But, nothing,' she gasped between coughs.

'We still love each other.'

Horatia waited impatiently for her coughing to subside. 'No,' she spat, 'I don't love you. I hate you!'

'Horatia!'

'Well I do!' Coughing again, she darted jerkily to her room and slammed the door behind her.

In the west Devon port city of Plymouth, Captain Horatio Charles Nelson Blanckley of the Royal Marines reclined on the tousled bed of his small, Emma Place apartment. He'd chosen it because its proximity to Stonehouse Barracks allowed him to easily meet morning musters. Not that this would be an issue tomorrow, as he'd just started three weeks of leave. Half-wrapped in a cream faux Provençal quilt, and languidly sucking a cigar, he was revealed as athletically wiry for his forty-one years. His dark red hair and moustache were neatly trimmed, and his smile was easy.

'Orace,' a young, blonde snuggling at his side regarded him with wide, painted eyes. 'Do yer 'ave to go ter that village near Exmouth tomorrow?'

Smile no-longer-easy, his moustache twitched in irritation. 'Yes, I really must go. As I've already explained.'

'But I'll miss yer, and yer only just got back from Birmingham, and it's gonna be Christmas–'

'Joan, I don't want to go through this again. If you cannot be good company, then there is precious little reason for my bothering to spend time with you.' Brimming tears threatened to smudge her makeup further. 'Oh do pull yourself together,' he scolded.

'Yes 'Orace. Sorry if I'm being difficult. It's just that I so adore you, in't ee?'

He relaxed. This was the sort of thing he liked to hear.

'Tell me about yer old aunt again,' she propped herself up on her elbows, revealing more than she'd perhaps intended. He grabbed her bosom provoking a shriek of mock horror. 'Oh you cad, I only asked fer a story.'

'Well cover yourself up, if you don't want a bit of the other.'

'Give me some quilt then, in't ee?' She grabbed a corner of the counterpane and wrapped it round her naked torso. 'That better?'

'I can still feel you.'

'Hmm, well what shall I do about that?'

'I think there's some Scotch in the kitchen. Be a darling and and fetch it. Here, wear this.' He scooped his blue-collared, scarlet marines captain jacket from the floor, and threw it to her. It had been careless of him to leave it there, but he'd worry about that in the morning. Joan, looking deflated, donned it, and stalked off to retrieve the spirit.

'So yer old aunt?' Joan asked when she returned with the whiskey and two glasses. 'Yer said she's an old witch?'

'Did I? Are you sure? I don't remember discussing her with you.'

'Yer don't?'

He considered it and shrugged. 'Nope. I have absolutely no recollection of talking to you about Aunt Henrietta."

'But we talked about 'er for ages. You were most particular.'

'Really? What do you claim I said?'

'"Claim?" I'm not making it up.'

'So tell me.'

'Umm, yer said she were a right old witch, and she'd always been nasty to yer and your sister, and yer said she's rich as the Queen of Sheba, and ripe to drop dead.'

'Hmm, it seems I really did talk of her to you. I have absolutely no memory of it. How peculiar! Pour me more whiskey.'

'I can't believe you'd 'ave forgotten all them plans.'

'What plans?'

'Yer really don't remember?'

'Do you think I'm playing a game?'

Joan looked suddenly uncomfortable. 'No, it's just I–'

'Tell me.'

'Here's yer whiskey.'

He snatched the glass. 'What is it that you have to say?'

'I don' wanna say nuffin.'

'Tell me immediately.'

She started crying again. 'I only did what yer said, honest.'

'And what exactly was this? Bearing in mind I have no recollection whatsoever of this *claimed* conversation.'

'Well, it were right afore you went to Portsmouth for that fancy dinner–'

'The annual dinner of the Royal Marines in May?'

'That were the one. Anyway, right before yer left, yer told me all about yer Aunt 'Enrietta and what an evil old cow she were, and 'ow she inherited everything off your granddad, and that it weren't fair coz the children from yer own grandma didn't get nuffin. Or summat like that.'

'Hmm, carry on.'

'Well, you were right narked about it all. Yer said you were the male heir to yer granddad, and the money shoulda come down to you. Not to 'er.'

'I own that this does all sound true,' he reclined back on the bed, easy smile resumed. 'Do have some whiskey yourself, Joan.'

She checked his face for suspicion, but her lover seemed to

have forgotten his query about what she'd done after their conversation last May. Surely they'd discussed it since? Her head swam. Yes, she remembered having told him, excitedly, how she'd done it, and him laughing delightedly. Clapped her on the back. Kissed her with passion. He had to have known... otherwise it didn't make any sense.

Horace eyed her blearily. 'Pour yourself some Scotch, then come here.' She obediently filled her glass, but, on turning back to him, found he was already asleep. She exhaled with relief, then, aware of her overly frayed nerves, swigged the whiskey anyway.

****

Forty-miles away as the seagull flies, though considerably further by train, Henrietta was restlessly pacing her parlour. Although her house was small, she preferred it to her previous out-of-town residence, which had become too remote for her ageing mobility to endure. Here, on Budleigh Salterton's high street, she was in close proximity both to village life and to the health-giving airs of the shore. Bored of staring through her twin parlour windows willing Ratia to arrive, she fidgeted with the baubles on her Christmas tree until realisation struck that her constant tweaking was making the overall effect worse. Her holly-wreathed grandfather clock, tick by tick, continued to inch forwards reminding her of every passing second. The sharp sound of clattering hooves on cobbles propelled her back to the nearest window. Was it them? No, it was an age-worn grocer's cart. Her view was momentarily obscured by a mother with two children traipsing past. She craned her neck to see further down the street. There was a scuttling errand boy, and a pair of businessmen strutting past the holly-bordered windows of the Feathers Hotel opposite, dressed in the style she thought of as dandy. Dandily dressed also was her jovial neighbour, Mrs. Taylor, resplendent in a scarlet hat pinned jauntily atop her extravagant coiffure. Mrs. Taylor was chatting to Widow Chown beside the fruit-bedecked kissing bough the villagers had erected further down the high street. Disappointed not to have seen Horatia, she considered distracting herself with needlework, but knew instantly that she was in no mood to concentrate on it.

'Bradford!' she called. Voice, as ever, loud as church bells. 'Is the guest bedroom aired?'

'Yes, Ma'am.' A thin young woman with unruly brown hair answered promptly from her station equidistant between Henrietta's fussing and the front door.

Oh, where were they? Henrietta wondered again. She realised, wryly, that she would be hopping up and down like an excited child if her old body permitted it. Calm down, old woman, she told herself. Surely, by this age, she should be able to await visitors in dignified repose? She succeeded in calming herself, until, a brief moment later, it occurred to her that their train may have crashed. There had been a terrible rail collision at Wigan earlier in the year, and another somewhere in Nottinghamshire in August. Also, people on trains could get murdered. What had been the victim's name? Briggs, maybe. Oh, why had she persuaded her dear friend to undertake a journey of such high peril?

****

Horatia was travel-worn and exhausted. Their journey from Bath that morning had begun well with the Bristol & Exeter Railway connection arriving punctually. Their first-class compartment had been very comfortable, despite the necessity of squeezing four adults, five girls, one baby, and an unruly spaniel into a space designed for eight. However, the train had been delayed for half an hour, and relief at its eventual departure was short-lived because, after chugging along for half an hour, it screeched to an unscheduled stop in the middle of nowhere, and remained there stationary for a full hour. It had been impossible to find out the reason for the delay because they were locked into their compartment. Pulling the communication line to demand attention had felt inappropriate. Her granddaughters were soon desperate to relieve themselves.

'Mama,' Ethel had wailed. 'You do not know how much I suffer!'

Horatia was similarly discomforted, but too polite to admit to it. Several rounds of A Frog He Would A Wooing Go, which Patch had amusingly howled along with, and Tori reading aloud from a newly-published children's story by some man named Lewis Carroll, had quietened the children until the emergence of a pungent aroma from Baby Alice. Her stink, and increasingly angry cries, had caused Patch to whine and the little girls to hold their noses. Kajri changed Alice's nappy behind the improvised screen of Tori's tent-like skirt, and the ayah threw the soiled rag out of the carriage window. The baby seemed happier after this and accepted a bottle of modern formula milk. Things had then been peaceful until Evie had begun to sob loudly about *wanting to go, and right now,* until distracted by the train's screech back into motion.

Their final arrival at Exeter hadn't come too soon. They were so happy to be there that their good mood wasn't even dampened when the stationmaster told them they'd missed their connection to Exmouth. They'd all agreed that relaxing in the station's first-class cafeteria would be much nicer than boarding another train. Poor Cousin Susan seemed utterly fagged, and Horatia herself was quite exhausted by this point. Her arthritis had flared, causing all her joints to hurt as if they were on fire. She had shooting pains in her back and shoulders, and her head throbbed and fuzzed so it was hard to even think.

On top of all of this, was the gnawing pain of William's absence in Madras. She spared Tori her worries, but was secretly terrified that this time, without Tori there to nurse him, his weak liver would finish him off, just as had happened to her poor, dear youngest boy, Philip, eight years ago.

It had been a blessing to relax in the first-class cafeteria and sip tea, but the trials of their journey from Pinner to Budleigh Salterton continued. Both the first and second-class carriages on the next Exmouth train were full because of the rush of families travelling home for Christmas. Horatia and her party had had no option but to cram into third-class. The Christmas rush had filled the cheap seats too, and they'd been forced to sit in an unpleasantly cramped fashion with their hooped skirts jammed together to form a long, asymmetric bulge. Standing passengers had crowded in on them. The carriage was stinky, stuffy and hot, despite the coolness of the December day. Knowledge that this last stage of their journey was short had escaped the notice of Baby Alice, who'd screamed for the entire duration. On top of that, Patch the spaniel had growled menacingly at everyone who came near, which, considering the jam in the carriage, had been a constant cause of concern for the unhappy dog.

Horatia had started to seriously question the wisdom of the trip. Rietta had persuaded her it would be quick and easy, but the journey had been an ordeal for all of them. Cousin Susan's eyes had sunk into dark hollows, Tori was clearly fraught, and even her excitable grandchildren looked like they were flagging... apart from plucky, little Ethel. The key attraction of the Exeter to Exmouth track was the view of the Exe estuary, but it wasn't visible to them because of the press of people around them. Ethel had shamelessly climbed up onto the bench-seat between Kajri and Susan, and loudly exclaimed that the view was marvellous.

Horatia was very relieved when the guard announced their

arrival at Exmouth, and heartily glad to disembark from all trains for the time being. Now all she had had to do was help steer her grandchildren onto the platform, locate a porter, and find transport for the final four-and-a-half miles to Budleigh Salterton, late as they were.

Horatia observed the twilit streets of Exmouth as her party followed the hired porter out of the hectic station. So this was where her father's wife, Lady Nelson, had spent her last days. Horatia felt glad to have been spared the awkwardness of meeting her, though she'd been a good friend to her Matcham kin, and she'd borne Lady Nelson no ill-will. Lady Nelson's plight as her father's publicly discarded wife had been pitiable. Of course, society blamed Lady Hamilton entirely for her father's romance with her. There really was no logic to people's habit of blaming women for affairs, whilst maintaining that men had mastery of their emotions. Horatia shrugged. Men could always do as they pleased, and women paid the price. Lady Hamilton had paid a very great price indeed. Even Chambers's dictionary defined her as a conniving harlot – or words to that effect – in their definition of Nelson, which, of course, portrayed him and his estranged wife as paradigms of virtue. 'Poor Fanny!' everyone lamented of Lady Nelson. Horatia remembered seeing her portrait in *The Times*. A proud, point-nosed, jowly woman with dark hair and more lace around her head and neck than a lion's mane. Should she visit her grave during her stay with Rietta? It would be a Christian gesture to leave flowers, if any could be found in December, but would Lady Nelson's spirit wish her shadow to touch her last resting place? Horatia thought not and sighed. Reminders followed her like ravening ghosts.

The party of nine plus one baby hired two Hackneys for the four-and-a-half mile journey from Exmouth to Budleigh Salterton. Horatia and Susan took the first carriage with Nellie, Ethel and Carrie. Tori and Kajri took the second with little Evie,

Ada and Baby Alice. The midwinter light was fading rapidly and the view dwindled into darkness as they left Exmouth's gaslit centre. Before long, it was pitch dark. Horatia gripped the edge of her seat. Rising wind and deep pits in the track were causing the coach to rock madly.

****

Henrietta was frantic. She'd grown more and more certain that Ratia and her family had suffered a fatal accident. She alternated peering through the windows with restless pacing and morosely staring at her lap, hands clenched, berating herself for murdering her friends. To say that she was relieved to hear loud knocking on her front door would be an untruth, because she thought it was the police with bad news. She wrapped her arms protectively about herself when Bradford went to see who had come. Henrietta was genuinely amazed to hear the tired voice of a cabbie announcing, 'Mrs. Ward and Mrs. Moore here for Miss Blanckley'.

She ran to the door with no thought for dignity. There she was, dearest Ratia, peering out of a Hackney looking frightfully pale, but definitely alive. And there was Susan, peeking past Horatia's black-clad shoulder, and also looking pale, but alive. Henrietta opened the carriage door herself. 'Friends! You can have no idea how happy I am to see you both here safe and well!'

****

Tori was also very relieved. She, her girls and Kajri were at last safely installed in the Rolle Hotel. A sleep-tousled porter had escorted them to their first-floor rooms before going back for their luggage. She was happily surprised to learn that Aunt Henrietta had, most generously, reserved three suites for them. There was one for Kajri and the infants; one for her older girls; and one for Tori's sole use. What luxury! She closed her suite door and collapsed into a sumptuously upholstered chair. She kicked off her shoes and unfastened the clips in her hair so it hung loose. Her feet throbbed and she didn't want to move them, but she stood up to extract herself from her tight-fitting, bustled dress and the corset beneath. She retrieved a linen nightgown from her trunk and let it fall over her head and down her body like gentle rain. It felt marvellous. Feeling relaxed for the first time that day, she laid herself happily down on the large, comfortably-sprung bed. The pillows were soft and plump, the covers had the pleasing feel of quality, and the mattress was pleasantly firm. The distant crashing of waves on the adjacent beach felt like the kindly beat of a protector's heart. She was sound asleep within minutes.

CHAPTER SEVEN

Tori tossed in her sleep. In her dream, she was in the sunny garden of the new country house. The air was perfumed with tangs of freshly cut grass and sawdust. Papa, dressed informally in a loose linen shirt, was balancing on a wooden ladder to help the builders with the verandah roof. Mama and Aunt Susan were sitting on the lawn wearing lacy cotton caps to shade them from the sun. Cousin Acheson, white-blond and a year her senior, was clinging to Aunt Susan's black skirt. Aunt Susan's older son, Cousin Alexander, was playing with her six-year-old brother, Horace. They were running to and fro along the edge of the steep slope down to the river, flying gayly-coloured paper kites. The kites looked very pretty fluttering in the air. Tori ran to them, wanting to grab one for herself. Mama cried out, 'Stay away from the edge!' But three-year-old Tori didn't listen. All she wanted was to hold one of the pretty kites in her hands. Suddenly, her foot slipped on the edge. Losing her balance, she screamed in terror. Mama rushed to reach her, but was hampered by her fat belly which had a baby in it. At last Mama was there, stretching her hand to save her, but she lost her own footing and tumbled over the edge. Head over heels over head. Red dress catching on the brambles. Blood on her white face. 'Mama!' Tori cried, 'Stay!' But it was too late. Her mama was gone into the river and lost forever.

Something soft was prodding her cheek. Tori realised she'd been having that awful dream about View Cottage, which she'd not had for years. The soft thing, she realised was a hand. She thought at first that it was William's, but remembered he was gone. She wondered if it was his recent departure that had prompted her to dream of View Cottage and her mama again.

'Mama, wake up!'

Tori opened her eyes to behold an unfamiliar bedroom, and blue eyes very close to her face. She was completely disorientated, until she remembered she was in the Rolle Hotel in Budleigh Salterton.

'Mama, you were asleep.'

'Yes, sorry, Ethel. Is it late?'

'Kajri said it is half-past-eight already, and you'll never guess what?'

Mind still troubled from her dream, Tori immediately panicked. 'What is it?'

'The sea's right outside! Nellie said I shouldn't wake you, because we got here really late last night, and you probably need to sleep, and Kajri said so too, but I just knew you'd want to see the sea. Come and look out the window!' Ethel skipped to the heavy brocade curtains and tugged them apart, flooding the room with painfully bright blue-white light. 'Come and look, Mama, you can see the sea from the window!'

Perhaps her nightmare had been a prophecy that her daughters would fall into the sea here and drown.

'Mama!'

Unable to resist her daughter's excited urging, Tori rose from her bed in her white lace nightgown and, squinting against the light, joined Ethel at the window. As expected, she saw the sea, although it was further away than Ethel had led her to believe. It lay as a sparkling, oddly brown-hued sheet beyond the flat, winter-dulled expanse of the hotel's lawn. Well, at least her girls were in no direct danger of tumbling into it from a hotel window.

'Isn't it marvellous?' Ethel enthused. 'May we go and play on the beach, Mama? I do so very much wish to. I really do.'

'Yes, we shall, of course, visit the beach, but not right now. I must dress and have breakfast. Have you breakfasted yourself?'

'Oh no, Mama. Kajri said we must wait for you to join us.'

Tori cringed.

Ethel prattled on. 'But I already know where the breakfast is. I went downstairs and asked a maid, and she showed me, and it's ever such a big dining room, and you can see the sea through the windows!'

'I'm sure it's very impressive. Now, Ethel dear, go and ask Kajri to help me dress. You may tell your sisters I'll be along in a few moments to accompany you all to the dining room to break our fasts.'

'Yes, Mama!' The six-year-old, pleased to be entrusted with this important errand, dashed off at full pelt.

Tori frowned at the unclosed door. Ethel was such a very bright spark, but she feared her heedlessness would lead her into trouble.

****

Horatia, who'd had an exceedingly good sleep, ran her arthritically-gnarled hand along Rietta's pianoforte. 'Your house is very charming.'

'It's small, but I like it. Please do be seated.' Horatia sat beside

Susan on a Swedish Rococo-style settee. Rietta alighted on a window seat. 'I'm the only person to have tenanted this building. This little row of four houses was built five years ago by a local man called Charlie Webber. I like that I can make it entirely my own, without the imprint of former inhabitants hanging in every corner, as it were. I also like that the amenities are thoroughly modern. We have piped water, an efficient kitchen range (which Cook, of course, adores), and you'll have already benefited from the internal flush toilet. I kept a second, larger home at Little Knowle on the cliff above the village, but I let the lease expire when I realised I was sleeping here all the time. As a girl in Algiers, we kept both town and clifftop residences. It was for this reason, I think, that it felt proper for me to maintain a pair of similar lodgings here. That is until I realised that, as an old maid, keeping an out-of-town perch was impractical and pointless. So here I am as you find me in my little nook. I do regret having no room to house Tori and her daughters, but I trust they're comfortably accommodated in the Rolle. I suspect the girls will enjoy its beachfront location.'

Rietta paused to watch a warmly-bundled family traversing the high street outside the twin parlour windows. When Henrietta spoke next, Horatia thought her booming voice sounded wistful. 'I recall my child-self peering through a hole in the carved wooden screen of our Algiers town-house to spy on the narrow, bustling medina outside. I suppose I gained my penchant for spying on passers by all those years ago in Algiers. Perhaps this is what drew me to live directly on the high street in a house whose parlour has two, large, glass-paned windows? They're so much better for spying through than those miserly Algerine trellises!'

'Your house certainly has a foreign feel.' Susan had wandered to the mantle-shelf. 'Some of your ornaments appear decidedly exotic.'

'I believe you're referring to the silver rosewater sprinkler, and repoussé hamam bowl? They are indeed souvenirs from my girlhood in Algiers. The red and blue embroidery on the back of the settee is, in fact, an eighteenth century Algerine turban cover, if you'd believe it? Or, at least, this is what Papa told me. Your bed covers too are Algerine. I have a few other Ottoman artefacts: plates and jewellery items for the most part. I doubt they're of any commercial worth, but they're of sentimental value to me.'

'I think all your things are quite lovely!' Susan declared, examining the hammered designs on the silver hamam bowl. She turned her gaze to a gilt framed watercolour festively bedecked with ivy. It depicted a smartly dressed gentleman beside a plump, younger lady with short-cropped, chestnut-coloured hair. 'Those are your parents?'

'Yes, Susan dearest, your eye is shrewd. The sketch was made by a talented young Italian who stayed with us for a time in Algiers. His name, I'm afraid, escapes me, although his painting is dear to my heart.'

Horatia lent forwards to see the painting better. 'Oh yes, I hadn't noticed it before, but the likenesses are very good. My, doesn't Lizzie take after her grandfather?'

'I'd not tell her so,' Rietta chuckled, 'but yes, I think she does share his long face and high cheekbones. As do all we Blanckleys, including Tori.'

Susan scrutinised the portrait. 'Yes, I do see something of Tori in the lines of his face. Quite remarkable!'

'I very much admire your Christmas decorations,' Horatia said. 'The overall effect is striking, but homely. I believe you, too, have an artistic eye.'

'Thank you. Humble as it is, my home is, as they say, my castle. And I like it to be furnished with care. Are you both rested after the ordeal of yesterday's horrendous journey? Which I must apologise for again.'

'And I, Rietta dear, repeat that you cannot be held to fault for the mismanagement of the railway system! And, yes thank you, I'm feeling much refreshed this morning.'

'As am I,' Susan supplied.

'Then perhaps you might enjoy a short perambulation to the seafront?'

'This sounds a marvellous plan,' Susan smiled. 'I do so love the sea. Could we perhaps also call at the hotel to enquire after Tori and her girls?'

Rietta's smile displayed her formidable set of yellow teeth. 'This was my exact thought.'

'Oh splendid. I'm looking forward to seeing the sights of your village.'

'It is small and mercifully flat, situated in the valley bottom as we are. The town itself is quite pleasant, with a brook running along the centre of the High Street in a walled ditch,' Henrietta gestured towards the windows, 'You can see it from here. The seafront itself is charming, with fishing boats winched up on iron chains. On fine days, one can see as far as the lighthouse at Portland Bill in Dorset, but,' she treated Horatia to an impish grin, 'people here don't care about how others behave. No one judges, well, not much, anyway! Ratia, as promised, this is your place to be free!'

Horatia doubted this, but didn't resist when Henrietta bossed her and Susan into knitted whatnots, tailored coats and firmly secured hats, and harried them outside. The High Street was moderately busy despite the drizzly coldness of the late December morning. The buildings either side were, for the most part, small, well-presented, and of modern design. The road was split in two by the neat walled ditch Henrietta had described, which efficiently channelled a loudly gurgling stream of water down the little street.

'So this is Budleigh Salterton?' Horatia remarked. 'It seems very pleasant.'

Henrietta tilted her head to see beyond the wide rim of a blue hat she'd squashed over her orange wig. 'It suits me well enough. The architecture is neat, and I'm spared the challenge of traversing hills. I like that the sea is close to hand, and...' she nudged Horatia and Susan before raising her voice several decibels, 'I don't give a hoot if I shout in the street! The locals like me better for being what they call a "character"!'

Her public outburst caused Horatia and Susan to freeze and cringe, but a well-dressed man on the other side of the street turned to Henrietta with a broad smile. 'Good morning, Miss Blanckley!'

'Ah, Mr. Woodman!' she boomed back, with an equally wide grin, 'May I introduce my friends from up country? Mrs. Ward and Mrs. Moore, who remain fearful that displaying their feelings in public will constitute making a ruckus!'

Mr. Woodman doffed his bowler hat. 'Welcome to Budleigh Salterton, Mrs. Ward and Mrs. Moore. We're no sticklers for etiquette here, and prefer smiles to stiff upper lips!'

Susan was happily enchanted. 'Then this does seem a very lovely place indeed!'

Horatia refused to believe that everyone in Budleigh Salterton was as easy going as Mr. Woodman and Rietta, but nonetheless felt a spring in her step for the first time in years.

****

Tori was startled from her porridge by Patch's sudden bark, quickly followed by Aunt Henrietta's church-bell voice. 'Toriana, good morning! I see you and your daughters are still breaking your fast.' Looking up, Tori beheld her three elderly relatives encroaching towards her across the Rolle's spacious dining floor.

Ada tumbled from her seat and threw her chubby arms around Henrietta's substantial midriff. She patted Ada's golden curls affectionately, while Patch, who'd made a cowardly retreat beneath the table, pretended to be brave and growled.

'Tori, darling,' Aunt Susan gushed excitedly, 'What a grand dining hall! And just look at that enormous Christmas tree! Such an extravagance to have its candles lit during the day!'

'It is certainly most festive,' Horatia concurred, 'but I don't wish to disturb Tori and my granddaughters' repast. Tori dear, shall we return later?'

'No, no, it's quite alright. I am afraid I slept in very late this morning, but we're almost finished. The girls are keen to visit the beach.'

'I want to see the sea,' Ethel clarified through a mouthful of grilled mackerel.

'And so you shall!' Henrietta smiled. Then added, after glancing to Tori, 'If your mama permits?'

'Why, of course my girls shall enjoy the beach, although with due caution for safety.'

'What, precisely, will "due caution" entail, Niece? As a child, I thoroughly enjoyed playing on the beaches of Algiers with gay abandon. Does modern parenting deny children this simple, wholesome pleasure?'

Susan intervened. 'Did you say, Tori dear, that your brother will be arriving later today?'

'Umm, yes, I received a letter from him before we left Pinner.'

'Who's your brother, Mama?' Ethel asked.

'Why, your Uncle Horace, of course.'

She scowled. 'I don't like him.'

'Ethel Mary Ward, we do not speak unpleasantly of our elders.'

'But Uncle Horace really is horrible, Mama–'

'Ethel!'

'Sorry, Mama, I didn't mean to be rude. It's just that... well I don't like him at all.'

'Refrain immediately from speaking ill of your uncle.'

'I honour my uncle,' Nellie interposed ingratiatingly. 'He is a hero of the Royal Marines.'

'Will Augusta be with him?' Susan asked.

'Alas, I think not.'

'What a shame, I do like Augusta. I've not seen her for a very long time. Do you know how she is?'

'I'm afraid not, Aunt Susan. I believe my brother, also, has not seen Augusta for some time.'

'Is their separation a mutual choice?' Henrietta enquired. 'I ask because your brother has always seemed to be a man who enjoys female company.'

****

Susan's fretful mutterings about Tori's brother continued onto Budleigh Salterton's pebble beach. Horatia had felt exhilarated to stand with the sea wind in her face and her dress billowing about as if she was a native girl on some far-away island where no one worried about decorum, until Susan broke her reverie by saying, 'poor, dear Horace. I fear his mother's death was very hard on him. He was of a fragile age, and dear Harriet doted on him so. I cared for him as my own after... we lost her, but as soon as he turned eight, Edward enrolled him in a boarding school in Devon, near the Rogerses, who were distant cousins. I fear poor Horace was deprived of motherly support when he needed it most.'

Horatia struggled to recall Tori's brother. She'd last seen him when he stood as father-of-the-bride at Tori's wedding to William nine years ago. She could vaguely picture Horace as a smartly dressed Royal Marine looking proud to take the place of Tori's – and his – father. Horatia thought it peculiar and, if she was honest, irritating that Susan considered him permanently damaged from childhood tragedy. 'I find it hard to believe the loss of his mother still affects him as an adult.'

'Oh, but I believe it without a doubt, Horatia dear.' Susan brushed away a strand of snow-white hair that had come loose in the wind. 'He's forever seeking ladies to admire him, yet seems unable to remain close to any. It's very sad.'

Horatia raised her downy brows. 'What of his wife?' She could picture Augusta at Tori and William's wedding in '64 as a fashionably slender young lady with an aquiline nose and tinkling laugh.

Susan watched the incoming waves collapsing tirelessly onto

the pebbles. 'I fear poor Augusta has been ill-used by Horace. Tori said he's refused to see her for several years now.'

'The poor woman! Do you know why?'

Susan shrugged. 'Tori said Horace has evaded talking about it.'

'Yet you see him as decent?'

'I see him as... wounded, but, yes, decent considering the toll of his hurts.'

'Aunt Henrietta!' Ethel, pink-faced and bright-eyed, was stumbling towards them across the ankle twisting pebbles. 'There are funny metal things at the top of the beach with chains coming out of them!'

'They're for winching boats clear of the high tide,' Rietta supplied. 'It keeps them safe from storms.'

The six-year-old took a moment to observe the line of cast-iron winching machines fixed along the top of the beach. Sure enough, small, beached fishing boats clustered around every machine. Heavy rusty chains could be seen running from them down the beach's steep course.

'Aunt Henrietta, why do the pebbles come in patches of different sizes?'

'I confess I know not why, Ethel, but I can tell you that local people call them "Budleigh buns".' Rietta stooped to pick up one of the smaller stones. 'See, it's shaped like a round bun?'

Ethel laughed, delighted. 'Hard to bite into though!'

'You know, Budleigh beach with its bun-like pebbles is a popular draw for amateur geologists.'

'What are geologists, Aunt Henrietta?'

'People who study rocks, dear.'

Ethel lost interest and stumbled her way back to Patch, chortling, 'I'm bouncing on Budleigh buns!'

The three old women regarded the sea for a time in silence. The sound of waves breaking on the pebbles was loud and deep. It resonated through Horatia's feet, and up through her whole body, as a crashing, rolling drum roll. Though the sky above was heavy with black clouds, the sea itself was oddly pink-hued beneath the white crested waves.

'Do you know why the sea looks pink?' Horatia asked Rietta.

'It's because of those cliffs.' Henrietta pointed westwards towards a series of dark, reddish brown cliffs at the western extent of the bay. 'The sea churns them up. The beaches over there, at Dawlish and Teignmouth, have red sand as a result, and, when the weather's rough, as it often is at this time of year, the sea's coloured pink by it.'

Horatia watched the rolling pink waves, mesmerised. 'I don't think I've ever experienced anything quite like this before. It really is quite dramatic.'

****

Kajri had magicked Tori's daughters into a reasonably organised greeting party in the Rolle's foyer when the incoming Exmouth Omnibus was sighted.

Horace alighted in a gaudy dazzle of scarlet, ginger and navy blue and strode straight up to them in the lobby. 'Do you enjoy drama?' He demanded of the girls, without bothering to introduce himself. The little girls stared back at him solemnly. 'Drama,' Horace prompted, 'theatre. Bright lights. Christmas pantomimes. You have heard of these things?'

'Yes, Uncle Horace,' Nellie supplied.

'And do you enjoy it?'

'Oh yes, Uncle Horace.'

'Well, I have a surprise for you,' he beamed, but the confidence of his smile wavered when the little girls stared back with dull-eyed blankness. He at last acknowledged Tori. 'They're a solemn bunch, aren't they, Sister?'

'I'm happy to see you arrived safely.' Tori stood on tiptoe to kiss his cheek, but he dodged away. Sighing, Tori clapped her hands. 'Girls, are you going to ask what surprise Uncle Horace has been kind enough to bring you?'

'Yes, Mama,' said Nellie. 'Uncle Horace, please may we know what your surprise is?'

Nellie's polite attention kindled the return of Horace's broad smile. 'I have arranged dress circle seats for the Christmas pantomime at the Theatre Royal in Exeter! It sounds quite splendid, "Harlequin, Sinbad the Sailor!"'

Tori gasped. 'This is indeed very generous of you, Brother.'

Her thanks appeared to cheer him even more. 'I have a friend in the industry who owed me a favour,' he winked. 'I wasn't sure how many tickets to demand, I mean *request*, so I asked for twelve. Will this suffice?'

'I am certain this will be quite ample, Brother. Your thoughtful generosity is greatly appreciated. Your uncle's surprise is marvellous, isn't it, girls?'

'Yes, Mama. Thank you, Uncle Horace.'

'Brother, would you care to take some refreshment in the

dining room, or would you prefer to go straight to your room? Aunt Henrietta has kindly invited us to dine at her house this evening at six p.m.'

He scowled. 'I shall go directly to my suite, Sister, and await you in the lobby, at half-past-five. Good day to you,' he began to stride off.

'Brother, a kiss for your sister?'

'Of course.' He lent back to peck her briefly on the cheek, but bounded away before she could ask any more.

CHAPTER EIGHT

A skinny blonde, and a curvaceous brunette were chatting in an otherwise empty theatre dressing room. The waif-like blonde dealt her companion a scrutinising, no-holds-barred stare. 'If yer 'alf bruvva marries this heiress, I'll get a cut of the money, yeah?'

'Christ's sake, Joan,' the other woman snapped at the blonde, 'We don't even know if anything's gonna play out, in't ee?'

'But if ee do?'

The brunette sucked on a silver-tipped pipe, kindling orange embers and a pungent cloud of smoke. 'I don't bloody know, does I?'

Joan waved the smoke from her face. 'Yeah, but if that rich wench does marry yer 'alf bruvva, I wants cash cos it was me that gave yer the tip, din't I?'

'Yeah, yer tipped me off, I'll own that. We're mates, in't we?' She shook her mass of dark brown curls. 'I'll do me best ter make sure me 'alf bruvva gives yer a share of any cash ee gets, but I can't make 'im do anything what wiv me being our farva's bastard.'

Joan looked up from the bundle of folded costumes she was slouched on. 'But yer dad looks after yer, don't ee, and ee's proper rich?'

The brunette laughed harshly. 'That old bugger? Ee sees me as chattel. Someone what ee can use cos ee thinks I'm bound ter 'im out of family loyalty.'

Joan thought on this. 'Ee gives yer money though, don't ee, Amanda?'

Amanda's shrug sent a cascade of shivers through her mane of brown curls. 'Yeah, ee gives me a bit, though not much, mind. Miser that ee be. To be fair, ee did get me this acting job through 'is cousin. Eased 'is conscience I reckon. Ee likes 'aving me owe 'im one, too. But ee in't gonna set me up with no good marriage, I can tell yer that. Ee don't want my likes being associated too closely with 'im.'

'But yer'll get a pay off if yer 'alf brother marries that bitch I told yer about?'

'Yeah, yeah, don't go on about all that again. I said I'd sort it, alright?'

****

Horatia was in a high-backed, upholstered chair for which Rietta had apologised, saying, 'Tis not a dining chair, but intended for a dressing table.'

'You know, I'm actually very much enjoying things being topsy-turvy here.' Horatia's smile was relaxed. 'It's a refreshing change from the rigid etiquette of Pinner. Did you know that Mrs. Beeton, famous for her book on household management, would have been my near neighbour, but for her tragically early demise.'

Rietta arched her brow. 'Mrs. Beeton made a grand job of codifying polite behaviour! I got a headache from reading just a single page of her book!'

'I suspect she'd have soon had an awful headache if she'd come to Budleigh Salterton on account of how relaxed everyone is here!'

'Well, I much prefer your company anyway!' Rietta's toothy smile took in her assembled dinner guests, comprising five adults and all of Tori's children, bar Baby Alice, seated on mismatched chairs around two tables covered with Algerine tapestries. The room was cosy with the ambient glow of dimmed gas-lamps and a table candelabra festively adorned with holly sprigs. Rietta's maid, Bradford, efficiently cleared their soup bowls and served a second course of winter salad and cheese fingers on hammered silver plates.

Susan squinted at the silverware. 'Are the plates Algerine?'

Rietta seemed pleased by the question. 'You're very observant, Susan. It's good to have an opportunity to use my little collection of Ottoman tableware.'

'It's lovely, isn't it?' Tori smiled to her girls.

'Is Aunt Lizzie coming?' Ethel asked.

Rietta patted Ethel's hand. 'Not this evening, dear, but she will be joining us for Christmas.'

'Oh, I was hoping to talk to her about our Blanckley ancestors. She promised to tell me more when she was in Pinner, but she never did.'

'Are you interested in genealogy, Ethel?'

'What's gen… genea..?'

'Genealogy is the study of ancestors.'

'Oh yes, Aunt Henrietta. I'm very interested in this.'

Horace leaned in from his seat at the head of the table. ‘You don’t need to wait for your Aunt Lizzie to answer your queries. You can ask me.’

Horatia noticed Ethel wriggle in her chair and avoid Horace’s eyes. It seemed her spirited niece had some issue with her uncle. Curious! Rietta also singled out Horace. She pierced him with her keen, steel-rimmed glare, and said, ‘I suspect a number of us present have information about our Blanckley ancestry. I, for one, knew your grandpapa, Henry Stanyford Blanckley, or H.S.B., as he liked to be known. Your Aunts Susan and Ratia knew him too, although I perhaps knew him somewhat better, because he was my own papa!’

Horace looked affronted, although he kept his voice even. ‘I was trying to be pleasant, Aunt.’

‘Well some people don’t actually have to try,’ Rietta quipped back, fast as a striking adder.

Horatia flinched inwardly, fearful of Rietta and Horace's discord escalating.

Horace fixed Rietta with a beady glare of his own. ‘And some of us should perhaps try a bit harder.’

To Horatia’s immense relief, Rietta clapped and chortled. ‘Touché, Nephew, well played! I do enjoy a good war of words.’

‘Your aunt,’ Susan told Horace, ‘has resolved to be pleasant to you and your sister. Haven’t you, Henrietta?’

‘What? Oh yes. I just keep forgetting. It’s my age, you know. I find it hard to remember things.’

Ethel took advantage of the ensuing pause to enquire, ‘Aunt Henrietta, was your papa my great-grandpapa?’

'That's right, Ethel. You have quite the genealogist's mind!'

'Thank you, Aunt Henrietta! So your papa is the same relation to me as Lord Nelson?'

Mention of her father caused Horatia's heart to jolt. She hoped no one noticed, for she didn't want to appear weak of mind. She placed a steadying hand on the tapestry-covered table and focused on breathing slowly whilst the conversation carried on around her.

Rietta said, 'You are again correct, Ethel, but don't forget to name George Matcham too, or your Aunt Susan may sulk for her own father being left out.'

Susan brightened. 'My mama, Mrs. Matcham, was Lord Nelson's sister, so you're related to Lord Nelson through both your mama and papa!'

'So I've got more of Nelson in me than Blanckley?'

'It's not a competition!' Tori tutted, giving Ethel a hard look.

Susan changed tack. 'My papa was very good friends with Henrietta's papa, whom everyone called H. S. B.'

'They were indeed,' said Henrietta, 'And we had a lot of fun touring Europe together when we were girls. Ratia joined us for a bit, didn't you, dear?'

'We had a marvellous time,' Horatia confirmed. 'It was then that Rietta, your aunt Susan and I forged our friendship.'

'And here we are now after all those years!' Rietta chirped. 'Ah, here's Bradford with the fish course. I hope you all enjoy it. It's a whole salmon stuffed with figs, and served with potatoes in a Hollandaise sauce. Do we need more wine?'

'Whiskey for me.' Horace sounded somewhat imperious, as if

their hostess was his waitress, but Rietta took his command with good grace.

'Bradford, bring a glass of whiskey for my nephew.'

'Sorry, Ma'am, but I don't think we've got none.'

Horace *hmphed.* 'Well, what do you have?'

'Umm, we's got sherry, Sir, and port...'

'Either will do, just bring the bottles.'

Rietta called to Horatia across the table. 'How is your salmon? Cook, who's usually excellent, assured me fig combines well with the fish, but I'm not personally convinced.'

Horatia pronged a flake of salmon with a fish fork and chewed it. 'It's an unusual combination I'll own, but not unpleasant.'

'Aunts, Mother,' Tori said, 'has my brother told you of his surprise?'

The three old ladies turned to find Horace looking smug. Henrietta replied, 'He's said nothing to me, Niece. Horace, would you care to illuminate?'

He raised himself importantly. The dimmed gas and candle lighting softened the contrast between his scarlet jacket and pale face, but he was an impressive sight nonetheless. Smile twitching beneath his auburn moustache, he took a long moment to savour the attention. 'I have reserved twelve dress circle seats for the Christmas pantomime at the Theatre Royal at Bedford Circus in Exeter for Monday 29th December, for which a special train is scheduled to run from Exmouth.'

'That's my birthday!' Ethel objected. Tori hissed at her to hush.

'Pantomime,' Susan murmured, 'I haven't been to one of those for many years… why Tori, do you remember we went to a Christmas pantomime in Brighton one year? You would have been nine or ten, I think.'

'Why yes, Aunt Susan, I do recall it. Alexander came too, although he was by then a nearly-grown man and objected quite heartily. I remember he complained you were dragging him to "drivel for small children and sops"!'

'Did he really say that? Oh what a prig he could be!' Susan laughed. 'I recall him enjoying it, however, despite himself. What was the show? Do you remember?'

Tori frowned for a moment, then smiled. 'Harlequin Somebody, I think… or was it perhaps Harlequin Nobody?'

'The story was always the same with Harlequin and Columbine trying to flee her silly parent, Pantaloon, who was hampered by his, or her, servant called Clown, and a useless policeman. I wonder if pantomimes still follow the same form?'

'Little has changed, Aunt,' Horace told her. 'The contemporary production, for which I've procured tickets, is entitled Harlequin, Sinbad the Sailor! and includes the standard cast of Columbine and Pantaloon, et al.'

'Sinbad the Sailor, hey? You like Sinbad tales, don't you girls?' Rietta queried her five youngest dinner guests.

Ethel studied her plate, but Nellie was less taciturn. 'Oh yes, Aunt Henrietta, we very much love tales from the Thousand And One Nights!'

'As do I,' Rietta smiled. 'Nephew, I declare you to have made an excellent choice.'

'It might be fun,' Susan concurred. 'Though it's such a long time since I've been to a pantomime.'

'But you have frequented other theatrical productions since Brighton?'

'I have not, Nephew. I've not felt at all drawn to bright lights and spectacle.'

Horatia, who'd not been to a theatre for more decades than she cared to count, chose not to comment.

Horace addressed Tori. 'Sister, I trust that you, at least, have taken your children to the theatre?'

'Fear not, Brother, there was a theatre in the British cantonment at Jaulnah. We went to it frequently before our return to England last year. Our girls watched many performances. There was little else to entertain us there, besides.'

'Didn't take me,' Evie objected.

'Evie, I did, in fact, take you. You fidgeted a lot, but were quite enchanted by the lights and music. You were perhaps too young to remember?'

'And what of young Ada?' Horace pressed.

'Well, she was only a babe in India. We haven't had an opportunity to attend a production since our return.'

'Well, well, I am quite at a loss for words... theatre is a tonic to the soul!' Horace inhaled deeply, and tossed his head back to pronounce theatrically, 'I prescribe, with utmost urgency, your universal attendance of a major theatrical performance, and hereby declare that the pantomime at Exeter is the precise and timely medication you all most desperately need!'

Tori laughed. 'Brother, you're still quite the dramatist! Have you continued to participate in amateur productions?'

'Sister, alas, I've not been on stage now for some years, although I remain a fervent audience.'

Nellie looked impressed. 'Have you acted on a real theatre stage, Uncle?'

He smiled grandly. 'Indeed I have, Niece.'

Susan cast him a charming smile. 'Might you, Horace dear, indulge us with a dramatic recital?'

'I should not wish to disrupt proceedings...'

Rietta caught his eye. 'A recital would be quite splendid, don't you think, Ratia?'

Horatia smiled. 'Yes, please.'

'Very well.' Horace cleared his throat, and declaimed:

Break, break, break,
On thy cold grey stones, O Sea!
And I would that my tongue could utter
The thoughts that arise in me.

O, well for the fisherman's boy,
That he shouts with his sister at play!
O, well for the sailor lad,
That he sings in his boat on the bay!

The adults, Nellie and Carrie clapped. Ethel smiled blandly, and little Evie and Ada seemed more amused by the clapping and "bravos!" than Horace's preceding recital.

'Tennyson!' Susan enthused, 'A perfect choice. You are certainly very talented, Horace, both in oratory skill, and in your memory of prose.'

Horace replied silkily. 'I'm just a humble amateur, Aunt Susan, but I thank you for the indulgence of your praise.' He sighed with satisfaction and poured himself another measure of port.

'Do you hear them?' Ethel cried.

'What, dear?' Tori asked.

'Christmas waites outside!'

'Oh yes!' Susan exclaimed. 'They're singing Once in Royal David's City!'

'That's one of my favourites,' Nellie cried. 'Aunt Henrietta, please may we go out to listen to them?'

'Oh, yes please!' Carrie enthused.

'Very well, children, I think this will make a splendid finale to Horace's charming poem. Bradford, do we still have gingerbread pieces in the pantry?'

'Yes, Ma'am.'

'Good! Bring the gingerbread to the front door. Come, children, let's go and listen to these waites.' The older girls hopped excitedly from their chairs, and Tori followed with little Evie and Ada. Smiling to each other, Horatia and Susan rose too. Horace, though, took a deep swig of port and remained seated.

Rietta's front doorway was a squash of billowing, bell-shaped skirts by the time Bradford arrived with a basket of gingerbread. 'Open the door,' Rietta told her.

The maid picked her way through the sea of skirts, and pushed the door open wide to reveal a group of singers and an accordionist rendering Once in Royal David's City. Their voices were hearty, despite the biting wind and rain. The waites were a motley bunch of locals. Male and female, young and old, but uniformly swathed in thick coats and woollen hats. Clouds of vapour punctuated their every breath. The gaslit windows on the far side of the street behind them were adorned with evergreen boughs. The rich smell of roasting chestnuts wafted from a cart down the road. Horatia stood with Rietta and her other guests listening enraptured. They clapped heartily at the carol's end.

'Oh, that was marvellous!' Susan declared. 'I feel decidedly more festive for hearing that lovely carol.' The carollers looked pleased.

'May I offer you gingerbread?' Henrietta asked them.

'Thank you, Ma'am,' an older member of the troop inclined his head. 'Gingerbread would be welcome.'

Bradford proffered the basket so they could help themselves.

'Can we have another song, please?' Ethel begged.

'Ethel Mary Ward,' Tori hissed, 'it's not your place to command the waites!'

But the lead waite bent down to her with an avuncular smile. 'And is there a particular song you'd like, young Miss?'

Ethel beamed. 'Sir, I should very much like to hear Silent Night.'

He nodded, and the accordionist squeezed the opening strains of the tune. United, they sang:

Silent night, holy night!
All is calm, all is bright.
Round yon Virgin, Mother and Child.
Holy infant so tender and mild,
Sleep in heavenly peace,
Sleep in heavenly peace…

****

Horace felt much better thirty minutes later when he regained his family's admiration by gallantly forgoing the remainder of Aunt Henrietta's strong drinks to escort his sister and nieces back to the hotel. When they reached the first floor, his sister summoned that tasty-looking ayah of hers to see to the girls, then surprised him by saying, 'Brother, might we have a quick word?'

He still felt magnanimous. 'What can I do for you, Sister?'

'May we talk in my room?'

He stepped backwards. The thought of entering a lady's private chamber for non-intimate purposes felt unsavoury, especially as the lady in question was his own sister. 'It would be more appropriate to adjourn to the dining room,' he boomed.

Tori flinched for some reason, and flicked her eyes to the closed doors of the suites her children occupied. 'It's past ten o'clock,' she whispered, 'I shouldn't wish to disturb the staff at this importune hour.'

He clicked his tongue at her naivety. 'This is an hotel. We're paying them to cater to our needs, be it day or night.'

'In point of fact, Aunt Henrietta is paying them, and we should, for that matter, respect her reputation within this village.'

'I'm quite sure our fearsome aunt is capable of protecting her own reputation.'

'Point taken, Brother. Yet I would not feel comfortable disturbing the staff by descending on the public dining room at this late hour.'

'In that case, we can just talk here,' he boomed.

'On second thoughts, perhaps you are right about the permissibility of using the dining room.'

He offered her his arm. 'You see, I'm always right.'

'Quite so,' she whispered, and allowed him to steer her down the stairs.

'So what is the subject you wish to broach?' Horace demanded as soon as they arrived in the cavernous expanse of the dark dining hall.

Tori untucked her arm and faced him. 'My query is about View Cottage. I should like to know if it is currently let.'

'What? Oh, you mean Papa's old place? Everyone calls it Lutton House now.'

His sister frowned. 'Has permission been sought to change our cottage's name?'

'I have no idea, but it's been known as Lutton House for some time. Makes it sound grander. Good for our rents.'

'Is it currently let?'

'Yes, my agent has been diligent in ensuring its ongoing tenancy. Have you not been receiving your share of the rents?'

'It's not that, Brother, it's just that... I should like to visit it whilst in the county.'

'I can assure you my agent has been seeing to its upkeep.'

'My wish to visit View Cot... I mean Lutton House, is for personal reasons.'

'May I help you, Sir, Ma'am?' A sleepy-looking bellboy had

sidled up.

Horace beamed. ‘Ah, good, service at last! But I’ll have you know I’m Captain, not Sir.’

‘Sorry, Captain.’

‘I’ll have Scotch with ice. Make it large.’

‘Right away, Captain. Ma’am?’

Tori, for some reason, looked embarrassed and her reply was a whispered squeak. ‘Nothing for me. Thank you.’

‘Why on Earth do you wish to visit Lutton House for personal reasons?’ Horace asked when the bellboy scuttled off. ‘Everything of worth was auctioned after Father’s death.’

She closed her eyes. ‘Because it was my childhood home.’

Horace was running out of patience. ‘And now you’re an adult. So what?’

‘It is of sentimental importance.’

‘I can’t imagine why. It’s just a decrepit old shack in the middle of nowhere.’

‘I thought you said it has been well-maintained?’

‘I used poetic licence.’

‘So it’s not decrepit?’

‘Damned if I know, but my agent says it’s fine, and the rent keeps coming in. That’s the important thing.’

‘I should still like to see it.’

‘As I told you, it is tenanted.’

'Do you happen to know the name of the current tenant? If they'd be amenable to a friendly visit?'

'I really have no idea. I leave my agent to deal with all that. Come, Sister, as you pointed out, it's late. Let's retire to our suites.' He marched back towards the darkened stairwell at a quickstep, but stopped suddenly and shouted, 'Where is that damned bellboy? I need that Scotch!'

The lad scurried out of a side door looking flustered. 'Won't be a minute, Captain!'

'Change of plan. Bring it up to my room. Name's Blanckley.'

Horace charged up the stairs without pausing to bid his sister good night, and bolted his room from the inside. He threw his scarlet jacket over a chair and punched the flock-papered wall violently. He was dismayed to feel unmanly tears streaming down his face. What had possessed his thoughtless, tactless sister to talk of their childhood in View Cottage? There were things, such as that, which should never be remembered at all.

CHAPTER NINE

Horatia woke slowly, savouring the luxury of not having to hurry. She'd had a pleasant and refreshing sleep, and felt very happy. She realised that she'd had no nightmares since coming to Budleigh Salterton. The sea air was assuredly a tonic, as was not giving a hoot about what passers-by thought of her, and, of course, the company of dear friends.

****

'Wake up, Mama!' Tori was disoriented. She'd been deep in a dream of her young girlhood when her mama was alive with a baby in her big tummy, and Horace and Cousin Alexander were running to and fro along View Cottage's lawn with bright, paper kites. 'Wake up!' the voice demanded again. She realised Ethel was pulling her shoulder. 'Umm… what is it?'

'It's Christmas Eve!'

She suppressed a groan and attempted to sound excited. 'Yes, dear. So it is.'

The six-year-old was bouncing up and down on her. 'That means, it's Christmas tomorrow!'

'Yes, dear.'

'And Aunt Lizzie's coming today, isn't she Mama?'

'Yes, dear.'

'Oh good. I'm so very happy, Mama!' Ethel beamed down at her. 'It will be very good to see Aunt Lizzie, because I can ask her about genealogy.'

'Umm, but we talked to you of genealogy at dinner at Aunt Henrietta's–'

'Yes, but Aunt Lizzie makes it more interesting.'

Tori sighed.

****

Lizzie was holding a scented lace handkerchief to her nose, feeling uncomfortable inside and out as she endured the airless throng of the overcrowded horse-drawn omnibus ride from Exmouth to Budleigh Salterton. She was squashed between a sharp-elbowed maid and an obese woman reeking of rotten cabbage. The bell of the fat woman's dirty skirt was pressing disagreeably over Lizzie's own blue silk. The bench opposite her was crammed too, and the central floor space was stacked high with baskets, cases, and hampers, including Lizzie's own. She averted her eyes when an ill-kempt labourer-type leered at her suggestively. In addition to the cabbage-stench of her gross neighbour, the air was acrid with tobacco, rancid sweat and a trace of vomit. She wondered why she'd thought it might have been jolly to join the Christmas throng on the omnibus, and resolved to take a private cab for the return journey.

On top of this considerable unpleasantness, Lizzie was further distempered by the knowledge that she'd soon be confronted with Cousin Horace. She'd delayed visiting Budleigh Salterton for as long as she politely could, but now, with it being Christmas Eve, and her aunt desirous of her being there for Christmas Day, she could postpone no longer. Unwanted recollections of Tori's wedding nine years before haunted her mind. What had possessed her to let him kiss her, and in a way that first cousins really should not, especially those of the better classes? She'd simply been comforting him. He'd looked so forlorn talking about his wife and when he'd admitted the despicable thing he'd caught Augusta doing with their maid, and naked! Well, that was when Lizzie had dropped her guard and found him kissing her. It was all so sordid and embarrassing. She flinched when the conductor yelled, 'Rolle 'Otel! End of the line!'

The majority of passengers jumped off the benches before the bus finished its juddering halt in front of a two-storied building with white painted walls and point-topped windows poking from its slate roof. Lizzie knew from previous visits to her aunt that the other side of the hotel possessed a large lawn and sea vista. This side, however, was blessed only with views of the buildings opposite and the muddy street. Her attempt to rise sedately was scuppered by the cabbagy woman who, having already risen, lost her footing in the melee to vacate the bus and toppled backwards onto her. Lizzie was at first grateful when someone took her elbow to steady her, until the helping hand tried to grope her bosom and she realised it belonged to the leering labourer type. She pushed him away as best she could within the tightly pressed crowd, and stood back until it had dissipated enough for her to retrieve her luggage from the middle of the grimy wood floor. All she now wanted was to gain her hotel suite as soon as possible in order to compose her thoughts before facing Cousin Horace. But her heart jolted when she spied a scarlet jacket through the disembarking throng. When an elderly couple moved, Lizzie gained a clear view of the jacket owner. He was, as she'd feared, Horace. Worse, he was actively scanning the crowd exiting the rear of the horse-drawn bus. There'd be no evading him, so she gritted her teeth and descended the metal steps with slow dignity.

She affected surprise when he exclaimed, 'Hoy, Cousin Lizzie! Tis a delight to see you arrived in "bloody Salterton"!' He proffered a hand, oblivious to the fact that she was using both of hers to carry her cases and large wicker hamper.

Lizzie nodded stiffly. 'Cousin. Tis fastidious of you to await me.'

'I'd do anything for my dear cousin.' Horace had the effrontery to look pointedly at the extended hand she'd failed to take.

Her luggage was feeling heavier by the moment, but she refused to let her oafish cousin see her struggle. She scoured the dispersing crowd for a porter, but they were all busy with other people's bags. Her right hand, which was clutching two suitcases, hurt tremendously. The cases' hard handles were digging into her palm. Her arm and shoulder muscles felt like they were on fire. Cousin Horace was still staring stupidly at his empty hand. Lizzie had a strong desire to slap him in the face, but, apart from anything else, couldn't because of the cases he'd failed to gallantly take from her.

'Cousin Lizzie!' The new voice was female and bright. Tori was hurrying towards her with her gaggle of little girls. Tori glanced from Lizzie's cases to Horace with raised brows to signify her understanding of her predicament, before saying, 'tis good to see you. We've been excitedly awaiting your arrival!'

'Cousin, Nieces, tis good to see you too!' The smile Lizzie returned was strained.

Tori pushed her third-born forwards. 'Carrie, do you have the pretty seashell you wished to give your aunt?'

'Yes, Mama. It's in my pocket.'

'Perhaps your aunt might like to see it now?'

Sudden understanding of Tori's ploy caused Lizzie to smile broadly. 'I should very much like to see this pretty shell,' she told Carrie, and placed her heavy bags on the pavement.

'Here you are, Aunt Lizzie,' Carrie handed her a tan-banded limpet shell. 'I found it on the beach this morning.'

'Why, Carrie, it's beautiful. Thank you for gifting it to me.'

Her five-year-old niece grinned back.

'Come, Cousin,' Tori invited. 'I suspect you must be tired after your journey in that crowded bus?'

'Oh, it was dreadful!'

'Shall we adjourn to the dining room and call for tea?'

'That, dear cousin, would be very welcome!'

'Brother dear, would you please find a porter to see to Lizzie's bags?'

'What? Oh... of course.' Although Horace complied, he both looked and sounded annoyed.

Lizzie's sigh of relief was small, not just because she'd still be trapped in Cousin Horace's company for the duration of Christmas, but because her fashionably tight-laced corset made it impossible for her to breathe in deeply. At least Cousin Tori and her girls would cocoon her from Horace's indelicate attention for the time being. She released another shallow sigh, and looked westwards towards Aunt Henrietta's High Street house. It was for her, and her alone, that Lizzie had come here. She had to keep her geriatric old aunt sweet to secure her dream wedding. She noticed a tall, smartly-dressed, and somewhat stocky man with bushy, black mutton-chop whiskers standing on the corner where Rolle Road branched down towards the shore. He pulled his top hat firmly down and strode off towards the High Street.

****

Henrietta and her houseguests were startled from their cosy parlour conversation by a loud rap on the front door. Her maid came to the parlour doorway a moment or two later. 'Ma'am, your niece is here.'

'Lizzie? How splendid!' Henrietta smiled. 'Bring her straight in.'

Her red-headed niece rushed in and embraced her. 'Oh, Aunt, I'm very glad to see you!' Lizzie pulled away to greet Henrietta's house-guests, 'Mrs. Ward, Mrs. Moore, tis good to see you both as well.'

'How are you, my dear?' Henrietta enquired. 'Did you actually travel here by omnibus?'

'Oh, I did, Aunt, and it was perfectly Hellish!' Lizzie chuckled. 'I was a veritable fool to assume the Christmas Eve omnibus might feel festive.'

'My poor girl! But the important thing is that you are here now for Christmas. I am so happy that you are.'

'And me too, dear Aunt Henrietta.' Lizzie hugged her again. 'I couldn't imagine spending Christmastide without you.'

'You truly are a treasure to me!' She patted Lizzie's flawless cheek.

'Whatever is that ruckus?' Susan exclaimed.

Everyone hushed. Muffled, angry shouts could be heard from the street outside. Henrietta, spritely despite her age, nipped to the right-hand parlour window and pulled the curtains apart just enough to peer through. 'Oh my,' she whispered, 'it looks like trouble at The Feathers!'

'The inn opposite?' Horatia queried.

'Yes. There's a scuffle going on outside it.'

Susan joined Henrietta at the window. 'Oh yes, there certainly is a kerfuffle out there!'

Horatia rose stiffly from her chair, soon followed by Lizzie, to join the others at the slit in the curtains. She commented, 'Young men are always so full of vitriol!'

'And alcohol,' Susan added, 'or, at least, in this case I think, Cousin.'

The pavement and road opposite the window were occupied by a dozen men, of whom two were angrily pushing and punching each other, while the others formed a loose semicircle around them.

'We have such a good view!' Susan declared, 'It's like watching theatre.'

'Although these are not actors,' Henrietta cautioned. 'It would be prudent, I feel, to keep the gap in the curtains narrow so they don't notice that we are watching.'

'Would they be aggressive towards us if they did notice?'

'Susan, dearest, please remember that these shouting men have come out of a tavern selling alcohol, and, as such, are unpredictable.'

'Is this then a dangerous place to live?'

'I've had no problems here, and do enjoy my proximity to the community's beating heart.'

'Even at times such as this?'

'Especially at times such as this,' Henrietta's grin was rakish, 'I do love to observe neighbourhood dramas.'

A woman suddenly ran out of The Feathers crying, 'Leave 'im alone!' but a tall, stocky man with bushy black sideburns stepped in front of her and said something too quiet for Henrietta's party to hear. A pair of burly men wrenched a thin man onto the street and kicked him into the gutter.

'Oh dear, that's Albert,' Henrietta said. 'He is, or was, the inn's yardman. Nice chap, but it seems genial Albert will be my neighbouring yardman no more.'

'And on Christmas Eve,' Susan sighed. 'What tragic timing. I hope he doesn't have a family to support.'

Lizzie frowned. 'How am I to return to the hotel? I didn't think, Aunt, when I decided to visit you that I would need to walk back alone in the dark with that public house outside your front door.'

Henrietta clutched Lizzie's sleeve. 'I'm sorry not to have invited you to stay here as you usually do.'

'I know it means a lot to you to have your friends staying with you for Christmas, dear Aunt.'

'You are a dear, sweet girl,' Henrietta approved. 'I'm happy to escort you safely back to the Rolle.'

'But who should then escort you back here, Aunt?'

'Dear Henrietta,' Susan interposed, 'I'll gladly accompany the both of you.'

'If you don't mind,' Horatia said, 'I'll remain here keeping vigil by the fire. My arthritis–'

'We quite understand, dear Ratia, please remain in comfort. We shall return before very long.'

****

Horace strutted into the Rolle's dining hall feeling tall and splendid in his scarlet marines jacket. 'Good evening, Sister. I have received a telegram!' he announced to Tori, who was sitting with his nieces at a long table close to the candle-adorned Christmas tree.

She rose to greet him politely. 'Good evening, Brother. I'm glad you have joined us.'

He eyed her rowdy girls with ill-ease, and began to say, 'I have determined to…' but stopped short upon spying Cousin Lizzie in the foyer. He called out her name, but she seemed not to hear him.

'Ah, there she is!' Tori smiled, 'We were expecting to meet her here at six o'clock.'

'She is joining you for dinner?'

'But of course, Brother. Do take a seat.' She nodded towards the largest of her multiple daughters. 'Nellie has a seat ready for you beside her.'

'Very well.' Horace crossed around the table to sit beside his largest niece. He coughed to regain his sister's attention, 'Would you like to know from whom the telegram I received came?'

'Please enlighten me, Brother.'

He held up a slip of paper and, unfolding it, read, 'Mr. Thomas Matthews Esquire.'

'Pray tell, who is Mr. Thomas Matthews Esquire?'

'He is the current tenant of Lutton House!'

'View Cottage?' His sister's surprised gasp made him smile.

'The same.'

'You wired him for me?'

'I did,' he continued to smile benignly, enjoying the lime-light.

'What is View Cottage, Mama?' The second biggest niece asked.

'Tis the country house we lived in when I was a small girl.'

Horace spoke before his niece could query further. 'Sister, would you like to know what Mr. Matthews says?'

'Very much.'

'He says, "Your sister welcome to visit. Home all this week".'

Tori looked happily excited. 'Oh goodness. It has become real!'

The second biggest niece, however, seemed less happy. 'What has become real, Mama?'

'Ethel dear, I am planning a short trip to visit that country house,' her mother explained. 'It is in south Devon, so not far from where we are.'

The second biggest niece brightened, 'When are we going?'

Tori breathed out slowly. 'Darling... darlings,' she addressed her daughters around the table, 'I shall be going alone.'

They all gasped, and the second biggest niece protested, 'But Mama, you cannot go without us!'

Tori sighed again. 'Ethel, I do not know what I shall find when

I reach the village. It may be very rustic. I mean to visit the house briefly then return straight here. It is not a suitable journey for you girls to accompany me on.'

'But it's my birthday on Monday!'

'I promise I'll come back for your birthday. I have a very special gift for you.'

The second biggest niece's eyes widened. 'A gift for me? May I please have it now?'

Tori stroked the little girl's golden ringlets. 'You must wait until I return from South Brent on December twenty-ninth.'

Quick as storm-chased cloud, the second biggest niece's mood switched from joy to grief. 'You won't be here when I wake up on my birthday? Who shall look after me?'

'Why Kajri shall, of course.'

'And so shall I!' Horace found himself declaring.

Tori looked to him with gratitude, and something that looked very much like admiration. 'Brother, I thank you.'

'It's not fair!' The second biggest niece protested.

Tori glared at her. 'Ethel Mary Ward, control yourself!'

The second biggest niece glared back.

'Ethel Mary Ward,' Tori repeated, 'do you wish to be sent to bed without supper?'

The little girl thought on this for a moment. 'Yes. Yes I do. For I am now too upset to feel hungry at all.'

'Oh, for goodness sake, Child!' Tori sighed again, 'Is it really that bad?'

'Yes, Mama,' the second biggest niece sniffed. 'My heart is quite broken.'

Horace began to chuckle, but was promptly silenced by the raw force of the little girl's reproachful stare. His sister's tone became steely. 'Ethel, come here.'

The second biggest niece, appearing to have sensed her mother's freshly-summoned mettle, obediently slipped from her chair and went to stand before Tori, head bowed.

'Look at me, Ethel!'

The child raised her face to meet her mother's unblinking eyes.

'Now listen to me well. You are a wild child. Many would say far too wild, and that I allow you more freedom than is proper–'

'But, Mama–'

'Do not speak over me–'

'Sorry, Mama.'

'You will rein your wildness in. Do you understand?'

'But, Mama–'

'Do you understand?'

'Yes, Mama.'

'Furthermore, you shall rise above your objectionable feelings. Do you hear me?'

'Yes, Mama.'

'You will thank Uncle Horace for offering to care for you in my absence.'

The second biggest niece stared at the carpet.

'Ethel, do you hear me?' Silence prevailed. 'Ethel, you will answer me immediately!'

'Yes, Mama.'

'Now thank your uncle.'

The little girl glanced vaguely towards Horace and mumbled, 'Thank you.'

Horace, used as he was to parade ground discipline, was unsure how to respond. Did his second biggest niece's muttered "thank you" constitute sufficient manners? His sister seemed to think it did.

'Good,' she told the little girl. 'Now return to your seat and partake of supper.'

'Yes, Mama.'

'Ah, look,' Horace said brightly, 'Cousin Lizzie's coming to join us at last!'

CHAPTER TEN

'Wake up! wake up!'

'William, is that you?'

'No, Mama, it's me, Ethel.'

'Oh, yes, of course. What is it, dear?'

'It's Christmas Day!'

'But Ethel, it's still nighttime.'

'Kajri says it's already six in the morning!'

'Does she? Well, how marvellous.'

'Mama?'

'Yes, Ethel?'

'May we please go to Aunt Henrietta's now?'

'I think it's a bit early to disturb her, and, besides, we must first attend morning service at the chapel.'

'Oh.'

Although it was too dark to see it, Tori sensed Ethel's disappointed frown.

'Mama, do you think Father Christmas will have known where to leave our gifts, as we are not at home?'

'I am fully sure Father Christmas will have found Aunt Henrietta's tree, and known to leave your gifts there… but have you been a good girl?'

'Of course, Mama,' she said earnestly, but paused. Tori could feel her fidgeting. The six-year-old shifted herself so her knees jammed into Tori's abdomen, and spoke again, 'Mama, may we go down for breakfast now?'

'Ethel, I am not even dressed, and there is no light with which to see.'

'Can't you see anything, Mama?'

'No, dear, I cannot.'

'Guess what colour dress I'm wearing.'

'Pardon?'

'Guess what colour dress I'm wearing.'

'Umm… pink?'

'That's right, Mama. I'm wearing my best, pink dress because it's Christmas Day. May we please go down to breakfast now, Mama, because I really am very excited.'

'Ethel, darling, I know you are, but I really cannot see at all to dress myself.'

'Do not worry, Mama, I shall send Kajri to help you.'

****

Christmas morning, Horatia thought, stirring from a deep, refreshing sleep, *a day on which to celebrate, with loved ones, all that is good in our Christian world, and to cast aside regret and woe. I'm so happy to be reunited with dear Rietta, and to have many members of my beloved family here with me in Budleigh Salterton.* She raised herself from her bed, gritting her teeth against the arthritic objection of her limbs.

Budleigh Salterton's small Anglican chapel of ease stood a block north of the Rolle on a high stretch of grass. Tori, her six children, Horace, Lizzie and the ayah were standing amid the merry, Christmas morning worshippers thronging the grounds, resplendent in best clothes. When Horatia approached them with Ratia and cousin Susan, Tori's face lit with a broad smile and she steered her party to join them. 'Merry Christmas!'

'God bless!' Cousin Susan exclaimed, 'Merry Christmas to you all!'

'Aunt Susan!' effervescent, little Ethel rushed up to her. 'It's Christmas!'

'Yes, dear one, it certainly is, and a merry Christmas to you!'

'Oh, don't you all look a picture?' Horatia declared. 'What a joyous morning!'

Ethel bounded up to her like an excited puppy. 'Why aren't the bells ringing, Grandmama? It's very quiet for before Christmas service.'

'This is just a chapel-of-ease, darling, the main church is... oh dear, I realise I'm not sure.'

'All Saints in East Budleigh,' Rietta supplied. 'I hope you can stand it here for Christmas without ringing church bells, Ethel?'

'Oh yes, Aunt Henrietta,' the little girl told her sincerely, 'for I do love the beach and the pretty streets with holly and ivy in every window!'

Horatia smiled. 'I must say that I find it peculiarly refreshing that there aren't bells ringing this Christmas Day. It feels a part of Budleigh Salterton's topsy-turvy charm.'

'Then I am glad,' said Rietta. 'And merry Christmas to you all!'

They followed the happy crowd into the plain, whitewashed interior of the little chapel-of-ease. They found space on a pew near the back of the wood-beamed building. They were lucky to have done so, for many of the congregation, on this most busy of mornings, were obliged to stand. Baby Alice began to cry loudly, causing Tori to wince with embarrassment and Kajri to carry her outside. When Tori turned to watch the ayah's awkward exit with the squalling baby, she caught the eye of a well-dressed gentleman with raven-black mutton chops in the pew behind. He doffed his hat genially. She smiled politely, and returned her gaze to Reverend Hitch at the altar.

Her husband, Reverend Philip Ward, was delivering his annual Christmas sermon in St. Mildred's in Tenterden. Horatia, with their eight beloved children on either side, listened enraptured to her husband's impassioned speech. Her heart soared in ecstasy at the picture of heavenly benevolence his resonant voice joyfully described.

Horatia realised, with a jolt, that she'd drifted back into the past. *Oh, but I'd so hoped to have stopped doing that! I should be focused on the present. Yet, can it be an evil to think of my dear husband's past sermon, whilst in another church celebrating the very same mass? How can such recollections be categorised as either holy or unholy? Is there a line that can be drawn, and if so where? If no line can be drawn, are all my recollections holy according to Christian diktat, or should I consider them all unholy? I cannot, in my heart of hearts, believe that recalling the righteous sermons of my late, beloved husband could ever be an unholy act.*

So are all my recollections, therefore, godly? She was surprised to feel a surge of excited joy fire upwards from her gut into her heart. *Are all my recollections then Godly?* She queried again, and now a peculiar, although not unpleasant, tingle shot through her, as if sheets of heavy matter were slaking from her head and heart. It felt as if old, hard ice, thawed by sudden sun, was sliding softly from the stone or tree it had been bound to. She felt blissfully lightened. Aware now of the surrounding congregation singing Hark The Herald Angels Sing, she joined her own voice lustily with theirs:

Mild he lays his Glory by,
Born that Men no more may die;
Born to raise the Sons of Earth,
Born to give them second Birth...

Uplifted from their joyous communion, the congregation spilled from the chapel, now keen to return to their homes, both humble and grand, for private celebrations of this most holy of Christian days.

Henrietta smiled to see the joy on Horatia's face, thinking it more than she could have ever hoped for. She'd been right to persuade her old friend to come to Budleigh Salterton for Christmas and, she realised with a catch of breath, she was at peace to pass from the world before the next year was out as the strange waif had foretold.

Susan smiled too to see Horatia's happiness, but her flash of joy was brief because her thoughts were tugged to her son, Alexander, who like Tori's William, was posted far away in India. Susan saw her sorry echoed in Tori's eyes. T'was the plight of military mothers and wives to pine for the men they loved most.

Horace's thoughts were closer to home. He stole another glance at Lizzie thinking her a fine looking mare. Why, though, had she been so reserved with him of late? He suspected there'd be ample opportunity to rekindle their intimacy during the course of the day's celebrations in their old aunt's high street house. His moustache twitched at the thought and he tried to catch her eye, but she was staring resolutely towards the vicar. He had a sudden sense of being watched. There was a well-dressed man, with bushy, black mutton-chop whiskers sitting immediately behind Lizzie in the next pew, but he too was staring straight ahead.

****

'Aunt Henrietta,' Ethel clamoured as soon as Bradford let the party into No. 44 High Street, 'Please may I go and look under your Christmas tree?'

'Patience,' Tori placed a much-practised restraining hand on her shoulder. 'We haven't even removed our cloaks.'

Ethel wrenched her cloak off and thrust it at Bradford. 'Take this quickly, please!'

'Did Father Christmas come here?' Carrie pulled at the fastening of her own shawl.

Little, dark-haired Evie joined in. 'Father Christmas?'

'You're too impatient,' the eldest sister, Nellie sniffed, 'Little girls should be seen and not heard.'

'Then you should not speak,' Ethel was in no mood for her older sister's haughty airs.

Tori, in no mood either, snapped, 'Ethel Mary Ward, enough!'

'Come in everyone,' Henrietta boomed, 'I think I saw some mysterious parcels laid beneath my Christmas tree.'

Ethel ripped the final shreds of paper from the parcel Father Christmas had left for her under Aunt Henrietta's tree, 'I've got a beautiful china doll, so I must have been a very good girl, even if people have sometimes said I wasn't!'

Nellie was over the moon that Father Christmas had given her a zoetrope machine that played animated scenes. Carrie was delighted to have been given a wooden model of Noah's ark with carved animal pairs. Evie was similarly delighted by a charming, miniature tea set. Little Ada was at first perplexed, then enchanted by the kaleidoscope in her own brightly wrapped parcel. Baby Alice, however, was oblivious to the woollen booties Father Christmas had so kindly left for her, and bawled angrily at her sisters' clamour, obliging Kajri to remove her from the room. Susan began to say something, but changed her mind, instead commenting, 'Tis a delight to witness your daughters' enjoyment of Father Christmas's gifts, Tori darling.'

'Yes, the heart of this holy day is reflected in the joy of innocent babes,' Horatia concurred.

Tori allowed herself to relax, but Horace was frustrated because Lizzie had jammed herself between the old lady guests so he couldn't sit next to her. Henrietta, although flustered and tired from the uncustomary and relentless social interaction, was satisfied that her hospitality plans were proving robust. The delicious smell of roasting turkey wafted from the kitchen. The distant sound of waites singing carols drifted in from outside. And all felt well in the moment.

****

There was a collective *ooo* when Bradford placed a holly-decorated platter of roast turkey on the joined tables.

Evie jumped out of her chair in her excitement. ‘It’s actually Christmas dinner!’

Susan said, ‘It looks and smells heavenly!’

‘Bradford, please take a seat and join us for the feast.’ Henrietta nodded towards a spare place between Carrie and Kajri. The maid bobbed, awkward with her temporary promotion, expected though it was, and joined the others at the table. Henrietta continued. ‘Horace, dear, as the man of the party, would you please carve the bird?’

‘My pleasure, Aunt.’ Bradford switched instantly back into the role of maid, and replaced Horace’s dinner plate with the turkey platter and a carving set. Puffing himself up as if about to recite prose, he set to work with the oversized cutlery to dismember the roasted carcass, slice by careful slice.

They relaxed in Henrietta’s cosy parlour after dinner. The adults drank sherry and everyone played charades. It was Tori’s turn to mime. She opened her hands to indicate a book, and stood by the curtains with one hand cupped to her ear and the other gesticulating in front of her, as she opened and closed mouth.

‘Talking?’ Susan suggested, but Tori shook her head, and repeated her mime.

‘Listening to neighbours?’ Horatia suggested doubtfully.

Tori smiled encouragement.

‘And talking about them?’ Henrietta chuckled.

Tori pointed vigorously between the curtains, cupping her ear again.

‘Spying on neighbours?’ Horace strode to the window and

peered out at the pitch-dark street. 'There's not much to report outside,' he shrugged.

Tori, suddenly alert, gestured at the window again. Horace brightened and called the others over.

'What is it?' Lizzie demanded. Horace tried to grab her waist, but she side-stepped away. And then, plain to all ears, came the haunting strains of distant carollers.

'How beautiful!' Susan gushed. Then recognition sparked. 'A Christmas Carol – the book by Charles Dickens!'

Tori was so relieved that she nearly collapsed.

Ethel spoke up quickly. 'May we please talk about the Blanckleys now?'

'Do not pester adults,' Tori clucked.

'Oh, but bless her keen persistence,' Henrietta interposed. 'Lizzie, would you indulge our studious niece?'

'Very well,' Lizzie patted Ethel's golden hair. 'Did you know we're descended from Sir Walter Raleigh?'

Ethel grinned from ear to ear. 'Oh no, Aunt Lizzie. Who is he?'

'His name is pronounced *roar*-leigh!' Horace declared.

Lizzie wrinkled her nose as if there was a bad smell, but Tori laughed. 'I remember Papa saying Sir Walter's name had a roar in it like a leopard. We were discussing the arms Papa was awarded, which feature a speared leopard head.'

'Roar!' Ethel cried. 'I'm a Blanckley leopard with a spear in my head! Roar, roar!'

Lizzie coughed to regain her attention. 'Sir Walter was a great favourite of Queen Elizabeth I. Have you heard of her, Ethel?'

'Oh yes, Aunt Lizzie.'

'Good. When Catholic King James took the throne after her, he threw Sir Walter into the Tower of London and beheaded him.'

Nellie screamed and Carrie started to cry, but Ethel was hungry to hear more. 'Did his head roll across the ground?'

'Ethel Mary Ward!'

'Sorry Mama, but it's ever so interesting! Aunt Lizzie, is Walter *Roar*-leigh in our family?'

'Our Blanckley line is descended from him,' Lizzie said proudly.

'Our family inherited some of his personal possessions,' Tori added. 'A ring bearing his coat of arms came to me.'

Henrietta grinned. 'Ethel, do you know where Raleigh was born?'

'Why no, Aunt Henrietta!'

'He was born right here!'

Ethel's eyes were wide as saucers. 'He was born in this house?'

'Not in this house, Ethel, but in a much grander residence named Hayes Barton. We villagers were entertained two years ago when an artist called Millais came here to paint a depiction of him as a child. He set his easel up at the top of the beach close to your hotel.'

Nellie was suddenly interested. 'May I please speak, Aunt Henrietta?'

'Of course, Nellie.'

Tori's eight-year-old, oldest daughter, was far more cautious in her manner than Ethel. 'Thank you, Aunt Henrietta. I'm wondering if you saw the artist, Millais, at work on his painting?'

'Everyone in the village did,' she chuckled. 'The poor man had little peace. He did, however, succeed in producing a lovely painting despite our clamour. He called it "The Boyhood of Raleigh".'

'Is this why you moved here, Aunt Henrietta?'

'Ethel, are you asking if I moved here to see the artist painting Raleigh's boyhood?'

'Because he used to live here, Sir Walter Raleigh, I mean. Did you want to live here too because he was family?'

'Hmm, good question. Now I think upon it, the Raleigh connection did weigh in Budleigh Salterton's favour when I was deciding where to live.'

Ethel resumed her interest in genealogy. 'Was Sir Walter Raleigh my great great-grandfather, Aunt Henrietta?'

'It's all rather complex. My father – your grandpapa – H.S.B., was the cousin of his first wife, Mary Rogers. They were both descended from Sir Walter, but it was she who inherited lands from his Irish estate. I have the papers in the attic, including the property details. It's all in there. You may be interested to see them, Toriana.'

Tori looked up. 'I recall Papa telling me the mortgages fell through during Grandpapa's time away as British Consul.'

'That's right, my dear. He was very distressed.'

Tori sighed. 'Papa said this too.'

'What may also interest you are letters that came into my possession after my sister's demise–' Henrietta paused in respectful silence, 'They written from your grandmama – Mary Rogers, that is – to your grandpapa.'

Nobody noticed Lizzie blanch, as all eyes were on Henrietta and Tori, who said, 'I should dearly love to see those letters!'

'I'll bring the box down during your visit, if time permits. If not, they should go to you, and Horace,' she smiled to her nephew, 'once I pass on.'

'Please don't talk of such things, dear aunt,' Tori admonished. 'You are yet hale.'

Susan looked away, but Henrietta nodded, 'You're correct, Niece. This is not a thing to talk of on Christmas Day.'

Horatia shifted higher in her cushioned seat. It was a joy that her joints were as trouble-free as her heart had become. 'Friends, family,' she addressed the room cheerfully, 'I wholeheartedly agree with Cousin Susan. Now is the time for joy!'

****

Three days later, and tense as a coiled wire, Tori welcomed the incoming Exeter-bound train as the first step on her newly-mapped route to internal peace. 'Horace,' she touched her brother's scarlet sleeve, 'it's not too late for you to change your mind. You could come with me,' but she felt him flinch.

'This I do not wish,' he affected an air of genial blandness. 'My only wish is your own speedy return.'

'Am I making a mistake? I'm sure Horatia was displeased when I told her of this trip, though, of course, she was too well-mannered to say so. But I expected her to give me her blessing and she turned away instead.'

'Why on Earth would Horatia give a hoot if you want to go off in search of your past? Not that I, myself, approve! You know my thoughts very well.'

'Yes, Brother, you believe the past to be dead and buried, and that no good can come from poking around in it and stirring up God knows what.'

Horace brightened. 'You've summed my feelings up in a perfect nutshell!'

'You'll keep an eye on my girls?'

'My word is my bond.'

'Thank you,' she pecked his cold cheek with a chaste kiss.

He returned the kiss stiffly. 'Fair you well, Sister.'

'Good bye!' Waving bravely, she boarded the steaming train.

CHAPTER ELEVEN

Francis Thomas Cooke looked distinctly distressed. His usually bushy sideburns were squashed flat by the palms of his large hands, 'But Father, pantomime is for children!'

Elderly Otho Cooke, skinny as a bunch of twigs in his throne-like chair in Withycombe House, near Budleigh Salterton, brooked no arguments from his son, 'I'm asking you to mind your sister.'

'*Half*-sister.'

'She is born of *my* blood, so sister to you.'

'But she's not born of my mama, God rest her soul.'

'Yes, yes,' Otho was no fan of nostalgia. 'I've recognised my daughter, so she's your goddamned sister. Understood, Boy?'

'If Amanda insists on performing on stage, I shouldn't be expected to mind her.'

'Don't speak back! You promised to seek out that eligible heiress while you're there.'

'I think her unlikely to attend a pantomime, unless she's twelve-years old.'

'What did I say about not speaking back?'

'Sorry.'

'I happen to know she'll be attending, don't I, Julia?' He

prodded a bony, yellow-nailed finger at a demure young woman hunching beside him.

'Yes, Husband.'

'That's what I like, respect and no arguing back!' He prodded his wife's ribs again. 'Julia, lift your face so Francis can look at you! See this pretty young thing? Only two years older than you! Do you know why she married me?'

'Yes, Father,' his voice was strained.

'Well, spit it out then.'

'Because you knew how to manage her inheritance.'

'Hah! So she can thank me for the luxury she lives in, while I benefit from her warming my sheets! You need to get out there and find a rich, young filly. Damn it, she doesn't even need to be young. Marry a toothless old crone, for all I care. Just make sure the wench has money.'

Lacking the mettle to stand up to his tyrannical patriarch, Francis dug his fingernails into his black sideburns. 'I shall, of course, do as you say.'

'The crone Amanda told us of?'

'I took a room in the inn opposite her house. She's a short, fat dumpling with a ridiculous, satsuma-coloured wig, blue steel glasses, and a voice like a trumpet.'

'Spare the boring details. Have you met the niece?'

'Umm, two young women have been visiting her, and I'm as yet unsure which, if either, is the heiress-to-be.'

'Have you acquainted yourself with these dubious wenches?'

'I sat behind them in chapel on Christmas morning. I

succeeded in catching the eyes of both women, and nodded greetings. And fear not, Father, I'm maintaining close surveillance on the entire family.'

'Good boy!' Otho's skull-like grin revealed brown teeth.

****

Ethel longed to run free on the beach without supervision. The white painted frames of the dining hall's tall windows felt like jail bars. How could Mama have abandoned her so cruelly to Uncle Horace's control? Mama had never gone off without her before, so why was she doing so now? It was Christmastide as well, and her birthday tomorrow. She'd promised to be back in time for the stupid pantomime Uncle Horace was making everyone go to on her birthday, but would she truly be back in time. Trains were often late. Mama's selfishness had quite spoiled their holiday.

****

Horace had had a headache all morning. He lent on the jamb of the dining hall door to regard his multiple nieces. He was mindful that his sister had left them in his charge, but he was completely inexperienced with childcare, and had no idea how to tell if he needed to do anything about any of them. Why had he volunteered to do this? His stomach knotted. He scanned his sister's dispersed brood. The biggest one, whatever her name was, was seated apart from the others writing in a book (so no obvious problems there). The two smallest ones, apart from the baby, were with the next smallest one (was she called Carrie?) and their exotic nursemaid, whose name escaped him. She really wasn't too bad to look upon, although she could be a bit whiney, especially with regard to cold weather. There should be five walking-around nieces and a baby. He spotted the baby in the Indian nursemaid's arms, but the location of the fifth walking-around-one eluded him until he spotted a small girl sitting alone by one of the windows. He supposed it was probably one of his sister's brood and that he should go and see if it's happy or something. As he approached the window he saw the girl had dark golden hair that had been neatly twisted into face-framing ringlets. She wore a short, pale lavender dress, which produced a pretty effect until he looked at her face, which was scowling at him. He took a moment to compose an appropriate avuncular remark, and settled on, 'Good morning, Niece. How are you today?' But the little girl carried on scowling as if there was something despicable six-feet behind him. His first instinct was to flee her presence, but he remembered his duty, and attempted to engage her for a second time. 'Niece, I notice you are sitting alone. Your mama has tasked me with watching over you, so I must ask if you are well.' When she continued to ignore him, he lost patience. 'Niece, I don't care what has caused your ignorant behaviour, but it will stop now, do you hear me?' The girl's eyes widened, but her lips remained closed. 'I have had enough of this!' He pronounced, raising his voice so that everyone in the dining room – which, by good fortune, wasn't crowded – turned to see what the fuss was about. 'Listen to me well, Niece, if you do not speak to me immediately, I will send a wire to your mama informing her of your extreme rudeness.'

'You don't even know my name,' the girl accused.

'Ah, so you do have a tongue?'

'And I have a name too, yet you don't know it,' the little girl retorted.

Horace scowled back. 'Of course I know your name.'

'Well, what is it then?'

'I do not take orders from little girls!'

'And I don't take orders from uncles.'

'Yes you damned well do, as your mama has left you in my charge! Do you wish for me to send her a wire?'

The little girl blanched, but held her ground. 'And what would you tell her? That you cannot control a six-year-old child?'

He turned red. 'Why… I… you…'

'Yes, Uncle?'

His vain struggle to formulate a reply was mercifully curtailed by the appearance of the largest niece who, ignoring the other one's angry look, enquired, 'Uncle Horace, is my sister behaving herself?'

'She has been perfectly charming,' he lied, with no trace of irony.

'I'm glad to hear this, Uncle Horace. My sister can be impertinent at times.'

'We shall get along just fine, shan't we Niece?' he asked the other one.

'Yes, Uncle,' she said meekly. 'I wish to retire to my room to read… with your permission.'

Horace exhaled slowly. Had it really been so easy? 'Of course,' he pronounced magnanimously, 'off you go.'

The girl scampered away. To all appearances, as merry as a May colt.

****

'Ratia, dear friend, are you well?' Henrietta queried Horatia, who'd scarce said a word during breakfast.

She was slow to reply, and when she did, her voice held the brittleness of spun-sugar. 'I am perfectly merry! I must thank you for the tonic you prescribed me of time with you, and dear Susan, of course! I feel better than I've done in years.'

Henrietta caught Susan's eye with frown, before addressing Horatia. 'Ratia dearest, I'm not sure how to put this but–' she trailed off, unsure what to say.

Susan stepped forwards. 'I think what Henrietta wishes to say is that she had hoped, I mean we both have, that coming here for Christmastide would help you to–'

Henrietta found her voice again. 'Ratia dearest, the three of us know you have, well, things to reflect on…'

Horatia stood up as abruptly as her arthritis allowed. 'I've no wish to reflect on anything! Brooding has been the cause of my woes. Coming here has made me realise that I can be, and am, perfectly happy if I completely cease brooding.'

Henrietta stood too. 'I invited you here to scream your secret frustrations at the sea. If you do not, to use your word, "brood" on things to call your demons to the fore, I shall consider you most ungrateful,' she winked, but any good humour was lost on Horatia.

'Poppycock, fuss and nonsense! I've had a life-time's fill of brooding and moroseness. The past is gone. Whatever my foolish daughter-in-law has in mind, going to South Brent is a foolishness, and I will not indulge myself that way. Those we've lost are in paradise. We should just get on and enjoy our lives.'

'Horatia,' Susan interposed, 'we didn't mean to upset you. But, well, I must say I agree with Henrietta that it would be healthy for you to take time to, as it were, exorcise your demons.'

She shot her a look of cold fury. 'And what of you, Cousin? Will you too partake of personal exorcism here? For I know you have a horde of nasty, little demons brooding in your bosom.'

Susan was startled. 'I... I do not know... I had not thought–'

Horatia slumped. 'Oh dear, forgive me, Susan. I was rude and out of turn. Perhaps the freedom of Budleigh Salterton has rubbed off on me too much? Please think nothing of my harsh words. If neither of you mind, I'll go back upstairs to have a little lie down.'

Susan's brow was furrowed when she returned from powdering her nose a little later that morning. 'Is Horatia not with you? I thought she'd gone to lie down in the guest room, but she's not there.'

Henrietta frowned. 'Where could she be? Bradford, have you seen Ratia?'

Bradford, neatly attired in a blue dress and an ankle-length starched white apron, came promptly to the doorway. 'I think she went out, Ma'am.'

'Out? Where did she go?'

'I don't know, Ma'am, I didn't think it my business to ask her.'

'I suppose it wasn't,' Henrietta conceded. 'Susan, where do you think she might have gone? She was in a peculiar mood earlier.'

'Perhaps she felt a need for solitude?'

'Perhaps she's taken my advice and gone to scream at the sea?'

'I really don't think she will be. Not after the things she said earlier.'

‘Hmmm, we shall see,’ Henrietta said thoughtfully. 'And, pray, Susan dear, how are you? Ratia was rather abrupt with you.’

‘Well, I confess Horatia’s words did shake me a bit.’

‘Would you care to share?’

‘Oh, well, it is nothing of major consequence. What Horatia said caused me to recall my sister. I was remembering her wedding to Edward.’

Henrietta brightened. ‘It was a marvellous occasion! Was it in Malta?’

‘Naples. In the British Ambassador’s house… what was his name? Mr. À Court, that was it.’

‘I remember him,’ Henrietta laughed, ‘He was a little, balding man, only just taller than me! Though he had quite a presence, and was unfailingly courteous. Do you remember all those handsome young naval officers in glittering, gold brocade?’

Susan turned back from the window, smiling. ‘How could I forget them? My sister, Catherine, married John Bendyshe from that party in Paris the next year!’

‘You know, I was very jealous of her,’ Henrietta confided, ‘He was so very handsome.’

Susan came to her side. ‘I didn’t know you were sweet on John Bendyshe?’

‘It was just a girlish fancy,’ Henrietta tilted her cheek to hide her blush.

‘Why did you, yourself, not marry, Henrietta?’

Henrietta’s mind was immediately flooded with the memory of rough hands wrenching, pushing, and pulling at her skirts, and Daniel's knee jammed between her thighs. She refused to let the hurt show on her face and stared resolutely at the fire. 'I was engaged to someone, but only briefly.'

'I'd no idea! What was his name? Was he very handsome?'

Henrietta attempted to breathe out through her nostrils, but part choked, and hoped Susan didn't hear the resulting, unladylike grunting. 'He was called Daniel. An army man.'

'What is his family name? Do I know him?'

'Actually I don't remember.' Henrietta released another forced chuckle. 'But I'm certain you don't know him.'

'Was he very dashing?'

'He was, but I realised I'm not the sort of woman who could be happily bridled to a man. You know me!'

'Oh, dearest Henrietta, I can't picture a man getting the better of you!'

****

Horatia was alone on Budleigh Salterton's broad, pebble beach, but not shouting at the sea as Henrietta had hoped. She was, instead, quiet as a mouse as she gazed, unfocused, at the curiously pink outgoing tide.

'Grandmama, what are you doing on the beach all by yourself?'

Horatia was surprised to find Ethel and the girls' little spaniel looking up at her. The six-year-old looked pretty as a picture in a knee-length dress with puffed sleeves, whose light purple colour contrasted strikingly with her golden ringlets. 'I could ask you the same question,' she told Ethel, 'and why are you not wearing a coat? Tis cold.'

'I don't feel cold at all, Grandmama, and see, my dress has long sleeves, and poor Patch hasn't had a walk today. Did you know that dogs need to go for walks every day?'

'Does Kajri know you're here? Or your uncle, Horace?'

'No, Grandmama, I saw you from the window of my room, and decided to get Patch and come and and join you.' The spaniel barked happily at the mention of his name, and wagged his stubby tail vigorously.

'Do you feel you should have told your uncle or Kajri before doing so?'

She considered the question. 'Maybe, Grandmama, but I'm quite safe, because I've got Patch with me, and the hotel's just there,' she waved vaguely behind her, 'and I didn't think I needed to disturb them.'

'And what if they look for you in your room and find you gone?'

'They would see me if they looked out the window.'

'Hmmm, I think I should return you to the hotel before they worry, and before you catch a chill.'

'Oh, but Grandmama, you see… well…'

'Yes, Ethel?'

'It's just that I really don't like Uncle Horace. I like you much better.'

Horatia could not help but smile at her granddaughter's twisted compliment. 'Ethel, tis not decorous to speak ill of your elders.'

'But I really don't like him at all.' Her blue eyes were wide with sincerity.

'Do you have a specific problem with him? You may confide in me.'

Her brows puckered in thought. 'I am not truly sure, Grandmama... but he... he seems like he's pretending to be friendly, when he isn't, and he doesn't even know our names!'

'Do you feel that he should know your names?'

'Why yes, Grandmama, I do. It would show that he paid us proper attention.'

'And you wish him to pay you proper attention?'

She shrugged, unsure. 'It would be polite, wouldn't it, Grandmama? Or, at least, it feels rude that he doesn't know our names.'

'Maybe, if you engaged with him, he would pay more attention to you?'

'Hmmm, maybe... though I still don't like him... and, Grandmama?'

'Yes, Ethel, dear?'

'It's bad, isn't it, that he doesn't see Aunt Augusta at all, because she's his wife, so he's supposed to live with her, isn't he?'

Horatia's heart skipped. 'Your own Papa has left you to rejoin the army in India.'

Ethel frowned. 'Yes, but... Papa did live with us as much as he could... but Uncle Horace doesn't want to live with Aunt Augusta at all.'

Horatia sighed, recalling her own father's infamous departure from his wife in favour of Lady Hamilton.

'It is wrong, isn't it, Grandmama?'

'Ethel darling, sometimes people find themselves unhappy with the person to whom they are wed and so step away from their wife or husband, and yet they may still have good souls.'

'But, Grandmama, marriage is meant to be forever and ever.'

'I know, darling... but sometimes people find that they just cannot live happily with their wife or husband, no matter how hard they try.'

Ethel, bless her dear heart, looked deeply troubled. 'But Grandmama, if they got married and promised to God, then they're not allowed to stop trying.'

'Ethel, darling girl, you have a good heart and a sharp mind, but please be kind to your Uncle Horace.'

'Why, Grandmama? You say that sometimes married people can't like each other, even if they try: well, I can't like Uncle Horace, even if I try!'

'And have you tried, Ethel?'

She shuffled her feet. 'Well, not really, Grandmama... but I really, really don't like him.'

'Ethel, your uncle has had a lot of pain in his life; a lot of loss, and it would be unchristian of you to behave unkindly towards him.' Horatia was encouraged to see that Ethel appeared genuinely interested.

'What has he lost?'

'He lost his mama – your other grandmama – when he was just a small boy. The same age as you are now.'

'But my mama lost her mama too, and she was younger than

Uncle Horace.'

'This is true, but your mama stayed with Aunt Susan, who adopted her, but your Uncle Horace was sent away to school with no mother to care for him.'

Ethel thought on this. 'That would have been hard for him. Poor Uncle Horace!'

'So do you think you can be more kind to him?'

'I can try, Grandmama. It would have hurt him a lot to lose his mama and then be sent away to school without anyone to love him.'

'Yes it would, Ethel dear.'

'Grandmama?'

'Yes, dear?'

'Were you hurt when Lady Hamilton died?'

The question impacted like lightning from a clear sky. Panicked, she countered, 'What do you know of this, child?'

'Aunt Susan said Lady Hamilton was your guardian, and she died in Calais with just you there... and you were only thirteen-years-old... and now everyone hates her, except Aunt Susan doesn't... and Mama. Aunt Susan says she knew Lady Hamilton and that she was a good person... but we don't speak of her much, I think it's because nearly everyone else hates her, including my papa.'

Horatia, deeply moved, wiped the tears she felt brimming.

'Do you hate Lady Hamilton, Grandmama?'

Oh, Ethel with your sharp mind and uninhibited tongue! She inhaled deeply, causing bitterly cold sea air to burn her lungs.

'No,' she said carefully, 'I do not hate Lady Hamilton.'

'Is that why you never talk about her, because you don't like people saying bad things about her?'

Horatia's voice hardened. 'Ethel, truly you are sometimes far too impertinent! Haven't you heard that little girls should be seen and not heard?'

Ethel was as dauntless as ever. 'Oh, but Grandmama, I merely wish to know if it upsets you a lot when people say bad things about Lady Hamilton, because then I can care for you better.'

Horatia was quiet for a long time.

'Grandmama?'

She wiped her eyes. The wind and salty sea air were most irritating. It was high time for both Ethel and she to return indoors. 'I am sorry,' she told the six-year-old more gently, 'but I cannot talk of this.'

'Why not, Grandmama?'

Horatia, emotionally bombarded, yet unable to release, felt herself spinning. What could she say to little Ethel?

'Ratia!'

Horatia was immensely relieved to see Rietta making her way towards them in a graceless amble across the rounded, fist-sized pebbles.

'I came looking for you, dear friend!' Rietta's voice rang loud across the beach, 'And here I find you with my favourite niece!'

'Thank you, Aunt Henrietta!' Ethel purred, 'I'm very happy to be your favourite niece, which means you think me even better than Aunt Lizzie!'

Henrietta opened her mouth to reply, but stumbled on the pebbles.

‘Ethel Mary Ward,’ Horatia chided, ‘vanity and boastfulness are sins. Now, let’s get into the Rolle and order tea!’

CHAPTER TWELVE

Tori was in a surprisingly empty carriage. The only other occupants being an elderly couple who kept themselves to themselves. Determined to at last enjoy the Exmouth line's famed view of the estuary, she found that her mind would not focus on it. Her churning thoughts demanded her attention on first one thing, then another. Were her girls coping without her? Was Ethel still being sullen? Wasn't it very dangerous to travel solo? Did her unchaperoned condition cause her to appear disreputable? On top of all this, was fear that the tenants of View Cottage would find her visit intrusive. She shook her head, and made another attempt to enjoy the famous estuary view. It really was very pretty, but her anxious thoughts churned on faster than the wheels of the chugging train. Would her lodgings at the Royal Oak Hotel be satisfactory? How would Horace cope as guardian of her daughters? Would Ethel behave decorously towards him?

Her heart leapt with joy when the train screeched into Brent station. She inhaled a hungry lungful of lost-home air, but coughed convulsively. She looked about her, squinting left and right beyond the steam-billowing locomotive. There seemed to be smoke coming in from outside the station. She wondered where on Earth it was coming from. She hailed the only cabbie in sight: a scruffy man loitering next to an equally scruffy Hackney. She directed him to transport herself and her cases to the Royal Oak Hotel. The jolting, horse-drawn vehicle turned right out of the station and almost immediately drew to a halt. The cabby called, 'The Oak, Ma'am!'

South Brent, she realised, was evidently not large. The Oak transpired to be a small building jutting out at the higher end of an unpaved street. She was dismayed to realise it was a public house, not a proper hotel. Reluctant to enter, she waited for the cabby to do so on her behalf. She explored the street with her eyes. Like the high street in Budleigh Salterton, it had a centrally-running drain, although this one was far more noxious. There was a terrace of small, slate-roofed buildings further down which seemed to be a mixture of private dwellings and shops. There was a grocer's with cartwheels stacked outside, and, several houses below this, a sign proclaiming 'Jennings' above what looked to be a newsagents. Her smile to spot a bakery and confectionery establishment next-door it vanished when a whiff of something rotten hit her from the open drain. The buildings across the road appeared to be solely residential, apart from – she craned her neck – the one at the very bottom of the block. Beyond this she could see shopfronts on a road running perpendicular to the bottom of the street. Looking uphill, she spied the entrance to the station on her left and, opposite it, a small terrace set back behind stone walled gardens. To her amusement a sign proclaimed this to be Nelson Place. Her esteemed great uncle had a memorial even in this backwater of darkest Devon!

'Ma'am,' the cabby had returned in the company of a portly, middle-aged man with greying hair, sideburns and stained teeth. He extended a podgy hand, 'Mrs. Ward, I presume?'

She touched his hand lightly. 'How do you do, Mr–'

'Arscott, Ma'am. I am the hotel's proprietor. Tis my great pleasure to personally welcome yer.'

Tori chose not to challenge his claim that this was a hotel. 'Would you show me to my room?'

Mr. Arscott's eyes darted left and right as if expecting to find help. 'Begging yer pardon, Ma'am, but yer room's not quite ready yet. Ellen, that's me daughter, she's making sure it's all spick and span for yer.'

'I see,' she said, feeling strong regret for having left Budleigh Salterton.

'May I invite yer to await in the family saloon, Ma'am?'

She hesitated, unwilling to enter a public drinking establishment.

'Ma'am, I can assure yer our saloon is a very decent room, and we 'as a nice fire going. Perhaps yer'd like a little tea? Me wife's made some dainty cakes especial.'

'How thoughtful of her. Please show me in then.'

To Tori's relief, the family saloon transpired to be a clean and cosy private parlour with a window opening onto a side lane. Several small, dark wood tables draped with unstained, white lace were placed around the perimeter, and a merry fire provided a welcoming glow. Mr. Arscott pulled out a chair which Tori accepted, glad to take the weight off her feet and be out of the cold December wind.

'Shall I send Sarah, I mean, Mrs. Arscott, with the tea, Ma'am?'

'Please do.' She removed her mid-length white gloves and stretched her bare hands towards the fire's blessed warmth, now feeling very much better about being in South Brent.

'Ma'am, Mrs. Ward?' A matronly woman bustled in with a tray of tea things and small cakes. 'Bill, I mean Mr. Arscott, told me yer were 'ere and you was wanting tea. I baked these little cakes especial, knowing we had a lady coming to stay.'

'Mrs. Arscott, I presume?'

‘That I be, Ma’am,’ the matronly woman bobbed. ‘And may I say it is an honour to ‘ave a lady of class staying at our ‘otel.’

Tori, embarrassed, was unsure how to respond, and was glad when her talkative hostess saved her the trouble.

‘Did yer have a good journey, Ma’am?’

‘It was quite pleasant, thank you.’

Mrs. Arscott set about adding milk to her cup, then steaming tea from the pot. ‘May I ask what brings yer to South Brent, Ma’am, if I int prying, that is? Would yer like sugar, Ma’am?’

‘One spoon, please, and to answer your question, I’m here to view a property.’

‘Yer thinking of comin’ ter live ‘ere, Ma’am?’

‘No, not at all,’ Tori was surprised that her words felt a lie, ‘I… the property is View… I mean Lutton House.’

Mrs. Arscott grinned. ‘Ah, you mean Blanckleys?’

Tori’s pulse quickened at her family name being used for her childhood home. ‘What did you say it’s called?’

‘“Blanckleys” is what they all calls it… or did. When I think on it, I been hearing more people calling it Lutton ‘Ouse of late. Big ‘ouse it be up Brent Hill. See, it were built by a fancy navy cap’n thirty or forty years back, and ‘is name were Blanckley. I weren’t around ‘ere back then. I were born in Buckfastleigh, up the road, but folks round ‘ere remembers ee well enough.’

Tori felt guilty to withhold her identity, yet compelled to encourage her garrulous hostess to reveal more. ‘They still talk of him?’

‘That’s right, Mrs. Ward. Oh, I do hope I’m not going on at yer.

Yer probably wanting to enjoy yer tea in peace. Do try a cake. I baked ‘em special.’

‘Thank you, Mrs. Arscott, you’re very kind.’ She cut a slice from one of the little cakes and nibbled it. It was heavy and greasy. ‘How delicious,’ she lied. ‘Mrs. Arscott, I’m very interested to hear more of what the villagers have said of this Captain Blanckley.’

‘Well, as yer asks, they says ee were a fine old gent what always had time fer people and that. Not too up in himself, he weren’t. And ee ‘ad a wife too–’ Mrs. Arscott frowned, ‘or were that two? I mean, I think the first one, poor thing, died and then ee ‘ad another.’

Tori’s heart hammered. ‘Did the villagers say anything of these two wives?’

‘Wife!’ Mr. Arscott strode in with a bundle of logs, ‘I 'ope yer not pestering our guest! Off with yer, Woman, and leave our good guest in peace!’

Mrs. Arscott scuttled away before Tori could think of a reason to halt her.

****

The room she was eventually taken to was small but clean and warmed by a crackling fire. Tori sat down on an upholstered chair by the hearth.

She woke with a start realising she’d fallen asleep. She shook her head vigorously, determined to stay awake. Tired as she was, she had less than twenty-four-hours in South Brent, and didn’t want to sleep through any of the precious, mid-winter daylight. Happily the sky outside was still light. She rang the servant’s bell, and the Arscott’s daughter appeared promptly.

'Please call a cab. I wish to visit View… I mean Lutton House.'

'Yes, Ma'am. I'll send the boy to fetch ee right away.' The eighteen-year-old curtseyed clumsily, and scuttled off.

The cab that came was the same Hackney and scruffy driver that had transported her to The Oak from the station earlier that day. 'Af'noon, Ma'am,' the old cabbie doffed his battered cap. 'Is it Lutton 'Ouse yer after?'

'Yes, please.'

'Right you is, Ma'am, but I'll warn yer the track's mighty steep, and it can be right cledgy this time of year and slippy as a veesh.'

Tori did her best to decipher his thick Devon dialect. 'Is the track too slippery for your carriage?'

He scratched his greasy head, 'That I can't tell yer, Ma'am.'

'Would it be safe?'

'Well, I couldn't promise. Track's likely proper cledgy after all 'em rain.'

'I see. Thank you for you honesty.' Tori was reassured that her winter boots looked sturdy. 'Take me to the foot of Brent Hill.'

'That I can do, Ma'am, but ee'll be dimpsey soon, and the track's proper dangerous in the dark when ee's cledgy.'

Surmising that "dimpsey" meant dark, Tori realised he was right. 'I thank you for your caution. Are you able to recommend alternative transport to View Cottage?'

'View Cottage, Ma'am?'

'This is what I said.'

'I in't 'eard ee called that for years, Ma'am. Folks round 'ere been calling ee Lutton 'Ouse of late.'

'Oh, yes, of course. I forgot.'

'We can't 'ave yer risking life and limb going up to ee when it's near dimpsey. How about I takes yer first thing tomorrow?'

'Very well, Sir. I suppose shall just have to wait.'

The grey-haired cabbie eyed her thoughtfully from beneath the peak of his age-worn cap. 'Yer seems mighty keen to get ter Lutton 'Ouse.'

'I am,' she admitted.

'Is they family of yers up there?'

She was surprised to realise she wanted to be completely candid with this stranger from her former home village. 'The house was, I mean still is, my family's. It was my childhood home. I wish to revisit it for sentimental reasons.'

The cabbie broke into a gap-toothed grin. 'Well, I'll be damned if yer in't little Miss Blanckley? I can see it now in yer face. Yer the spitting image of yer pa!'

'Tis I!' she cried, the villager's recognition having lifted her heart in a most unexpected way.

'Let me look at yer, cheach,' the cabbie clasped her shoulders gently with rough hands, and beamed at her. 'Yer all grown up! I remembers yer from when yer was a tiny tot running round on the grass up View Cottage.'

'You remember me?'

'Yes, my love. I'm 'Arry Soper. I were one of 'em boys doing up the 'ouse fer yer pa. Just a cheach I were then. I 'ad sandy-coloured ‘air, and I used ter play with yer brother. What were ‘is name? ‘Orace, that were ee, and I recall yer ‘ad cheach cousins too.’

‘Alexander and Acheson,’ she smiled. ‘I grew up with Alexander after my mother–’

He bowed his head. ‘Lovely lady, your ma were. God rest ‘is soul.’

A lump rose in Tori’s throat. ‘Did you know her?’

‘Course I did. Like I say, I were working on the ‘ouse. I recall yer cousin’s ma was a very sad lady.’

‘Aunt Susan lost her husband. It broke her heart.’

‘Sad times, sad times,’ he shook his head as if to shake them away. ‘But I shouldn’t be waylaying yer. It’s proper cold, in’t ee?’

‘No, really, I am very pleased to speak with you. It’s hard to explain, but coming back here after all these years and finding out that you remember me and my family means an awful lot. I sincerely wish to acquaint myself with you further.’

‘Wassat?’

‘I am delighted to speak with you, Harry.’

‘Are you certain, Ma’am?’

‘Please call me Tori.’

He brightened. ‘Well, if yer sure, Miss Tori, but yer gotta call me ‘Arry, in't ee?’

‘Harry it is, then,’ she beamed.

‘I knows my wife’ll wanna see yer. Yer might not remember ‘er. Eliza Maddick she were afore she became Mrs. Soper. Orphan she were, poor cheach. Used ter do maiding. I know ee'll be right vexed if I don't take yer to say 'ello.'

Tori was happily entranced. 'I should love to meet your wife.'

'Then yer must come for supper. But…'

'You look troubled, Mr. Soper?'

'Just that yer a fanty-sheeny vurriner, and we in't got no place for the likes of yer.'

'Harry,' she touched the rough weave of his sleeve. 'I'd be honoured to be a guest in your home.'

'Really? I mean, yer joking me, right? And, well, we in't got nuffing good in to eat.'

'I should like, if you'll permit, to gift you a Christmastide joint of meat.'

'Why, Miss Tori, that'd be proper welcome for Mrs. Soper and our cheaches. But I'd not wanna presume of yer.'

'I'm truly happy to gift this.'

'Proper Blanckley, yer too!' he flashed his gap-toothed grin. 'Me cousin Bill's got a grocery shop on Church Street. That's the main street. It's round the corner past the Anchor Inn yonder. Ee'll 'ave some nice meat in for sure. Yer can walk down with me, or…'

'I should be delighted to walk there with you,' she tucked her arm affectionately beneath his. The uneven road demanded her full attention lest she slip. She smiled to Harry. 'I recognise these buildings. It's as if a thick fog in my mind has suddenly cleared.'

'Wassat you say?' Harry guided her around a heap of horse dung, 'Thick fog? It's all 'em mills, in't ee? Wind's blowing the smoke right at us. Does that sometimes. We's got six mills 'ere nowadays, and most of 'em uses coal instead of water, so it do get a bit foggy!'

'I did wonder where all the smoke came from. I was saying, however, that I think I blocked many of my memories after Mama…'

'Terrible thing what 'appened, God rest 'is soul. No wonders yer forgot. Good thing is yer back 'ere now. I thought all yer Blanckleys were gone like morning dew in the sun. It's proper good yer 'ere now, maid!'

'This it is, Harry. I feel I've come home after far too long away, and my heart feels bright!' Gone was the grinding pain of *Mummy-is-gone*. In its place was her inner three-year-old's certainty that *Mummy-is-here.* Nodding joyfully at every passer-by, she skipped past the blue-painted Anchor Inn, and down the main street towards Harry's cousin's shop. She neither knew nor cared that mud had splattered the skirt of her tailored day dress. The stench of midden heaps and open drains conveyed to her the wholesomeness of Earthly paradise. The mangey, growling dog, which Harry kicked away, was a darling pup in her eyes, and the bare-footed children were not the vile paupers Lizzie would spurn, but dear unfortunates whom she wished to buy shoes for. 'Harry, that hill rising up behind those cottages at the end of the road: I remember that too!'

'Ugborough Beacon, ee be. Our 'ouse in't far now, and me Cousin Bill's shop is just across the road. Come on, me love,' Harry steered her gently over planks bridging the street's drains. 'Ere we are!'

Tori was confused and a little alarmed because there was no shop where Harry had indicated, just a small terraced house.

'Lez see if ee's 'ome.' Harry banged on the low, weather-worn door.

‘You said he has a grocery shop?’

‘This ‘e do, love. Ah, but I can see yer looking flummoxed on account of ‘im not ‘aving a sign out front?’

The cottage’s wooden door creaked outwards to reveal a skinny, pock-faced woman in a greasy, grey dress. She assessed Tori without expression, but grinned to see Harry. ‘Cousin, good ter see yer, boy. Yer brought us some custom?’

‘Cousin Eliza!’ he squeezed the pock-faced woman in a bear hug, ‘This ‘ere’s Miss Blanckley, what used ter live up View Cottage!’

‘Well, I’ll be damned!’ Eliza’s breath reeked of vinegar. ‘I thought ‘em Blanckleys left Brent fer good? What yer wanting 'ere, Ma’am? We in't got much fanty sheeny stuff in, sorry ter say.’

Tori felt out of her depth. ‘I am seeking to purchase meat to contribute to Harry’s family supper.’

The woman shot Harry a hard look. ‘In't a butchers ‘ere.’

Harry patted Tori’s arm. ‘I remembered I gotta talk ter me cousin about summat in private. Family stuff. Would yer mind?’

‘No, of course not.’

He let out a sigh. ‘Cousin Eliza, might I step inside with yer a minute?’

Eliza shrugged and stood aside to allow Harry in. She gave Tori a cool look, and closed the door leaving her startled and alone on the muddy step. However, when the door reopened a minute or two later, a far less dour Mrs. Soper emerged. ‘Miss

Blanckley, please forgive me rudeness afore. I thought yer were someone else.'

Nonplussed, her only response was, 'Oh.'

The pock-faced woman affected a brown-toothed smile and ushered her in. The front door led directly into a dark, dank, stone-floored room with a battered table in one corner. Crude shelving fixed to rough-plastered walls was stacked with boxes and jars, whilst the skirting boards were partially obscured by a multitude of hessian sacks, some full, and some nearly-empty.

Harry, waiting by the table, greeted Tori with his gap-toothed smile. 'I 'ope yer weren't put out by me cousin's caution, but she's gotta be careful when 'er 'usband in't 'ome.'

Tori refrained from asking exactly what threat a loan gentlelady had posed, and put it down to countryside eccentricity. She smiled in what she hoped was an encouraging manner.

The pock-face woman cleared her throat. 'Yer after meat?'

'Please, if you have some?'

The woman hopped onto a three-legged stool to retrieve a grease-proof paper parcel from a top shelf. 'Got a chicken 'ere, if that's any good?'

Tori waited for her to unwrap the bundle for inspection, then, realising she wouldn't, looked to Harry for confirmation. 'Cousin Eliza stocks lovely fresh chickens. Lotsa folk around 'ere keeps 'em, and Eliza buys 'em when they wants ter make a few pence, in't ee Cuz?'

Eliza shrugged noncommittally.

'Very well, I would like to purchase this chicken.' Eliza's

unflinching gaze flustered her. 'Umm, I should like to purchase some vegetables too... if you have any in stock, that is?'

'We 'as.'

'Umm, might I ask what... I mean which vegetables you have?'

'We's got a few turnips, some teddies, swedes and apples in 'em sacks. Dried: we got raisins, sultanas and prunes. Pickled: we got cabbage (red and white), marrows, carrots, peas, trout and blackbirds.'

Tori thought she'd misheard. 'Sorry, what was the last pickle you named?'

'Blackbirds.'

'Pickled blackbirds?'

'Yup.'

'Are they popular?'

'I likes 'em.'

'Ah, I see... umm... Harry, does your family like–'

'We don't like 'em pickled blackbirds one bit, Miss Tori!'

'Umm, I was going to ask if you like the other things your cousin listed.'

He relaxed. 'Ah, right yer are. We likes 'em all, apart from 'em pickled birds.'

Eliza folded her arms and glared at him, 'Yer in't even tried 'em.'

'Well, that's coz we don't want to!'

'Ain't nuffin' wrong with pickled songbirds.'

‘I’m sure there’s not,’ Tori intervened, ‘but I am purchasing food as a Christmas gift for Harry’s family.’

‘Right grateful I am,’ Harry doffed his cap.

Eliza *hmph*-ed, and Tori took quick advantage of her silence. ‘I should like to purchase five pounds each of potatoes, turnips, swedes and apples–’

Harry gasped. ‘Yer can’ buy all that!’

‘Would it be too much to give you? I don’t wish to embarrass you, Harry.’

‘We wouldn’t want to be greedy, in't ee?’

‘Would you accept it as my gift to a dear friend from a childhood I cherish?’

‘Wassat?’

‘I should like to gift these things as a token of the high value I place upon our shared history, and the happy circumstance of our having found each other again.’

He continued to look confused. ‘Weren’t expecting nuffin, Miss Tori.’

‘Would one pound of each be better for you?’

Harry relaxed. ‘That’d be very kind, Miss Tori.’

‘Very well. One pound each, please, of potatoes, turnips, swedes and apples.’

The pock-faced woman scowled her assent and set to work grabbing vegetables from various sacks and dumping them into the pan of a rusty set of scales on the table. ‘Anything else?’

‘Do you have any bread?’

'Got a loaf.'

'May I please purchase it?'

Eliza seemed annoyed by the request. 'Someone might be wanting it.'

'Umm, I am someone who wants it.'

Eliza stared at her unblinkingly for approximately half a minute, then *hmph*-ed and said, 'I sold it already.'

'The loaf?'

'Yeah.'

'But... I mean... you said you had one just a few minutes ago?'

'Yeah, but I forgot, in't ee?'

'So you don't have any bread?'

'No.'

'I see... umm... do you have tea?'

'No.'

'Do you have–'

'No.'

'You have nothing else?'

'That be right.'

'Shall I pay for what's on the counter?'

'Yes.'

****

'Mind yer feet now,' Harry Soper watched Tori with an eagle eye as she transversed back across the rough planks bridging the drainage ditches. 'I can tell yer it in't nice at all ter fall in ter that cledgy muck!' He shifted her paper-wrapped purchases under one arm in order to proffer a helping hand to guide her to the low door of one of the terraced cottages facing his cousin's front-room grocery shop. 'Our 'ouse is right 'ere.' He pulled the door open and called, 'Eliza! I brung us a visitor, in't ee?'

Tori panicked that Harry's pickled blackbird-selling cousin was simultaneously his wife. She was immensely relieved when a small, gaunt, grey-haired woman appeared in the doorway and said, 'Wassat?'

'Wife,' Harry beamed, 'yer'll never guess who this be!'

'Bailiff?'

He chuckled. 'Eliza, ee be Miss Tori, Cap'n Blanckley's little cheach from View Cottage. All grown up now, in't ee?'

'Yer what?' Eliza Soper peered up at Tori. 'Is yer really Miss Blanckley?'

Detecting none of the other Eliza Soper's prickliness, Tori smiled. 'I am she, although I'm now Mrs. Ward.'

'Yer's married?' Harry sounded first amazed, then anxious, 'Course yer are, fine lady like yerself, I were right improper ter imagine yer in't got married. Please forgive me, Miss... I mean Mrs. Tori.'

'No offence taken, Harry. The fact is that, being here in the village of my youth, I felt myself again to be Miss Blanckley.

And please do call me "Miss Tori".'

Harry's wife was staring at her, eyes agog. 'Yer really Miss Tori who was a little cheach up View Cottage?'

'Do you remember me?'

'Course I do, in't ee?'

'Miss Tori bought us some dinner from Cousin Bill's and all,' Harry grinned.

'Wha' from 'cross road?'

'Yeah, Cousin Eliza saw to us.'

'Ee din't sell 'er no pickled songbirds, did ee?'

'Don't be afeared. I warned 'er not ter buy 'em. Din't I, Miss Tori?'

'Umm? Oh, yes, you can be assured that I didn't buy any of her pickled blackbirds.'

Harry's wife visibly relaxed.

'She got us teddies, turnips, swedes, apples, and an 'ole, umm, chicken, in't ee?'

Her eyes widened further. 'Yer din't 'ave ter do that!'

'I wished to. As a Christmastide gift to my childhood friend, and his family.'

Harry squeezed Tori, grinning broadly. 'Din't we always say 'em Blanckleys was good folk?'

'That we did, 'Usband.' Although Eliza nodded earnestly, she still looked uncomfortable.

'I do not wish to intrude,' Tori assured her.

A squall of chill wind blasted them from Ugborough Beacon. Harry tugged her arm. 'Come on in outta the cold.'

Tori's confidence wavered. The sunken parlour was dark as ink and didn't look welcoming at all.

CHAPTER THIRTEEN

The old friends had been enjoying little cakes and hot tea in the Rolle's cosy ladies' salon, when Henrietta decided to tell Horatia the strange tale of the waif who'd accosted her outside her home. 'So, you see, she appeared to have had a truly prophetic vision!' She concluded to the astonished Horatia.

Horatia sipped from an elegant, gilt-edged teacup. 'You believe this odd woman had a prophetic vision about your mistreatment of your half-brothers' kin, and–' her eyes teared, 'your own imminent doom?'

Henrietta smiled ruefully. 'I do. How else could that that wretched woman have known I'd been unkind to the children of my half-brothers? Her prophecy must be true!'

'What a frightful thing!' When Horatia clasped Henrietta's hand, her black taffeta cuff was dark as crow feathers on the salmon-pink velvet of Henrietta's sleeve.

Henrietta mustered a brave smile. 'Tis my good fortune to be able to make amends to my half-relatives who still survive: Toriana, Horace, and Henriette in Versailles. I've written to Toriana's barrister cousin, Nelson Matcham, with instructions for a new will with them named as beneficiaries.'

Horatia, although sceptical of the waif's prophetic ability, saw no harm in the plan, and smiled encouragingly.

Henrietta continued. 'I've also decided to include provision for

Baby Alice once she reaches her majority. In this way, I hope to rectify the hostile neglect I'm ashamed to have inflicted on the families of my half-siblings.' Henrietta squeezed Horatia's arthritically-gnarled hand back. 'So you see, I am so very glad you came to spend this Christmastide with me, for I shall not–"

'I'm here, dear Rietta!' Horatia said quickly, not wanting to hear her friend's next words.

Henrietta's blue steel rimmed eyes glistened. 'Your presence means the world to me.'

'As your presence was for me during the anniversary of Trafalgar! Tis selfish, I know, but I can't bear to think of spending the next October twenty-first without you. May we pledge, Rietta dearest, to toast each other on that day, even if we're apart?'

Henrietta stared at the table cover for a long moment. When she finally looked up, she was resolute. 'I cannot alter my fate, dear friend, but I promise you that I will hold onto life with every scrap of stamina and determination I can muster; and you know that I am a stubborn old mule once my mind is set! So I solemnly promise, dear friend, to do my utmost to be here, there or wherever next October twenty-first so as to raise a toast to you.'

It was Horatia's turn to be tearful. She struggled to find her voice. 'Oh, my dearest, dearest friend! I promise too that I shall raise a toast to you on the anniversary of that most ominous of days.' The love she projected was wet with tears. 'You, my dearest Rietta, and Susan too, are the only tonic I've needed! I confess I was in something of a slump before you came to Pinner, and then dragged me here… No, Rietta, let me continue! Yes, I know you have an ambition for me to brood on things.'

'The word I used was "reflect"!'

'Please don't quibble. I need to say this. It's important and I'm struggling to find the correct words, so please be patient. It's a truth I'm not proud of, but before you stormed back into my life – in a thoroughly welcome and agreeable way, I should add! – I was doubting my sanity.'

Henrietta set her teacup on its saucer in a clatter of porcelain on porcelain. 'My dear, what a dreadful thing to have felt!'

'I'm relieved you've not judged me ill for my weak mind. But here's the thing, Rietta dear, I thought I was losing my proverbial marbles because I'd been brooding on my past. Call it "reflecting" if you prefer, but it was this that was making me go mad. Truly! So when Susan and you coaxed me into doing more of it, well, obviously I didn't want to! And I apologise again if I was rude to you earlier, but can't you see, dear Rietta, friendship is the simple, wholesome tonic I've needed all along! I used to dread sleeping for fear of reliving ancient memories, but since coming to Budleigh Salterton, my memories have been at bay, and my sleep's been peaceful. It's simply marvellous to wake each morning feeling calm and happy!'

'Oh, Ratia, this is excellent news!' Henrietta's blue steel framed spectacles jiggled up with her exuberant smile.

'Shall we make a toast now, do you think?'

'To Other Days?'

Horatia's grin held the vibrance of youth. 'I say forget Other Days, let's drink to true friendship!'

****

On the floor above, Horace was not happy in the slightest.

He'd been lying on his luxurious Rolle bed for several hours, heedless that the mounting gloom had deepened into night. His nieces were exhausting in the extreme. He wondered what the Devil had possessed him to volunteer to be their minder. His head felt like an iron-bound steamship barraged by high-calibre guns. He wondered how his sister coped, and actually felt in awe of her stamina. For his part, he was decommissioning himself until his metaphoric coal-store was resupplied. The ayah would just have to damned well cope alone with those miniature banshees in the interim.

'Uncle Horace?'

He realised that one of his wretched nieces had pushed her way into his room and was standing silhouetted against the bright gas-light of the corridor outside. He cursed himself for not locking the door, and demanded. 'What do you want?'

The child confused him by replying with a question. 'Are you hurt from what happened before?'

'What? Yes, yes, that's why I'm in my room. On my own.'

'It's very dark in here. Shall I light the lamp?'

'No, I have a headache. The light would hurt my eyes.'

'Poor Uncle Horace.'

'Do you want anything?'

'I came to be nice to you because you were hurt.'

'Well, that's very thoughtful, I'm sure, but if you really want to be nice to me…'

'Yes, Uncle Horace?'

'Then go away.'

****

'Are you still there?'

'Yes, Uncle Horace.'

'Why are you standing there in the dark?'

'Because you didn't want the light lit, Uncle Horace.'

'Why didn't you go away when I told you to?'

'Because... I want to be nice to you, but I might not ever want to again if I go now.'

'You find being nice to me difficult?'

'Almost impossible, Uncle Horace.'

'Oh... umm, why is that?'

'I shouldn't tell you if I'm trying to be nice to you.'

'Is it important to you to be nice to me?'

'Not really, Uncle Horace. That's why I know I'll never try to be nice to you again if I go away now.'

Horace tutted and fumbled for a match to light the lamp. The resulting glow revealed the second-largest of his nieces blinking in the sudden light. 'There, is that better?'

'Thank you for lighting the lamp, Uncle Horace. I hope it doesn't hurt your head too much?'

'Hmph. Do you want to sit down?'

'Oh yes, Uncle Horace!' She hopped nimbly onto his bed and swivelled to face him. 'You have a very big bed, Uncle Horace.

Mama's is very big as well, but they only put thin beds in our room.'

'Fascinating, I'm sure. Did you want to talk to me about something important?'

'Beds are important, Uncle Horace. If it weren't for beds, we'd have to sleep on the floor.'

'Niece, I do not wish to talk about beds. Is this clear?'

'Yes, Uncle Horace.'

'You are the niece who was moody with me earlier, aren't you?'

'Oh yes, Uncle Horace.'

'Yet you say you now wish to be nice to me, is that right?'

'Yes, Uncle.'

'Why did you suddenly wish to be nice to me when I'd closed myself in a darkened room with a headache?'

'Because of Grandmama Horatia.'

'Aha, now we're getting somewhere! And what precisely did your Grandmama Horatia say to you?'

'She said I should try to be nice to you because you were hurt when you were my age, and–'

'Hold on. What did she say to you?'

'She said you were very hurt after your mama died, and–'

A sudden tightness constricted his chest. 'I am quite fine.'

'You said you were hurt when I first came in, Uncle Horace.'

'I meant I was hurt by you and your sisters' clamour! Your

grandmama had no business telling you to be nice to me because I was hurt as a child for the reason that I was *not* hurt as a child. Is this clear?'

'You don't want me to be nice to you, Uncle Horace?'

'What? Umm, well, you should be nice to me out of respect, but not because you feel sorry for me.'

'What should I do if I don't respect you, Uncle Horace?'

He propped himself higher on his pillows. 'Do you not respect me?'

She considered his question. 'Well, it's difficult because you don't seem to respect us.'

'How so? I got you theatre tickets, and volunteered to mind you while your mama is away–'

'But Uncle Horace, you bought theatre tickets for tomorrow without knowing it's my birthday, and you don't even know our names, do you?'

He frowned, deflated, until a lucky strike of revelation came to his rescue. 'I do know your name! You're Ethel Mary Ward, aren't you?'

The girl lunged forwards without warning and threw her arms around him. 'Oh Uncle Horace, you do respect me!'

'Well, umm,' he spluttered, craning his head away from her clinging body, 'I... yes, actually, Ethel Mary Ward, I do respect you. I respect that you are strong-minded and clever. Now will you please stop squashing my head?'

'Yes, Uncle Horace,' she released her hold and snuggled next to him on his pillows, dark blonde ringlets pooling on his white sleeve.

'Are we friends now, then, Ethel Mary Ward?'

'Oh yes, Uncle Horace. I'm glad I didn't go when you told me to. Will you come down to dinner with me, Uncle Horace?'

He grimaced at the thought of meeting the entire pack of nieces in the dining hall. 'My head still aches awfully. I think I shall eat in my room.'

'Are my sisters too noisy for your head, Uncle Horace?'

'Very much so.'

'I can make them be quiet for you, Uncle Horace. And you really should eat with us because you're minding us.'

He blew out a sigh. 'Very well, we'll mind them together, shall we, Ethel?'

'Oh yes, Uncle Horace, we can keep them all in place. Even Nellie!'

****

Horatia was surprised when Ethel and Horace entered the dining hall together. It seemed the little girl had heeded her advice, which was marvellous. Ethel was doing her best to keep her right hand proprietorially on her uncle's scarlet sleeve, but their height difference forced her to keep hopping up to hang off his arm like a monkey in a frock. Ethel tapped her uncle's hand and whispered something in his ear when he bent to listen. He frowned and followed the direction of her pointing finger. 'Nellie!' He reprimanded as they drew closer, 'Do not slouch!'

Nellie straightened. 'Sorry, Uncle Horace.'

Horatia saw Ethel suppress a smirk before turning to face the hotel's enormous Christmas tree as if to admire its myriad candles. Poor Nellie looked mortified.

The ayah, Kajri, hurriedly took Ethel's elbow and ushered her to a vacant seat between Carrie and Nellie, saying, 'Sit here, Miss Ethel.'

But Ethel resisted. 'I should like to sit beside my uncle, we are such very good friends. Aren't we Uncle Horace?'

'What?' Horace had been beelining to an empty seat next to Lizzie.

'May I sit beside you, please, Uncle Horace?'

'Umm, the majority of places are already taken.'

To Horatia's quiet amusement, nothing seemed to daunt plucky, little Ethel, who said, 'Kajri, would you move the chairs around, please?'

The ayah, however, was perfectly capable of withstanding the pressures of pushy little girls. 'You have a seat here already, Miss Ethel.'

'Oh, but–'

Kajri put on her sternest look. 'Your place is waiting.'

The six-year-old turned to her uncle in desperation. 'Oh, Uncle Horace, I do so want to sit beside you. You are such a very fine uncle!'

Horace lapped up Ethel's flattery like a cat given cream. 'Kajri, dear girl, look here! There's space for my niece to squeeze in beside me.'

Lizzie seemed hasty to pull her chair away from Horace to

make space for Ethel. 'Ethel dearest, perhaps I could tell you more tales of our Blanckley ancestors?'

'Oh yes, please! Thank you, Aunt Lizzie!' Ethel looked to be having the time of her life.

'Is your party ready for dinner, Sir?' An immaculate waiter had sidled up, 'We have twelve courses tonight. The first is crab soup.'

'Yuck,' Carrie mumbled, 'I don't like crab.'

Horace barked at her as if she was a subordinate marine. 'I'll not have you making a fuss, Niece!' Carrie looked like she might cry, and squeaked something inaudible. 'Speak up!' Horace barked again.

Horatia coughed to gain Horace's attention. 'My dear, she's just a five-year-old girl.'

Carrie turned to Horatia with imploring eyes. 'Why did Mama go away without us?'

Horatia felt a surge of anger that Tori had abandoned her daughters for the sentimental whim of visiting South Brent. The pain and confusion on poor Carrie and Nellie's faces was plain to see. What on God's Earth did Tori expect to achieve by abandoning her daughters this way? Brooding on the past was akin to opium addiction, for both drew you in and sucked out your soul. Tori, she realised with a shudder, was being led by Satan himself.

The quiet was broken by Ethel's imperious tone. 'Pass me the salt, Nellie.'

Nellie, looking flustered, reached for the salt bowl, but missed and knocked it over, spilling precious salt on the white linen.

Horatia heard Ethel whisper to Horace. 'Look, Nellie spilt the salt because she wasn't being careful. Mama would be very cross!'

Horace fixed Nellie with a cold glare. 'Niece, you must be more careful.'

Nellie hung her head.

'Well?' Horace pressed her. 'What do you say?'

'S…sorry, Uncle Horace.'

Ethel hid a smirk behind a napkin.

****

Kajri was tired. Dinner in the Rolle's dining hall had been going on for hours, and she'd been up since six in the morning looking after her lively, little charges. Mrs. Ward would have let her retire with Baby Alice before dinner, but she'd gone off to some place called South Brent leaving her brother in charge, and Major Blanckley had said Baby Alice must attend dinner. The baby, of course, hadn't wanted to stay on her lap at the table all this time, and neither had she wanted to keep her there, but it wasn't their place to decide. Her back ached from sitting upright on the hard dining chair supporting the weight of Baby Alice for all these hours, and her head was tired too. Kajri had hoped that the plates of fish in white sauce would be the final course, but the waiters had just come back with a fifth course of casseroled meat and vegetables. How much longer must they all sit here like flies trapped in resin?

'I don't like cabbage!' four-year-old Evie complained.

Kajri's lip started to twitch, but she stopped it. It wouldn't do to let anyone see that she was annoyed. She was a servant, and of especially little worth because she was a brown-skinned woman born in India. Her colour, gender and cultural heritage placed her at the bottom of the British Empire's social pile, lower in rank than white-skinned prostitutes and criminals from the poorest of slums. It was not her place to voice opinions. Doing so would, in fact, jeopardise her employment. She, more so than the children she minded, must be seen and not heard. In fact, it was better if no one saw her. Her only worth and, therefore, security lay in Mrs. Ward's assessment of her effectiveness as a nanny to her little girls. Her role was to be invisibly efficient in steering the young girls in her charge to be almost as invisible as she was.

Goodness yes, she did love these little girls, but it could be hard sometimes, like now, not to be annoyed at their too-easy life. They were not appreciative of all the good things they had, like having more nutritious food in one hour than her home village might see in a month. They were sitting here at their fancy table settings complaining that they didn't want to eat this nutritious vegetable or that luxury soup because they didn't like its flavour. Imagine if some shiny-dressed waiter came to Jaulnah offering people more than five courses of food with fresh crab soup to start? Would they be moaning? No, they would be dancing in the streets praising Lakshmi for their great good fortune! Kajri contained another lip curl. She reminded herself to feel joyous that these innocents didn't know what hunger was, but, goodness, it was sometimes very difficult for her to remain silent when they complained about silly, little things. Ah, but no one in this blessed England knew what it means to want for food!

Of Mrs. Ward's six daughters, Kajri's favourite was Ethel. Not that she ever said so, of course. Kajri took quiet pleasure in Ethel's outspoken honesty. She liked that Ethel spoke from her heart in a way that she, herself, could never do if she wanted to keep her job. She liked Ethel's warm heart too, and that Ethel treated her as an equal. Ethel never spoke down to her because she was a servant, or because of her dark skin.

'It's my birthday tomorrow!' Ethel suddenly chirped. She looked very small between her aunt and her new favourite, Uncle Horace. Her golden ringlets bobbed back and forth as she spun her head to address one then the other. By the looks of it, she was failing to keep them simultaneously engaged. Kajri noticed also that Lizzie seemed to want to put as much distance as she could between Horace and herself, which surely wasn't aiding Ethel's efforts to maintain a three-way conversation. The little girl nudged Horace. 'Uncle, may I please request your aid?'

Horace puffed himself up. 'Certainly, Niece, I am ever the one to aid a fair maiden in distress!'

'Oh Uncle Horace, I don't know what to do because I can't talk to both you and Aunt Lizzie at the same time, and I do so want to talk to you both.'

Horace looked happier still. 'Perhaps we could swap seats so I am next to Lizzie?' Kajri saw Lizzie flinch, but neither Horace nor Ethel seemed to notice. He continued, 'This way, Ethel, you could address your questions to both of us at the same time.'

'Oh yes, please, Uncle Horace,' Ethel jumped from her seat and grabbed his arm to hasten the swap.

'Cousin Lizzie,' Horace smiled oilily as he lowered himself into place beside her, 'you look very fine this evening.'

Lizzie took a dainty sip of wine. 'Thank you, Cousin Horace.'

'Aunt Lizzie?'

'Yes, Ethel dear?'

'Please may I hear another Blanckley story?'

Kajri saw Lizzie grimace, though her words remained polite. 'Let me think, Ethel dear...'

'I know a good tale!'

Ethel clapped her hands excitedly. 'What's the story, please, Uncle Horace?'

He puffed himself up even more. 'Well, Ethel, have you heard the story of the princeling Papa – that is, your grandpapa – rescued from the devastation of Rangoon in Burma after the British stormed it in eighteen-twenty-four?'

Kajri stiffened not wanting to hear that depressing tale again, but Ethel lent towards her uncle eagerly. 'Why no, Uncle Horace, I've never heard about it. Did my grandpapa really rescue a prince?'

'Picture this,' Horace looked around the table catching eyes where he could. 'It was a scorching, humid Burmese summer day, and my father, along with ten thousand other brave men, sailed up the Irrawaddy River to Rangoon thinking that taking the capital city in one swift, surprise swoop would hand them all of Burma!' He looked pleased that most of the party were listening enraptured, but frowned when his eyes fell on Kajri, who couldn't bring herself to pretend to enjoy his story. His look of disappointment deepened when he realised the smaller girls were looking bored.

'Please tell me more!' Ethel urged, and his smile returned.

He cleared his throat. 'But the slippery Burmese had burnt their city to the ground and fled into the jungle!'

'Oo!' Ethel gasped.

'And it was then, whilst walking over the smouldering ashes with his fellow officers, that my papa came upon a tiny native baby lying all alone. When he picked it up, he discovered that it was dressed in the most exquisite clothes so must be some poor princeling who'd been dropped by its attendants in their panic to flee!'

Kajri, mindful to hide her indignation, lowered her head to observe sleeping Baby Alice. Maybe, she thought, that poor Burmese baby had needed rescuing, but Mrs. Ward's father treated him like a slave when he took him back to England because of his brown skin. Not that these people could see that, of course. She knew they'd praise Captain Blanckley like one of their saints.

'How marvellous of Grandpapa!' Nellie exclaimed, 'He was very kind to rescue the princeling!'

'Where's the prince now?' Carrie asked.

'Who knows?' Horace scoffed indulgently, 'Your grandpapa set him up in London as a tailor. He employed his services for new jackets and whatnot. He took me along with him once or twice. I recall the princeling tailor was a swarthy man, but very civilised, and impressively deft with his scissors. He was always excited to see Papa.'

'Might we visit him?' Nellie asked eagerly. 'I should like to meet him if he knew Grandpapa.'

'I have no idea where he now is, but he is of no import to us.'

Kajri thought he was very important to her, but spoke not.

CHAPTER FOURTEEN

Tori steeled herself to step down into the darkness, heart telling her to embrace her South Brent heritage despite her fear.

'It's right dark in 'ere, in't ee?' Harry interrupted her thoughts. 'Eliza, in't we got no candles? What about coal or a faggit of vuzz fer the fire? Let's get our 'ouse a bit brighter fer our guest!'

Harry's skinny, pale-faced wife disappeared into the black room. She became visible again when she neared the weak fire. She clanked and fiddled for a moment, then dumped an armful of something in the grate which made the fire blink out completely. The room fell into a blackness so complete that Tori felt she was standing at the bottom of a deep well filled with tarry smoke. Her throat tickled, but she resisted coughing because she didn't want the Sopers to worry any more about their home's fitness to receive her. Thankfully, further clattering from the direction of the hearth culminated in Mrs. Soper, bellows in hand, being suddenly illuminated by a bright burst of flame.

Harry took her arm and steered her to a rude chair beside the hearth. 'That's better now, don't yer think, Miss Tori? Tis loads brighter in 'ere with the vuzz blazing, in't ee?'

The Soper's front room smelt of damp earth and smoke, although the details of its layout were hard to make out in the dim light. She could see some small figures hovering near the smoky, guttering fire, but the rest of the room was dark as pitch.

Harry shouted to his wife. 'Eliza, where's that candle? Let's get it real bright in 'ere for Miss Tori!'

'Just a minute,' Eliza called back.

'Chillern!' Harry cried, 'Say 'ello ter our guest. She's a fanty-sheeny lady, so mind your manners, in't ee?'

'Yes, Da!' The figures, now revealed as children, approached with the sound of leather slapping rough stone. Tori was pleased that it sounded like they had shoes on their feet. Multiple pairs of eyes, illuminated in the hearth-light, regarded her from the inky gloom. 'Pleased ter meet yer,' said one, and another said, 'I'm Lucy, 'ello.'

'This is my cheaches,' Harry sounded proud, though it was too dark to see his face. 'Good as gold they be. Me eldest 'ere, Billy,' Harry may have pointed to one of the shadows, but Tori couldn't see which, 'got ee-self work as a shoemaker, same as my old dad used ter do. Ee's apprenticed to old Veale, in't yer, Billy?"

'I is, Da,' a boy's voice replied.

Harry's wife bustled back in and poked a candle in the fire to light its wick. 'I'll stick it up 'ere on the mantel-shelf,' she decided. Its flickering light illuminated a ragtag bunch of hollow-faced children staring earnestly at her. The Sopers' all purpose front room was rudely furnished, and the whitewashed walls were discoloured in places with stretches of black mould. A threadbare rug covered the centre of a stone floor. Kitchenware was neatly stacked and hung from a shelf on one side of the hearth, and there was a small table with a wall bench on the other side of it, near a sixteen-pane sash window looking onto the street. Dim grids of reddish light told the location of hearth-lit rooms across Church Street, one of which almost certainly belonged to Harry's fearsome cousin with the pickled blackbirds. Harry's family were grouped in front of the window, their faces looking pale as butter cream in the candlelight.

'These others are me youngest cheaches: Lucy, Mary, George and John. Scholars, they is. All of 'em. Some folks don't bother with their own chillern, but we make ours go to school regular, coz they can get good work when they grows up if they gets an eddy-f'cation, in't ee, Miss Tori?'

Tori was impressed. 'Quite so, Harry. Education is of high importance. My older girls share a tutor with their cousins.'

'Yeah, it's good fer girls ter learn stuff too, in't ee Lucy?'

One of the little girls, presumably Lucy, answered without enthusiasm. 'Yes, Da, but it's right boring, in't ee?'

'Mind your manners, young madam!'

'Sorry, Da.'

'We've got two other chillern, as well. Our eldest, 'Arry ee's called, same as me and my own dad before me. Anyway, ee's working on a farm, so ee's staying there. Strong lad ee be. And we've got another girl, name of Sarah. Ee's fifteen now and working up the shoddy mill. Ee'll be 'ome before long. Good girl ee is, bringing in a wage ter 'elp feed us all.'

Tori thought fifteen sounded awfully young to be working in a mill, but hard work was a virtue for the poor.

The street door suddenly burst open and a thin teenager rushed in. 'Ma, Da, it's blowing a proper gale out there! You got the room right bright and toasty!'

Harry nudged Tori. 'Just as I said, tis our Sarah come back from the shoddy mill! Hey Sarah, maid, we've got an fanty-sheeny guest! Ee's Miss Blanckley what used ter live up View Cottage, would yer believe?'

Sarah hung her cloak on a wall peg and stepped closer. Tori saw that her cheeks were very hollow. 'Welcome to our 'ome, Miss Blanckley,' she curtseyed.

'Umm, thank you,' Tori said, not comfortable with being treated like a celebrity.

'Are yer comfy, Miss Tori?' Mrs. Soper peered at her anxiously, 'Like I said, we in't got no fine 'ouse 'ere and we weren't expecting no vurriner guests, but we wants yer ter be comferble, in't ee?'

'She in't no vurriner,' Harry declared, 'cuz she live yer as a cheach, in't ee?'

'Thank you, Harry! It means a lot to be accepted as a local,' Tori beamed, and told his wife, 'I'm very comfortable, and it's a true pleasure to be here.'

'And we're very pleased to 'ave yer 'ere, in't we?' Harry patted her shoulder. 'You'll never guess, Sarah, but Miss Tori brung a load of frawzy, including a chicken, din't ee?'

Eliza grinned. 'I got a cauldron of soup already 'anging on the fire. I can add 'em nice veggies and chicken right into ee. It'll make a proper frawzy feast. Much obliged, we is.' Her face fell, 'In't got no tay in. I 'ope yer don't mind. We've got spring water though, if yer'd like a cup?'

'A cup of spring water would be welcome, thank you, Mrs. Soper.'

Harry nudged his wife. 'Yer might wanna strip the *chicken* outside by the, umm, spring, while there's still a bit of light?'

It seemed to take Eliza a moment or two to get her husband's meaning; although precisely what this was eluded Tori. 'Yer what? Oh, of course, good idea! If yer'll 'scuse me, Miss Tori, I'll go and see ter preparing that chicken you so kindly brung. Lucy, come with me out back and fetch our guest a cuppa water from the spring.'

It was little Lucy's turn to look confused. 'What spring, Ma?'

Eliza lowered her voice to a whisper, but Tori heard her anyway. 'The ditch out back, in't ee?'

Sarah, who'd been sitting at the table stretching her legs in front of her, stood up. 'Want me to do the chicken fer yer, Ma? Let you 'ave more time fer entertaining?'

'Yer a right good gal,' Mrs. Soper approved, 'and I needs to see to the fire and get the table laid proper for Miss Blanckley too.'

Harry smacked his forehead. 'I'm such an addle 'ead! I keep forgetting our guest's Mrs. Ward now! Please forgive me, Miss Tori!'

'Don't worry, Harry, I actually quite like being named Miss Blanckley here, for this was my name when I lived here, very young as I was.'

'It's a shock to think of the sweet, little cheach from View Cottage being all grown up and married too! I bet ee's a proper good bloke ter be married ter a Blanckley!'

Tori pulled her thoughts together. 'In fact, he's my second cousin. You know my mother–'

'God rest 'is soul.'

'Yes, indeed, God rest her soul. Well, her mother was Catherine Matcham, who was Lord Nelson's sister.'

'God bless Lord Nelson. Ee was a proper 'ero, ee was! It don't surprise me ee were your relative.'

'Thank you, Harry... umm, well, my husband, William, is actually the grandson of Lord Nelson.'

'And Lady 'Amilton's grandson then too! God rest 'is soul.'

'Excuse me?'

'Everyone knows that Lord Nelson's little daughter were Lady 'Amilton's cheach, in't ee?'

'Umm... do they? I mean...'

'That Lady 'Amilton, she were a proper fine lady, weren't ee? Did loads of good fer England in the war, and that... though lots of folks say mean stuff about 'im, in't ee?'

'Lady 'Amilton?' Mrs. Soper had returned with a folded cloth, and an armful of dried bracken. 'Ee were the princess of us poor people. 'Arry told me all about 'im. I won't 'ear nuffin bad said about Lady 'Amilton, I won't!' She dumped the furze into the fire so it blazed brighter.

'Guess what, Eliza, but Miss Tori's married to Lady 'Amilton's grandson!'

'Yer not?' Mrs. Soper's jaw dropped so low that her chin was nearly resting on the neckline of her dress. 'Yer actually married ter a grandson of Lady 'Amilton?'

'Umm, well... that's what some say.'

'What do yer mean "some say"? Surely yer either married ter 'im, or yer in't... unless yer 'ad one of they nonconformist weddings?'

'Goodness no, Harry! Our marriage was Church of England.'

Harry visibly relaxed. 'Good ter 'ear it, Miss... I mean Mrs. Tori.'

'What I meant was that some people claim Horatia; that is, my mother-in-law, is Lady Hamilton's daughter, but–'

'Course ee is!' Harry proclaimed. 'It's only stupid people that think ee in't. All 'em addle 'eads what think Lord Nelson magicked 'is daughter outta thin air!'

Eliza chuckled. 'They's not able ter cope with Lady 'Amilton. They don't like ter believe a poor-born woman did well for ee-self, in't ee? But we're not so fickle 'ere. God bless 'im, we say. And God bless yer for marrying 'is grandson, in't ee?'

'Thank you,' Tori said, not knowing what else to say.

Harry scratched his head. 'I suppose if people did think Lady 'Amilton was the mother of Nelson's daughter, they might not treat 'im nice coz of all their addle 'ead ideas about Lady 'Amilton being bad.'

Eliza was unconvinced. 'But everyone's surely gotta know the truth, in't ee? It's as plain as the nose on my face!'

'And I can't see the nose on yer face at all right now!' Harry shot back, 'Fire's gone down again, in't ee?'

'Damned vuzz don't burn long at all,' Eliza grumbled. 'I'll fetch some more.'

Harry turned his attention back to Tori. 'I'm right pleased to learn yer in't turned against Lady 'Amilton yerself! Always knew you Blanckleys were a decent bunch.'

Tori was cheered. 'Aunt Susan; my mother's sister... you said you remember, Harry?'

'You mean the sad lady?'

'Yes, the same. She adopted me after–'

'Terrible thing it were yer ma dying,' Harry bowed his head. 'God rest 'is soul.'

'Amen,' Tori mumbled. 'Well, Aunt Susan always spoke very highly of Lady Hamilton. She said society has treated her unfairly.'

Harry nodded emphatically. 'That they 'as.'

Eliza returned with Sarah, Lucy and more furze. Lucy presented Tori with a cup of water whilst her mother and Sarah busied themselves at the fire. The blaze illuminated Sarah's thin hands dropping strips of dark-looking meat into a cauldron suspended above the flames.

Eliza noticed Tori watching. 'That chicken'll cook in a jiffy. Stew's already started bubbling again. Fowl cooks right quick, it do. Let's everyone be seated.'

Harry ushered his family into places around the little, dented table, which Eliza had attempted to cover with a very small, blue and cream checked cloth. Tori and Harry had the honour of using the family's two chairs, while Eliza insisted she was fine perching on an old, wooden packing crate, and the five children squeezed onto the bench against the hearthside wall.

Eliza scooped a ladle-full of stew into a chipped, yellow bowl and placed it in front of Tori. 'Eat it while it's 'ot,' she advised. 'No offence to the church and that, but we don't wait fer grace 'ere, not in the winter anyway, coz food cools down quicker than prayers. 'Ope you don't mind?'

'Umm, not at all,' Tori said politely. She studied the contents of the bowl. The chicken she bought from Harry's cousin was oddly dark in colour. She squinted against the smoke billowing from the fire and gave Eliza a warm smile, 'This broth is delicious, Mrs. Soper.' The other bowls in use around the table were far more battered. She noticed that only Harry and she had been given metal spoons. Everyone else was making do with ones made from whittled wood. She was humbled to realise the good family had given her the best they had, meagre as it was.

'Ta very much, Miss Tori,' Eliza smiled back. 'Ee's our family soup. Ee were 'Arry's ma's before ee came to us, in't ee, 'Usband?'

'That's right,' Harry confirmed with evident pride.

Tori hoped she'd misunderstood. 'Are you saying that the soup in your cauldron once belonged to Harry's mother?'

'That's exactly it, Miss Tori,' Harry grinned. 'Ee's our lucky, family soup. This 'ere cauldron,' he indicated the battered iron pot dangling on a chain over the fire, 'in't been allowed ter run empty fer… I don't know 'ow many years.'

Tori felt giddy. 'Are you saying that the soup in our bowls was started decades ago?'

'Wassat?'

'A decade is ten years,' Lucy supplied.

Comprehension dawned on Harry's amicable, gap-toothed visage. 'Might be more than an 'undred years old! We've kept our family soup going since at least the time of my ma's gran.'

Tori's stomach lurched at the thought of eating soup that was at least a century old.

'We scoops the soot out when it falls in,' Harry elaborated.

'Of course ee's always changing, in't ee?' Eliza said. 'I'm afraid we in't 'ad no salt ter put in 'im fer a while, but 'em veggies and chicken what yer kindly brung 'as made 'im right frawzy again.'

'I do, umm, greatly appreciate this food–'

'We's proper honoured yer eating our family soup, Miss Tori,' Harry's tone was reverent, 'but I'm ashamed we's only got plain water ter offer you.'

'No, really, it is all wonderful for me. The soup is... umm, a treasure. I am honoured... umm, truly, and the water tastes... pure... real... wholesome... I apologise, I cannot find the right word.' Tori wondered if it would be exceedingly impolite to run away.

Harry beamed around the table. 'Did you know, chillern, that Miss Tori 'ere's married to the grandson of Lady 'Amilton?'

Lucy scrunched her face, 'Mrs. Winter says Lady 'Amilton was an imm... a very bad person.'

Tori sighed. Why of course Mrs. Winter would think that, whoever she was. The whole world thinks of Lady Hamilton as immoral and bad.

'She's our teacher,' the Sopers' younger girl, Mary, explained.

'At the school what we goes ter, in't ee?' Lucy clarified.

Tori was heartened that the Soper girls were opening up, albeit via a subject she'd prefer not to discuss. 'Is Mrs. Winters a good teacher?'

'She whacks our 'ands with a stick if we don't sit up straight and pay proper attention,' Lucy told her.

'Oh, I see. That doesn't sound pleasant.'

'It in't, Miss Tori, but I'm leaving school ter work in the shoddy mill with Sarah soon, so she'll not bother me then.'

'She'll still bother me,' Mary muttered.

'How old are you, Lucy, if you don't mind my asking?' Tori queried, thinking Lucy looked exceedingly young to be leaving school to work in a mill.

'I'm nearly fourteen. It's only chillern up ter thirteen's gotta go school, in't ee?'

'In't fair,' Mary whacked her wooden spoon on the table so hard that broth spilled out of her tin bowl.

'Be'ave yerself, Mary,' Harry chided.

'I wanna leave school too, in't ee? In't no point learning writing and that when I just wanna work in the mill like me sisters.'

'Me too,' little John said earnestly. 'It in't fair they make me go ter school. I wanna work, in't ee?'

'Education is important…' Tori began, but trailed off fearing she sounded pompous and out of touch with the children's reality.

'Wha's the good of knowing letters, Miss Tori?' Lucy asked bitterly. 'I spend all 'em years going to blinking school–'

'Watch yer language!' Eliza scolded.

Lucy carried on. 'What's the point of it, though?'

Tori considered this. Was there a point? Surely education would open better opportunities for them? She turned to the eldest of the children present. 'Billy?' the lad looked up from his stew, 'You're an apprentice shoemaker, is this right?'

'Yes, Ma'am.'

'Did you learn to read and write in the school?'

'A bit, Ma'am, but it don't 'elp me make 'em shoes.'

'Umm... but you could handle accounts, or write receipts?'

He shrugged. 'Maybe, Ma'am, but Mr. Veale in't asked me ter do nuffing like that.'

'Yet Mr. Veale could do? I mean, you could do more than just make shoes if it was required?'

'I suppose so, Ma'am, if there were a call.'

Tori felt like she was getting somewhere. 'So Lucy, Mary, John: education allows you to do more things.'

'This is what I've kept telling yer, chillern,' Harry beamed his gap-toothed smile, 'School's right important, just like Miss Tori says.'

'Yes, Da,' his children mumbled, unenthused.

Quiet descended as everyone settled into eating the ancient soup. The only noises were the clink of metal and wood on china and tin, and furze popping in the smoky fire. It was several minutes until anyone spoke, and this was Eliza, curiosity sparkling in her eyes. 'Miss Tori, you got chillern yerself?'

'I do, Mrs. Soper. I have six girls.'

'Six gals? And I thought we had a lot with our lot!' Eliza smiled warmly at the five children squashed elbow-to-elbow on the bench, 'You in't got no boys?'

'Alas, no. My husband, Major Ward–'

'Major, is ee?' Harry gasped. 'No surprise though being as ee's the grandson of Lady 'Amilton and Lord Nelson!'

Eliza nodded her agreement. 'That be true, 'Usband… but, Miss Tori, where's your gals to now, if yer don' mind me asking?'

'I don't mind at all. My girls are in Budleigh Salterton, which is a village on the south Devon coast close to Exmouth. They're in the care of my brother, Horace, and their ayah.'

'Please excuse my ignorance, Miss Tori, but what's an ayah?'

'An ayah is an Indian nursemaid. She journeyed with us from Madras.'

Eliza was wide-eyed. 'Yer got someone come all the way from India ter look after yer chillern?'

'Yes. Our daughters are quite attached to her.'

'I never 'eard anything like it!'

'Where's yer 'usband to, if yer don' mind me asking, Miss Tori?'

She sagged, 'He had to go back to India.'

'Yer don't look too 'appy about that,' Harry observed.

'Alas, I'm not. His health suffers in the Indian climate. I worry for him.'

Harry reached across the blue and cream checked table cloth to pat her hand reassuringly. 'I can see it's a big worry, Miss Tori. I wish 'im the best of 'ealth.'

She mustered a brave smile.

****

The night was black as Indian ink when Tori wished the Sopers fond goodbyes. Harry had insisted on taking the mantel-shelf candle to escort her back to The Oak. Tori had at first declined his offer, despite dreading the idea of picking her way along the dark, ditch-pocked streets alone. She told him, 'I'm worried your family won't be able to see, because that's your only candle.'

Harry squeezed her arm. 'They'll be fine, don't cha worry, Miss Tori. They's still got the fire ter see by, in't ee?'

'What about upstairs when they to go to bed?'

He chuckled good-naturedly. 'We can feel up 'em stairs like we's bats or summat!'

'Please hurry home though, Harry dear. I feel bad hogging your only candle.'

'I'll see yer to the door of The Oak, Miss Tori. Make sure yer safe. Look, 'ere we is now.'

Sure enough, The Oak's jutting edifice loomed in the light of Harry's improvised lantern. 'Thank you, Harry. You and your family have been wonderful hosts. You've made me feel truly welcome in South Brent.'

Though she couldn't see his face behind the candle's yellow glow, his voice conveyed embarrassment. 'It's no trouble, Miss Tori. Proper honoured we all was, in't ee? Mind yer step, love,' he held the inn's door open for her.

Disregarding the smell of stale tobacco and the men huddled round the glowing hearth, she boldly pecked him on the cheek. 'Good night, Harry dear.'

He moved to kiss her back, but stopped himself. 'And good night ter yer, in't ee? I'll pick yer up in the morning and take yer up View Cottage, if yer still wants ter go there, that is?'

'Oh, Harry, thank you. I still very much wish to go there.'

'Well, good night then, Miss Tori. I'll see yer in the morning and that, in't ee?'

'Good night, Harry. Good night.'

CHAPTER FIFTEEN

Susan approached the crib. Cold, weak light from the February sun scarce lifted the shadows. She knew the form of the wooden cot more from memory than what her eyes now saw. Anxiety pulsed with every heartbeat. Death peered around every corner. Infants were easy prey. The baby had been silent for a long while. She'd been distracted. She reached the dark crib and peered in...

Susan woke in a cold sweat, realising she was in the gas-lit parlour of Henrietta's high-street house. Her hostess's loud voice boomed, 'Did you say something, Susan dear?'

'Oh, it was nothing,' Susan's tone was purposefully light. 'I think I nodded off. I hope I didn't sleep-talk! How embarrassing!'

'I confess to having nodded off too,' Henrietta chuckled.

'Well, your parlour really is very cosy, and old ladies such as we are wont to sleep a lot!' Susan examined the mantel clock. 'It's past nine o'clock, and Horatia's not yet back from the Rolle.'

'I suspect she's enjoying time with her granddaughters, though I must say I'm enjoying your quiet company here by my hearth,' Henrietta yawned contentedly.

****

Susan held her sister's tiny baby to her breast. 'Look at the pretty vase, sweetums, it has such bright colours... no, you don't want to look at it, do you? How about this colourful mask? No, actually that might be a bit scary, and, oh my goodness, don't look at the mummified children! Look, here is a pretty shell. Isn't it big?' Susan, frantic to calm her newborn nephew, paced to and fro between the glass-fronted cabinets of her brother-in-law's famed museum of curios. 'Hush, hush, sweetums,' she crooned, 'hush now, little one.' But the baby wouldn't let up his wailing. She sighed, 'I'm going to have to take you to your poor mama, because you're hungry, aren't you?'

She left the museum room with Baby Nelson still hugged protectively to her bosom. She was reluctant to ascend the state-of-the-art wooden staircase that led up to the second-floor bed chambers. She'd not heard her sister sobbing or vomiting for some time and was loath to disturb her rare peace. However, little Nelson was hungry, so what choice did she have? She approached the staircase tentatively. There was so much luxury and frivolity in their shiny, new house, but what was its use if Harriet was going to die? Why couldn't Edward lift his finger to find a wet nurse? And what was he thinking getting Harriet pregnant again at thirty-eight years of age? Hadn't her darling sister already provided enough children for his vanity? She realised she was being uncharitable. Her sister had wanted this new baby too, and just look at him! Wasn't he just the most perfect, little darling she'd ever seen? But she didn't want her beautiful sister to die. Not her as well! Oh good Lord in Heaven, please save her.

The sound of brisk footsteps approaching down the wooden stairs heralded the approach of Mary the assignee from the Female Orphan Asylum. Mary was a skinny, fretful girl with permanently grubby hands. Though she swore she was fifteen, she looked only twelve. She appeared paler than usual against the fashionable green paintwork. 'I's taking this fer washing, Ma'am,' she nodded her pointy chin at a wicker basket hugged in her arms.

'Is my sister...' Susan faltered, unsure whether to enquire whether Harriet was well, because everyone knew she wasn't, and never would be again. She swallowed a sob. 'Is she awake?'

'She's sleeping, Ma'am, God bless 'er. Cap'n Blanckley's in with 'er.'

Susan sagged knowing she must wake her poor, tortured sister, just as she'd feared. Baby Nelson let forth a distressed scream as if in confirmation. 'Thank you, Mary. You may be on your way.' Nelson continued screaming as Susan ascended to the second-floor. Edward appeared from Harriet's door before she reached it. Grey skinned and red eyed, he looked not to have eaten or slept for many days. 'She's asleep,' he whispered.

'I don't wish to disturb her peace, but the baby...'

His tension lessened as he regarded his three-day-old son, but only for a moment. 'Can it not wait?'

She bristled. 'I have kept him waiting for as long as I feel I may, but I'm afraid his hunger is now fearsome.'

'Why not give it something from the kitchen?'

Susan rolled her eyes. This was the man who'd compassionately carried a rescued infant princeling from Burma all the way to Plymouth! 'One must be extremely careful with what one feeds tiny babes.' Realising how haughty she'd sounded, she adjusted her tone. 'Harriet was clear that she wishes to feed your baby for as long as she may.'

He paced the floor. 'Yes, yes, she did request this, but I hate to have her disturbed.'

'Have you made enquiries about a suitable wet nurse?'

He shook his head morosely, 'She made me promise not to.'

It was hard for Susan to think above Baby Nelson's relentless wails. 'How is she?'

Edward wiped tears from his cheek with a rumpled kerchief. 'She has been in very much pain, yet mercilessly clear of mind.'

She struggled to find a suitable reply, but forgot everything the moment her sister called out from her chamber. 'Susan?'

Her first instinct was to rush in, but she remembered propriety and looked to Edward for permission. He nodded, almost imperceptibly, and pushed the door open for her to enter. Susan took a moment to straighten the crying baby against her bosom before entering the darkened chamber.

'Oh Susan,' Harriet whispered. 'My own body is burning me to death!'

'Mama!' A small body hurtled into the room. 'Mummy!'

Susan realised it was little Toriana and reached a hand to stop her, but missed.

'Tori, you're not allowed in there!' A boy's voice shouted. Was that one of Susan's sons, or was it Tori's older brother, Horace? Several sets of feet could be heard running towards her down the passageway.

Edward's deeper voice commanded. 'Stop this nonsense immediately!'

Then Harriet – darling, darling Harriet – said, 'Tori, sweetheart! No, be very careful of my belly!'

Hearing his mother's voice prompted Baby Nelson to scream

even more loudly and wriggle frantically against Susan's bosom.

'Oh Harriet!' Susan rushed to the bed. 'My poor, sweet sister!'

'Mummy!' Tori grabbed Harriet's limp hand, and pressed her little head against her shoulder to breathe deeply of her mother's scent. Harriet stroked her three-year-old's dark curls. The strain was clear on her pale face. Her breaths were quick and shallow. She was lying on her back with her knees up, endeavouring to lessen the pain of her swollen abdomen. Susan tried not to look at her sister's stomach, but her eyes were drawn there against her will. Bare of all covering, it was swollen as if carrying triplets full-term. The skin looked cruelly hot and taut.

'She just ran in,' Susan explained. 'I'm sorry if I woke you. It's Baby Nelson–'

'Would you place him on me, mindful of my belly?'

Susan positioned the squalling newborn against Harriet's breast as gently as she could, but Harriet winced nonetheless. 'I am sorry, Sister, I didn't mean to hurt you.'

Harriet forced a smile. 'Oh Susan dearest, even thinking hurts right now! I should have more laudanum…' she panted after every few words, 'but I want my babe to suckle… before the drug passes into my blood… though God knows my body… is poisoned enough already!' Harriet caressed her suckling infant's tiny head, but the removal of her comforting hand caused little Tori to screech, 'Mummy!'

'Tori darling, Mummy's here,' Harriet soothed. She said to Susan, 'Sister dear, I… I don't have long left.'

'But, Harriet–'

'Please hear me out… I don't have much time… or energy.'

'I am listening, Sister.'

'Mummy, Mummy!'

'Hush now Tori, darling… Susan,' Harriet fixed sharp green eyes on hers, 'May I prevail…'

'Anything, Sister.'

'Will you care for little Nelson… and Tori and Horace after…'

'Gladly. I would guard them and love them as my own, but–'

'No buts, we know… I am not long for this world… no, hush! We know this,' Harriet attempted a smile, 'What will give me peace is… knowing my children will be cared for… if you will care for the little ones…'

'You have my word, dearest Harriet.' She planted a gentle kiss on her sister's fevered cheek.

'Mummy!' Tori grabbed her mother's limp arm to help pull herself onto the bed.

Susan saw Tori's foot swinging up towards her sister's grossly distended belly as if in slow motion. 'No!!!!' she cried.

Harriet turned her eyes at the moment her daughter's little foot was about to impact. Then it hit. Harriet juddered and screamed. 'Babies,' she muttered, 'Protect my babies,' and then the light left her eyes, and her body went limp.

'Mummy fall!' Tori sobbed, 'Mummy gone!' She pressed her head onto Harriet's soft, unconscious shoulder, 'Mummy fall right down. Want Mummy!'

Edward burst in. 'What by God has happened?'

'She fall,' Tori told him tearfully. 'Mummy fall.'

'Why are you sitting on your mother's shoulder?' He lifted her none-too-gently and dumped her on the floor. Tori grabbed his leg, but he brushed her aside. 'Harriet, oh Harriet,' he leant his face close to hers and placed two fingers on her neck, 'She has a pulse! Where is Mary? Susan, you must stay here with the baby. I will fetch a doctor!' He bounded from the room like a greyhound unleashed on a hare.

Susan surveyed the aftermath. Baby Nelson was suckling as if nothing had happened. Where is Tori? Ah, there she is, poor thing, snivelling on the floor below poor, dear Harriet's head. Oh Lord, but please let my sister be alright. Please let her recover.

****

'Uncle Horace?'

'Uh?'

'It's me, Ethel.'

'What're you doing in my bedroom in the middle of the night?'

'Oh, Uncle Horace, I had ever such a bad dream! There were giant jabberwockies trying to catch me and eat me!'

'Oh… umm, what are jabberwockies?'

'The jabberwocky is a fearsome monster in Through the Looking-Glass, and What Alice Found There. Have you read it, Uncle Horace?'

'Umm, no. I can't say I have.'

'Oh, Uncle Horace, you really should. It's very good.'

'I'm sure it is very good,' he said without enthusiasm. 'Now run along back to bed.'

'But in my dream there were six jabberwockies, and they all wanted to eat me, and they had ever such big teeth!'

'Well, that does sound scary.'

'Uncle Horace?'

'Yes, Ethel?'

'Please may I sleep in your bed?'

'What?'

'My dream has made me very scared, and I would feel safer in your bed because you're a strong Royal Marine captain, so you can protect me.'

'Umm...'

'Mama says I should never feel scared and alone, and lets me sleep in her bed if I've had a bad dream, and you've got ever such a big bed here, Uncle Horace.'

'Hmph, very well then...'

'Oh, thank you, Uncle Horace!'

He winced when a heavy weight collided onto his head and chest. His second-biggest niece had certainly grown more friendly. He was sure his sister would be very pleased with his proficiency at minding her daughters... 'Ouch, that was my hand!'

'Sorry, Uncle Horace.'

****

'Uncle Horace!'

'Ugh. Who's there?'

'It's me, Ethel. I slept in your bed.'

'Ugh, umm, yes... what... umm...'

'We have to get dressed, Uncle Horace!'

'Umm, do we?'

'Today is my birthday, Uncle Horace! I'm now seven-years-old!'

'By Jove, it's the pantomime today! How perfectly splendid!'

CHAPTER SIXTEEN

Emma reeked of rancid wine and was snoring loudly on the tatty sofa. There was an empty bottle on the floor below her sprawling fingers.

'You are meant to protect me,' Horatia told her. 'Sometimes I really hate you.' Admitting this felt liberating – a breath of bold freedom – even though Emma was too insensible to have heard. She turned from her and went to the window. A gibbous moon was riding high and free in the sky beyond the grimy panes. 'Hate,' she told the moon, reverent of its freedom. She turned back to the lumpen, drunken, useless form of Emma. 'Hate,' she said again. She twirled around to encompass the entirety of their pathetic accommodation. 'Hate!' she repeated with relish to the empty air, enjoying the way the final 't' bounced on her teeth like a concealed weapon. 'Hate, hate, hate. Hate! I hate this horrible building, and I hate being stuck in it, and I hate...' she shied from naming the woman on the couch, 'everything!'

She collapsed in another of those blasted whooping cough fits. She hated them too. But her unleashed wrath felt powerful and releasing. She'd felt nothing but frustrated despair for long, cruel months. Hatred must be the key to her salvation. If she held onto it, perhaps there was hope after all.

She raised her voice to a shout when her coughs subsided. 'Hate!!!' She tensed, fearful that Emma had woken, or that a neighbour had heard, but silence prevailed. She smiled and raised her arms to the moon beyond the dirty glass. 'Hate!' she cried again, 'Hate! Hate! Hate!'

Horatia woke with a jolt. She'd had another episode, despite her naive hope that her lunacy had been cured. Her heart thumped, and she felt sick to her stomach. She clawed herself to a sitting position, with her arthritic joints screaming their objection.

'Are you awake, Horatia dear?'

'Susan? Yes, I am.'

'We seem to have woken before the larks! I wonder what the time is? Shall we light a lamp?'

'I think a little lamplight might be cheering. I'll find the matches.' Horatia felt for the top drawer of the little chest beside her bed where a matchbox was stowed. A rattle of matchsticks in the cardboard box followed by the scratch of a struck match resulted in a burst of yellow fire and puff of sulphurous smoke. The match's little flame seemed sun-bright in the darkness. Horatia's hand glowed red for a moment, but the match spluttered and went out.

'Drat,' said Susan, but the second match Horatia struck held its flame long enough for her to light the oil lamp on her bedside chest of drawers. 'Oh, thank goodness!' Susan approved.

'Why, Cousin Susan, you look somewhat fraught.'

Susan grimaced. 'Oh dear, do I? I confess to having had some not-too-pleasant dreams.'

'Poor thing,' Horatia told her with feeling, 'you looked quite harrowed.'

'I do confess to feeling quite harrowed, Horatia dear. I think it must be because of Tori going to South Brent, but I keep dreaming about... well, about the dreadful time when Harriet... you know, when my poor sister passed away.'

Horatia pursed her lips. 'I fear my daughter-in-law's excursion caused a similar dream for me.'

Susan plonked her feet onto the bare boards, apparently heedless of the December cold. 'Oh Horatia, how dreadful! I know how happy you were to have ceased having troublesome dreams since coming here!'

'It seems Tori's mission to relive her past is dragging us back there too.'

'I should have tried to talk her out of it,' Susan fretted. 'Though, to be honest, I doubt she'd have listened. She was determined to go. As you know.'

Horatia nodded gravely. 'I'm loath to speak ill of my daughter-in-law, who's as a daughter to you, but I confess to being… well, in truth, I'm annoyed at her recklessness. It was heartbreaking to see poor Nellie and Carrie last night. They were so sad and lost that their mama had gone away without them.'

'The poor mites! Did her other daughters seem distressed too?'

'Well, Baby Alice was fast asleep the whole time. Little Evie and Ada didn't seem to notice anything beyond their food, and Ethel, God bless her, was enjoying herself tremendously.' Horatia found a smile, 'Would you believe it, but she's wrapped her uncle round her little finger, and insisted on sitting between him and Lizzie and commanding both of their attentions!'

Susan, who was struggling to pull on plain cotton drawers, smiled too. 'That girl is a force of nature! I confess that I can't help but admire her spirit, although society, of course, thinks ill of little girls – and ladies – who speak their minds!'

'Of Ethel's many graces, the virtue of being seen and not heard is one that's assuredly passed her by!'

The old ladies chuckled, and Susan said, 'It's very sad that poor Nellie and Carrie were distressed last night. Is it not a virtue for mothers to put their children's needs before their own?'

Lady Hamilton appeared bright as day against the dark background of the guest room. She was bending close, imploringly. There was something she wanted Horatia to accept, but she'd kept refusing. Lady Hamilton's eyes flashed crossly before she turned her head away.

'Horatia, are you hale, my dear? You looked quite white for a moment, as if you'd seen a ghost!'

Susan's question brought Horatia back to Henrietta's lamp-lit guest chamber. 'It was nothing,' she lied, panicked to let even Susan know she'd had another past-vision, and this time whilst awake.'You know, Cousin dear, I think we owe it to ourselves to put Tori's reckless mission from our minds, and set about enjoying ourselves again. We are on holiday here, after all.'

'You're right!' Susan agreed with gusto, 'And I've just remembered, it's Ethel's birthday. We should have a party for her, even if her mama's away.'

'Good idea, we can provide Ethel with a birthday luncheon in the Rolle. I have a china doll to gift her.'

'Oh goodness, there's something else!' Susan said with a shudder. 'We have to go to the pantomime tonight!'

Horatia laughed despite herself. 'Oh Susan, is that all? I thought you were about to tell me that the world was about to end!'

'Do I sound like a ninny? Oh golly, it's just that the idea of being crowded in with all those people is utterly terrifying to me! You know me, I prefer my quiet little cottage on Gipsy Hill.'

'You don't sound silly at all when you put it like that. As you know, I prefer my own quiet existence. Out of the limelight, as they say. Coming here for Christmastide has been a wonderful tonic – for the most part, at least, but, much as I'm enjoying the topsy-turvy freedoms of this little seaside town, a rowdy pantomime does not sound appealing at all!'

A loud, gurgling roar caused both old ladies to freeze like rabbits caught in lantern light. The rumbling gurgle repeated, and Susan slammed a hand over her mouth. 'Oh my!' she whispered, voice shaking with suppressed laughter, 'it's Henrietta snoring!'

The gurgling rattle sounded again and Horatia gripped her midriff to stop it shaking with her own laughter. 'Oh goodness, I'd thought we'd been invaded by demons!'

'Shh,' Susan hissed, 'let's not wake our snoring hostess! But, I say, shall we dress and venture downstairs? I could do with a cup of tea. I've no idea what the time is, but Bradford will surely be up by now.'

'Why yes, hot tea would be marvellous!' Horatia set about assembling her day garments, and Susan lit another oil lantern for the dressing table. She squinted at her reflection in the tilted mirror, 'I declare my eyes look to have been washed with claret!'

Horatia tutted, not bothering to look up from the petticoat she was easing herself into. 'Now you really are being a ninny! Everything looks orange by oil lamp. I'm sure you look perfectly beautiful. As you always do.'

Her cousin chuckled wryly. 'I am seventy-one-years-of-age. I certainly have not looked "perfectly beautiful" for decades! And am unsure I ever did.'

'Your modesty is becoming, but all you Matcham girls were blessed with cherubic looks, and you especially resemble a porcelain doll.'

'Me? Oh, surely not! Well, perhaps a doll whose face has been cracked all over like an old dinner plate!' Frowning, but with good humour, she smoothed lavender-scented cold cream into her soft wrinkles. 'I know it's vain of me to make a fuss of my toilet, but how are we ladies supposed to uphold society's expectation of pale, clear complexions and rosy cheeks? The truth is that, unless we are extremely young and blessed with naturally wholesome looks, we must secretly daub ourselves with ointments! You say I'm modest, but did you know I'm the subject of a painting entitled "Omnia Vanitas"?'

Horatia now did look up. 'You never mentioned it.'

Susan cast her a shy glance. A floorboard creaked with the shift of her weight. 'I was embarrassed, and I didn't find out about it until we moved to Gipsy Lodge... when was that? About eighteen-fifty-five, I think. Tori turned twenty shortly after we moved there.'

'I recall you visiting us in Kent around that time.'

'The proximity of the Gipsy Hill to the line to Kent was one of my reasons for choosing to live there. You've been such a dear comfort to me over the years, darling Cousin.'

'As you've been for me.'

'Oh, I now recall that first visit we made to you from Gipsy Lodge. Poor Toriana lamented your William's absence even then. They were always in love, weren't they?' Both women smiled. 'I wondered that they didn't marry sooner.'

'William was determined to secure a living before proposing.'

'It's ironic, in a way, isn't it?' Susan mused. 'The good living he secured has caused them further separation.'

'They misjudged the reality of raising a family in India. All is clear with the wisdom of hindsight, is it not?'

Susan sighed. 'Yet how else could they have been together? It's so sad when loved ones are forced apart because of military service. I confess to longing to return to Gipsy Lodge to see if a letter from my Alexander has arrived. Ah, the plight of womankind to wait forever helpless for news of men at war!'

Horatia fastened a fine-wool chemise over her corset. 'You were telling me about being the subject of a painting entitled "Omnia Vanitas"?'

'Oh yes, of course. My story meandered. We moved to Gipsy Lodge because an old friend of ours from Paris, an artist chap, was lodging in The Oaks, which is the house next to it. He arranged the tenancy for me, you see? He'd been looking out for me since… after the terrible events that happened when Tori was tiny.'

'He was a Frenchman?'

'A Scot, in fact, but he'd become our family friend when we were living in Paris. William Dyce. You may have heard of him?'

'Do you mean the man who established the South Kensington system of art?'

'Yes, yes,' she flapped her hands as if to hurry Horatia's questions away.

Horatia raised her eyebrows. 'You sat for William Dyce for a painting entitled "all is vanity"?'

'No, no, of course not… and he told me he meant the painting's title to translate as "all is emptiness". "Omnia Vanitas" can mean this too, you see?'

Horatia stepped into her black, cotton dress with some

difficulty. 'Susan, I confess to being quite lost. You say you were the subject of his painting, but didn't sit for him?'

'He painted me from memory.'

'And, pray, did he explain why he chose to do so?'

'He was most apologetic, but said he'd been haunted by the, umm, grief he sensed in me after… after that terrible time,' she met Horatia's eyes shyly.

'Oh Susan, that was an awful time for you!'

'He said he'd felt moved to make my grief the subject of a painting.'

'Tis not a happy portrait then?' Eyes meeting, both giggled, and another loud snore from the direction of Henrietta's front bedroom caused them to laugh even more.

'Oh, Cousin!' Susan dabbed tears from her cheeks, 'Tis not a happy scene at all! I'm portrayed wistfully laying my hand on a human skull.'

'A skull? How frightfully sombre!'

'One could not wish for a more sombre rendition of oneself!'

'You saw the portrait in his house?'

'Far worse, it was his diploma piece, and he took me to see it in the Royal Academy's public gallery!'

'I'd no idea, Susan, that your likeness has been so prolifically observed!'

'I am grateful at least that Will didn't attribute my name to it. He told the art world it was a depiction of Mary Magdalene.'

'Mary Magdalene caressing a skull?'

'Outer beauty perishes, so it is both nothing and a vanity,' she winked.

Taking an oil lamp each, Horatia and Susan tiptoed down the stairs, stifling giggles every time the stairwell reverberated with another of Henrietta's snores. The parlour's gaslighting was already lit. The maid was kneeling in front of the cold hearth busily blacking the grate.

'Good morning, Bradford,' Horatia whispered.

The maid dropped her rag as if a gun had been fired. 'Spare me!' she screeched, and leapt to face them with the poker brandished like a sword.

'Tis just us,' Susan assured her, 'we woke early.'

'Oh, Mrs. Moore, you gave me a fright!'

'We didn't mean to alarm you,' Horatia said, still whispering, 'if the kitchen stove is lit, we can make ourselves tea.'

Bradford gasped. 'Miss Blanckley'd 'ave me guts for garters if I let you make yer own tea, and not that I'd want you ter do anyway. Sit yerselves down. I'll get the fire lit in 'ere in a jiffy, then I'll fetch yer tea, and there's warm rolls ready in the side-oven.' True to her word, the fire was blazing within a minute and she bustled back in soon after with a little table so they could eat and drink without leaving the newly-lit fire's warmth. The freshly-baked rolls were delicious, as was the steaming tea. Horatia, who's habit was to sit properly at a dining table to eat, enjoyed the informal picnic arrangement as another of Budleigh Salterton's topsy-turvy liberties. She realised it had been silly to worry that one dream and a brief memory flash signalled a relapse of insanity. After all, everyone dreamed and had recollections. She'd become overwrought and was jumping at shadows. Breaking dawn lit the street outside Henrietta's twin parlour windows in pinkish-gold highlights.

Rietta arrived a while later, brightly-dressed and puff-faced, with her steel-rimmed spectacles awry on the top of her pointed nose. 'You're already up,' she observed without first pausing to greet them.

'Good morning, Henrietta,' Susan rose to peck their old friend on the cheek. 'We awoke before the larks.'

'Were your beds uncomfortable? Was your chamber too cold?' Rietta asked anxiously.

Horatia resisted a playful urge to mention Rietta's loud snoring, and said instead, 'Good morning, dear friend. Our accommodation is exceedingly comfortable, but sleep evaded despite this. Bradford looked after us excellently, despite our disturbing her morning chores.'

'Then I shall give Bradford a boon for her diligence,' Rietta declared. 'I hope you're both well?'

'I, for one, am very well,' Horatia pronounced. 'I'm not too proud to admit that the holiday you prescribed has proven to be the exact remedy I'd needed.'

'I knew I was right!' Rietta declared immodestly.

'I am fully ready to embrace the liberal joys of Budleigh Salterton!' Horatia strode to the nearest of Henrietta's parlour windows to take in the view. A man with dark, bushy black sideburns was looking straight back at her. She recoiled, tottering backwards away from the window. When she looked again, the high street was devoid of life.

'Horatia has a very merry plan in mind for today,' Susan said, oblivious of Horatia's fright.

Rietta clapped her hands. 'Pray tell.'

Her hostess's expectant scrutiny sent Horatia into panic. A lifetime of avoiding limelight made all attention feel like a threat. But then she remembered this was her childhood friend who knew her dark past and didn't judge her in any way. And the plan Cousin Susan referred to was a life-affirming and happy thing of which Rietta would heartily approve. She realised she was smiling, and this felt good. 'Today, dear Rietta, is Ethel's seventh birthday. It troubles me that her mama isn't here for her because of her ill-considered jaunt to South Brent. My plan, as the poor mite's grandmother, is to make her birthday special despite her mama's absence. I'm thinking of asking the powers that be in the Rolle to lay on a special luncheon for Ethel. My treat.'

Rietta was enthusiastic. 'What a marvellous idea!'

'You could ask them to provide blancmange. Tis Ethel's favourite food,' Susan suggested.

'I shall make sure the Rolle provide her with a blancmange the size of a Christmas turkey!' Horatia laughed, but a loud rat-a-tat-tat on the front door made her heart jolt.

Rietta examined the mantel-clock. 'Tis only half-past-seven! Who on Earth would be calling at this early hour?'

The maid, Bradford, could be heard walking quickly from the kitchen in her hard-soled shoes. There was a murmur of voices before Bradford appeared with an envelope. 'Telegram, Ma'am,' she told Rietta.

Rietta held her hand out to receive it. 'How peculiar!' I cannot think of anyone who'd have a reason to message me so early, and during Christmastide!'

'It's for Mrs. Ward,' Bradford clarified, and proffered the envelope to Horatia.

Horatia's heart hammered. She took the telegram gingerly, as if it might bite her.

'Who's it from?' Rietta adjusted her spectacles.

Horatia wanted to ignore it; pretend it hadn't come, but everyone was watching her expectantly. She had no choice but to open the envelope and force herself to read the message it contained:

> *DEAREST MOTHER –(STOP)–*
>
> *GOOD NEWS –(STOP)– MR. ARCHIBALD HAS AGREED TO ACCEPT JACK INTO ETON IN JANUARY WITHOUT YOUR WRITTEN TESTIMONY –(STOP)–*

Horatia breathed a sigh of relief. She'd not realised how much anxiety the pressure to write the testimony had given her.

'You're smiling,' Rietta observed, 'I surmise it's good news?'

Horatia carried on reading:

> *WE ARE INVITED TO HIS NEW YEAR'S EVE DINNER –(STOP)– YOUR VERBAL TESTIMONY THERE WILL GUARANTEE NELSON'S ADMITTANCE –(STOP)– CONFIRM YOUR ATTENDANCE BY RETURN –(STOP)–*
>
> *YOUR LOVING SON NELSON WARD*

'Ratia?' Henrietta asked, concerned, but Horatia didn't hear.

She was scowling at Emma. 'Why do you keep writing your stupid letters? Why can't we just retire with dignity? Have you no concept of my humiliation?'

'We cannot retire, because, as you know very well, my stipends from Sir William and your good father are not being paid. What are we supposed to live on: fresh air?'

'We can at least save what money we do have. Why do you keep employing tutors for me? We could use the money for food.'

'Your dear father bequeathed a stipend specifically for you, and I spend that money on you only. Your education is of utmost importance for your future.'

'Well, you should at least stop throwing parties and getting drunk.'

'You know very well that I must to entertain our supporters–'

'Don't you know that no one will ever honour Nelson's last codicil?'

'It will be our salvation, darling. Once it's granted and the government gives us the honour we deserve, everyone will be our friends again, you'll see! We'll live comfortably and respectably as your dear father wished,' Emma smiled at the thought. 'Don't you see, they simply must honour his last wishes. He died for our country and, in return for his great sacrifice, he asked only that we be provided for. The Prince of Wales, once he becomes King–'

'Oh do shut up going on about the fat, smelly prince and that wretched codicil!'

If Emma was shocked at Horatia's rudeness, she didn't show it. She threw up her hands, 'But what else can I do?'

CHAPTER SEVENTEEN

'I don't feel good about this, Tom,' Mrs. Elizabeth Matthews, a plump, early middle-aged woman, complained to her husband as she paced up and down in front of the French windows. Her ankle-length skirt swooshed hither and thither over the painted boards. Her expression was petulant. 'Why does our landlady suddenly want to inspect our home? What does she want from it? From us?'

Tom Matthews, grey combed-over hair protruding above today's copy of The Times, clicked his tongue. 'I don't know, Wife, but I'm sure she means us no ill. As you know, I arranged for her to stay at The Oak, instead of here, so she can't snoop when we're not about. Come sit awhile, your walking to and fro is dizzying me.'

'Oh, but I cannot! I'm worried for the security of our babes. What if this Mrs. Blanckley decides to throw us all out on the street?'

Forty-year-old Tom Matthews frowned at his patently hysterical wife, 'As I have already told you, her name is Mrs. Ward, not Mrs. Blanckley. She is the married daughter of Captain Edward Blanckley who built this place. She co-inherited it with her brother, and it's he, not she, who the rental agent answers to. We have no reason to fear her throwing us out onto the street. Calm yourself.'

'Oh, but Husband, what if–'

'Enough, Woman! If you do not calm your hysteria voluntarily,

I'll have to throw a jug of cold water at your face. Do not disturb me until you're sure she's arrived.'

Mrs. Elizabeth Matthews returned to the French windows and pressed her rubbery cheek to one of the cold panes. The view through the glass was obscured by myriad water droplets, and sounds drowned by the drum, drum, drumming of the hurling rain. She squinted at the squall for a long minute or two before saying, 'I think there are people under the verandah, Husband, but I can't quite see.'

Tom clicked his tongue again. 'Woman, I told you not to disturb me until you're certain our visitor's arrived.'

'Oh, but Husband, I am quite sure!' She pressed her cheek back against the glass, 'And I can hear voices. I'm sure of this too!'

He rolled his eyes. 'Woman, your "sure" is the rational world's equivalent of baseless speculation.'

Mrs. Matthews looked crestfallen. 'But what if Mrs. Blanckley's here? I want to be ready. Do I look presentable?'

Deigning finally to raise his eyes from the newsprint, he sighed and shook his head sadly.

'Husband,' she prompted, 'am I presentable?'

'Is your hair supposed to look like that?'

Blanching to an even paler shade of blancmange, she pawed frantically at her greying ringlets. 'What do you mean?'

'It looks like a monkey has died on your head. Is this the effect you desire?'

Her lower lip wobbled. 'Must you be cruel to me?'

'Pull yourself together. It was a joke.'

'Well not a very funny one.'

'Lighten up,' he stretched his lips into the semblance of a charming smile, 'You were saying our guest may be here?'

Mrs. Matthews actually jumped (though not very high). 'Oh my goodness, I'd forgotten! My hair, does it truly look like a dead monkey?'

'It looks–' Mr. Matthews began, but a pair of adult figures passing the French windows caused both parties to forget about the appearance of Mrs. Elizabeth Matthews' hair.

****

Tori looked up at the verandah's under-roof with wonder. 'I remember Papa helping the workmen build this. Mama was here too, so I could have been no more than three years of age. It was a hot sunny day. Mama and Aunt Susan were sitting on the lawn with wide bonnets to keep the sun off their faces. Mama's tummy was very fat because of the baby. Horace and Alexander were playing with a paper kite, running to and fro along the top of the steep bank.' Her smile was wobbly as if she might cry. 'I wanted to grab the kite from them because it was so prettily coloured.'

'Like as not, I was there and all,' Harry grinned. 'I remember yer dad was right 'appy to muck in with us builders. Not all 'igh and mighty, ee weren't. Not like some folk. Good bloke ee were.'

She swallowed. 'Harry?'

'Yes, my love?'

'Were you here when... when my mother had her fall?'

He scratched his wet head. 'Fall, Miss Tori?'

'Umm, you know... when she fell down the bank.' She gestured at the impenetrable fog on the far side of the lawn.

'I never 'eard that she fell, Miss Tori.'

'But, I mean, you are aware of her death, Harry?'

'Right sad that were,' he met her eyes with compassion.

'And did you not... did you hear how she died?'

'That we did, Miss Tori.'

She frowned. 'Tell me, please Harry, what it was that you heard.'

He shuffled and bowed his head. 'Well, Miss Tori, what we 'eard is that she fell foul of childbed fever after 'aving yer baby brother in Plymuff.'

She stared open-mouthed at the grey, blank space across the lawn.

'Miss Tori, my love,' Harry touched her white cheek with his dirt-ingrained hand.

Focus came back to her eyes. She turned to face him. Her taut smile conveyed wonder. 'I remember the last time I saw my mother. It was at Raleigh House in Plymouth. Not here. Just like you said, Harry... but,' she deflated like a slow-punctured rubber balloon, 'my mother's death... that is to say, I have remembered...' she stuttered, tremulous, and flicked him a shy glance, 'it was because of me that she died. I was stupid, selfish and clumsy. She died because of me.'

She stared at the featureless grey of Lutton House's December-sparse lawn. Why had she thought her mother had died here? Why had she been plagued by nightmares of her mother tumbling down the steep bank to her death? She hoped the current tenants wouldn't think her too peculiar if she elected to inspect it.

Harry stood quietly by her side under the narrow verandah roof. He had a folded oilcloth tucked beneath his arm which he'd been using as a rainproof cape. It was releasing rivulets of water down his already-soaked legs. The verandah roof was doing little to protect Harry and her from becoming even wetter than they already were. The downpour, which had relentlessly intensified from drizzle into a torrent of bullet-like shards, was now assaulting them from all angles. Tori had just noticed that her teeth were chattering when the chipped boards of the front door swung open to reveal a scowling, hatchet-faced maid with unruly snakes of grey hair crammed into a too-small mobcap.

'Whatcha be wanting outside the front door 'ere?' The maid's voice screeched like slate on granite. The walls of the short hallway behind her were hung with dated rococo wallpaper patterned with lurid pink roses on arsenic green leaves. Tori felt resentful, because the hallway used to be papered in blue and white.

'This is Miss Tori, Ma'am.' Harry doffed his sodden cap. 'Ee's expected 'ere, in't ee?'

The hatchet-faced maid continued to scowl. 'Yer's 'Arry Soper who's a railway station cabby of late, in't yer?'

'That I am, but, like I said, this 'ere's Miss Tori, and ee's expected, and it's right rainy and that out 'ere, in't ee? So are you going to let 'im in?'

'I don't know nuffin' about no "Miss Tori" being 'spected,' Hatchet-face *hmph*-ed and marched back into the warm interior without so much as a by-your-leave.

Tori wanted to snap at the maid to let her into her own house, but contained herself for the sake of propriety.

Harry was more outspoken. 'Where's yer off ter, woman?' He bellowed at Hatchet-face's retreating back. 'Whatcha doing leaving a fanty-sheeny lady out in the rain?'

Hatchet-face turned to face him. 'Tis no call for the likes of yer ter be shouting at me.'

'And there's no call fer an 'ousemaid ter be leaving a gentlelady rudely out in the cold!'

'I said we in't bin expecting no "Miss Tories". So shut yer gob and let me go and ask the master if ee'll see 'im.'

Tori felt a need to speak. 'He might be expecting me as "Mrs. Ward".'

Hatchet-face eyed her coldly. 'In't expecting no one by that name, neither.'

'What's all this commotion?' A skinny gentleman with greasy combed-over hair strutted into the lobby.

'There's a strange woman and a railway cabbie come to call, Sir. I was just about ter come and ask yer if yer expecting a "Miss Tori" or a "Mrs. Ward", Sir.'

The skinny man stared from Tori to Harry confused. 'You say there are two women arrived?'

Hatchet-face *hmph*-ed again. 'Just this one, Sir, but ee changed 'is name while I stood 'ere, in't ee?'

His eyes widened. 'Are you Mrs. Ward?'

'I am, Sir.'

'Good grief, Hawton! What were you thinking leaving her out in the cold? This is our landlady, and honoured guest!'

Hatchet-face had the decency to look marginally contrite. 'I thought yer guest were called "Mrs. Blanckley", Sir?"

'I do not care what idiocy you thought, Hawton. Show our esteemed guest inside immediately, and take her man to the kitchen and tell Cook to give him a biscuit or something.' He treated Tori to an oily smile, 'I am deeply sorry for my maid's incompetence, Mrs. Ward.'

'It was really no inconvenience,' she lied.

'Please, please, come in. Hawton, take her cloak and hang it by a fire to dry.'

The first impression Tori had of the parlour was of a cacophony of blue wallpaper peacocks on acid green screaming for attention behind islands of dark hardwood furniture. She spied a pair of rococo revival scroll-carved settees and what looked to be a real Henry Pape pianoforte, which she stared at dumbfounded, convinced it had been her mother's.

A plump middle-aged woman rose from one of the rococo settees. The hooped skirts of her dress ballooned as she stood in an expanse of blue, which might have appeared bright had it not been for the gaudier peacocks on the wall behind her. 'Mrs. Blanckley,' she beamed, 'we are deeply honoured by your visit.'

'Ee says ee's Mrs. Ward, Ma'am,' Hatchet-face mumbled.

'What did you say, Hawton?' The blue-dressed woman's chins wobbled when she swivelled to face the maid.

'Ee said ee's called Mrs. Ward, Ma'am.'

She appeared nonplussed, but the skinny man with the comb-over spoke quickly. 'Wife, how many times have I told you that our esteemed guest married a man by the name of Ward?'

Her lips quivered. 'Mrs. Ward, I humbly apologise. My memory is that bad. I have had it in my head that you're called Blanckley. Please, take a seat by the fire.'

'Hawton, you haven't introduced us,' the combed-over man scolded the maid.

Hatchet-face bobbed. 'Sorry Sir. Mrs. Blanckley, this is Mr. and Mrs. Matthews, what lives 'ere.'

'A pleasure,' Tori intoned politely before lowering herself into the warm hearthside seat indicated.

Mrs. Matthews took charge. 'Hawton, fetch the dainties.' She turned, chins wobbling, back to Tori 'We're right honoured by your visit, M'lady…'

'Umm, I'm not as such a Lady… I mean–'

'Nonsense,' Mr. Matthews came to his wife's voluminous side, 'You are the child of a Royal Navy Captain, are you not, M'lady?'

'Well… yes, but–'

'And a great-niece of Lord Nelson himself?'

Mrs. Matthews released a little squawk. 'The blood of our great hero! We are honoured all the more!'

'Thank you. You are very kind.'

'We are overjoyed,' Mr. Matthews began, but was interrupted by the sudden emergence of raised voices from the hallway.

'I told yer, ee won't like 'em!' A man said heatedly.

'They is sent over special from France,' a woman objected.

'My foot are they! It's my cousin, Eliza…'

Mr. Matthews strode briskly to the doorway and bellowed, 'Whatever is this ruckus?'

'Sorry, Sir, it's the coachman what Mrs. Ward brung up from the village with 'im. Ee's arguing about the dainty food what Mrs. Mathews requested.'

'Do you have a problem, Mr... whatever your name is?'

'I'm 'Arry Soper, Sir, and I do 'ave a problem coz I know Miss Tori...'

Tori, unable to contain herself further, rushed to join Mr. Matthews at the drawing doorway. Before her stood Harry, hands adamantly on his hips, facing Hatchet-face clutching a silver platter bearing round-cut toast topped with something shiny. 'Harry, please do not worry for me. I am certain that the dainties my hosts have provided for my repast will be entirely satisfactory.'

'But, Miss Tori–'

She held up a hand. 'Harry, I insist. I appreciate your concern for my well-being, but I am perfectly fine.'

'Shall I take the dainties in, Sir?'

Mr. Matthews cleared his throat, 'Right away, Hawton.'

Harry looked anguished, but Tori laid her hand gently on his rain-sodden sleeve. 'Harry, please return to Cook in the kitchen and warm yourself by the fire.'

'But, Miss Tori–'

'I insist.'

He bowed submissively and retreated. Mr. Matthews sighed loudly with relief, and clasped Tori's arm to steer her pronto back into their rococo drawing room. ‘Place the platter on the table near Mrs. Ward,’ he told hatchet-faced Hawton.

Mrs. Matthews clapped her podgy hands in delight. ‘The dainties! Oh Mrs. Blanck... I mean, Ward, these are a treat indeed!’

Tori surveyed the proffered platter with interest. The round-cut toasts were topped with dripping or lard, and dark, shiny mounds of something with pale grey and reddy-orange patches. Were those little clawed feet sticking out? Oh my goodness, were those beaks? ‘I am intrigued, Mrs. Matthews,’ she managed to say, ‘What, pray, is this delicacy you have so generously bestowed?’

Mrs. Matthews’ double chins swelled with her smile. ‘They are a rare treat indeed.’

‘How marvellous,’ Tori concealed her wariness behind a gracious smile, ‘Are they a type of meat, perhaps?’

Her hostess grinned broadly. ‘They are pickled robins!’

‘Oh,’ said Tori, simply. Her gratitude to Harry for having attempted to save her from eating these monstrosities was immense.

‘If you don’t mind my saying, M’lady, you look a little uncertain,’ Mrs. Matthews observed, ‘but do not worry, you can eat them whole. The bones turn soft in the vinegar, isn’t this right, Husband?’

‘What? Oh, yes, very soft. They are something of an acquired taste, I’ll own. Very tart on the tongue. Distinctly slimy too, and yet crunchy and chewy at the same time. Really quite delicious once one is accustomed.’

‘Oh,’ Tori said again.

'They are very expensive,' Mrs. Matthews confided. 'Hawton's cousin in Dartmouth imports them all the way from France, where they are quite the fashion, isn't this so, Hawton?'

Hatchet-face shifted from foot to foot. 'Yes, Ma'am,' she mumbled, avoiding Tori's eyes.

'And we are fortunate that her cousin deigns to spare us the odd jar, what with them being so highly sought after. The Duke of Devonshire is one of his keenest patrons, is he not, Hawton?'

'Umm, yes, Ma'am. Shall I bring the tay?'

'Tea, ah yes!' She clapped her podgy hands again. 'Do you like tea, Mrs. Ward?'

'I like tea very much,' Tori told her honestly.

'Oh good! We adore tea here too, don't we, Husband?'

'What? Oh yes, tea is sublime!'

'Mrs. Ward,' she fixed Tori with keen eyes, 'Please do partake of a pickled robin on toast. They are a delicacy enjoyed by royalty, as Hawton will attest.'

'Just off ter fetch the tay, Ma'am,' the hatchet-faced maid darted out the door.

Unperturbed by her maid's abandonment, Mrs. Matthews pressed on relentlessly. 'I insist you at least try a bite. We instructed Cook to prepare them in honour of your visit, M'lady. We reserve them for only the most exalted of occasions, of which your visit, of course, is one.' The dumpy hostess grabbed the platter and, with a rustle of royal blue silk, pushed its grisly contents under Tori's nose. 'Mrs. Ward, I insist.'

'Wife!' Mr. Matthews interjected, 'It is impolite to force food on a guest.'

The blancmange-pink hostess stepped back, the tray of grotesqueries mercifully receding with her. 'Mrs. Ward, pray forgive my poor hospitality!'

'Do not fret,' Tori was hasty to assure her, 'I am really not at all hungry. I should like, with your permission, to view the whole house.'

However, Mr. Matthews now assailed her instead. 'We do have some tiny, gentry-friendly pickled Jennies, I mean wrens–' he began at the same time that Mrs. Matthews said, 'But M'lady, our children are upstairs, and might disturb your tour.'

'I have children,' Tori attempted a reassuring smile, 'and do not mind being disturbed.'

'Or a tiny, little pickled goldcrest?' Mr. Matthews went on.

'I cannot!' Tori flinched at the snap in her own voice. Host and hostess regarded her with astonishment. Gentlelady visitors who raised their voices were almost as peculiar, she supposed, as fairground ladies with beards. However, of all the company, Tori was the most surprised by what she said next, 'I'm with child.'

Oh my giddy goodness, she thought, but I really am with child! I have not had my courses since October. Why did I not notice this before? Goodness me, but we will have a seventh baby by… July. Oh Lord have mercy, how will I cope? Oh William, where are you? How are you? All your little children! I wish you home, my love!

CHAPTER EIGHTEEN

'Wake up you stupid woman!' Horatia tugged Emma's inert shoulder and slapped her slack face 'Wake up!' she repeated, and grabbed a fistful of Emma's greying hair to yank her head up. Emma mumbled inaudibly, batting uselessly towards her head. 'Wake up you stupid, fat cow!'

'What? Who is it?' Emma half-opened an eye. 'Horashya, what is it?'

'It's you,' she spat, 'you're a stupid, fat, old woman getting drunk all the time instead of looking after me. I hate you!'

'Horaysha, what you saying?' Emma attempted to raise herself, but fell back on the sofa.

Horatia watched without pity. 'You're too drunk to even sit up, you stupid, fat, old woman. Lord Nelson asked you to protect me, but you can't even protect yourself. I hate you!'

Sobered by her violent wakening, Emma succeeded in raising herself to a sitting position. 'Oh my poor head!'

'Who cares about your "poor head"? No one does. Everyone hates you. I hate you. I disown you. You are not my mother. I wish you dead. You are nothing to me.'

'Horaysha,' Emma protested, but Horatia had already turned her back and was storming towards her room.

'Ratia?' Rietta's loud query propelled Horatia back to the present as if she'd been slapped across the face. Her heart skipped a beat. Her waking visions had come back with merciless force. She hadn't escaped insanity after all. She prayed that God would preserve her sons and grandsons from society learning of her shame. She had to hide her insanity for their sakes, not hers. 'I'm perfectly fine,' she lied.

Rietta squinted at her through her blue steel-framed spectacles. 'We need strong tea!' she declared, and rang for her maid.

Horatia doubted tea would help. She distractedly worried her lace cuff, and a fragment of verse looped in her thoughts, like sheep's wool snagged on rough bark:

Cold as the cold Decembers,
Past as the days that set,
While the only one remembers
And all the rest forget, –
But one remembers yet.

'Did you ever allow yourself to grieve?' Rietta's loud question made Horatia flinch, and Susan stop her listless examination of Algerine mementos.

'For whom?' Horatia's reply was brittle.

'For Lady Hamilton.'

'Henrietta!' Susan gasped, 'Whatever has got into you this morning?'

'Was I blunt again?' Rietta sounded a little sheepish, 'I didn't mean to be. Ratia, I'm sorry if I was blunt. It's just that I so dearly wish for you to find the peace you hoped to find here.'

Horatia raised her hands. 'I'm know you mean well, but the peace I've sought is right here and, at the risk of sounding very blunt myself, questions such as yours are the only things getting in the way of it! So, yes, thank you for inviting me here for Christmastide. I've already told you that you were right that I'd needed this break, and it truly has worked wonders. But what I continue to need is freedom from scrutiny and second-guessing. I am not a science experiment to observe under a microscope, but a mature woman who is quite capable of knowing what she needs, and this is to be let alone!'

Rietta was contrite. 'I apologise, dear Ratia. Please disregard my clumsy question.'

Horatia was happy to do just this. The parlour sank into extended silence. The mantel-shelf clock ticked away the time. Horatia returned her attention to the cuff of her black dress and contented herself in quiet, thought-free meditation of its stitching until she heard Rietta whisper something to Cousin Susan. She perked her ears and heard Rietta say, '...fed up with complying with her unspoken decree that no one may talk about the blatant truth!'

'Hush,' Susan whispered, 'Horatia's not deaf.'

Horatia was irritated. She most certainly was not deaf. Why wouldn't Rietta just leave her be? It was her relentless meddling, as well as Tori's ill-considered trip to South Brent, that had caused the memory attacks to come back. She'd come to Budleigh Salterton to forget all that nonsense. She needed to relax! Even Rietta had admitted this. So why wouldn't she just shut up and let her do so?

'Ratia looks cross,' Rietta observed, loudly.

Susan breathed out sharply through her nose. 'I surmise that this would be because she heard what you whisper-shouted to me. Is this so, Cousin Horatia?'

'What do you mean by saying I "whisper-shouted"?'

Susan's reply held affectionate humour. 'Henrietta, my dear, you cannot be quiet even if you try to be!'

'Quite so!' Horatia's own humour had returned. 'Rietta, much as I do truly love you, you're hardly a shrinking violet, I mean, not with your orange wig, and you have the volume and tact of a foghorn!'

'"Foghorn"?' Rietta shrieked, 'I'm shocked at how mean you're both being to me!'

Horatia tried not to laugh. 'Surely you must know that your voice is naturally loud?'

Rietta stood up abruptly. 'You really are being cruel! Well, I have no mind to take it! I apologise if you found me insensitive, but there's no need for either of you to name-call me.' She glared at Horatia and Susan, 'I organised this holiday for you. Selflessly, I might add! Yet you see fit to accuse me of being a loudmouth!' Rietta's mood worsened when Susan collapsed into giggles. 'You're behaving like a pair of rude and unruly children!'

Horatia managed to suppress her welling laughter. 'Oh, Rietta, it's my turn to apologise for being insensitive. You've been an exemplary hostess, and we're very grateful, aren't we Cousin Susan?'

Susan pulled herself together. 'Yes, of course!'

Horatia decided a change of scene was needed not just for Rietta's benefit, but because she wanted to distract her from bringing up the subject of Lady Hamilton again. 'I say, the Rolle's kitchen staff will be getting lunch prepared by now. It's high time for me to ask them to make a special, birthday luncheon for young Ethel. Do either of you fancy accompanying me there?'

****

Horace was attempting to teach Ethel to play as-nas. Ethel was sitting cross-legged on the cream-coloured Provençal quilt covering his hotel bed, struggling to hold a hand of Persian cards neatly. 'Uncle Horace, am I ready to play for real money yet?'

He inhaled deeply from his cigar. 'Tis not considered decorous for ladies… or little girls, to gamble money.'

'Why not, Uncle Horace?' Her blue eyes scanned his imploringly. 'I should very much enjoy the fun of playing for money. It would be unfair to be disallowed just because I'm a girl.'

He exhaled a satisfyingly perfect smoke ring. 'Tis not about fairness,' he told her pompously, 'but about propriety, and propriety is based on intellectual and emotional capacity. It is well known by science that women and girls possess lower intellectual capacity, though higher emotional vicissitude.'

His newly turned seven-year-old niece frowned. 'What does "vicissitude" mean, Uncle Horace?'

'It means skitting from one thing to another.'

Eyes suddenly alight, she smiled broadly. 'Oh yes, Uncle Horace, I am very skittish indeed, but I should still like to play as-nas for real money. I should like that very much, and it is my birthday, after all.'

He nodded and looked about to say yes, but coughed and said instead, 'I think your mama will be home soon, Niece.'

Ethel hurled her whole body, cannonball-like, onto his head and clasped it tightly with limbs, chin and forehead. 'Oh, Uncle Horace! I love you so much more than Mama! I don't want her to come home and stop me being with you!'

Horace's heart swelled. 'We have done well, have we not, Ethel?'

'I do hope so, Uncle Horace,' she sniffed. Her hot breath was close to his skull above his right ear. 'Mama will be very pleased with me... I mean *us*, when she gets home... don't you think, Uncle Horace?'

'I am certain of this.' He unleashed one of his radiant, moustache-stretching smiles, 'Your mama will without doubt be happily amazed at the close friendship we've forged.'

Ethel's eyes shone like nuggets of sapphire in the glow of his bedside gas lamp. Her exposed teeth gleamed like tiny, hard pearls. 'Do you think Mama will be cross with Nellie for behaving badly?'

'Without doubt, Niece.' He patted her head again.

She squeezed his head more tightly. 'Oh, Uncle Horace, I love you!'

'Release my head immediately, Niece! You are squashing my moustache.' Fortuitously, a loud rap on his suite door shocked Ethel into letting go of him completely. 'Come!' he barked.

The door opened and a spotty-faced bellboy in the Rolle's green livery slipped in and bowed smoothly. 'Captain Blanckley, good morning, Sir. Miss Blanckley and the Mistresses Ward and Moore wish to inform you of their presence in the dining room.'

'Why the devil do those old crones want me to know where they are?' Horace snapped.

The bellboy cringed. 'Sir, they said something of a special luncheon–'

'You may inform them that I am happily engaged in my suite with no interest in their luncheon plans!'

'Very well, Sir, but if I may say also that they spoke of their luncheon being in honour of a niece of yours–'

Ethel leapt off the grand bed in a flash of pink silk and golden ringlets. 'It must be for me because it's my birthday today! Uncle Horace, please may we join them immediately?'

****

The birthday girl entered the Rolle's dining hall with one small, pink hand imperiously clutching her uncle's scarlet sleeve. The hotel's enormous, candle-laden Christmas tree glimmered like a tower of living gold. In front of this was a row of smiling faces seated at a long, linen-covered table. 'Everyone's here!' she squealed. 'There's Grandmama and Aunt Susan, and all my sisters, and Kajri, although Mama isn't here, of course...' she scanned the table again, 'and I can't see Aunt Lizzie.'

'Happy birthday!' everyone cheered, and Ethel brightened.

Horatia rose awkwardly, hampered by her arthritis, and opened her arms for a hug. 'We thought it might be nice for you to enjoy a birthday luncheon, even though your mama's away until the evening.'

Ethel wrapped herself around her grandmother's thin, black-clad frame. 'Oh, Grandmama Horatia, I'm so very pleased that you've all come to make my birthday special. Did you know that I'm actually seven-years-old now, which means I'm nearly as old as Nellie?'

'Yes, my dear girl, you are now very grown up, and very pretty indeed!'

'Thank you,' Ethel purred, 'though Mama says vanity is a very bad thing so I'm not allowed to think I'm pretty, which is a shame because I know I am.'

'Omnia vanitas!' Susan laughed.

Horatia smiled. 'Quite so, Ethel. Well, I hope you'll enjoy your birthday luncheon. I asked the kitchen to provide a blancmange for dessert.'

'Blancmange?' Ethel was so excited that she jumped up and down, 'Why, that's my most favourite thing of all, Grandmama Horatia!'

'That's why we asked them to provide it for you, dear girl. Your birthday's a very special day, after all!'

'It's going to be the best birthday luncheon ever if there's blancmange!'

Horatia's warm smile held a flicker of dissatisfaction. 'Know, dear one, that I – your grandmama – will always be here for you, even if your mama is absent.'

Five-year-old Carrie whimpered, 'When's Mama coming back?'

'Fear not, Carrie,' Susan said, 'your mother will be home in a few hours. Her train will bring her back to Exmouth in plenty of time to join us here by early evening.'

'The poor children!' Horatia sighed, 'And such a shame for you, Ethel, having to spend your birthday without your mama!'

Ethel disentangled herself from their embrace, and eyed her grandmother steadily with a smile flicking at the corners of her mouth, 'Do not worry for me, Grandmama, for I have been having the very best birthday ever with Uncle Horace, who is the best uncle in the world!' Horace grinned broadly. 'He has been teaching me how to play as-nas!' Horace's smile faded.

'What, pray, is as-nas?'

'Oh, Grandmama Horatia, tis a very interesting game from Persia that has special cards, which are ever so pretty, and people can actually bet money on them!'

Henrietta chuckled, but Horatia was not amused. She frowned at Horace, who was standing just behind Ethel looking sheepish. 'Is as-nas a gambling game?'

Horace's ginger moustache twitched. 'Rest assured that I have not permitted my niece to play for money!'

Ethel pouted. 'It isn't fair because it's my birthday!'

'Ethel Mary Ward,' Horatia admonished, 'no respectable lady plays cards for money, so you certainly may not, even if it is your birthday. Look, here comes the waiter with our first course. I asked for cheese fingers, which I noticed you enjoying during your aunt, Henrietta's meal.'

'Sit next to me here,' Susan patted the chair beside her invitingly.

Ethel eyed the vacant seat without enthusiasm. 'But where will Uncle Horace sit, Aunt Susan?'

'Why, at the head of the table, of course! See, the chair there's empty and waiting for him.'

'Shouldn't I sit at the head of the table too, Aunt Susan, for it is my birthday and this luncheon is for me.'

Both Susan and Horatia opened their mouths to object, but Horace spoke first, 'Quite so! My favourite niece should certainly sit at the table's head beside me! I say…' he gave Ethel's elder sister a puzzled look as if he couldn't remember her name, '…Niece, how about you sit there beside your aunt, Susan, so Ethel can take your chair beside me?' Nellie's lips began to wobble, but she controlled her expression and politely vacated her chair. 'Good show!' Horace beamed, 'Come along, Ethel, and sit down here. It looks like the waiter's brought us cheese cut into thin slices with some vegetable stuff.'

'It's winter salad,' Horatia informed him, sounding a bit vexed.

Horace pushed the vegetable matter aside with his fork and skewered a cheese finger. 'I must say, this cheese is rather good.'

Ethel was uncharacteristically subdued during the meal until the arrival of the blancmange, which caused her to jump out of her chair and run to kiss Horatia's withered cheek. 'Grandmama, thank you! I can not tell you how happy I am to have blancmange!'

Horatia smiled broadly. 'I'm so glad to see you enjoying your birthday, Ethel dear. Perhaps we could take a walk on the beach after luncheon?'

Nellie was enthusiastic. 'This a marvellous idea, Grandmama. Poor Patch has been locked in our suite and I'm sure he'd very much like to visit the beach.' However, the sky outside grew suddenly dark and a torrent of rain began battering the dining hall's tall windows.

'I think nature disagrees with your plan, Ratia dear!' Henrietta's booming voice drew everyone's attention.

Horatia eyed the rain soaked window glass. 'I have an even better idea, Ethel. How about we adjourn to the ladies' parlour and I teach you how to play whist? It's a highly popular card game that is not played for money.' She shot Horace a hard look.

'"Ladies' parlour"?' Horace parroted gracelessly, 'I can't say I fancy the sound of such a place.'

Nellie, infinitely more discreet, coughed delicately and touched Susan's arm. 'Please may I be excused to see to Patch, Aunt Susan? I'm concerned that he's upstairs all on his own.'

'You're such a sweet and dutiful girl!' Susan gushed. 'I say, Horatia dear, we won't begrudge Nellie abandoning us for her pet spaniel, will we?'

'You need to take him out for a walk as well,' Ethel told her, 'I can't do it because it's my birthday.'

Nellie lent close to Ethel and whispered. 'It's always me who thinks to take him out anyway, little sister.'

Ethel glared at Nellie and patted Horace's arm, but the decibels of Henrietta's voice once again drew all attention to her. 'Ah, look! My niece, Lizzie, is standing in the reception! I was wondering where she was. Lizzie!' she barked, even louder. All eyes followed the direction of her bellow through the dining hall's doors to Lizzie standing, arms akimbo, in the lobby with her red hair elaborately coiffed and a waist so fashionably thin that it looked like her top half might snap off and tumble onto the plush carpet.

'Where have you been, Niece?' Henrietta projected her enquiry so that everyone in the hotel could hear it. Lizzie made a rapid, beckoning motion with her gloved hand, and Henrietta bounded towards her like an excited puppy. The others watched their interplay with interest. Though what Lizzie said was too quiet to reach them, Henrietta could be heard saying things such as, 'I quite understand,' and, 'a carriage sounds like a marvellous idea!'

'Is Cousin Lizzie going to join you in the ladies' parlour?' Horace sounded eager.

'I do hope so,' said Ethel, 'for I like Aunt Lizzie very much indeed.'

However, Henrietta bounded back, with surprising nimbleness considering her short, rotund stature and advanced age. She informed them, 'I am taking a carriage home with Lizzie, who is suffering a fit of delicate health.'

'I think that has answered your question,' Horatia told Horace wryly as Henrietta scurried back to her niece in the lobby. 'However, we can still make the birthday girl's afternoon fun, even without your cousin, Lizzie and dear, old Rietta!' She eased herself upright and smiled broadly, 'Let us adjourn to the ladies' parlour!'

Horace's moustache twitched. 'With your leave, I'm sure you understand that ladies' parlours are not a good fit for me. I'm a captain of the Royal Marines after all! I shall return to my suite.'

Ethel grabbed his scarlet sleeve. 'Uncle Horace, please may I accompany you? I would very much like to play more as-nas.'

'Your company is very welcome.' Horace patted her golden hair and ushered her towards the lobby.

'Oh dear, we seem to have lost the birthday girl,' Susan said to Horatia.

'In addition to Horace, Nellie, Lizzie and Rietta,' Horatia sighed.

The ayah broke her meal-long silence to say, 'With your leave, Mrs. Ward, Baby Alice is starting to stir. I should take her to the nursery for her milk.'

'Yes, of course, Kajri dear,' Horatia waved her on her way and summoned a bright smile for the three young girls still present, 'Well, Carrie, Evie and Ada, what do you say we have a little party in the ladies' parlour?'

Four-year-old Evie perked up. 'Will there be cake?'

Horatia smiled indulgently. 'Would you like me to send for some?'

'Oh yes, please, Grandmama!'

Susan prodded Horatia's arm. 'It looks like your grandmother skills are appreciated by someone here! Though how young Evie can still want cake after the delicious meal we just had is beyond me!'

'I confess it's not the merry gathering I'd envisaged, but we can still make a merry time for the little girls, can we not?'

****

The ladies' parlour was cosy and quiet, bar the happy prattle of the little girls, crackling logs in the fireplace, and the occasional voices of people traversing the street outside. Horatia soon gave up teaching whist to her young granddaughters because the rules confused them and they were more interested in picking out the picture cards and playing with them like dolls. 'The queen of hearts is looking for Alice in Wonderland!' Carrie decided, 'but the bad jack of spades wants to steal all her gold.'

Horatia half-listened to the girls' play as she sipped on the sherry Susan had persuaded her was an appropriate afternoon drink during Christmastide. Susan had drifted off to sleep, and Horatia was beginning to nod off too. It was a shame, she admitted to herself, that Ethel had elected to spend her birthday afternoon with her uncle instead of her, but she'd clearly developed a bond of strong affection with Horace and this, she smiled to herself, was because of her intervention. So, in this light, she was a very effective grandmother. This was the one role she excelled at. Tori's absence, regrettable as it was, had enabled her to step forward as a positive, guiding force in her granddaughters' lives.

****

A tall man with bushy black sideburns hummed the tune of A Frog He Would A Wooing Go as he appraised himself in his dressing mirror. He stroked his bushy, black sideburns. 'Your nose is a smooth rose petal,' he murmured, imagining his reflection was the speaker and himself a trembling heiress enchanted by his poetic flattery. Straightening his back, he caused his reflection to direct him a smoky gaze. 'Your lips are pink cauldrons inviting me to dine.' He paused. Might that perhaps have been indelicate? He cleared his throat, 'Your hands are twin goslings fluttering softly on the bank beside a gentle forest stream.' Good, good, he thought, I am a veritable Hugo! That heiress, whichever wench she transpired to be, would be powerless to resist him. He clutched his top hat to his lap with an excited energy he was not accustomed to. His decrepit father had said he would countenance his marriage to the heiress-to-be, meaning he, Francis Cooke, would soon be the possessor of a wife to do with as he wished. He clutched his hat harder, picturing the broken subservience of his father's young bride. How marvellous it would be to have a woman of his own to bend to his will. He considered the scenario, the process of breaking her spirit and bending her to the mastery of his will would, without doubt, be much more satisfying than procuring her inheritance.

CHAPTER NINETEEN

Emma was out of her mind with drink and shouting incoherently and kicking the wall and punching it. Her greying hair was a mess of greasy tangles. Her body bloated. Her dress unkempt. Mood suddenly switching, as was her drunken wont, she began crying piteously in great, body juddering shudders. Horatia had learned it was pointless to reason with her when she was like this, as was happening more and more often. The best thing to do was maintain a low profile and ride out the storm. Too late, she'd noticed her, 'Horaysha! Lovely Horaysha!"

She remained still, hoping Emma would forget about her again.

'Horaysha, come to me. I am sore sorrowful in my heart.'

Horatia stepped backwards, but found her retreat blocked by the mildewy, sponging-house wall.

'Come to me now!' Emma's mood switched again, as quick as flint lighting tinder. She swayed unstably and reached for Horatia with clumsy arms, 'I told yer to come to me.'

'I don't want to. Leave me alone! You're drunk.' Horatia snapped.

'I am not drunk. I just want a hug from my own daughter. Is this too much to ask?'

'Oh, just go away!'

'Don't speak to me like that!'

'Well leave me alone then.'

Emma exploded back into tears. 'Why does everyone turn on me?'

Horatia relaxed. Although unpleasant, her mother's drunken tears were easier to deal with. 'Let me help you to bed,' she tugged the heavy woman's shoulder to prompt her to stand.

'You're such a sweet girl,' Emma slurred without resistance.

'Yes, yes. Let's get you into bed.'

Nellie sat at the dark-wood hotel dressing table heedless of Patch hunched dejectedly at her feet. Her outward attention was focused on the way her spinning zoetrope transformed a cardboard strip printed with a series of posed ballet dancers into a magical animation of a single dancing lady. It was spellbinding. She watched, determined to avoid recalling the dire happenstance of Ethel's dictatorial rise during Mama's absence. Mama had been gone for longer than a day, and would not return until late afternoon. How much more mischief might Ethel conjure in the interim? It was safer to remain up here in their hotel room, all alone. Ethel herself had scarce set foot in their shared suite since her inglorious bonding with Uncle Horace. She had even slept in his bed. It was all so unfair. Whilst Nellie had always striven to be courteous, demure and obedient, Ethel gave not a hoot for decorum. She'd behaved in a most beastly manner towards poor Uncle Horace until Mama's departure, but had now wheedled her way into his good books, and manipulated him to punish and humiliate her in front of everybody. Fat tears blurred the zoetrope's hypnotic animation. Patch whined his sympathy, though Nellie, distracted as she was, heard him not.

Her anguished solitude was curtailed abruptly by Carrie pushing the door open, without knocking, and screaming that Baby Alice had turned blue.

'What do you mean, "turned blue"?' Nellie snapped at the excited five-year old.

Her little sister sobbed. 'Kajri's scared!'

'Why is she blue?'

Carrie struggled to articulate. 'Bad… Baby Alice is dying.'

'Dying?'

'Kajri's scared,' Carrie repeated. 'Need doctor.'

Nellie's heart hammered. 'Are Grandmama Horatia and Aunt Susan with Kajri?'

'They went to sleep in the parlour. Took Evie and Ada up to Kajri, and Baby Alice turned blue!'

'You took Evie and Ada up to Kajri on your own?'

Carrie quailed. 'Was I bad?'

'Oh dear, I don't know! What a fix! I need to see Kajri and Alice!' Nellie bounded down the corridor to the nursery suite without another word. Baby Alice's high pitched screaming rang out loud and clear. Kajri was hovering over the squalling infant who'd been laid flat on one of the beds. Little Evie and Ada were sitting on the floor near the ayah's sandalled feet.

'She go blue,' Kajri whispered, dark eyes wide with fear. 'She breathe too fast, then she go blue.'

Nellie peered at the baby. 'She doesn't look blue.'

The ayah shrugged. 'She was blue. Now she just pale. I'm very worried.'

'Do you think Baby Alice is well now that she's stopped being blue?'

Kajri frowned. 'Baby Alice always difficult. Not feeding properly. Not sleeping. Crying too much.'

'Mama says it's because England is colder than India.'

'Maybe it is this, but why she go blue?'

Nellie realised she could play the role of helpful, eldest sister again. 'I will go to Grandmama Horatia and Aunt Susan.

They'll know what to do.'

She hurried off, mindful, despite the urgency, to descend the stairs one step at a time as a young lady should. On attaining the ground floor she beelined towards the ladies' parlour. Aunt Susan was snoring loudly in an armchair, but Grandmama Horatia looked to be awake.

'Please come quickly!' Nellie cried. 'I'm sorry to interrupt, but Kajri says Baby Alice turned blue and I think she might be very ill!' But Grandmama Horatia didn't react at all. Nellie realised her grandmother had fallen asleep with her eyes open. It felt impolite to disturb her, but it was an emergency, so she tentatively touched her black sleeve and said, 'Grandmama, please wake up.' But Horatia remained as still as a cliff. 'Oh, please! Please, wake up, Grandmama!' She dared to shake the old lady's shoulder, but it was as if she was trying to move a sack of clay. Nellie despaired. She was just a little girl and an adult should be in charge. She felt very small and weak, but then an idea struck: she could go to the hotel's reception and tell them a doctor needed to be sent for urgently.

She hurried to the mahogany reception desk at a brisk, but dignified pace. She was dismayed to find it unmanned. She rang the brass bell three times to indicate urgency, proud of her resourcefulness. A young man in bellboy livery duly appeared, but scowled when he saw her. 'The bell in't for playing with.'

Nellie, who hated being told off, overcame her fear and summoned a steely glare that would have made her great-aunt Henrietta proud. 'There is an emergency. My baby sister has turned blue. A doctor must be sent for immediately.'

The bellboy's gawp caused his wispy facial hair to form a yellow ring around startlingly brown teeth. 'Wassat?'

'We require a doctor post-haste,' she snapped. 'If you won't go yourself, tell me where to find him and I will fetch him myself.'

He at last galvanised into action. 'Right away, Miss. I will run and fetch 'im!' The bellboy sped off towards the hotel's grand front entrance.

Nellie was powered up like a coke-filled steam-train on trackless ground. She had a burning need to act, but no idea what actions to take. She hurried first one way, then another, across the foyer's carpet until she thought to tell Uncle Horace about her baby sister's blueness. She dashed for the stairs, then stopped. What if the bellboy returned with the doctor and didn't know which rooms they were in? She should have told him! She peered left and right in the hope of seeing another staff member, but the lobby was devoid of life. Why was nobody around? It all felt hopeless, but her eyes caught on the front entrance. The doorman would be standing guard outside it. She bolted to the grand double doors, and pushed one with all her might. Her whole body pressed against it in her effort to force the heavy mahogany and glass door slowly open. A broadening stream of cold, wet late December air assaulted her through the growing crack. She spied the doorman's green livery, but his back was to her. 'Help, please!' she called, straining to hold the door open against the wind, but he didn't hear her. 'Help!' she cried again. 'Help!' At last he turned. His eyes widened when he saw her and he swiftly took hold of the heavy door and pulled it wide so she could step through. 'It's my baby sister,' she sobbed. 'She has turned blue. The bellboy's run for the doctor, but I daren't go upstairs to check on her because the doctor won't know which room to go to.'

'Wassat?' The doorman squinted at her with one hand cupped to his ear. 'You say a babby's took poorly?'

'Yes, Sir,' Nellie caught his eyes imploringly. 'I am very worried.'

'Yer needs a doctor?'

'Yes, Sir, right away.'

He rubbed his chin. 'There's a doctor staying in the Rolle, in't ee? Dr. Lowe's 'is name. Down from Gloucestershire ee be ter see 'is folks fer Christmas. Let's go ask the maids. They'll know where ee be.' He ushered Nellie to follow him back into the hotel. 'Bessie! Meg! Got us a little girl what needs us ter find a doctor coz 'er babby sister's took proper poorly!'

A blonde haired maid hurried to meet them. 'What's all that 'ollering, Fred?' she grumbled, but her face softened when she caught sight of Nellie. 'My, but you look proper worried, my little love!'

The doorman tutted. 'I told yer, Bessie, 'er babby sister's took proper poorly. I need yer to fetch that doctor what's down from Gloucester quick as yer can!'

Nellie paced the lobby floor distractedly. Every second felt like an hour. What if no doctor came? What if Baby Alice actually died? Should she be trying harder? What else could she do? Then, finally, she saw a grey, besuited man descending the Rolle's red and gold papered stairwell with Bessie the blonde maid. She rushed to him. 'Are you Dr. Lowe, Sir?'

He didn't even look at her. 'Hurry along, my business is urgent.'

Unperturbed, Nellie persisted. 'Is your business, Sir, to check on Baby Alice who turned blue?'

The besuited man paused. 'What do you know of this, child?'

'She's my baby sister. It was I who sent for you, Sir.'

'You?' He peered at her through *pince nez* glasses. Nellie noticed that he smelled strongly of carbolic soap. 'Is there no responsible adult present?'

Nellie, having shrunk under his critical gaze, answered a little breathlessly. ‘Kajri, that’s our ayah, is with Baby Alice.’

‘Are you holidaying here with no British guardian?’

‘Uncle Horace is standing as our guardian,’ she squeaked.

‘Where is this Uncle Horace of yours?’

‘I think he is in his suite, Sir, with my sister, Ethel.’

‘Is he alerted of this alleged medical emergency?’

Nellie was surprised to find herself countering the doctor. ‘Shouldn’t you attend Baby Alice quickly, Sir?’

‘This is for me to judge, girl. Do not evade my question. Is your uncle aware of his baby niece’s illness?’

‘Umm, no, Sir,’ Nellie wished fervently to sink into the patterned carpet.

‘Why not?’

‘Umm, because, Sir, he does not like me disturbing him.’

‘Well, don’t just stand there snivelling, girl. There is a sick baby for me to attend. Escort me to her immediately, then fetch your uncle. Post haste!’

****

Uncle Horace at last answered Nellie’s persistent knocking. ‘I instructed you not to disturb us.’

Nellie for once held firm in the face of adult rebuff. ‘It is an emergency, Uncle.’

Ethel appeared at his side. ‘Let me guess, you have mislaid a doll?'

The eyes that turned to regard her were simultaneously flame hot and ice cool. 'Why no, Sister. Baby Alice turned blue, and I was obliged to summon a doctor, who is with her now. I should not have bothered your important seclusion, but the doctor demanded that I do.'

Horace and Ethel stared at her for a long moment, until Horace at last cleared his throat. 'My baby niece turned *blue*?'

'Yes,' Nellie told him levelly, 'but you needn't worry for the matter is quite in control.'

'But... but, your mother entrusted me as guardian to you all...'

'Never mind, Uncle Horace,' Nellie patted the white linen of his jacket-less sleeve. 'Mama will see we managed without your having guarded us at all. I bid you a pleasant day.' She turned her back on them as if they no longer existed, but when she reached the nursery suite, she realised that her uncle had followed her.

'Are you the doctor?' Horace demanded of the grey-haired man bending to examine something on one of the single beds.

'I am Dr. Lowe.' When he straightened, the doctor, the grey-haired man was revealed to be several inches shorter than Horace. 'Are you the infant's elusive guardian?'

'Captain Blanckley of the Royal Marines, Sir!' Horace saluted as if addressing a military superior.

'Hmm,' Dr. Lowe fiddled to light a pipe. 'It's as well one of the children in your guardianship sent for me. It's bad news, I'm afraid, Captain Blanckley.'

Horace paled. 'Good grief, is it dead?'

The doctor took a long suck on his pipe and exhaled a cloud of smoke. 'Not yet, old chap! Could be worse, hey? But the infant's got a dicky heart, sorry to say. Means it's fragile. No medicine to help it, I'm afraid, but beef tea's good for the heart. If you want it to live, you'll need to make sure it doesn't get excited. Tricky to achieve with females because of their proneness to hysteria.'

'Yes, yes, quite so,' Horace nodded. 'I shall inform my sister of your diagnosis.'

'Very good.' Dr. Lowe examined a watch on a gold chain pinned to his waist. 'I'm afraid I must fly, Captain Blanckley. Family gathering. Mustn't keep 'em waiting, hey?'

Nellie clung to Horace's shirt sleeve and whimpered, 'Poor Mama will be ever so upset.'

He ruffled her hair. 'Tis fortunate that your mama has four or five other daughters.'

'Five,' Nellie supplied. 'Mama has six daughters in total.'

'Yes, yes, of course. So the threat of losing the smallest one will not feel as grave to her as it would to a mother possessing just one or two female offspring.'

Uncle Horace's dismissive attitude surprised Nellie greatly. 'But Mama is very fond of Baby Alice.'

'Why, of course your mama is fond of her baby. Such sentiments are par for the course for mothers, but the salient point is that none of her children, prolific as you all may be, are sons.'

Nellie stared up at him, trembling. 'Do you mean that Mama doesn't love us as much as she would love sons, Uncle Horace?'

He patted her head again. 'How could she? No parent is happy until a son is born.'

'Oh, Uncle Horace, I am sorry.'

His ginger moustache twitched. 'How so?'

Nellie flinched. 'It's just that you have no sons.'

Horace was quiet for a long moment. 'My wife proved unfit.'

'I'm sorry to hear she is unfit to have children, Uncle Horace.'

'She is unfit to be near!'

Nellie didn't know what to say. She cast an eldest sister's surveying eye to little Evie and Ada. Carrie, God bless her caring nature, had them quietly occupied in a den she'd fashioned from bedspreads, cushions and a side table. 'Look,' she was saying to them as she held up their much loved copy of Edward Lear's Nonsense Songs, Stories, Botany, and Alphabets. 'The owl and the puss-cat are in a boat. Can you see the puss-cat's stripy tail?' Evie and Ada, transfixed, peered dutifully at the proffered page. Ada jabbed a finger in the book's general direction. 'Clever Oddy!' Carrie praised, 'Who can see a pot of honey?'

'I can see the honey!' cried Evie, who hated to be outdone by her bright younger sister.

****

Ethel was alone and bewildered in Uncle Horace's suite. Her mama would be awfully cross with her because she hadn't been there when Baby Alice turned blue... but why should she have been there? It was her birthday after all, and it was actually Mama who'd disappeared completely, not her. She'd actually been a very good girl, because Uncle Horace had been pleased with her. She smiled through her tears. Nellie had always been a bully. Why would Mama be cross with her at all? Ethel now positively grinned. She straightened her back to stand taller, but a different remembrance caused her to slump again. It had maybe been a little bit bad to encourage Uncle Horace to lock his room to everyone else, and it was because of this that they hadn't known Baby Alice had turned blue. Ethel slid dispiritedly down the flock-papered wall to squat on the floor, knowing now that her mama would deem her very, very badly indeed. Worse, Mama would view Nellie as a heroine. Ethel clasped her head in both hands and wept. She'd so wanted to be a heroine. And it was her birthday! Everyone was supposed to think she was the best daughter today. It wasn't fair that smug, bullying Nellie had won yet again!

****

Kajri, exhausted, stroked the soft, downy hair of Baby Alice asleep on the bed. She thanked holy Parvati that the baby had turned British pink again, that the doctor had said she would live, and that one of those wondrous, modern telegrams had been sent all the way to Mrs. Ward in the distant countryside so she could know of this trouble and hurry back on a steam train. What a wonder was this modern British world! How marvellous it was that white babies had such super care. But what of brown babies? Who cared for them? Kajri wondered if she was being bitter. She knew she loved Baby Alice and her sisters with all her heart. Of course she did. She would not be a human being if she didn't love them... but what of that poor, little Burmese prince Mrs. Ward's father dragged back to England on his ship? Did anyone send a doctor for him if he fell sick after he was forced to work as a pageboy for some rich, English Memsahib? If that Captain Blanckley had truly cared for that poor baby he'd have kept him in his house as a child of his own. But he didn't because the poor boy had brown skin. The ayah continued to stroke Baby Alice's peach-soft cheek.

The sweet, little angel didn't know how lucky she was to be born pink not brown.

****

On the floor below, Horatia continued to be oblivious to her surroundings. Her eyes were glazed, though she sat bolt upright.

Emma missed her chair, and would have fallen to the floor if she hadn't grabbed the table's edge. Horatia suspected this had been more through luck than judgement. 'You are always drunk!' she accused.

'Well make sure you tell everyone this after I am gone.'

'Don't talk of such things. You'll get better.'

'There's no getting better for me,' Emma laughed blackly. 'My old body's done with this world.'

'If you'd just stop drinking so much–'

'Horatia darling, you know I cannot. Every morning I wake shaking until I've had a drink. My body won't let me be without it. The numbness it brings is my only solace.'

Horatia bristled. 'Of course I am no solace for you.'

'Darling, you are the greatest solace of all, but I am feeble and cannot endure the prevailing... heartless hypocrisy and... spite that the rest of the world throws at me. And,' she fixed Horatia with a lucid glare, 'I will serve you better in death.'

'Don't say that!' Horatia grabbed her shoulders, hauling her up to better behold the earnestness in her face. 'Do you think I don't love you, Mother? Do you really think I'd be happy if you died?'

Emma turned her head stubbornly to the wall. 'How many times have I told you not to call me that?'

She clasped Emma's head. Her hair was greasily slick, but she cared not. 'Look at me. You are my Mother. It's ridiculous to expect me to pretend otherwise. People aren't stupid.'

Emma smiled bitterly. 'People will believe anything they like if it accords with their own views. Mark my words, their views will never accord favourably with the illegitimate daughter of the infamous and detested Lady Hamilton.'

Horatia flinched at her mother's brutal self-defamation. Collecting her thoughts, she replied, 'They will ask me what you told me about my mother.'

'Tell them I wouldn't say,' she shrugged. 'Tell them I was insensible with drink.' Emma's bloodshot eyes burned with lucidity. 'Tell them you begged me to reveal the identity of your mother on my deathbed, but I refused to disclose it.'

'But... but, I don't want to. It would be a lie.'

Emma hung her head, deflated. 'For this I am sorry, Child. I see no other way. It's clear the world has come to hate me. I was a fool to believe they'd love me forever. My name's become poison! Your only hope is to distance yourself as far as you are able from the taint of my name. Tell them how much I've caused you to suffer.' She fixed Horatia again with that resolute stare. Her eyes flashed hot like flame. 'Tell them I was a useless drunk who was solely responsible for our poverty. Remember those expensive parties I threw vainly trying to woo support? Tell people of my stupidity in having thrown them. Tell them I was remiss in your care. Tell them you hate me.'

'I shall do no such thing. I have given my word that I will not name you as my mother. I shall hold to that promise, though it hurts me to the core. I shall not, though, ever tell people I hate you.'

Eyes now dull, Emma broke her gaze. 'Well, just do not support me. Will you promise me that?'

CHAPTER TWENTY

Horatia was horrified to realise she'd drifted into yet another immersive memory. Rain hard as hammer-driven nails was assaulting the window glass, and the early afternoon was nearly dark as night. 'Pardon me?' she said, hoping to dear God that she'd misheard, but Cousin Susan's sorrowful whimper boded ill. She elaborated her query, 'I thought you said Baby Alice turned blue, but I assuredly misheard.'

'Alas, you heard true. Poor Nellie says we were both dead to the world when she came to alert us!'

'I didn't like to disturb you, and I'm sorry if I did wrong,' Nellie muttered. Horatia realised the eight-year-old was standing beside Susan with her head bowed and her hands tightly clasped over the pink sash around the waist of her knee-length dress.

Susan wiped her eyes. 'Nellie, my dear, dear girl, if it wasn't for your quick-thinking courage, who knows how much worse things could have been!'

'I confess I'm at a loss,' Horatia tried to keep panic from her voice. 'It's my fault for, umm, falling asleep. That was very remiss of me. But how is it that you, dear Nellie, came to be the heroine of the day, as your aunt says? And, oh dear, where are little Carrie, Evie and Ada? We were supposed to be minding them. Anything could have happened to them!'

Nellie lifted her head just enough to meet Horatia's eyes shyly. 'My little sisters are with Kajri and Baby Alice in the nursery.

Carrie was reading to them when I left.'

Horatia shuddered to think of those tiny children must wandering through the hotel unsupervised to reach the nursery, whilst she'd been immersed in a memory. They could have got lost. They could have been abducted! Minding them had been her one duty, but she'd failed it.

'Our girl here was ever so brave!' Susan indicated Nellie with adoring eyes. 'When she found us fast asleep and insensible – silly, old fools that we are! – she went to the reception on her own and rang the bell for attention, isn't this what you told me, Nellie dear?' The eight-year-old blushed and stared at her polished, black shoes. 'Then the bellboy ran to find a doctor at her bidding, but our brave, clever girl realised the emergency was too great to leave anything to chance, so she sought the help of the doorman too, didn't you Nellie, dear? And the doorman knew there was a doctor staying in the hotel, and it's because of this that a doctor reached Baby Alice so soon! Nellie, you should be very proud of yourself!'

Lady Hamilton was standing right in front of Horatia, impossibly tall, and as young and fresh as a spring garden. *Remember!*

Go away! Horatia shouted in her mind, you're a figment of my insanity. You're not real. Dragging her focus to the reality of Cousin Susan and Nellie, Horatia exhaled forcefully. 'We must do what we can now to help Baby Alice. We should go to the nursery immediately to see how the poor babe is, and a telegram should be sent to Tori in South Brent. Do we know where she's staying?'

'Not I,' said Susan, already on her feet and heading for the door. 'Maybe her brother knows, it was he who set her up for the trip.'

'The damned fool!' Horatia muttered.

Horatia tackled the stairs without any care for decorum, and with the energy of a woman fifty years her junior. Nellie and Susan were hurrying after her, but were still only half way up when Horatia burst onto the first floor. She barged into the nursery suite like a bullet. The room was dark and eerily quiet. The first person she noticed was Horace pacing the small floor space like a caged tiger. He looked strangely diminished. She realised it was because he wasn't wearing his scarlet jacket. Behind Horace, on a window seat, the Indian nursemaid was clutching Baby Alice to her scarlet sari-ed breast. 'Why is the baby not moving?' Horatia demanded.

Horace paused his manic pacing long enough to bark, 'Good god, Aunt Horatia, but it's been a nightmare! The damned thing went blue, and who knew if it'd live after that? Thank goodness a doctor came quickly!'

'Grandmama Horatia!' Little Carrie rushed to greet her. 'Baby Alice got really poorly!'

She ruffled the five-year-old's hair distractedly. 'Why is she so still? Does the doctor know?'

The ayah answered tiredly. 'Baby Alice is sleeping, Mrs. Ward, thank Lakshmi! Doctor said she needs sleep now. He said sleeping's a very good thing for her.'

Horatia peered down at the baby in the Indian nanny's arms. 'Is she now well?'

'Good god, but no!' Horace said as he paced passed her. Then, during his return pace: 'Damned baby's going to be weak all its life! Might die any minute! Damnable bad luck! The only silver lining is that it isn't a boy.'

Remember! Emma hissed in Horatia's ear. 'Stop!' she realised she'd shouted out loud. 'I mean we should stop all this confusion and worry. Horace, have you sent a telegram to your sister in South Brent?'

'Good idea, Aunt,' Horace said. Horatia was relieved he hadn't responded to her as if she was mad. It had come down to this. Regardless of the very real danger to dear, little Alice's life, Horatia had the ever present dread of family members noticing her insanity. No matter how hard she tried to resist, her thoughts kept slipping back into her distant past. Reality and recollection were flicking from one to the other at giddying speed. Her young teen self was currently clinging to a mast, terrified of being tipped into the boiling waves.

The flimsy boat had finally rocked its way out of the Thames estuary to join the North Sea at Kent. She had never been in a boat at sea before, and wasn't finding the experience pleasant. The waves were hefty, making the boat tip crazily. The salty spray had drenched her so she was cold to the bone, and the heavy lurching made her increasingly queasy.

Emma was incongruously jubilant. She flung her heavy arms around Horatia. 'Finally we've escaped that most cursed and ungrateful kingdom! We can start anew in Calais, darling, you'll see.'

Although Horatia hoped her mother's speculation would prove accurate, she could think of little else right now beyond growing nausea and the panic of being swept overboard that kept her clinging to the mast.

Horatia shook her head vigorously to dislodge this latest memory. The scream of her arthritic neck joints for once made her happy, because it rooted her into the here and now like a skewer through her flesh. 'I'm so happy that Baby Alice is sleeping peacefully and no longer blue,' she told the ayah, who looked nearly as exhausted as the white-faced baby clutched against her scarlet sari. But then her mind slipped again.

****

Mrs. Matthews opened the door at the end of the upstairs corridor with a clumsy flourish. 'The master bedroom, M'lady.'

Tori's heart hammered. She looked eagerly for the stars Papa had painted on the ceiling to comfort her three-year-old self during sleepless nights. But instead of stars, there was drab, greying paint wrought with cracks. 'May I see the view?' She stepped forwards before her hosts (her tenants) had a chance to reply. Walking through her parents' former bedroom evoked a tingling sensation beneath her sensible green day dress. The room resonated of "home" but its decor and furnishings were jarringly wrong.

'Of course you may see the view, Mrs. Bl... Ward,' dumpy Mrs. Matthews called after her, 'although the view is sadly hidden today by all this dastardly rain.'

The sash-window, at least, was unchanged. Tori felt a warm thrill when she recognised its distinctive pattern of eight large panes bordered with ones of half the width. She knew the window looked onto hedged fields below a wide sky, but, as Mrs. Matthews had pointed out, the heavy rain veiled the view. Everything beyond the jutting verandah roof was diminished to dully defined greys tinged with aqua and ultramarine. She was reminded of those modern, blotchy paintings daubed by artists such as Monet and Sisley, which art experts criticised, but she actually quite liked. Fat rain hurled incessantly at the window glass and streamed down, down, down, dispersing their substance like myriad tear trails on dead blue cheeks. The sky was crying for her lost mother, she heard herself think. She shook her head to clear away such maudlin nonsense. She addressed the cold glass before her, with her voice raised so her hosts/tenants would hear. 'Is the house comfortable to live in?'

Mrs. Matthews whispered something to her husband, but he shushed her and said, 'Lutton House is very comfortable, M'lady. We are grateful to your family for renting it to us, aren't we, Mrs. Mathews?"

'Oh yes, Mrs. B… Ward, we are very grateful indeed.'

Tori continued to stare unfocused at the drizzle-obscured view from the master bedroom. In her mind's eye, she was three-years-old and leaning against Mama's soft shoulder as they reclined on the big bed beneath the star-painted ceiling. Separate shafts of sunlight illuminated individual sections of their combined whole. Mama's soft cheek. Tori's hand and wrist. A section of Mama's loose, wavy, honey-gold hair. A patch of her own cream silk skirt, brightened to white by the sunbeam. Mama's fat tummy with a baby inside. 'Tori, Tori, Tori,' Mama crooned. 'Oh my darling, little girl. Know your mama loves you so much more than all the world.' A foraying beam of light illuminated her eyes so they shone the same vivid green as the leaves of the hazels hemming the lawn.

'Mrs. Ward? … Ahem, umm, Mrs. Ward?'

Tori at last heard Mr. Matthews' attempts to gain her attention. 'Oh, please forgive me. I confess I was lost in my thoughts.'

'Why, you have absolutely no need to apologise, Mrs. Ward. As we have said, we are deeply honoured by the kindness of your visit.'

'We would not interrupt you, M'lady,' Mrs. Matthews joined, 'but a boy's run up from the village with a telegram what was sent to you at The Oak.'

'A telegram? For me?'

'Would you wish to read it, M'lady?' Mr. Matthews proffered a folded slip of paper.

Tori gathered her wits. 'I am much obliged.' She took the folded paper. The Matthewses watched eagle-eyed as she unfolded it and scanned its contents. 'My baby!' she wailed. 'My darling, little baby turned blue.' She stared at the paper as if it was a strange, malignant butterfly alighted between her fingers. 'The telegram is from my brother, Captain Blanckley… he is supervising my children during my absence.' She sought her tenant-hosts' eyes for confirmation that it was acceptable to leave tiny children in a brother's care. However, to her chagrin, they merely stared back, affirming nothing. Her panic exploded. 'My baby turned blue! She turned blue! It cannot be good for a baby to turn blue, can it?'

'Sweet Jesus!' Mrs. Matthews' gasp caused her blancmange-pink chins to wobble. 'A baby turning blue is very bad indeed!'

Tori spoke slowly, as if her mind was running through thick mud. 'I am sorry. I will have to… I mean, it is necessary… for me to return…'

Her fat tenant/hostess smiled. 'I understand, Mrs. Bl… Ward. You need to rush to your baby's side.'

Tori's eyes welled. 'If you will forgive me, Mrs. Matthews, I do. I'm very concerned for her.'

'I cannot, of course, speak for my good husband,' she glanced to Mr. Matthews.

Mr. Matthews patted her podgy hand. 'I believe my good wife may speak for me in this instance.'

'Thank you, Husband,' Mrs. Mathews' pink, gelatinous features wobbled into a multi-chinned smile. 'Mrs. Ward, I should like to say that I heartily sympathise with your need to hurry to your baby's deathbed.'

'Deathbed?' Tori shrieked. 'The telegram says she is recovered.'

'My humblest apologies, M'lady. Pray, forgive my clumsy hyperbole.'

Ignoring her obese tenant/hostess,Tori addressed Mr. Matthews as propriety dictated. 'With your leave, Sir, I wish to leave post-haste.'

'Of course, M'lady.' He rang the servants bell and barked, 'Hawkins!' when his dour, hatchet-faced maid arrived. 'Instruct Mrs. Ward's man to ready her carriage, then escort her to the front hall. Is her cloak warmed and dry?'

'Yes, Sir,' Hatchet-face bobbed.

Mr. Matthews returned his attention to Tori. 'Mrs. Ward, it really has been an unprecedented honour to have you visit us. Hasn't it, Mrs. Matthews?'

'We have been exceptionally overjoyed,' his wife simpered. 'Most exceptionally.'

'Oh Harry,' Tori clasped her new friend's old hands as soon as he rejoined her in Lutton's House's luridly-papered hallway. 'My brother sent a telegram to say my tiny baby turned blue. Can you imagine? I'm so worried for her! I must take the very next train.'

Harry's eyes oozed sympathy. 'What a fright fer yer, Miss Tori! I'll get yer to the station dreckly!'

'Oh Harry, you are my stalwart ally!'

'Wassat?'

'I am very grateful for your friendship, Harry.'

'In't nuffing, Miss Tori. You're one of us, in't yer?'

Harry's words struck a deep chord. The idea of being an

accepted local of South Brent thrilled her to the core. But then she remembered that her baby had turned blue and panicked. She had to get to her baby as soon as was humanly possible. She shouldn't have travelled to South Brent at all. It was remiss to be so far from her offspring. Emergencies like this could and did happen and she was so far away. She should have known Baby Alice was prone to illness. She'd always been delicate. The British climate wasn't good for babies. She should have stayed in India with William. But all that mattered now was that she got to her as soon as possible.

'I'll getcha ter the station dreckly, Miss Tori. Don't yer worry. Come along ter the stables with me. Yer can shelter from this dastardly rain while I readies me carriage.'

****

Harry drove his coach at break-neck speed down the steep, mud-slicked track from Lutton House to South Brent village. Tori gripped the doorframe with white knuckles. Thankfully, before long, the carriage drew to a halt and Harry banged on the rain splattered window. 'Next train's in 'alf hour, Miss Tori.'

'Oh Harry, you're such a good friend to me! Shall we adjourn to the waiting room?'

'Right yer is, Miss Tori, I'll get yer in ter the dry dreckly.' He held his dripping oilskin up to shelter her head.

The waiting room was sparsely populated and spartan with gloss painted benches and large windows for viewing trains. He guided her to an unoccupied bench. 'Let's sit yer down 'ere, Miss Tori.'

'Thank you, Harry. You'll sit with me?'

A besuited gentleman coughed and shot Harry a haughty

sneer. He shuffled uncomfortably. 'I dunno, Miss Tori, what with me being all wet. I'm making a puddle on the clean floor as it is, in't ee?'

'Sit, please,' she insisted. 'The floor's stone and the benches are painted. They'll all dry off with no damage done.' The haughty man coughed again, but Tori ignored him. She added, voice raised near to the volume of Aunt Henrietta's, 'You are my good friend, Harry.'

'But, Miss Tori, I've gotta go to The Oak fer yer luggage.'

'You said we have half-an-hour before my train is due?'

'Yes, Miss Tori, I looked at the station clock, see, and I knows the train times coz of cabbing 'ere.'

'Then pray sit for five minutes.'

When Harry lowered himself tentatively onto the bench, the haughty man coughed as if he'd swallowed a cupful of dust. 'What's it yer wants ter say, Miss Tori?'

Tori paused to frame her thoughts into words. 'I wish to talk to you about your daughter, Lucy.'

'I 'ope she din't offend yer, Miss Tori?'

'Not at all. She's a charming young lady.'

'Thank you, Miss Tori. We does our best to bring our chillern up proper.'

'I am hoping Lucy might consent to, umm, work for me.'

'Work fer yer, Miss Tori?' Harry gaped at her. 'Up in London town?'

'Umm, my wish is for Lucy is... to work for me as a correspondent.' Harry stared at her blankly. 'I mean, if she could use her schooling to write me letters?'

He brightened. 'She can do all 'er letters, Miss Tori. Proper clever she be.'

'I am in need of a person I trust to post me regular letters,' she elaborated, not quite sure she was going, but hoping to find a way to financially support skinny, little Lucy and Harry's whole family by default. 'I should want her to tell me of events concerning the village and, umm, Lutton House.'

Harry scratched his wet hair, and lowered his voice. 'Yer wants Lucy ter spy?'

'Oh no, no,' Tori said hastily. 'I merely wish for the services of a trustworthy person, who's familiar with South Brent, to send me regular letters about, umm, how people are… how the village is… that sort of thing.'

'Hmm,' he scratched his head again, and attempted to dry his hands on his jumper, only to find it wet too.

'It's just that South Brent is very dear to me.'

Harry brightened. 'And yer's dear ter us too, in't ee?'

She returned his smile, heartened. 'It would be a great service to me if your Lucy would write to me every month telling me of village news. I'd pay her, of course.'

'Yer'd pay my Lucy ter do that?'

'Yes. I trust her, and she can write, so I consider her the perfect candidate.'

'Wassat?'

'I would pay her five pounds per month is she would do this.'

'Five pounds?' Harry gawped, astonished. 'That's more than

what the shoddy mill pays!'

Tori smiled.

'If it'd 'elp yer if Lucy does letters for yer, then I don't mind at all, Miss Tori.'

'Oh, marvellous! But one thing, Harry.'

He slumped as if expecting a poisoned catch. 'Miss Tori?'

'Lucy must keep going to school. I'll need her to keep her energy for writing good letters to me, so she must not work in any mills, nor in any other place that would tire her mind.'

A slow smile crept horizontally across Harry's careworn face. 'I'm sure I can make 'im say yes to that, Miss Tori.'

Tori retrieved a writing pad and fountain pen from her bag, wrote a few lines, tore off the sheet, and passed it to Harry. 'This is my address in Pinner. Do you believe Lucy will accept my job offer?'

'I'll make sure ee does, Miss Tori.'

She rummaged again in her bag and retrieved a five pound note. 'This is her indenture stipend.'

He raised a hand to scratch his wet head, but thought better of it. 'Wassat?'

'Money to help her start working for me. She can use it to buy candles, paper and stamps: all she will need to send her first letter.'

His eyes widened. 'Do letters cost that much?'

'I suggest Lucy purchases the necessary materials and sets a little aside; then – as she will be a wage-earner – contributes the remainder towards housekeeping.' She thrust the five pound note at him.

Harry stared at it as if it were a summer butterfly flown out of the December squall. 'I gotta say, Miss Tori, that we weren't 'specting nuffin like this from yer.'

'If your Lucy agrees to work for me, her services will be worth every penny. Please take the money to pass to her, Harry.'

The haughty man cleared his throat as soon as Harry closed the door behind him en route to fetch her luggage. Rising awkwardly, he laboured his bulk across the waiting room to where Tori sat. 'Petherick,' he extended a presumptuous hand that was large and pink with shiny, manicured nails. It reminded her of a boiled lobster claw.

She smiled faintly. 'Mrs. Blanckley...I meant to say Mrs. Ward. Pleased to make your acquaintance.'

Mr. Petherick looked at her askance. 'Ward or Blanckley?'

'I was born Miss Blanckley, but became Mrs. Ward.' She winced as icy water from her sodden hood trickled down her cheeks.

'Mrs. Ward, are you well?' The haughty man was so close that she could hear the movement of fluid in his nasal passages. 'I feel obliged to caution you against fraternising with paupers. It's well known that they are slovenly, untrustworthy and ignoble.'

She bristled. 'Perhaps you're not familiar with the writing of Henry Mayhew?'

'The wishful thinking of a liberal fool,' he sniffed. His nostrils were cavernous and glistening. 'It is patently obvious that paupers lack the mental faculty for hard work and frugality.'

'My personal observations have been to the contrary, Sir.'

He carried on as if she hadn't spoken. 'I can in no way condone the prospect of a gentlelady employing the services of a pauper girl as her correspondent. The very thought!' His gurgling chuckle sprayed Tori's already wet face. Revolted, she retrieved a handkerchief to dab herself clean.

'Miss Tori!' A small figure burst into the waiting room, pale face swamped beneath a battered bonnet too large for either fashion or her. A sudden fit of coughing stopped her momentarily in her tracks. 'Miss Tori!' She repeated hoarsely once the fit had passed.

'Lucy,' Tori smiled. 'I am so glad you came.'

'Is it true what Jimmy Arscott said?'

An ear-splitting whistle announced the arrival of the Exeter train.

'Did he tell you I wish to employ you to be my correspondent for a wage of five pounds a month?'

Her jaw dropped. 'Five 'ole pounds? Ee din't say that!'

'It's a serious proposition.' She paused to allow Lucy to ask 'wassat?' But the twelve-year-old returned her gaze solemnly, understanding apparent.

'Yes, Miss Tori,' she said. 'I'll work proper 'ard, I promise I will.'

'Good. However, you must promise also to take no other work. I need you to apply full energy to your employment with me.'

'Of course, Miss Tori,' Lucy nodded vigorously, but began coughing again.

'Your cough sounds troublesome.'

'It's winter, Miss Tori. Lotsa folk gets coughs, in't it? I can still work proper ‘ard, though. Yer’ll see.’

The guard blew the final whistle. ‘I must board the train, but I shall await your first letter. Good bye!’

CHAPTER TWENTY-ONE

Susan had a sore head thanks to the sherry she'd impulsively drunk in the ladies' parlour. She hoped the bracing sea air would pick her up, and was walking gingerly along the road flanking the beach. The pavement was slippery wet, and a chill wind was buffeting relentlessly. She chided herself for wearing a silly, little fashion hat that did nothing to protect her head and, instead, required constant attention lest it fly off. A decently secured cloak hood, or full-sized bonnet, would have served her much better. The windows she passed were festively festooned with evergreen sprays and aglow with candles which cast a delightfully golden light onto the ground. The sun went down so early at this time of year and it was already nearly dusk, but it was surely not yet past three o'clock.

She had a sudden sense of being watched. Every shadow and blur of rain felt malignant. She drew her shawl close. Hadn't she felt watched here before? Had there been a man; someone tall and dark with mutton-chop whiskers?

A figure dashed in front of her as if conjured from the squall. 'Are you a guest of Miss Blanckley?'

Susan stopped in her tracks sensing no threat despite the fear she'd been feeling. The hissing voice had been female, though no features were discernible beneath its tightly hugged cloak. 'Who, pray, are you?' she inquired bravely.

The cloaked figure contracted. 'Please do not ask who I am,' it wailed, sounding truly afraid, 'I should not be here. I shouldn't!'

'What do you know of Miss Blanckley?' Susan asked instead.

'I... I know she is in danger,' the tremulous voice confessed, 'and her niece as well.'

Susan tensed. 'To which niece do you refer?'

The cloaked figure shrank back further. Cascading raindrops veiled the air between them, and bounced on the dark fabric of her hood. 'I do not know. I am sorry.' The stranger's whispered voice was hard to hear above the clamorous rain, 'But there's a man who seeks her suit tonight. His intentions are not to her good.'

'Are you referring to Lizzie?'

The figure flinched. 'I do not know. I heard no name, but Miss Blanckley's niece should be careful of suitors at the pantomime tonight.'

Susan's blood felt cold. How could this stranger know of their plans to go to the pantomime in Exmouth this evening?

'I must leave.' The cloaked figure turned in a wet swirl and scuttled down a side alley before Susan could reply. Dumbfounded, she stared at the dim, rain-obscured blankness into which the strange, cloaked figure had vanished.

The beach was scourged by a much fiercer wind than the one battering Budleigh Salterton's sheltered streets. Bullet hard rain bombarded Susan from all directions. She wondered why she'd been drawn here on such a dark, hostile night. What solace could she hope to find on the cold, black beach? Devoid of clear purpose, she felt drawn, nonetheless, to pick her way down the slick scree towards the wave-lashed border of land and sea. The crashing tide's noise was immersive. It travelled up through her feet, and in through her ears. Her thoughts were drowned, and she thought this is good thing. Her thoughts had been too often melancholy. She shivered. Did she dare? A savage gust wrenched her silly, small bonnet from her head and hurled it with careless whim onto the dark waves. She regarded it bobbing like a child's toy boat. Gone! It was a stupid thing anyway. What was the merit of a bonnet too small to protect one's head? But the icy gale had other thoughts and tugged her bound hair with cold fingers, and whipped her eyes until they smarted and wept. I am here, she thought, why I know not, but I am! Her spoken voice came as if of its own volition. 'I am Susan Moore!' she felt herself shout, though all sound was instantly ripped from her face by the wind. 'I am Susan, born Matcham, and I have lived in pain for nigh forty years since my good husband died, and then...'

A vision of Harriet flashed so strongly that Susan gasped and stepped backwards. 'My babies!' Harriet begged, her face was sweat-slicked and white. Her hair, dark with damp, hanging in snake-like tendrils. 'Please... protect my babies.'

Susan shuddered. Why had she recalled that awful scene? What seed had Henrietta planted in her mind? Unlooked-for mettle straightened her spine and raised up her chin. What did she fear? 'I am sorry!' she shouted at the thunder-loud sea. Henrietta, I do own, your suggestion was sound. It feels wholesome to shout these secrets free from my heart. But I hope no one heard me! She looked to her right towards the town, and was relieved to see the beach deserted, but then, looking left, she saw a little girl with a dog. Could it be Toriana?

****

Ethel half-lugged and half-chased Patch along the storm-ravaged beach. The little dog was alternately cowed by the storm, and excited to have the opportunity to run and explore. 'You're having a nice walk, see,' Ethel reminded him. 'Nellie didn't bother to take you out, but I did. I am a very good girl, aren't I Patch?' Cold rain clattered on her face and ran down under the collar of her pink dress. 'It's a bit rainy, I think,' she confided to the spaniel.

'Ethel?' Aunt Susan appeared as if from nowhere. Patch, yipped excitedly and bounded across the wet pebbles to sniff the black cloth of her belled skirt.

'Aunt Susan, why are you here?'

'Oh, I needed to clear my head. The sea wind's good for that! I thought you were Tori, I mean your mama, when I saw you first. You know, you look much as she did when she was your age.'

'I look like Papa too,' Ethel retorted, having regained her wits. 'Everyone says so.'

'Why, yes you do.' Susan peered down at her, smiling. 'You have his eyes, and something of his nose.'

'Not so big I hope, Aunt Susan?'

'Worry not, your nose is tiny compared to your papa's. But pray tell, Ethel, what are you doing out in the rain without a cloak?'

Ethel stopped smiling. 'It's not cold, Aunt Susan, and I only stepped out because I had to walk Patch.' The little dog yipped at the sound of his name, and Ethel's smile returned like sorbet on white linen. 'I am walking him, Aunt Susan, because Nellie was meant to do it, but she didn't.'

'Oh, I see. Well it is very good of you then to walk Patch yourself.'

'Thank you, Aunt Susan. I consider it important to do what is good.'

'Quite so, but it's cold and wet out here, so let's get back to The Rolle and see how Baby Alice
is.'

'I saw her before I left, Aunt Susan, and she was sleeping. Grandmama Horatia was too, but sitting up and with her eyes open!' She laughed.

'Horatia's asleep with her eyes open?' Susan sounded concerned. 'We must get back to her immediately!'

Ethel placed a hand dramatically over her heart. 'Why, Aunt Susan, I'm afraid I cannot return to the hotel, because Aunt Henrietta must be told about Baby Alice turning blue, and there is only Patch and me to tell her!'

'Ethel, you should not spend any more time in the rain!' But Susan's command was fruitless because Ethel had already darted away.

****

Ethel was in the hallway of No. 44 High Street five minutes later, wet as an otter, and with an equally wet spaniel at her side. 'Great-aunt Henrietta, I have come to inform you of grave news.'

'Well, gracious me, dear girl,' Henrietta boomed. 'Come right in and tell us all about it!'

'Thank you, Aunt Henrietta,' Ethel smiled. 'I am most sorry, but Patch and I are very wet. I fear my ringlets are no longer nicely sprung, and Patch likely smells of very wet dog.'

'Come in right away.' She pulled Ethel's soaked sleeve. 'You need to sit by the fire and warm up. Why, but your teeth are chattering! In with you now!'

A trail of water marked Ethel and the little dog's journey to the blazing hearth. 'Aunt Lizzie!' She smiled when she saw her aunt reclining on the settee.

'Niece,' Lizzie's sweet smile didn't reach her eyes. 'You look frightfully wet. As does your dog.'

'Oh, but Aunt Lizzie, I am most frightfully wetted indeed, but I felt duty-bound to come here to give you news.'

'News?' Henrietta's voice was, as usual, cacophonously loud.

'Oh yes, Aunt Henrietta,' Ethel regarded her with wide, earnest eyes. 'A very bad thing happened to Baby Alice, and I thought I should inform you of it because I am a very good girl.'

Henrietta jolted like a frog leg pinged by an electric charge. 'What bad thing?' She demanded.

'She turned blue,' Ethel supplied.

'Perhaps it was the light?' The hearth fire rendered Lizzie's own complexion as orange as her hair. She examined her fingernails and yawned.

'The doctor–' Ethel began.

Lizzie spoke over her. 'Your dog is creating a puddle on your great-aunt's Turkey rug. Aunt Henrietta, should the beast not be placed in the kitchen, or in some other servant's domain?'

'Baby Alice turned blue?' Henrietta queried. 'And a doctor came?'

'Yes, Aunt Henrietta...'

Lizzie buffed a nail. 'I wonder why an adult did not come to impart such momentous tidings?'

'They're all with Baby Alice, Aunt Lizzie.'

'They permitted a frail, little girl to rove the darkening, stormy village streets alone?'

'Umm, yes, Aunt Lizzie... I mean, no.'

'Yes or no, child? You cannot answer both. People might think you a fantasist.'

'What is a fantasist, Aunt Lizzie?'

'Niece, enough!' Henrietta subjected Lizzie to one of her fierce, steel-rimmed glares. 'Young Ethel has evidently brought serious tidings.'

'The only thing evident, Aunt, is that she has brought a damp dog to make a puddle on your Turkey rug.'

'Lizzie, enough I said. What is the matter with you this afternoon?'

Sneering, Lizzie pulled herself upright to stand facing both Henrietta and Ethel. Patch, not liking her look, cowered behind Ethel's wet skirt. 'She's obviously attention-seeking,' Lizzie proclaimed, fixing Ethel with her own, spectacle-free steely glare. 'I'd refuse to countenance it, Aunt.'

Henrietta surveyed them both with a frown. 'Is your story true, Ethel?'

'Oh, it is, Aunt Henrietta. It is a terrible thing indeed.'

She scrutinised Ethel's face for a long moment, then pronounced, 'You appear guileless. I believe you to be telling the truth. But what should I do?'

'Get that wet mutt out of your front parlour, I'd suggest,' Lizzie muttered.

'Patch is not a mutt,' Ethel retorted angrily. 'And another thing I wish to say, Aunt Lizzie, is that I used to think you wonderful, but now I don't. You are very mean.'

Her aunt shifted closer, silk skirt dragging on the Oriental rug. 'You, a six-year-old child–'

Ethel raised her chin. 'I am seven years old, Aunt Lizzie, for today is my birthday.'

Lizzie smiled grudgingly. 'Happy birthday.'

'Why thank you, Aunt Lizzie! I am, in truth, very excited that it is my birthday today and–'

'Yes, very nice, I'm sure.'

'...And I am so happy that you have wished me happy birthday, because I was alarmed to have maybe vexed you...'

'And so you did.'

Henrietta tutted. 'Lizzie, for goodness sake! Can't you be nice?'

'I'm sorry, Aunt, but her dragging a dripping mutt, uninvited, into a civilised parlour, and speaking when not spoken to, even if it is her birthday, is rude in the extreme.'

Ethel tilted her shoulders back to face her aunt squarely. 'Patch is not a mutt, he is a spaniel. Aunt Henrietta invited us in. I have only spoken when addressed... and it is you who is rude.'

Lizzie gasped. 'Did you hear her, Aunt? She called me rude!'

Henrietta laughed raucously and clapped her hands. 'And quite right too! You have been thoroughly rude to poor Ethel since the moment she entered my home. What has come over you, Lizzie?'

'I cannot believe you are defending her, Aunt! Are you saying you are happy to have her hound dripping on your parlour floor?'

'Enough!' Henrietta clapped her hands. 'Young Ethel, Lizzie is quite right in saying that you shouldn't talk back to your elders. Lizzie, you can wipe that self-satisfied smirk off your face. It is neither ladylike nor becoming. What is all this bickering during Christmastide, and on Ethel's birthday too?'

'I am merely–' Lizzie began.

Henrietta glared at her. 'Enough! Ethel dear, you came here, in the pouring rain, to tell us that Baby Alice turned blue?'

'Oh yes, Aunt Henrietta. This is what happened. The doctor came and said it is most serious indeed.'

'Hmm, I must go to The Rolle immediately. Squally weather and darkness be damned. Bradford!' the scrawny maid appeared, seamlessly prompt. 'Fetch my cloak and walking stick. I shall embark at once.'

Lizzie and Ethel, frozen out of voice and action by surprise, watched their diminutive aunt's rapid departure as if observing a monkey in the zoo. There she is being helped into her dark blue cloak by Bradford. There she is tying the ribbon of her sensibly large bonnet firmly under her chin. There is Bradford reaching to open the door. There is Aunt Henrietta striding out of sight towards the doorway. There disappears the last glimpse of her long, cherry-red skirt. There is the sound of Bradford pulling the front door closed. There goes Aunt Henrietta passing in front of the parlour window closest to the front door. Her bonnet is pulled tightly down. There she is passing the other parlour window, with her expression grim. There is rain water streaming down her cloak already, and she's only just set out... 'You can't say here,' Lizzie pronounced unexpectedly. ‘Especially not with that mutt.’

Ethel treated her to her most fiery and impertinent look. ‘Aunt Henrietta did not ask me to leave.’

‘Yet,’ Lizzie raised her long nose as if sniffing, ‘I did not hear her give leave for you to stay in her absence.’

‘Did she give you leave to stay, Aunt Lizzie? For I did not hear her say it.’

'Your wet mutt’s smell is disagreeable.’

‘Your every word is disagreeable, Aunt Lizzie, but I was not going to be unladylike and complain.’

Her aunt’s pale cheeks coloured. ‘How very rude you are, little girl. I shall inform your mother of your bad behaviour.’

Ethel, defeated but uncowed, swirled her wet, mid-calf-length skirt towards the parlour door. She called for Patch, then craned her bedraggled head backwards to cast her aunt one final look. Blue eyes defiant, she poked out her tongue.

****

A tall, stocky man with bushy, black sideburns was admiring himself in a full-length looking glass. ‘The honour is mine, fair lady,’ he mimed claiming a dainty hand to kiss. ‘Madam, may I say you are a vision to behold? Your eyes are like diamonds glistening in a tiara… no, your eyes are like twin stars reflected in a midnight pool.'

‘What are you wittering on about, Boy?’ his skeletally-thin patriarch snapped from a throne-like chair beside the hearth.

‘I am polishing my charm, Father. You do wish me to ensnare the heiress at the damned pantomime you’re insisting I attend tonight?'

'Language, Boy! Of course I want you to ensnare the wench there, but if you spout that drivel at her, she'll laugh you out of the house for a sap.'

The tall, stocky man stiffened, and suppressed a frown. 'How then would you have me act, Father?'

'Show her you're a man, Boy. Ladies like a manly man, don't they, Wife?'

'Yes, Husband,' a timid voice squeaked from the shadows behind his chair.

'Tell her you find her acceptable for courting. Make sure you convey that the honour is hers, not yours. Forget every jot of spineless, begging poetry. Play the big man, and spare her no quarter to back away.'

The man with bushy black sideburns frowned. 'But what should I do if she refuses?'

'Just remember that all women can be mastered by men because God put them on Earth for that sole purpose. All you have to do is remember that you are her master and her knees will go weak! Raise your eyebrows to show your disbelief if she dares to refuse you. Tell her that you forgive her womanly foolishness, then offer her a second chance, this time naming the date and time of your next meeting (which will be here in my house, where I shall approve her). Present her with your dead mother's ring,' the stocky man flinched, but his father was oblivious, 'and that's that. She'll find herself engaged to you, so unable to escape. The trick is to allow her no time for independent choice or thought. Heed my instructions, Boy, and you'll be married within months of her senile aunt's death.'

'Which could be years from now, Father.'

The old man cackled. 'We know otherwise though, don't we? That crone aunt of hers will be dead within a year, haha! The fortune the wench will inherit will be ours by the spring after next.'

'I'm still not sure which of the younger ladies visiting the Blanckley crone is the heiress-to-be.'

'Well, what on Earth have you been doing, Boy? I told you to study them to work out who the heiress is. Are you an idiot as well as useless?'

The younger man winced. 'Father, I have done my level best to find out. As you know, I made sure to acquaint myself with both wenches in chapel during the Christmas morning service. And I've continued to watch the crone's house from The Feathers, and her guests at The Rolle–'

'Don't beat around the bush, Boy. Have you learnt anything of use?'

'Yes I have, Father. You might be pleased to know that one of the wenches – in fact, I must say, the prettier of the two – has departed, leaving the other with a man and a clutch of small girls.'

'So you've deduced the prettier wench is your game?'

He grinned. 'This I have.'

His skeletally thin father switched from genial to fierce in the blink of an eye. 'Boy, heed my words, pretty or ugly, your task is to marry the wench who inherits.'

The man with bushy, black sideburns lowered his gaze. 'Yes, Father, of course. It would merely increase my fortune if the heiress proves comely.'

'And child-bearing,' the old man leered. 'I want grandsons from the deal.'

'What if she is not of child bearing age?'

'Then the priority is money. Tell me, does the wench who departed look fertile?'

He stroked his cheek-hair thoughtfully. 'Tis hard to say, Father, but she looked to be before middle age. I'd wager my money on her ability to whelp.'

'Her money, Boy!' the old man cackled. 'Wife, my shoulders ache, give them a rub.' His young bride stepped out of the shadows to wordlessly comply.

CHAPTER TWENTY-TWO

Emma, yellow-skinned and piteously bloated, was unconscious again. Reeking of sour wine and snoring loudly, she had collapsed like a broken puppet spreadeagled on the alcove bed in their dingy Calais apartment.

Don't wake up, Horatia silently begged. I can't bear for us to argue more… but don't die. Please don't die. Just be well again, and calm of mind.

Tori's relief on reaching Exeter station died swiftly in the face of the ticket clerk's obtuseness. 'As I have told you, I am not seeking to change my existing ticket to Exmouth, but to purchase a new one for an earlier train.'

The clerk, a lacklustre fellow of uncertain age, returned her gaze with undisguised boredom. 'Yer can't change yer ticket, Ma'am.'

'I do not wish to change my ticket. As I've already explained.'

'Yer said yer's got a ticket already.'

'Yes,' she admitted, biting back bile, 'but I no longer wish to use it.'

The clerk scratched his head. 'Whatcha plan ter do with it, Ma'am?'

She pushed her shoulders back to draw herself taller. 'I plan to do absolutely nothing with it. Sir.'

'Yer wanna do nuffin with a valid train ticket, and first-class to boot?'

'You are correct.'

He rifled through a book of perforated tickets. 'New one'll cost you 12d, Ma'am.'

****

The final stage of the journey was mercifully smooth, but dragged nonetheless because Tori's heart yearned to be with her baby, and immediately so. When the cab from Exmouth at last halted outside the Rolle, she sped to it heedless of decorum, with her green, belled skirt flopping left and right like hammered dough.

'Mama!' An extremely wet pair of Ethel and Patch hurled themselves at her legs. 'Mama, I missed you so very, very much! And it's my birthday!'

'Happy birthday, dear. I am sorry I was away until now. Have you had a lovely day?' When she ruffled Ethel's hair, her hand came away sopping wet. 'What are you doing outside in the rain with no cloak and bonnet?'

'Oh, Mama, it has been most dreadful! I went to tell Aunt Henrietta that Baby Alice turned blue. She will already be here. Then Aunt Lizzie said I couldn't stay by the fire, and made Patch and me go back out in the rain! She is a monster!'

Tori sighed. Who knew what Ethel may have said to provoke Lizzie. She tugged Ethel's wet hand. 'Let's get you inside and have Kajri dress you in something dry. I must see Baby Alice immediately.'

****

Horace, who'd been pacing the first floor hall, chain-smoking cigars, drew to an abrupt halt when first Patch, then his sister dragging a wet-haired Ethel, charged out of the stairwell. He assembled the sort of smile he imagined a confident and diligent niece-minder would have. 'Sister, I am glad indeed to see you arrived. You received my telegram?'

Tori scarce acknowledged him, and beelined for the nursery suite door. 'My baby!' She grabbed the doorframe as leverage against the inertia of her wet, hooped skirt. She spied Kajri with a bundle clasped to her bright-sari-ed breast. 'Baby Alice,' she whispered (for it did not do to wake sleeping babes). 'Kajri? Is my baby well?'

The ayah regarded her with flat eyes. 'Doctor come. Say she just needing rest. Not in danger right now. Big danger before. She turned blue.'

'Did the doctor say why she turned blue?'

'He say you can ask at hotel desk. They send him. His name's Dr. Lowe.'

'But did he say what was wrong with her?'

The ayah straightened a gold-edged fold of her sari, but said nothing.

'Kajri!'

'Weak heart, Mrs. Ward. Baby's got to stay calm. Always calm. Heart not strong.'

Tori collapsed bonelessly on the carpet. Susan, who had been sitting quietly in a corner with Henrietta and the girls, gasped and rushed to her adopted daughter's side. 'Tori,' she whispered, gently patting her white cheek, but Tori lay as still as a corpse. Patch, still damp, licked her face, but Susan pushed him back. 'She needs the doctor now herself,' she whispered to the room at large. 'He must be fetched at once.'

Nellie stepped forward. 'I can go. I fetched him before. I know what to do.' She purposefully avoided Ethel's eyes, wishing to signal neither battle nor reproach. Ethel merely shivered and stared at the Baby Alice-shaped bundle in Kajri's arms.

'You are a veritable saint,' Susan told Nellie. 'Please do go and fetch the doctor as quick as he can come.' She returned her attention to her unconscious adopted daughter. 'Perhaps I should place a pillow under her head?'

'Please don't worry for me!' Tori struggled upright. 'I'm perfectly fine.'

Henrietta noticed Ethel's half-frozen state. 'Child, you are soaked through. Why did you not stay warming by my hearth?'

Instantly animated, Ethel flung herself onto her great-aunt, who, being only slightly taller than the seven-year-old, was engulfed in icy cold, sopping wet fabric, hair and skin. 'Aunt Lizzie said I had to leave!'

Tori cupped her head in her hands. 'I just wish everyone had harmonious relations. Ethel, you must stop talking back to people.' The seven-year-old opened her mouth to argue, but Tori held up a hand. 'I mean what I say, Ethel. You always have an argument, no matter what's been said, and this is a very poor habit. Little girls should be seen and not heard.'

Ethel changed the subject. 'Look, Grandmama Horatia's asleep again with her eyes open!'

Susan gasped. 'Golly, but I didn't notice her sitting there in the corner! She doesn't look right at all!'

'Oh dear!' Henrietta boomed. 'She seems to have gone into one of her blank states again.' She patted her old friend's cheek. 'Ratia?'

Emma, illuminated by the early evening sun, smiled radiantly. 'Horatia, my darling, but you are doing so very well! You are walking all by yourself, and so far! Good Lord Nelson will be so proud when I tell him; and I am proud too! God bless you, my darling! Come here and give me a hug!' She held her arms wide, encouraging her to toddle further, but caught her as soon as she stumbled, and drew her in close. 'Oh, you are such a clever, and very good girl!'

****

Horace ceased his pacing in the corridor outside the nursery suite. How could he have forgotten that the pantomime was this evening? He consulted his pocket watch. They were due to leave in less than an hour. He wondered if everyone would still attend after the todo of that baby turning green, yellow or blue, or whichever colour it had been. It would be a frightful shame for their pantomime trip to be called off because of such a small thing. Theatre was vital for the wellbeing of the soul. Too few people these days were privy to this fact. He scratched his ginger-haired head so hard that he drew blood above his left ear. They had to all go! He'd gone to such pains to procure the tickets. What a tragedy it would be if they forewent the opportunity simply because an infant briefly changed colour, and despite the fact that it had now turned pink again! He opened the nursery suite door with an excited flourish and declared, 'We must ready ourselves for the pantomime!' But not one person smiled. Not even the children. 'Pantomime!' he repeated as if to a bunch of lunatic asylum patients. 'We are due to leave in less than an hour. Chop chop! Get a move on!'

He was greeted by silence again, until his sister spoke, 'What are you thinking, Brother? My baby nearly died and now your aunt, Horatia, is in a bad way.'

'I'd prefer you not to speak about me as if I'm not here!' Horatia's unexpected outburst made Horace jump. 'It's not I who gallivanted off to South Brent leaving these poor little girls motherless!'

Hs sister knelt before her mother-in-law and clasped her gnarled hands. 'Mother, I am sorry. It was remiss of me to leave my girls, and poor Baby Alice!'

'It's my birthday today too!' Ethel plucky, little reminded her.

'Yes, yes, Ethel, happy birthday.'

'I should like to go to the pantomime, please, Mama.'

'Why don't you take her,' Horatia suggested to Tori. 'After all, you have a preference for being absent.'

Tori burst into tears and Susan said, 'There, there sweetums. Your mother-in-law didn't mean it. Did you, Horatia? We're all overwrought.'

'Well whose coming to the pantomime?' Horace demanded.

'My goodness, Nephew!' Susan snapped at him. 'There are frankly more serious concerns right now than a silly pantomime, which I recall none of us wanted to attend to begin with.'

Henrietta arched her eyebrows at her normally demure friend's sudden vitriol. 'Gracious me, but tempers are hot this evening!'

'I am thoroughly affronted,' Horace grumbled. 'I've offered you free tickets to a spectacular pantomime in Exeter's new, state-of-the art Theatre Royal, yet you seem to prefer the idea of staying in this cramped little suite!'

'Enough. Everyone!' Henrietta clapped her hands as if to a class of unruly Sunday school children. 'Tis past five o clock. Bradford will have our supper ready. Susan, Ratia, we'll take a coach to my house…'

Horatia held up a hand. 'If you don't object, Rietta, I'd prefer to walk alone.'

'What's got into you, Ratia? What's got into everyone, in fact? No, Ratia, I will not permit you to walk alone to my house. It's already night outside and there's a horrendous storm blowing in from the English channel.'

'It's not your place to give me permission, Rietta,' Horatia snapped. 'I'm perfectly capable of navigating wet and windy streets in the dark.'

Henrietta snorted. 'Perhaps you might find a tiny semblance of camaraderie in your stubborn old heart and consent to sharing a cab with Susan and me?' When Horatia didn't argue, Henrietta boomed out the remainder of her plan, 'The same cab can bring my niece back here because she, at least, certainly needs to attend the pantomime. I have not seen such a grumpy bones as Lizzie was to poor Ethel earlier!' Tori looked puzzled and Ethel tried not to smile. Henrietta continued in her brisk, Sunday school teacher voice, 'And I shall return here after supper in time to join your transport to the pantomime.'

Susan cocked her head and peered at Henrietta quizzically. 'You wish to attend it?'

'Why on Earth not? We could all do with a little light-hearted merriment in our lives. There's plenty enough gloom to contend with, and I don't just mean the infernal weather out there! I detest these early mid-winter sundowns! But my feelings aside, I can't imagine dear Toriana wishing to attend the pantomime, so someone's going to need to help Horace with the children.'

Tori flicked Henrietta a weak smile, and Horace said, 'Bravo!'

'Are we still going then?' Ethel asked hopefully.

'Of course you are, children,' Henrietta's tone brooked no argument.

Carrie looked up. 'Kajri will help Uncle Horace, Aunt Henrietta.'

Henrietta nodded towards the ayah, who'd fallen asleep on a single bed propped against the wall with Baby Alice gently snoring against her red sari-ed breast. 'I think the young Indian lady has had quite enough exertion for today.'

'Thank you, Aunt,' Tori murmured. 'I'll also need her for Baby Alice's feeds.'

'Good.' Henrietta brushed her hands as if ridding them of the last motes of uncertainty. 'Come along Ratia, Susan, my dears, we'll find that cab!'

Nellie clutched Tori's wrist. 'May I stay with you, Mama, please?'

Henrietta stopped in her tracks, brows raised behind the blue steel frames of her spectacles. 'You don't fancy the pantomime, Nellie?'

'I'm dreadfully sorry, Aunt Henrietta, and please excuse me, but I should prefer to remain here with Mama.'

****

The monotonous tick-tock, tick-tock of Henrietta's parlour

clock had caused the elderly cousins to nod off after a warm, wholesome supper.

'Promise!' Lady Hamilton said right in Horatia's ear. She cried out in fright.

Susan blinked. 'Are you well, Cousin?'

'It's that wretched wind rattling everything. It's making me jump at shadows.'

Horatia woke in the alcove bed in the little Calais apartment. Cold dawn illuminated the room in chill shades of grey. The fire was long dead and the room was bitterly cold. The blanket had fallen from her mother's shoulder, so she pulled it up, but when her hand touched Emma's skin it felt colder than ice. She leapt off the bed.

Susan mumbled, perhaps in response to a noise Horatia had made, and the fire crackled in the iron grate, but Horatia's mind inhabited a time fifty-eight years past.

She was staring helplessly at her mother's corpse. 'She's dead,' she told the air between them. 'They can't get her now.'

But her mind shied from the thought of her mother being dead. I surely must be mistaken, she thought. We've been through so much together, Mother. You have been so strong. You were always tenacious. So vital. How can you be dead? It cannot be possible. Oh, please move. Please be alive. Oh Mother, oh Mother, oh Mother. The single thought was sluggish, but unremitting.

There was a sudden hammering on the apartment door. 'Ouvrez la porte!'

Something was grabbing her hands. Horatia struggled to free herself. 'Get off me!'

'Gangplank's yonder,' the sailor pointed to his left. Horatia, already well-aware of the route the departing passengers were

taking, shuffled towards them in her ill-fitting, wood-soled shoes. She was careful to descend the gangplank in the close proximity of tall adults so as not to stand out lest one of her mother's debtors spotted her. When she made footfall on the wet flagstones of Dover harbour, she was dismayed to behold a vast, milling crowd. Where was her uncle? Then she saw him, darling Uncle Matcham stamping from foot to foot to keep warm with his wool jacket buttoned tight. Joy broke through the black clouds in her heart. 'Uncle Matcham!' She heard herself cry, as her legs ran towards him of their own volition and her arms reached out. 'Uncle Matcham!'

He scanned the crowd again, but seemed confused.

'Uncle!' Half-laughing, half-crying, she waved her arms manically as her wood-soled shoes battered the cobbles. 'Uncle Matcham, tis I!'

Recognition at last dawned on his beloved, craggy face. 'Horatia? Is that you dressed as a boy?'

She buried herself in the sweet sanctuary of his damp, woollen jacket.

'Darling Horatia,' his warmth enfolded her. 'I am so joyed you've reached me. Know that you are as mine own daughter. Mrs. Matcham wishes this too. Your most eminent father begged me to vow to protect you, just as he begged me to bar our sons from the military! But I'd protect you without that oath. You shall want for nothing. You are the same to us as our own children. Come, let's get you to the coach, then home to Ashfold Lodge!'

Someone was pulling at her. Their flesh felt enticingly warm and wholesome. She clasped their hands back.

'My poor child!' Uncle Matcham fussed as the carriage jolted towards Ashfold Lodge. 'I cannot imagine how very vile your time was with that despicable woman!'

Horatia suppressed the urge to tell her uncle to go to Hell for defaming Emma, but she remembered the promise her mother had coerced her to make.

The thing tugging at her hands was hostile. Horatia clawed at it, trying to pull it off. 'Get off me. Let me go! You Matchams didn't care about Lady Hamilton!'

'Horatia, what are you saying? You're hurting me!'

'Cousin Susan?' Horatia's vision swam back into focus. 'Is it you holding my hands?'

'Thank goodness you're looking at me now, Horatia dear! You've been staring through me as if I were a ghost. You've scared me half to death!'

They were standing in the rainy dark of Budleigh Salterton's high street. 'Why are we out here?' Horatia asked, entirely nonplused.

'You scared me,' Susan said again. 'We were dosing in Henrietta's parlour when you suddenly stood up and started shouting and waving your arms around as if someone was attacking you! With Henrietta being away at the pantomime in Exeter, I didn't think it right to tell her maid about your... umm, sleepwalking, I mean, we wouldn't want servants to gossip...'

'What do you mean "sleepwalking"?' Horatia demanded.

'Well, as I said, you stood up and started arguing with someone who wasn't there, and you didn't respond at all when I spoke to you. In fact, when I took your hands to try to calm you, you reacted as if I was attacking you and... well you said something unkind about my family! I didn't know what to do for the best.'

'I feel so embarrassed,' Horatia gritted her teeth for the shame.

'You've absolutely no need to.'

'Poppycock! From what you've told me, I behaved like a lunatic, and was cruel to you too!'

'No, not at all. We're all fraught at the moment. Didn't I say so earlier?'

'What is not lunatic about sleep-fighting imaginary adversaries? No, please don't assure me otherwise. This is something I've been concerned about for a long time. I've done my best to hide it. God knows, I haven't wanted my sons, and their sons, to be tainted with my lunacy, but despite my best efforts my madness is indisputable. Oh, Cousin, I thank you for your compassion, but the fact that I'm standing here with you now in the dead of night in the pouring rain, and with no recollection of how I got here, tells me that I really am a lunatic and that I can't hide it anymore.'

'This is not true at all!' Susan said with feeling. 'You have always been a paradigm of sense and sanity. So what if you sleepwalked tonight? I'm sure that everyone, including the greatest and best of us, sleepwalk from time to time. Doing so doesn't make them lunatic, and it doesn't make you so either!'

'Susan, dear cousin, my mind has been off it's bearings for far longer than this one evening. I am mortified to admit to it, but I've been slipping into the past for months. I thought I was cured when we first came here because my memory attacks stopped. I was so happy and relieved, and naively believed I'd cured myself of lunacy. But I was wrong. If anything, the power of my memory attacks has increased. This is the first time I've sleepwalked and talked during an attack, but... oh dear, perhaps I sleepwalked during earlier memory fits and no one told me! I'm so ashamed and scared.'

Susan hugged her. 'Oh Horatia, my dearest cousin, I'm so sorry you've suffered all this in silence. You should have known I'd never judge you! Come now, we should return to Henrietta's warm hearth before talking more!'

Emma was miraculously young again. Skin pale as porcelain. Her beautiful face was framed by lustrous auburn locks bedecked with orange blossoms. Her smile was indomitable as a summer breeze.

'Mother!' Horatia cried, overjoyed.

'Remember.'

'Horatia?' Susan, illuminated by the lanterns on the kissing bough, took Horatia's elbow and steered her gently, but firmly, towards Henrietta's house. Horatia pulled free and darted into the middle of the deserted thoroughfare. Her sodden dress clung to her frame like a lumpen, black shroud down which tendrils of her hair hung like white snakes. 'I'm useless! Useless! A failure all round!'

'Hush, Cousin!'

'Leave me be.'

'But people will hear–'

'Then leave me, Susan. There's no need for you to be tarred with the brush of my lunacy.'

'Horatia, please. You are not lunatic–'

'Susan, listen to me. There's no longer any point in my trying to maintain any air of sanity! Look at me standing here on the high street at night, in the pouring rain and shouting as if I'm a tavern drunkard! Jesus only knows what this exposure to the elements will do to your health. I am a burden and liability. I beg you, Susan, return to Henrietta's warm hearth. You can do nothing for me. My mind's broken. Save yourself.'

Susan made a more determined grab for Horatia's hands, and refused to let go. 'I will not leave you out here in the freezing rain. No matter how lunatic you think yourself. You're just distraught. You need to come with me back to Henrietta's house and change into dry clothes. You'll catch your death–'

Horatia laughed again. 'Oh, I think I caught that long ago!'

'What would Henrietta say?'

Horatia's expression turned hard and cold. 'Oh yes, I came here following Rietta's whim, but what happened? My daughter-in-law selfishly jaunted off to South Brent to dredge up past events which would have been better left buried. All those fine words Rietta spouted about connecting with the past and shouting it to the sea turned out to be dross. Connecting with the past is a recipe for insanity. There, I said it. Tori's trip to South Brent has made my sanity worse, not better.'

Emma was there again. Older now. More careworn. The orange blossoms in her hair had browned edges. Her skin was yellow and her figure had run to fat. 'Horatia darlin'! I've been waiting so long to see you.'

'You're drunk again, Mother.'

'Hah, and you are always one to disapprove.'

'I hate you being drunk.'

'Child mine, you are witness to the spite the once-admiring world now spews upon my very name.'

'How does being drunk aid this?'

'It allows me to escape. Within my mind, at least.'

'Cousin?'

Horatia, embarrassed to have been seen during an episode of lunacy, attempted to redirect Susan's focus. 'You suggested returning to the warmth of Henrietta's hearth. I think this a capital idea.'

'No.' Susan's negation thoroughly surprised her. 'I want to know if you blame Tori for your, umm, distraught state of mind.'

'You mean my lunacy? Yes, I do blame her. And Henrietta too. Their nostalgic fixation on the past has tipped me over the edge.'

When Horatia pulled Susan closer, she noticed that she was shivering violently. Her chattering teeth made her pronunciation clumsy. 'Horatia, you should know that I followed Henrietta's advice and shouted at the sea to purge my own secrets, and I've felt jolly well better for doing it.'

Horatia was momentarily dumbstruck. Susan was the last person she'd have expected to confess her secrets, even to the sea. She declined to query precisely how much she'd admitted.

'You should speak with Tori,' Susan advised.

'I'm sure she'd prefer not to see me,' Horatia said wryly. 'I was very rude to her when we last met.'

'So you must apologise. No, don't look at me like that! You've admitted you were rude, so you jolly well need to make things right for both of your sakes.'

'Horatia!' Emma pronounced her name – "hooray shah!" – with a skip and a beat so it sounded like an invocation of freedom. She was draped in white muslin with leaf-green trim, perching artfully on a bench beneath a trellised rose arch. Her sandalled foot rested on the seat.

'Mother, is it really you? It has been so long.'

'I know, darling.' Emma swung her foot to make space for Horatia to sit beside her.

CHAPTER TWENTY-THREE

Exeter's Queen Street station was chockablock with pantomime goers. 'I do so love the hustle and bustle of people at leisure,' Henrietta boomed approvingly.

Horace was less relaxed. 'Let's sally to the forecourt to hail a cab.' He strode briskly into the crowd without pausing to see if his party was following. They weren't.

Lizzie squinted at his departing back. 'How does he expect us to keep up?'

'I dare say he hasn't considered it at all,' Henrietta chuckled. 'Horace!' her bellow caused thirty heads to turn, but not his. Glimpses of his scarlet jacket could be discerned bobbing through the melee at breakneck speed. 'Stop that marine!' she commanded, causing more heads to turn. 'Him in the red jacket,' she pointed her umbrella. 'He is needed by his family, which is us.'

No one responded. The steam-train they'd departed emitted an ear-splitting screech. Then a man's voice cried, 'Stop the marine!' Suddenly, the platform rang out with calls for the marine to stop at once. Unfortunately, their combined effort had no effect on Horace, whose scarlet sleeve could be glimpsed ascending the steps to the street-level exit.

Henrietta frowned at his disappearing jacket. 'Fiddlesticks! We'll just have to hope he's waiting for us outside. He does, after all, hold the theatre tickets.'

'The man is an ignoramus,' Lizzie said tartly. 'If he didn't have the tickets, I'd be inclined to leave him for lost.'

'For good or ill, Lizzie, needs must we find your errant cousin. Come along children, we're off to find Uncle Horace and the pantomime!'

'Panty-mime!' Evie squealed happily.

Henrietta was blossoming in her role of affectionate family leader. 'Evie, Ada, take my hands. Carrie, you walk ahead with Aunt Lizzie and see if you can spot Uncle Horace in the crowd.'

****

Horace, panting heavily, had braced himself against a quieter section of the station's street-level facade. Behind him, the massing crowd jostled to hire Hackney cabs. Their combined noise was tumultuous. He fixed his gaze on the station's planked facade.

An eager-eyed urchin tugged his sleeve. 'Shine yer shoes, Sir?'

'No! Leave me be.'

'I can do 'em for fer tuppence, Sir!'

'Scarper!' The shoeshine boy fled, but then someone shouted his name and his hands balled reflexively into fists.

'What are you doing here? We couldn't find you!'

He realised Aunt Henrietta was standing in front of him with Cousin Lizzie, Ethel, and his three smaller nieces. 'The crowd…' he began, but didn't want to admit to the unmanly urge that had caused him to flee. 'I had a bit of a turn. Nothing serious. I just needed air. Let's get to the theatre!'

Henrietta regarded him keenly. 'You had a turn?'

'As I said, Aunt, it was not of import. Where are the cabs?'

'Yonder.' Lizzie flicked a hand lackadaisically at the thickest part of the throng. 'There appear to be far more customers than carriages.'

'Mayhap we could walk?' Henrietta suggested. 'The rain has ceased and, as I recall, the Theatre Royal is a short step from here.'

Horace brightened. 'Aunt, you are a treasure! Bedford Circus is only half a mile away, and all on the flat.'

'I'm tired!' Evie complained.

'Oddy is too,' Carrie indicated her two-year-old sister.

Horace regarded his smaller nieces. They looked wan and fragile in the December night's dark. 'I shall carry you both!' he declared, happy to have a chance to impress them.

'You can't carry both of them!' Carrie exclaimed. 'They are very heavy.'

'Uncle Horace can do it,' Ethel told her. 'He's a captain of the Royal Marines.'

Horace gave Ethel a wink and a salute, and scooped the tiny girls up, one in each arm. Evie giggled and Ada pulled at his ginger moustache.

'Good show!' Henrietta approved. 'You are a strong man indeed.'

He grinned broadly. 'Who wants to go to the pantomime?' His nieces squealed their assent, and with this they set off.

As the crowd converged towards the theatre's grand entrance, the increasing crush of bodies made Horace panic again, but his enthusiasm for the theatre was enough – just – to keep him on an even keel. He glanced back and saw Aunt Henrietta and Lizzie close on his heel with the third-smallest niece in tow. He felt rather than saw someone looking at him from further back. He caught a glimpse of a tall, pale-faced man in a top hat with bushy black sideburns. Then a laughing woman carrying a tiny tot blocked his view. Horace frowned, feeling sure he'd seen the man with bushy sideburns somewhere before.

****

The women's dressing room held more bodies than air, and the scant air that remained was hot and heavy with cheap cologne, stale sweat and tobacco smoke. Amanda Verlander, star-in-the-making – or so she liked to believe – pressed against the plank wall with her smouldering, silver-tipped pipe as two witches bustled past en route to the stage door. Her waif-like friend was sitting on a pile of costumes. 'I 'as ter go on in a minute,' Amanda told her.

'Yeah, good luck. Thanks for letting me stay 'ere, in't it?'

The gaslight lent Amanda's scarlet lipstick the appearance of dark claret. Her pallor was concealed by coffee-coloured grease paint, and her eyes and brows were smeared with thick, black kohl. 'Will I pass for a foreign princess, do yer think?'

Joan studied her bitten fingernails boredly. 'Yer've asked me that about fifty times, in't it?'

****

A flustered usher began leading Horace to the front row on the gallery's left. 'I need no directions!' Horace snapped. 'This way,' he instructed his party, happy to have regained control.

'Ladies before gentleman,' Lizzie muttered as Horace bounded ahead.

Little Evie and Ada were alarmed by the precipitous drop to the stalls, but Carrie coaxed them onwards. When all were seated, Horace sat back to admire the surroundings. The brightly lit auditorium was rapidly filling. The chaos was increased by a legion of hawkers blocking the part-filled rows and thrusting baskets of edibles at the incoming audience. Horace, pleased to be above the mayhem of the stalls, sat back in his luxuriously cushioned dress circle seat and closed his eyes. Ah, theatre, he thought, I adore you, but your hustle and bustle can sore vex my head!

Ethel stood to better survey the auditorium. Rows of chattering children were fussed over by mothers resplendent in soft-hued, off-the-shoulder dresses and high-knotted hair, but the menfolk outdid them with their higher top hats. 'Everyone's dressed very nicely, Uncle Horace.'

'Tis a place to be seen and admired, but those gentlemen should remove their hats. Otherwise, people will struggle to see the show.'

'It's very bright in here!' Henrietta's booming voice caused a score of well-coiffed heads to turn. 'What is it with those drab fittings high up on the ceiling? What happened to the glamour of chandeliers?'

Horace smiled, enjoying the opportunity to show off more knowledge. 'They were deemed obstructive, Aunt.'

'Like top hats, Uncle Horace?'

'Exactly, Ethel! Good girl!'

Henrietta frowned up at the plain light fittings. 'Chandeliers were deemed obstructive, were they? I can't say I care for these… what do you call them?'

'Sunburners, Aunt.'

'Hmph, well they do cast about as much light as the sun. It feels hot enough under them to burn too. How is one expected to focus on the stage with all this glare?'

'They dim them when the performance starts, Aunt.'

'What a novel idea! Well, they better had, or we'll see nothing but fellow theatregoers.'

'Look, Uncle Horace, the curtain's lifting up!'

Bright joy exploded within Horace as the sunburners dimmed. 'The show's about to start!'

'Oh, this really is fun,' Henrietta declared. 'The scenery and costumes are a veritable feast for the eyes. They transport me straight back to my childhood in Algiers when I used to listen, transfixed, to our janissary, Siddi Hussein, recounting his fabulous tales!'

'I knew you'd enjoy it, Aunt,' Horace beamed. 'Girls, are you enjoying the show?'

'It's very marvellous, Uncle Horace,' Nellie told him politely.

****

An exotically garbed woman sprinted the corridor from the subterranean dressing rooms to the steps up to the stage door. Tinkling bells attached to loose anklets offset the rapid tattoo of her feet on the wooden boards. Multiple black shadows lurched beneath her and behind, ever changing as she passed from one wall-mounted lamp to the next. A tall man with bushy black sideburns stepped suddenly into her path. 'Amanda?'

She flinched, but, intent as she was on reaching her destination post-haste, spared him not even a sideways glance. 'I'm in an 'urry!'

He grabbed her velvet-clad arm. 'Tis I, Francis.'

She slowed her pace so they might speak. 'I gotta go on stage.'

'Our father sent me to see to your well-being.'

'Well-being?' she snorted. 'You know what the only "well-being" is ee cares about?'

'His purse.'

Surprise registered in her kohl-rimmed eyes. 'Yer knows 'im true then.'

'He's my father. Of course I do.'

'Ow do yer put up with actually living with 'im?'

'I don't.'

'Come to me dressing room after this act so I can speak ter yer proper.' She sped away.

****

'Why has the curtain come down, Uncle Horace?'

'They are changing the scenery, Ethel. I can promise you that the curtain will soon lift again to reveal a brand-new scene.'

'What will it be?'

He studied his program. 'Aha, it will be the Pashah's palace where Sindbad will meet, and fall in love with, a dark-skinned princess.'

'I like princesses. I hope she will be beautiful.'

'As do I,' he concurred.

****

Amanda was waiting at the stage door with Wet John, the prompter. She felt thrills of adrenaline whenever the audience laughed and clapped. She knew the last laugh had followed a joke about knocking over three old women. She was due on soon. Her hand twitched for her pipe, but she'd left it on her dressing table. Something was prodding her bottom.

'Yer looks gorgeous,' Wet John leered.

'Yer touching my be'ind?'

He lunged his face onto hers. His breath was rank with old beer and decay. She pulled back, but his greasy fingers pawed her breasts undeterred. 'Yer know yer wants it. Yer actresses is all the–'

Her ankle bells jingled prettily as she smashed her foot into his groin. She smoothed her auburn locks back under her tiara, then kicked his collapsed, writhing body with her pointy-toed slipper. 'Don't yer dare do that again. Ever.'

The felled prompter whimpered, 'I'm… I'm sorry, Amanda.'

****

'Uncle Horace, look! The curtain's coming up again!'

'Prepare yourself for a spectacle!'

Ethel leant across her uncle's lap. 'Carrie, look the curtain's lifting. There'll be a really pretty new scene. Tell Evie and Oddy to watch.'

The orchestra switched from the jolly, ambient refrain to a peppy faux-oriental ditty which drew widespread applause and calls of 'Where's Sindbad?' and, 'Get on with it!'

'What fun!' Henrietta chirped. 'Look, Ada! Can you see the bottom of gold pillars?'

'Look, look!' Ethel was so excited that she was nearly screaming, 'There's actual jewels on the pillars. Look, Uncle Horace, there's people wearing colourful dresses!'

The risen curtains revealed a magnificent be-turbaned man with curled black moustaches and a fawning entourage. A fanfare blasted from the orchestra pit as a liveried man bounded front of stage to jubilantly declare, 'the pashah is returned to the Palace of Bungaboo!'

The be-turbaned man stepped forward in a twirl of scarlet and gold. 'I am back, returned from Dover! The journey was long, and I'm glad it's over!'

The audience tittered, but Lizzie did not. 'Are you enjoying the performance?' Henrietta boomed at her. 'You look a little strained.'

'I'm just a little warm, Aunt.'

'It is damnably hot in here, I agree. Has the heat of those sunburner lamps detracted from your enjoyment of the show?'

'Oh no, Aunt. The show's most spectacular, is it not?'

****

'All the world's a stage!' Emma tilted her head with expert grace so her pale skin and auburn curls formed a pretty tableau against the multicoloured roses pinned to the arch.

Horatia narrowed her eyes. Roses do not bear multi-hued blooms. I'm dreaming.

Emma raised herself up, supple as spilt cream. 'Of course I am real, darling.' She spread her milk-white arms wide in an inviting embrace. 'Impossible-seeming things may still come to pass.'

'Mother, look at you. You are, what? Thirty years of age?'

A wrought silver hand-mirror appeared in Emma's hand. She scrutinised her reflection for a moment, then turned her full, brightly smiling attention back to Horatia. 'You know, darling, I think you're right. I look thirty years of age, more or less.'

'Mother, I was not born until you were thirty-five.'

She shrugged. 'Perhaps then I am five-and-thirty, and have aged well?'

'I am not a newborn babe.'

She prodded her cheek affectionately. 'No, my love, you look to have about thirty years.'

'So this cannot be real, can it, Mother? We cannot, as mother and daughter, be of the same age.'

****

Amanda felt an electric surge bolt through her the next time the audience laughed. This was her cue. Sparing Wet John not a glance, she strutted over his whimpering body into the limelight. Robson, playing the Pashah, declaimed:

My Angelina, dearest child of charms,
Come to your royal father's royal arms,
My daughter's thinner then when I last seen her,
But still an angel, though an angel leaner.

Lizzie shifted awkwardly more upright, and leant across Ada to lightly touch Henrietta's arm. 'Needs must I visit the powder room.'

Henrietta spluttered in surprise. 'Pardon me? Oh, Lizzie dear, yes, of course. In fact, I also have a need to powder my nose.' Her booming voice caused multiple frowning heads to turn their way again. 'Ada dear, we're going to the powder room.'

The two-year-old clambered eagerly down from her seat. 'Go!'

'I need to go too,' Evie piped from Henrietta's other side.

'And I,' Carrie declared.

'Well, well, it seems we're to have quite an expedition! Ethel dear, we're going to powder our noses. Would you like to join us?'

Ethel glanced up, briefly, 'Oh no, Aunt Henrietta. I am far too interested in the pantomime to wish to powder my nose.'

Henrietta bounded through the auditorium's exit and down the red carpeted stairs ahead of Lizzie and the little girls. 'The ladies' powder room is just along here. No, Evie, not that way!'

****

Horace watched Amanda Verlander prancing daintily around the stage in her tin tiara and pointy-toed slippers. Her stage presence was magnificent, and she truly was beautiful. Glancing left and right, he saw that his companions were absent, bar Ethel who was as transfixed by the actress's performance as he was. He decided to take the opportunity to slip backstage alone.

****

A tall man with distinctive black sideburns nearly collided with Lizzie when she exited the powder room. 'I do beg your pardon, Mrs...' he began.

She smoothed her skirt self-consciously. 'I confess you gave me something of a fright, Sir.'

'I say, are you the young lady I saw at chapel in Budleigh Salterton on Christmas morn?'

She glanced at him shyly. 'Why, I do recall you. You were in the pew behind my party.'

He moved in closer. 'What a coincidence to run into you here. Please allow me to introduce myself: Francis Thomas Cooke Esquire of Withycombe House.' He treated her to a warm, white-toothed smile.

'Miss Broughton.' Lizzie curtseyed to hide the collapse of her knees.

****

Ethel was alarmed to realise that all of her party had vanished. Where had they all gone? Were they angry with her? But she had been a very good girl, and it was her birthday too. Perhaps there'd been an emergency? Was she supposed to be with them? Panicked, she bolted for the nearest exit.

****

Tori startled awake when Aunt Susan and Horatia tumbled

into the nursery suite drenched, shivering and excited.

'I hope we didn't wake you?' Aunt Susan's attempt at whispering was loud and breathless. Thankfully, neither Nellie nor Baby Alice woke, the latter lying in the equally somnolent ayah's arms. Susan plonked herself beside Tori on a single bed that had been requisitioned as a couch. 'I'm so sorry that we woke you.'

Horatia remained standing. 'Your aunt commanded me here to apologise to you, Daughter.'

'Oh,' said Tori, surprised.

'You were needlessly rude to her, weren't you, Horatia?' Susan prompted.

Horatia touched Tori's hand tentatively. 'I have been... well, your aunt's convinced me of a hard truth or two, and I wish to retract...'

Susan pressed Horatia's hand more firmly onto Tori's. 'Your mother-in-law is trying to apologise for her extreme rudeness to you earlier.'

'You were not rude in the slightest, Mother.'

Horatia cleared her throat. 'What your aunt says is true. I judged you ill for visiting South Brent. This was wrong of me.'

Tears beaded in Tori's eyes. 'It was I who was wrong, Mother. God forgive me, but Baby Alice nearly died in my absence. I was selfish and negligent.'

'You were not remiss, and you didn't abandon your children,' Susan said firmly.

Horatia, at last galvanised, hugged Tori close. 'The doctor said your poor, dear baby's heart was already weak. Baby Alice's attack wasn't caused by your absence, dear.'

'But I should have been with her!'

'Tori, dear, how was your visit to South Brent? Did you reconnect with your past?' Horatia now sounded tentative.

'Oh, Mother, it was wonderful! I felt restored there. I mean in the whole village. I felt as a thirsty wanderer must feel coming upon an oasis in a desert...' she cast Horatia a worried look, 'please do not feel my love for you, or William, or our girls has ever been anything but complete.'

'I do not doubt your love for William and your girls. Yet I just don't understand how any good can come from digging into old wounds.'

Tori paused to think. 'Perhaps, if you'll forgive an indelicate metaphor, some old wounds need lancing to release, ahem, poison.'

Horatia blinked. 'You think there's poison in me?'

'Oh, Mother, I cannot judge, but this is what it felt like for me. I'm probably making little sense. It's hard to explain, but when I visited my childhood home in South Brent, it felt like I'd let go of a burden of darkness I'd not even known I'd been carrying... Mother?'

Horatia's eyes had rolled up and her mouth had gone slack.

'What's happened to her, Aunt Susan?' Tori whispered.

'I confess it's a worry,' Susan admitted. 'Horatia's been... well, she's been going through something of an ordeal.'

'Why has she suddenly frozen? She's still sitting up. It's not a faint. Her eyes have gone white. Should we call the doctor?'

Emma's smiling face bobbed up. 'Darling, you absolutely need to know how immensely proud I am of you. I am grateful that you have kept your promise for all these long years.'

Horatia scowled. 'You demanded too much!'

'Sorry darling, I don't understand.'

'You obliged me, with forcible insistence, to promise many hard things.'

Emma studied her hands for a moment, puzzled, then met Horatia's eyes boldly. 'So I did, and so I praise you even more!'

Horatia bridled. 'You forgot?'

'Of course I did not, darling, I–'

'Do you have any idea how hard it has been for me to keep all the promises you required of me?' Horatia, angry at her mother's forgetfulness, averted her eyes to stare at the bench. Her heart caught. Could it really be? She ran her fingers lightly over the planks, and leaned closer to examine the joinery. It was the bench her darling Philip made during their first year at Tenterden! She felt his presence and looked up smiling. There he stood, young and handsome in his black Vicar's robe.

Philip smiled warmly. 'How could I ever forget you?'

'Or I you? Oh, Philip!' She rose effortlessly on young limbs and collapsed into the bliss of his unforgotten embrace. 'I have missed you so much.' His comforting weight was exactly as she recalled. The sharp angle of his shoulder blades beneath the heavy fabric of his robe. The clean scent of his skin. The soft curls of his hair. 'Oh my love, but how can you be real?'

Philip stroked Horatia's unlined cheek tenderly. 'Your heart should be whole, darling.'

Emma appeared beside Philip. 'I second that. Your heart, most certainly, should be whole.'

'Oh, Mother, please wake up!'

Tori's voice dragged Horatia's attention back into the improvised nursery. She was mortified that both Tori and Susan were watching her with concern. 'I apologise for drifting off,' she told them in as light a voice as she could muster.

'Oh, Mother!' Tori's exclamation caused Nellie to stir on the bed beside her. She lowered her voice. 'I'm truly happy that you're back with us.'

Embarrassment caused Horatia to snap. 'I didn't go anywhere.'

Susan snorted. 'Enough of your smoke screens, Cousin. You admitted that you've been reliving past memories willy-nilly. And you also promised you'd stop being rude to poor Tori.'

'I didn't mean to be. I apologise if I was.'

Tori touched her hands. 'Don't worry on my account, Mother.'

'I do though. I worry that I've been rude to you. I worry that I've failed as a grandmother. And I worry that I've lost control of my own mind!'

'Golly, poor you!' Susan gushed.

Horatia ignored Susan's pity and addressed Tori, 'Did you truly feel a sense of liberation when you visited your childhood home?'

'I did. Oh, Mother, it was wonderful. This may sound silly, but I felt my dear mother's presence with me there, right beside me, and she was full of love. I'd always worried she was angry with me.'

Susan was puzzled. 'Why on Earth would Harriet have been angry with you?'

'Oh, I don't know. It was my muddled girlhood fantasy that I'd caused Mama's death by making her fall down the hill at View Cottage, but when I went there, I remembered that it was in Raleigh House, not there, that poor Mama passed away.'

Susan dabbed at a tear, and Horatia said, 'It was a terrible tragedy.'

'My poor Mama suffered dreadfully, I fear, and it pains me to dwell on it, but all that black worry I'd been carrying around floated up and out of my heart. I feel so much lighter! I'm reminded of the Spiritualist belief that our lost loved ones wish to speak to us if we can but hear them.'

Horatia looked small and frail. 'If my lost loved ones have been trying to tell me something, I've failed to understand a single word!'

CHAPTER TWENTY-FOUR

Henrietta stopped in her tracks. 'Where is everyone?'

Carrie, quick to pick up on her great-aunt's alarm, studied the empty seats. 'Where is Aunt Lizzie?'

'Fiddlesticks!' Henrietta exclaimed. 'We appear to have lost nearly half our party. The adults are of less concern, but the whereabouts of young Ethel is of highest import. Carrie, when did you see your sister last?'

The five-year-old looked blank.

'Ethel,' Henrietta prompted. 'When did you last see Ethel, Carrie?'

'Ethel gone.'

'Yes gone, and a big worry that is.' The old woman turned back towards the exit, then thought better of it. 'Oh, double fiddlesticks and an oboe bow, but I can't go and look for her without leaving you little ones unattended.'

****

Horace inhaled the heady aroma of female sweat and... could that really be the smell of pipe smoke in a ladies' dressing room? Well, he'd be blowed, but there was a pipe on the dressing table! Bravo though, there was no one here. He could make himself comfortable to await the shimmering starlet's return. Easing himself into Amanda Verlander's chair, he didn't notice a waist-height pair of eyes watching him through the crack between the door and its jamb.

****

The man with the bushy black sideburns pulled back. 'I really do apologise, Miss Broughton. I have been holding your attention without thought.'

They'd been standing outside the powder room since he'd introduced himself as a fellow attendee of the Christmas service in Budleigh Salterton's chapel of ease. Lizzie, who was enjoying the attention of this tall, dark stranger, had no desire for him to withdraw. 'Mr. Cooke,' she simpered, 'I could call you many things, but thoughtless is not one.'

'You flatter me!'

'I meant not to, Sir. Though I confess I'm happy to have made the acquaintance of a gentleman such as...' she trailed off, self-conscious that her impulsive words may have caused her to appear forward.

'Why my dear Miss Broughton, your kindness humbles me.'

The warmth of his body was palpable through the silk of her bodice. She realised she was trembling. 'Oh, Mr. Cooke, I am feeling quite out of sorts.'

He inched closer. 'I swear that I meant not to startle you.'

****

Ethel started at the sound of approaching footsteps. A furtive glance revealed a man-sized shadow encroaching along the subterranean corridor. Panicked, she pressed herself closer to the splintery door jamb. The corridor comprised wooden walls without niches or obstacles behind which to hide. Stamp stamp stamp. Whoever was coming would spy her very soon. Looking back into the gaslit dressing room she noticed firstly that Uncle Horace was still engrossed with his own reflection and, secondly, that a mass of robes was hanging against the far wall. Ethel dived into it, but was surprised to hear a female voice exclaim, 'Ouch!'

To Ethel's surprise, there was a skinny, blonde woman already crouching behind the hanging costumes. The skinny woman acknowledged her, very briefly, and fixed her eyes in the direction of Uncle Horace, who could just be glimpsed through the hanging robes. Ethel froze too. Uncle Horace might well be annoyed if he knew she was there. Thankfully, he appeared not to have noticed her arrival. Ethel, relaxing, turned to the skinny blonde beside her. 'Who are you?'

The skinny woman hissed, 'Hush!'

'I'm Ethel Mary Ward,' she whispered back, 'and that man's my uncle. If you don't tell me who you are, I'll make a hullabaloo.'

The skinny woman flinched. 'I'm Joan, but please 'ush.'

****

The whole cast assembled on the stage to smile and bow. The audience cheered and clapped happily, while the sunburner lights lived up to their name by increasing their heat to a near-intolerable degree. A well-dressed man strode to the fore and pronounced, 'The interval will extend for half an hour, after which we shall be entertained by the comic shenanigans of a full harlequinade with Harlequin, Clown, Pantaloon and Columbine!' He paused to allow the audience to *oo* and *aah* appreciatively. 'Refreshments are being served for your convenience in our grand foyer. Please be reminded that this is a temperate theatre, so no alcoholic beverages are available for purchase, nor permitted to be consumed herein.'

Henrietta regarded her three young charges. 'Who fancies coming with me to look for Ethel?'

'I'm tired,' Evie whined.

'Well, you're all coming with me anyway.'

****

Ethel and Joan were startled by a thunderous crash which continued to grow. Uncle Horace, as far as Ethel could see, remained oblivious, polishing his brass buttons with a costume scarf, whilst whistling 'a life on the ocean wave'.

'It's the interval, in't ee?' Joan whispered.

Ethel returned her attention to her mysterious co-hidee. Her dirty cotton dress was loose on her thin frame, which seemed to mainly comprise elbows and knees. Her lank hair was of the palest blonde, and her hollow face was paler still. From this, big, dark eyes darted furtively between her and Uncle Horace. Ethel was determined to wheedle more information out of her. 'Do you know my uncle?'

She contracted like a bony spider. 'Yeah, but keep an 'ush on!'

****

Amanda Verlander kicked weasel-faced Wet John in the face as she swept through the stage door. Her beautiful, heart-shaped face sparkled with sweat. Costume diamonds twinkled in her mane of hair, and crimson silk trailed in her wake.

'She moves fast, that 'un,' Felix Pitt (aka Captain Hunkey Dorum) commented to Eddie Robson, who was hastily pulling off his pashah cloak.

'She's after smoking 'er bleeding pipe, like as not,' Eddie rejoined. 'Blimey, but it's 'ot on that bloody stage!'

****

Francis Cooke had drawn Lizzie against the wall to protect her from the stampeding exodus. 'It seems the interval has begun.'

'Oh dear,' Lizzie used her sweetest, most feminine voice. 'It may be a challenge for me to find my family.' Handsome Mr. Cooke appeared to be considering his reply when the throng pushed noisily onto them, with more than one elbow, knee and skirt knocking Lizzie in the process. She pressed herself further back against the wall, hampered by her belled skirt and unmentionable woman's malaise. Mr. Cooke opened his shapely mouth to say something, but was cut off by a booming voice.

'Lizzie dear!' Aunt Henrietta was battling through the contrary-thrusting crowd, wig bright as an orange beacon. She had tight holds on Evie and Ada's hands, and Carrie was clutching her jacket as if for dear life. 'How fortuitous to find you amidst this mayhem!' Noticing Mr. Cooke, she scrutinised him through her steel spectacle frames and said, 'I see you have found a gentleman.'

Lizzie was mortified to have been discovered unchaperoned. 'I, ah, this is Mr. Cooke. I ran into him upon vacating the powder room. He recognised me from chapel.'

He affected an unctuous smile. 'You must be the famous Miss Henrietta Blanckley. If I may?' He watched Henrietta's hand expectantly.

Henrietta cocked her head to better survey the tall stranger. 'Gallant are you, Mr. Cooke?'

'I believe gentlemen should respect their elders.'

She proffered a gnarled hand, but flinched when his lips brushed her skin. 'And youngers, I hope, Mr. Cooke?'

'I beg your pardon, Miss Blanckley?'

'I enquired as to whether you respect youngers as well as elders.' She indicated Lizzie.

'Why, of course, Miss Blanckley.' He treated them to a dazzling smile. Lizzie blushed.

'Very good. Well, I am sorry to bear bad tidings, but my great-niece Ethel has vanished.'

'How dreadful!' Lizzie sounded more irritated than sincere.

Francis Cooke, however, was a picture of concern. 'You have lost a great-niece? How worrisome! I, of course, offer my services in seeking it.'

'My thanks. Perhaps it would be prudent for us to search in different areas? I shall keep the children with me.'

'I could ask the usher if he's seen her,' Lizzie suggested.

'I shall accompany you…' Francis began, but Henrietta was

having none of it.

'It would not do for my niece to spend any further time unchaperoned. Lizzie, why don't you take Carrie with you?'

'May I be a chappy-rone, please?' The five-year-old asked eagerly.

Mr. Cooke's smile was slick. 'Being chaperoned by you, young miss, would be my absolute pleasure.'

'Ladies, gentlemen and children!' The chief usher was standing in the foyer with his feet planted firmly apart to brace himself against the crowd. 'Tonight's very spectacular harlequinade is commencing in fifteen minutes!'

****

Amanda's hellbent rush to reclaim her silver-tipped pipe came to an abrupt halt. There was a ginger-haired marine lounging in *her* chair and peering into *her* dressing mirror by the light of *her* gas lamp. 'What the flip are you doing in me dressing room?' Sparks all but flew from her tongue.

'Princess Angelina, I have been awaiting you. May I just say–'

She smacked him hard on the mouth. 'Get out me flipping dressing room. Now!'

A gaggle of costumed dancers picked the moment to appear at the door. 'Miss Verlander–' one began.

'And yer can all flip off as well! Good, there's me pipe!'

'But we need to get changed for the harlequinade–'

'Well, grab yer bloody clothes and change somewhere else.'

'Yes, Miss Verlander.' The chorus girls darted to a clothes

heap in the far corner and hastily grabbed an assortment of garments before fleeing.

Amanda glared at Horace. 'I told yer to flip off.'

He clasped his scarlet-jacketed heart. 'How can I leave when faced with one as fair as thee?'

'Yer can leave by walking out the bloody door, in't it?'

****

'Where on Earth can Ethel have got to?' Henrietta boomed musingly to her two infant charges. 'Aha, I spy the usher. Let's ask him if he's seen her.'

The usher, however, raised his megaphone before Henrietta had a chance to speak to him. 'Ladies, gentlemen and children! Tonight's extravanganzious harlequinade will commence in ten minutes!'

****

Carrie was increasingly alarmed by the narrow, dark corridors through which Aunt Lizzie and the tall stranger were leading her. She gasped when an angry cry sounded from a part-open door further up the corridor.

'Wait here,' the tall man told them importantly.

'Isn't he gallant?' Aunt Lizzie sighed as he strode towards the commotion.

****

Ethel was alarmed when the door opened to reveal a tall man

with bushy, black sideburns. The look he shot Uncle Horace was one of sheer rage. She cried out unthinkingly, 'He's behind you!' The skinny blonde hiding beside her clamped a bony hand over her mouth. Thankfully, however, no one had heard Ethel because the actress had shrieked 'Francis!' at the exact same moment of Ethel's warning to her uncle.

'Francis,' Amanda repeated. 'I 'ate ter say it, but I'm proper 'appy ter see yer. This man's refusing to shift.'

'Is this so?' The man with sideburn's surveyed Uncle Horace with a look of thunderous contempt. 'My sister wishes you to leave. As do I. Get out.'

If Uncle Horace was nonplussed, he didn't show it. 'Miss Verlander, I didn't introduce myself. I am Captain Horatio Charles Nelson Blanckley of the Royal Marines. I have theatre contacts which may be of use to you.'

Amanda clicked her tongue, but the dressing room door flew open again and a sandy-haired lad poked his head in. 'Five minute call!'

'Piss off!' Amanda snapped.

****

Little Evie and Ada, overwhelmed by the sights of their impromptu theatre tour, toddled mutely behind their diminutive, orange-wigged great-aunt as she led them through the dark maze below the stage. 'The usher told us Ethel went this way, or, at least that a little girl matching her description went thither,' Henrietta boomed jollily.

'Where Effel?' Evie asked.

'The truth is that I have absolutely no idea where your big

sister is. If your mama knew this, I dare say she'd serve me very cross words!'

****

Aunt Lizzie was oozing worry. 'Mr. Cooke has been a long time in that room. Do you think we should see how he is?'

Carrie had scant idea of what was going on. She felt simultaneously intimidated by the shouting from the room, and eager to please her glamorous aunt. She decided her best recourse was to be helpful, and that her aunt clearly wished to visit the scary room. 'Go room.'

'As this is what you wish, Niece.' Aunt Lizzie marched up the corridor and pushed the door open. Carrie followed, clinging fearfully to the lilac silk of her aunt's bustled skirt. Princess Angelina was standing, arms akimbo, facing two men. Carrie instantly recognised Uncle Horace. The other was Mr. Cooke, the stranger she'd been tasked to chaperone.

'I warned you to leave,' the stranger told Uncle Horace icily.

Princess Angelina noticed Aunt Lizzie. 'Who the flip are you?'

Aunt Lizzie stuttered. 'You are unseemingly rude, Madam.'

Princess Angelina's black-rimmed eyes flashed, but Mr. Cooke stepped forwards. 'Miss Broughton, what a surprise to see you in my sister's dressing room.'

'Your sister?'

'Hah!' Princess Angelina exhaled an extremely big cloud of smoke. 'Yer expected a gentlelady?'

Mr. Cooke smiled. 'Sister, allow me to introduce you to *Miss Broughton*.'

Princess Angelina lowered her hackles an inch. 'Nice ter meet yer, I suppose.'

'And this,' he told Aunt Lizzie grandly, 'is my half-sister, Miss Verlander.'

Uncle Horace looked surprised. 'You are the lovely actress's half-brother?'

A muffled thunder of clapping sounded from the auditorium above.

The grown-ups' chit chat had become boring, and Carrie's attention wandered. She spotted a rail of colourful clothes on the far side of the little room. 'Pretty!' she squealed, and dived at it. She grabbed a crimson, velvet robe, but the booming voice of her great aunt stilled her.

'Aha, look, Evie, Ada, we have stumbled upon the star of the show! And – how surprising! – your aunt, Mr. Cooke, Carrie and, gracious me, your uncle too!'

Uncle Horace dipped his head politely. 'Aunt Henrietta! I confess equal surprise at seeing you.'

'Oo's this blinking crone in the orange wig?' Princess Angelina snapped. 'What's with all you people coming in me dressing room uninvited?'

Uncle Horace flashed a big smile again. 'You'll be pleased to know I'm here with employment prospects for you. I have connections in Plymouth–'

'Don't want 'em.'

'But–'

Princess Angelina shook her auburn curls. 'No flipping buts. I've 'ad plenty of men like you try it on. They all think I'm easy coz I'm an actress.'

Suddenly, a woman in a voluminous orange and blue scarf shot from the clothing rail, crying, 'I was asleep, boyos!' in a peculiar accent, before fleeing the room.

Aunt Henrietta chirped, 'Well that was unexpected!'

****

'I am dead!' Emma's dramatic collapse onto the sandstone paving stirred a mass of fallen petals to dance as if reborn.

'For goodness sake, Mother.' Horatia tutted. 'You've been dead nigh on sixty years. Why are you making a drama of it now?'

Emma smiled up from her orange blossom pillow. 'It's about what's in your heart, darling.'

'Mother, I really cannot see how you think throwing yourself onto the floor like a dying swan will have any impact on my heart. I grieved you as a thirteen-year-old girl. What, pray, do you wish of me now? To grieve you afresh?' She prodded her with her satin slipper. 'Well I have, rest assured, never ceased grieving you, so your latest bout of histrionics is a waste of effort.'

Emma brightened. 'You acknowledge your grief for me?'

'Well...' she shifted uncomfortably, 'of course not... I mean, you made me promise not to.'

'You forsook me even within your own secret heart?'

Horatia studied her feet. 'I...'

'Tell me, child.'

'I'm not a child.'

'Look at yourself. At your hands.'

Horatia beheld her slim, unblemished hands and flung them up and out in a gesture of frustrated dismissal. 'Tis but a fantasy within my mind. As are you. I'm tired. I don't want to go over this. Be gone!'

Emma remained stubbornly solid-looking. 'I'm going nowhere until you face the truth.'

'What truth? The truth that the whole world despises you as a cheap, grasping harlot who lured noble Lord Nelson from his good wife's side?'

'Yes, that truth,' tears dewed Emma's eyes. 'The oath I pressed on you was to never defend me nor own me as your mother, for I knew the world would shun you and your descendants if you owned my "bad blood".'

'But keeping that secret has nearly torn me apart.'

Her mother touched Horatia's face with a sad, gentle hand. 'I know, my darling, but it's kept your children safe.'

'I've understood!' Horatia's loud outburst caused Nellie to mumble in her sleep, but Tori didn't notice for the surprise of her mother-in-law snapping out of her trance of her own volition.

Aunt Susan sounded as surprised as Tori felt. 'What do you understand, Cousin?'

Horatia stood taller than she'd done for decades. 'I now know what my remedy is, and I'm going straight out to get it.'

Horatia picked her way down the steep pebbles. The yellow beam of the oil lantern she carried swung crazily with each step. When she reached the frothing shoreline, she balanced the lantern on the pebbles so it lit the incoming foam in a bright lattice of gold.

The exalting smile that formed as her face muscles relaxed was lost in the dark, and witnessed by none. She finally felt stronger than the relentless cruel slights against Lady Hamilton sneered by family, newspapers, servants, and every corner. It felt as if a monumentally heavy bulk of icy weight had calved from her heart. Far greater than the sloughing she'd felt during Christmas mass. It was overwhelming. She stumbled giddily backwards and tripped on the pebbles to land ignominiously on her backside, gasping like a beached fish. *Oh my goodness, but I feel alive! I feel good. Why am I crying?* She wiped her eyes with her sleeve. *Oh Mother, I turned my soul inside out attempting to fulfil a promise you never asked!* She scrambled back onto her feet and squared her shoulders at the dark waves. 'I love you Mother, and I always have. I detested every hateful word said of you. I love you. I love you!'

CHAPTER TWENTY-FIVE

When Horatia woke at dawn the next day, her heart felt as light as thistledown in a flawless summer sky. Her consciousness coalesced with lazy ease. Her body, too, was eased of pain. Her slowly waking mind was puzzled that she felt so good, but then she remembered her epiphany and shouting it at the sea, just as dear Rietta had prescribed. She chuckled and it felt good. She realised she no longer cared if anyone heard her expressing her true feelings. That someone, in this instance, would be Cousin Susan snoring in the bed beside hers. *My dear cousin was a stalwart ally during my histrionics of last night. Goodness, but I was behaving like a mad woman!* Horatia propped herself up against the goose down pillows. *I'd feared for so long being seen as a mad woman, but Susan saw me thus last night and accepted it without judgement or condemnation. In fact, it was because I behaved thus that I found my way to salvation!*

A shuffle of bedding and a delicate cough preceded Cousin Susan's bleary enquiry. 'Are you awake, Horatia dear?'

'I am,' said she, 'and, before you ask, I feel marvellous. Thank you sincerely for your patient aid last night.'

Susan sat up with her quilt wrapped around her to ward off the cold. 'Think nothing of it, Cousin. I'm just glad, very glad, you feel marvellous. I can't say my head feels the same way, but that's my own fault for imbibing port yesterday, and my headache is a trifle, and I'm babbling. Forgive me.'

'There's nothing to forgive, Susan dear! Your garrulous warmth is cheering.'

'Golly, well, that's good to know! I say, though, we must have slept long to wake with the mid-winter dawn. I suspect it's past eight o clock.'

Horatia slid out of the bed and onto her feet as if her joints had never known arthritis. 'We should get to the Rolle post-haste.'

'Why rush? It's frightfully cold out there. I'd prefer to wait for Bradford to bring tea and light the fire.'

'Both Horace and Lizzie are leaving this morning. I don't wish to miss bidding them farewell.'

'Drat,' said Susan, 'And those marines are sticklers for early starts!'

****

Ethel was with her mother and sisters at their usual table near the gigantic Christmas tree in The Rolle's dining hall. The tree's candles, already lit despite the early hour, cast merry, twinkling reflections on the silver tinsel and multi-hued glass baubles. Her mama smiled broadly when she caught sight of Horatia and Aunt Susan approaching. 'Mother, Aunt, I'm joyed to see you both here in time for breakfast! Will you join us?'

'Good morning, everyone,' Horatia replied merrily as Susan rushed to hug first Tori, then Ethel and her sisters. 'Have Horace and Lizzie already left?'

'Oh no, Aunt Susan,' said Ethel with a forkful of kidneys on toast halfway to her mouth, 'they've not yet joined us. They are very lazy indeed.'

'Ethel Mary Ward, remember your manners!' Her mama's admonishment, however, sounded half-hearted, and mama's attention quickly returned to Grandmama Horatia and Aunt Susan. 'There are spare chairs aplenty. Please take seats, if you wish to join our repast.'

To Ethel's delight, the old ladies alighted between her and Kajri, who had Baby Alice balanced on her green sari-ed lap. Grandmama Horatia leant back comfortably against the upholstered panel on the back of her chair. She sighed happily and addressed Ethel's mama, 'Daughter, I wish you to know that I hold you in the highest esteem. I was remiss to have criticised you. Your boldness in visiting South Brent, and alone, was commendable. No, please don't argue! I regret each and every of the cross things I said to you...'

Ethel's interest was piqued, 'Did you say cross things to Mama, Grandmama Horatia?'

Her mama looked panicked and said, 'Umm...' but Grandmama Horatia had no such compunction about answering the seven-year-old's direct question. 'I confess I did say cross words to your mama, and I apologise for having done so. I judged your mama harshly for the simple reason that I didn't want to believe any good could come from revisiting the past.'

'But Mama went to a place called South Brent, not to the past, Grandmama. Tis not possible to visit the past because it disappears with every time the clock ticks.'

'Golly,' said Susan. 'What a profound thing to say!'

'Thank you, Aunt Susan,' said Ethel, very pleased at the praise.

'Profound, yes,' Horatia agreed, 'but not, I think, wholly true. The past, you see, lives on inside us. It remains lodged in our memories and in the ways we've learnt to see the world.'

'Like those fossils people find with the shapes of animals and plants from ages and ages ago, Grandmama?'

'Profound again, Ethel, yes. I believe the past stays inside us just as the shapes of animals remain in rocks as fossils.'

'But fossils aren't really animals, are they, Grandmama? They're just the shape of them. So, the past isn't really still there in our memories either. It's just the shape of what happened to us.'

Grandmama Horatia smiled broadly. 'Oh Ethel, you are perfectly correct that our memories only hold impressions from our past. You are a treasure indeed.'

'Thank you, Grandmama... but why would it be good, or bad, to visit fossils of our past?'

'Well, you see sometimes these fossils we're carrying around with us are heavy and weigh us down a lot so we're not happy.'

'But that's silly,' Ethel objected. 'Why don't people just drop their fossil memories if they're too heavy to carry?'

'Good question. I think it's because they believe they're too important to lose... or maybe they can't forget them, even if they want to, so those fossil memories of theirs keep coming back into their minds and making them sad. This is why I believed your dear mama was wrong to remind herself of sad memories by visiting South Brent.' Horatia shot Tori a warm, apologetic smile. 'It transpired, however, that the reverse happened, and going there made her heavy memories float away.'

'God's bones!' Uncle Horace was thundering into the dining hall brandishing a sheet of paper. 'Sister, this is for you. A telegram, would you believe it? The wretched bellboy foisted it on me before I made it into here. I'm not a messenger boy. God, but I need a coffee! Where's the damned waiter?'

'Good morning, Uncle Horace.' Ethel's chirpy greeting caused Nellie to twitch. Her annoying older sister being of firm mind that little girls should be seen and not heard.

As it happened, their uncle was too engrossed in his hangover to have heard Ethel anyway. 'Where is that goddamned waiter? I need at least a pint of coffee immediately.'

Mama succeeded in gaining his attention by standing up and grabbing his scarlet sleeve. 'You have a telegram for me?'

'What? Yes! Damned bellboy thrust it at me.' Uncle Horace waved the folded paper vaguely towards Ethel's mama, who took it with a quiet thank you and returned to her seat. All eyes watched expectantly, but she laid it neatly beside her place and asked Uncle Horace if he cared to join their repast.

'Are you going to read it?' Aunt Susan prompted.

'I shall read it after breakfast.' Mama took the porcelain cup containing her tea and lifted it slowly and carefully from its saucer towards her mouth, where she held it until her audience tired of watching her.

'Good morning!' Aunt Lizzie glided up to their table. The hard heels of her shoes thumped her pace on the parquet floor.

'Good morning, Aunt Lizzie,' Ethel's bright reply elicited another twitch from Nellie. 'I hope you slept well? You look very pretty today.'

'Oh,' said Aunt Lizzie, sounding surprised. 'I wasn't sure about this dress. Does the blue make me look florid?' Her dress glowed pale sapphire where caught in the window light, and mauve where illuminated by the Christmas tree candles. It was bustled at the back, and her corset was fashionably tight-laced.

Ethel, pleased to be getting along amicably with her aunt, told her earnestly, 'You don't look florid at all, Aunt Lizzie. Your complexion is like fine china, and your waist is ever so thin!'

'You look like you might snap in half.' Uncle Horace's bluntness made Aunt Lizzie look cross.

Mama spoke quickly to smooth Aunt Lizzie's mood. 'I'm very impressed by the thinness of your waist, Cousin dear. How do you manage to tie your corset so tightly without a personal maid?'

Aunt Lizzie, happy again, confided, 'I asked the maid who comes to fill the jug for my washstand. She's tight-laced me every morning, in fact. Thank goodness, because I'd not want to look a frump.'

Mama's smile dropped, just as Aunt Lizzie's had a few minutes earlier from Uncle Horace's bluntness. She stole a surreptitious glance at her loosely corseted midriff and took another, long sip of tea.

'I'm curious to know who sent you a telegram,' Aunt Susan urged her.

Aunt Lizzie was immediately interested. 'Did Cousin Tori receive a telegram?'

Ethel's mama continued to hold her teacup like a tiny, porcelain shield.

'Is it from South Brent again?' Ethel was now very curious too.

'Come on, Sister,' Uncle Horace cajoled. 'Don't keep us all in suspense. Read it now.'

'Very well.' Sighing, Mama returned her cup to its saucer and picked up the telegram. She began to scan it, but paled and quickly folded it again. 'I'll attend to it after breakfast.'

'But who's it from?' Ethel pressed.

'Ethel Mary Ward, enough!' Mama hissed.

Uncle Horace, however, outranked Mama because he was a man. He snatched the telegram and read it out, very loudly:

> *DEAREST SISTER –(STOP)–*
>
> *A FAVOUR TO ASK –(STOP)– MOTHER NOT REPLIED TO TELEGRAM SENT YESTERDAY –(STOP)– URGENT MATTER –(STOP)– MUST CONFIRM SHE WILL RETURN BY DECEMBER 31 FOR DINNER WITH ETON GOVERNOR –(STOP)– TELL HER MUST REPLY TODAY –(STOP)–*
>
> *YOUR LOVING BROTHER NELSON WARD*

Ethel saw Mama grimace, Grandmama Horatia tense, and heard Aunt Susan gasp, 'golly!' But Uncle Horace didn't seem to notice. 'Dinner with the governor of Eton? What a singular honour!'

'How thrilling!' said Aunt Lizzie, who'd seated herself on one of the dining chairs at an awkward angle to allow for her bustle. 'You must order a new dress and wear your best jewels.'

'Ah, here's a waiter at last!' Uncle Horace clicked his fingers at a smartly dressed man with a pristine, white cloth draped on one arm. 'I say, bring me strong coffee!'

'What's Eton, please?' Ethel asked Grandmama Horatia, who was sitting next to her and now looking stunned and ashen.

Grandmama Horatia seemed not to have heard, but Aunt Lizzie clearly had. 'Eton is the most prestigious college in the empire! Though I wonder why Horatia's been invited to dinner with the governor? All her sons are fully grown.'

'Oh, hush!' Aunt Susan's admonishment surprised everyone into silence, coming as it had from this genteel old lady who, as the saying went, normally wouldn't say "boo" to a goose. 'Horace, you were rash to read Tori's telegram to the table. Especially as she told you, very clearly, that she thought it best for her to read after breakfast.'

Uncle Horace spluttered on his coffee, 'Umm, what? But, I say, Aunt Susan, being invited to dinner with the governor of Eton is something to celebrate. Why all this fuss about secrecy?'

'No, there's no need for secrecy.' It was Grandmama Horatia's turn to surprise everyone by speaking out. 'There's been far too much secrecy in my life, and I'm sorely fed up with it.'

'But, Mother–' Ethel's mama began, at the same time that Aunt Susan cried, 'Cousin, you don't have to talk about this. You've already had such a–'

But Grandmama Horatia said, 'Pah, I can handle this. Though I thank you both for your concern.'

'I confess to confusion,' Uncle Horace owned. 'Aunt Horatia, I don't understand why my sister and Aunt Susan believe your invitation to dine with Eton's governor is a cause for concern.'

Grandmama Horatia sat up straighter. 'The governor will grant a place at Eton to my grandson, Jack...' she drew a deep breath and shifted so her back was ramrod straight and her chin proudly raised, 'if I testify that Lady Hamilton was not my mother.'

'Well, that's understandable.' Aunt Lizzie opined.

Uncle Horace gasped. 'I beg your pardon, Cousin Lizzie? You'd consider it "understandable" for my aunt Horatia, who is my dear mother's first cousin, to make that... that despicable calumny?' He addressed Grandmama Horatia. 'What does your son, Nelson, say to this, Aunt Horatia? Surely he's given the governor a piece of his mind for his rudeness?'

Grandmama Horatia held her upright stance, though her chin dropped slightly. 'My son is eager for me to give this testimony, as evidenced by his telegram pressing to Tori, in turn, press me to accept.'

'Have I heard you right, Aunt Horatia? Did you say your own son wants you to publicly disown Lady Hamilton as your mother?'

Ethel was excited. 'Is Lady Hamilton my great-grandmother? I do hope so, because she's ever so pretty in all the pictures of her.' But no one heeded her, for all eyes were on Grandmama Horatia who was deflating before them like a bolster pillow that had been slashed so its stuffing poured out leaving an empty, sagged case.

'Society detests Lady Hamilton,' Grandmama Horatia whispered. 'My son, quite rightly, wants the best for his son. If Jack is accepted into Eton, his future will be golden.'

Uncle Horace's face turned as red as his jacket. 'Nelson says his son's future will be golden if you besmirch Lady Hamilton's name? What a snake! You should tell him to go to Hell for demanding dear Lady Hamilton be further besmirched!'

Ethel thought Uncle Horace's words were marvellous, but her mama sounded worried when she spoke to Grandmama Horatia. 'Mother, if you wish, I could speak quietly to Nelson. I can catch a train from Exmouth this morning and be there before dark.'

Ethel was thrilled by mother's gallantry until it dawned on her that she'd have to go with her so her holiday would be over before it was meant to be. She was relieved when Aunt Susan nudged Grandmama Horatia gently and said, 'I say we should forget about Nelson's demands for now, Cousin. You've had a frightfully trying time and need rest. Come, let's return to Henrietta's cosy house and forget all this for now.'

Ethel fervently hoped her grandmother would agree, but instead she said, 'no.'

There was a collective intake of breath. Uncle Horace's hands started flapping, but Grandmama Horatia looked straight ahead as if she was a Spanish bull impervious to a bullfighters' cape. 'I shall deal with Nelson alone,' she announced, making eye contact with no one. 'I now know I must and, more so, that I can.'

Ethel was impressed beyond words. Her grandmama had shown herself to be stronger than all the other adults around the table, including Uncle Horace, who was captain of the Royal Marines. 'Oh, Grandmama Horatia, what will you do?'

Grandmama Horatia treated Ethel to a rare, bright smile. 'I'm going to deal with your uncle Nelson alone. It's high time I did so, and I know exactly what I need to do.'

'What is it? Oh, please tell me!' Ethel clamoured, but her grandmother simply smiled and tapped her lips with her middle finger.

Everyone, even Baby Alice, stared at Grandmama Horatia curiously as if her silence was a theatre curtain ready to rise. Grandmama Horatia did not, however, rise. She remained stoically still in her black widow's reeds. If a pin had dropped, the sound of it hitting the floor would have been audible to all. Uncle Horace, when he spoke, sounded very loud indeed. 'Will you at least assure me you'll refuse your son's demand?'

Horatia turned her head, very slowly, to meet Uncle Horace's ginger browed eyes. 'I shall tell him that glory without integrity is a palace built on mud.'

His ginger eyebrows scrunched with his frown. 'Huh, what? I don't understand.'

'In other words, Nephew, I shall tell Nelson "no".'

****

The dark, January morning was bitterly cold. The ground was slipperyy with refrozen slush. A strong north-wind bit with teeth of hail, but Horatia's heart was warm. 'Here we are,' she told Jack.

Her nearly eight-year old grandson looked up with a broad smile. His thin face was pale beneath his school uniform top hat. The white silk of his shirt collar peeped over the top button of his black, wool coat. 'The school looks like a palace!'

Horatia saw what Jack meant. The red brick edifices of the ancient school, seen through its glossy black, wrought iron gates, were towering and grand. The grounds were a monotone expanse of neat angles and frozen slush. The school loomed above on a rise of land. The space below was thick with top hatted boys in long, black coats jostling to join one of the stone staircases which led up to the grand entrance. Horatia took hold of the wrought iron gate to pull it open. The metal was surprisingly warm, having already been clasped that morning by a hundred or more incoming boys. 'Are you ready to go in?'

Jack frowned. 'Papa said I was going to an important school called "Eton".'

'Your papa realised that Harrow School is just as good as Eton. Did you know this school was built in the reign of Elizabeth the first? Have you heard of her, Jack?'

He brightened. 'Why yes, Grandmama, she's nearly as famous as Lord Nelson!'

'My, aren't you the scholar! And do you know what's especially good about Harrow School?'

'No, Grandmama Horatia.'

Her grandson's trusting, innocent smile made Horatia's heart feel fit to burst. 'Harrow School is only a short carriage ride from your home, so you can visit your family at weekends. If you went to Eton, you'd only see them during school holidays.'

Jack regarded her solemnly. 'Promise you won't tell my sisters, but I think I'd miss them a bit if I only came home during school holidays. I mean, they are very annoying, but I actually do quite like them.'

'So you're happy to be staying near your home?'

'Oh yes, Grandmama Horatia. I do declare that I am!'

AFTERWORD

Horatia's Secret is fiction woven from facts scavenged from archives, old texts, and my mother's recollections of what her great-aunts, Evie and Ada, told her during her childhood holidays in Lutton House. Tori and William were my second great-grandparents via 'Baby Alice', who died young from congenital heart disease.

Lady Hamilton was defamed by prudish Georgian and Victorian society. Whilst Nelson was all but canonised, Lady Hamilton was demonised. If you'd like to learn more about her rise and fall, I provide a summary of her life on emmahamiltonsociety.co.uk/herstory.html

Nelson and Lady Hamilton hid their parentage of Horatia by claiming she was adopted from a crewman, and pretending she was three-months older than she really was and born on 29th October 1800 during their very public overland journey home from Naples. Nelson later claimed paternity. As a man and a hero, society easily forgave him, but they'd never have forgiven Lady Hamilton if she'd admitted to being Horatia's mother. We can never know what Horatia truly knew, or felt in her heart of hearts, but Victorian society would certainly have spurned her, and her descendants, if she'd named Lady Hamilton as her biological mother.

Thomas Joseph Pettigrew, one of the few people who hadn't bought into the anti-Lady Hamilton propaganda, wrote in 1849:

'That Horatia was the daughter of Nelson no one has been disposed to entertain a doubt, but the evidence in connection with the birth of the child has been purposefully obscured and mystified.'

The Matcham descendants of Lord Nelson's sister, Kitty, were about the only other inhabitants of the British Empire who viewed Lady Hamilton favourably. Both Tori's mother, Harriet, and her aunt, Susan, were Matchams. Susan's son, Alexander George Montgomery Moore, is quoted by the editor of an 1891 reprint of Sichel's Memoirs of Emma, Lady Hamilton:

'Lady Hamilton was a frequent visitor at my grandfather's (Mr. Matcham) place, Ashfold Lodge, Sussex, for years after Lord Nelson's death, and my mother always spoke of her periodical visits to them as gala days, which the children of the family always looked forward to. In 1811 she was godmother to my uncle, Mr. Nelson Matcham, the youngest son of Nelson's sister.'

According to Horatia's biographer Winifred Gérin, Susan was godmother to Horatia's fifth child, William George Ward. Further, Susan, of all the Matchams, maintained the closest, lifelong contact with Horatia. She fostered Tori after her sister Harriet's death of childbed fever in 1838. Tori would have accompanied Susan on visits to Horatia and thus have known William well prior to their 1864 wedding.

The precise views of Horatia and her children are hard to ascertain, but there's a clue in a letter to The Times, dated 29th March 1888, from Hugh Herbert Edward Nelson Ward quibbling his father's obituary:

'I was astonished to read in the obituary column of The Times of to-day regarding the death of the Rev. Horatio Nelson-Ward the following sentence:—"His mother was the Little Horatia whom Lord Nelson bequeathed to the nation, whether she

was his natural daughter by Emma, Lady Hamilton, or the daughter of Lady Hamilton by one of her other admirers, and his adopted child." As to the first of these theories, I am beyond measure astonished that it should be again offered to the world, in spite of the solemn statement made by Mr. Hazelwood (Lord Nelson's most intimate associate and confidential advisor) to Horatia that he was permitted at any rate to assure her "that she certainly did not owe her being to Lady Hamilton." This was the only satisfaction which Horatia's passionate appeal produced from Mr. Hazelwood, bound as he was by oath to secrecy. Apart from this, Lady Hamilton herself never claimed to be the mother of the child; in fact, she left behind her in writing an emphatic denial of her right to the relationship…'

Tori was brought up with Aunt Susan's positive view of Lady Hamilton on one side, and society's prevailing negativity on the other. Tori seems not to have shunned Lady Hamilton. One of the few relics which came down to us is an eighteen-eighties albumen print of Lady Hamilton, with a note on the back that it was framed for 'Mrs. Ward' (Tori).

Teenage Horatia's flight from Calais, dressed as a boy, to escape Lady Hamilton's debtors after her death is included in Sichel's 1882 Memoirs of Emma, Lady Hamilton. Sichel attributes Horatia's rescue to Nelson's elder brother, Earl Nelson. He is again refuted by a descendant of George Matcham, in this case, William Eyre Matcham of New House in Wiltshire. His copy of Sichel's Memoirs, complete with handwritten corrections, remained in New House's library until recent years. On page 312, under an editorial footnote that most of Sichel's statements were entirely untrue, William Eyre Matcham wrote: 'Quite true. Horatia came to England in boy's clothes.' On the next page, he penned: 'Mr. Matcham, not Earl Nelson, went over to Calais, and brought back Horatia to England dressed in boy's clothes.' There is, however, no corroborating evidence that George Matcham met Horatia in Calais. In my narrative, I place him in Dover waiting to greet her. His telling Horatia, 'I cannot imagine how very vile your time was with that despicable woman!' is inspired by his 1830s diatribe, recorded in The Nelsons of Burnham Thorpe, by Mary Harriet, sister of William Eyre Matcham:

> *'The connection which [Nelson] formed with a certain lady has been the cause of much blame and much ungrateful calumny... if Lady Hamilton had not artfully endeavoured to inveigle it, some other female would... Lady H.'s disposition was satirical, not I believe from malignity (or) temper, but from an affectation of point and wit. Her letters and even casual notes were never free from this despicable propensity...'*

Horatia would have been swamped with strong, contradictory opinions about Lady Hamilton when the Matchams fostered her after Lady Hamilton's death, and whisked her around Europe with them. Gérin's detailed description of their tour tells that the Blanckleys helped them find a house in Boulogne-sur-Seine, for the annual rent of £116, and a carriage into central Paris for £5 a week. The Matchams and Blanckleys sent their daughters to a Parisian school in between their excursions around post war Europe. It was during this time that young Henrietta Blanckley would have first met Horatia. They enjoyed picnics and visited Portugal, where Horatia was much admired by suitors. The Matchams and Blanckleys travelled on to Naples, where Tori's parents-to-be, Harriet Matcham and Edward Blanckley, married in April 1819. Horatia, however, had returned to England to the family of Lord Nelson's other sister, Susanna Bolton, in Burnham Westgate, Norfolk. Here she met a young curate named Philip Ward and married him in February 1822. When the Matchams eventually returned to England, George Matcham went into business importing wine, vegetables and olives from the continent.

Henrietta was born circa 1804 on the island of Minorca, where her father, H. S. B. (Henry Stanyford Blanckley), was British Consul to the Balearics. Spain's decision to side with Napoleon forced the Blanckleys to flee Minorca in January 1805, shortly after Henrietta's half-brother, Edward, joined the navy as a midshipman.

Edward Blanckley was the youngest of six children born to H. S. B.'s first wife, Mary (née Rogers). Edward's mother had suffered a long illness and died in the health spa of Bristol Hotwells in March 1798. H. S. B. remarried a younger woman, Mary Richards, in Sulham, Berkshire, England in March 1800. Henrietta's childhood is vividly detailed in her full-sister, Elizabeth Broughton née Blanckley's memoirs, Six Years Residence in Algiers (1839). From this, we learn that the Blanckleys paused in Malta before H. S. B. was made British Consul to Algiers; that their Italian cook accidentally cooked their pet eagle which had been mistaken for a guinea fowl; and that the family had clifftop and town residences, of which the latter had marvellous potential for spying on the street outside.

I used artistic licence to make Henrietta's mother the illegitimate, orphaned daughter of a remote relation of the Sulham Wilders. Mary Richards' birth records are elusive. Her marriage to Henry Stanyford Blanckley was presided over by Dr Wilder and took place in Sulham House, which the Wilder family owned. Her father isn't named in the few records that remain of their marriage.

Mary Richards's animosity towards the children of H. S. B.'s first wife, is inspired by an 1875 letter, held by Princeton University, from the daughter of Edward Blanckley's full-cousin, Mary Philippedes Cammenos, to another full-cousin, Henriette Blanckley in Versailles:

'Lizzie spoke as if she had expectations of our cousin Mrs. Graham [Mary Rogers's niece], which I thought strange, but as she was very

much with the family, I supposed it was only one more instance of the way the first family has been supplanted by the second.'

Edward Blanckley captained an expedition to South America between May 1831 and June 1834. Horace was born in Versailles in his absence. His Matcham sister-in-law, Susan, wed the wealthy Alexander James Montgomery Moore in April 1832. The couple appear to have settled in Versailles too, because her father-in-law, Nathaniel Montgomery Moore died there 1834. Susan's husband didn't long outlive him, and died in February 1837 in his estate at Sedgehill, Wiltshire, England. She was left with two young sons, Alexander George, and Acheson.

Edward Blanckley returned from South America with a stash of cash and a lingering tropical illness. He and Harriet had the address of Raleigh House in the fashionable new build of Union Road in south-west England's naval port of Plymouth.

Tori was born there on 5th May 1835. It was at about this time that Edward Blanckley purchased, and extended, a property called View Cottage on Brent Hill, overlooking the south Devon village of South Brent. British Listed Buildings says 'Lutton House (formerly View Cottage) is circa 1830-40'. This ties in with my grandfather's recollection that Edward Blanckley constructed it as a hunting lodge. The 1838 tithe map records Edward Blanckley as the owner occupier of View Cottage.

Susan adopted Tori after Harriet's death in August 1838. Susan's younger son, Acheson, died of typhus in Worthing, West Sussex, on 18th January 1839. The fate of Tori's baby brother and Susan's subsequent reclusiveness, along with the story of the Burmese tailor prince which Kajri cringed to hear Horace recount, will be explored in the next book, Susan's Silence.

Horace was boarding in an Exeter school in 1841, and joined

the Royal Marines in 1848. He was part of a military troupe performing a comedy in Plymouth Theatre Royal in 1853, and sponsored theatrical performances in later years. His marriage to Augusta née Polkinghorne seems not to have worked out. Census records show them living apart, and the main beneficiary of his will is surprising to say the least. He had a new will drawn up, at the age of sixty-seven, four days before his death in June 1899. His address at that time was in Heaton Chapel, Lancashire. After specifying bequests of £500 each to Mrs Augusta Blanckley and someone named Mrs Estelle Emilie MacDonald, both residents of London, he bequeathed the remaining £2,100 of his estate to his "friend" Nellie Lowe, a spinster, also of Heaton Chapel. Nellie Lowe transpires to have been a twenty-eight year old living with her parents, Christopher and Betsy. Intriguingly, her elder sibling is Horace Arthur Lowe. Might she and her older brother have been Horace Blanckley's biological children?

Lizzie, Elizabeth Henrietta Blanckley Broughton, was born in Edinburgh in 1844. Her only sibling, Mary Elizabeth, was ten years her senior. Their father was dead by the time the 1851 census listed seven-year old Lizzie living with her sister, their widowed mother, and aunt Henrietta, in St Johns Wood, London.

Horatia, in the meantime, was the vicar's wife of Tenterden in Kent. They kept a frugal household, but paid the wages of three servants, of whom one was Walter Honeysett, who Horatia still employed, as a butler, in 1873. They struggled to finance futures for their five sons on her husband's clerical salary, which was sorely stretched by financial problems inherited with his posting. He home schooled his children, and funded further education for their firstborn, Horatio Nelson; and third son, Nelson, for careers in the clergy and law respectively. The problem of financing careers for their other three boys was solved by a national appeal, nicknamed 'the Horatia fund', launched in 1850 to rectify the government's failure to honour Nelson's dying wish for Lady Hamilton and Horatia to receive state pensions. Horatia asked for the fund to finance careers for her sons Marmaduke, William and Philip. Marmaduke embarked on a career as a naval surgeon; and William and Philip were awarded East India Company cadetships. The subcontinental climate, unfortunately, wreaked havoc on their livers. The severity of William's illness resulted in him being granted twenty-months sick leave, during which he married Tori in Clevedon on 15th November 1864. She returned to India with him and bore him five daughters in the British cantonment of Jaulnah. Philip was less fortunate, and his liver illness killed him in 1865.

After Reverend Philip Ward died in January 1859, Horatia's lawyer son, Nelson, urged her to move near to him in the new-build Woodridings estate north of Pinner. Honeysett accompanied her. The Nelson Wards had eight children. According to Gérin, Horatia's cup of happiness was filled when William and Tori returned from India, with their five little girls, and settled near her in Woodridings.

Kajri, is my invention, but a list of incoming passengers, published by the Naval & Military Gazette on 27th April 1872, names 'Major and Mrs. W. G. Ward, five children and servant'. Although the servant's role isn't specified, it was standard practice for British families returning from India to bring their ayah with them. Unfortunately for these ayahs, many were then cast adrift with no means to pay for tickets home. The situation became so dire, with cast out ayahs forced to beg on the streets, that a charitable institution, named the Ayah's Home, was opened in London circa 1891.

Henrietta had moved to the Devon seaside resort of Budleigh Salterton by 1870, when Morris and Co.'s Commercial Directory and Gazetteer listed Miss Blanckley at Barnhayes

Cottage, Little Knowle: a clifftop house above the village. The 1871 census, however, lists Miss Henrietta Blanckley in a house on Budleigh Salterton's High Street. The 1881 census's listing of her neighbours pinpoints her address to No. 44, which, fortuitously, was a deli cafe when I visited the village in November 2018. It was an oasis of warmth after viewing the surprisingly pink sea from the pebbled beach. I drank hot tea and ate a tasty little cake whilst peeking at The Feathers Inn through the twin front windows.

Henrietta's family gathering at Budleigh Salterton is my invention, although the detail of the Feathers yardman being sacked just before Christmas was inspired by a notice in The Exeter and Plymouth Gazette on 26th December 1873:

> *WANTED, immediately, a middle-aged steady MAN for the yard, and to make himself generally useful.—Apply to G. C. PERRIAM, Feathers Hotel, Budleigh Salterton.*

Francis Cooke's elderly father, Otho, did indeed live in nearby Withycombe House,. He married a young heiress, Julia Garnault, in September 1872, eight months after Francis's mother's death. Julia was two years older than Francis.

Tori's excursion to South Brent is also my invention, though the names and addresses of the people she met there are real. The more exotic dialect is gleaned from Germon's 1995 guide to the dialect of Ashburton village, fifteen-miles from South Brent, entitled Zee 'ee Dreckly. The poor sanitary conditions are based on Dr Parsons' detailed 1881 report of typhus fever in the village. Brent had five mills dotting the course of the River Avon, including one for manufacturing cheap shoddy cloth.

After Edward Blanckley died in 1845, his second wife called for his possessions to be transported from London for auctioning in View Cottage. The property was then rented to a series of tenants. When the Strutton family rented it in the 1850s, it was named Higher Lutton House – not to be confused with a nearby farm of that name. It's named 'Blanckleys' at the end of that decade, when a son of new tenants, the Maxwells, was baptised in the parish church. It's named Lutton View Cottage in the 1861 census, and Lutton House thereafter.

There really was a pantomime entitled 'Harlequin Sindbad the Sailor!' in Exeter Theatre Royal for the Christmas season of 1873, which had a special train laid on from Exmouth on 29th December... Ethel's seventh birthday. The actors' lines are quoted verbatim from a review in the Exeter and Plymouth Gazette. Princess Angelina was played by Miss Verlander, though I invented her first name, Amanda, and her relationship to Francis Cooke. Joan, and her fake prophecy, are also my invention.

The narrative was informed by knowledge that Henrietta died on 21st October 1874: the anniversary of Trafalgar. Lizzie was the main beneficiary in Henrietta's will, but she left £200 to every living child of her half-brothers: Henriette in Versailles, Tori and Horace, but left nothing to Mary Philippedes Cammenos, the daughter of her half-sister Maria Tonna née Blanckley. Henrietta's only other bequests were £200 each to Tori's husband, William, and to her 'great niece Ada Blanche Ward daughter of the said William George Ward... as and when she should attain the age of twenty one years old.'

Lizzie married Francis Cooke in Pinner on 8th April 1875, less than six moths after Henrietta's death. Tori and Horace stood as witnesses. Francis Cooke is recorded as a resident of Budleigh Salterton, and Lizzie as resident in Pinner. It's likely she'd been a guest in Tori's house at No. 1 Cornwall Villas prior to her wedding.

Lizzie destroyed the Blanckley family papers shortly after her marriage to Francis Cooke. Mary Philippedes Cammenos, in her 1875 letter to her cousin Henriette Blanckley, explains:

> *'Lizzie told me that after the death of our aunt Henrietta, all the private papers left by our grandfather came into her possession, and that she had torn & burnt them all, — including letters from our grandmother to our grandfather, as well as those from her own grandmother. —I was surprised, & expressed myself so, but as the thing was done it was useless to complain. We do not know what these papers might have revealed, & I must say I think you or I, or Horace —as the only male representative of the family should have been consulted.'*

Her account is corroborated by Tori's daughter, Ethel, in a 1937 letter to my great-aunt Phyllis:

> *'A wretched half cousin of mother's destroyed all mother's family papers from spite & it does not matter now does it? But it was very hard on mother.'*

Horatia's grandsons, Jack and Tom, both attended Harrow School and went on to become lawyers like their father. Nelson Ward junior, aka Jack, and Tori's eldest daughter, Nellie, were co-executors of her will.

Please kindly take a moment to rate Horatia's Secret. Without ratings, it won't be found by other readers.

Printed in Great Britain
by Amazon

16395639R00210